A Critique of Christian Fundamentalism
Pilgrim Simon

© 2022 Culturea Editions

Illustration de couverture : © domaine public

Edition : Culturea, le patrimoine des lettres (Hérault, 34)

Contact : infos@ culturea.fr

Retrouvez notre catalogue sur http://culturea.fr

Imprimé en Allemagne par Books on Demand,

In de Tarpen 42, Norderstedt.

Design typographique : Derek Murphy

Layout : Reedsy (https://reedsy.com/)

ISBN : 9791041940332

Dépôt légal : decembre 2022

Tous droits réservés pour tous pays

A CRITIQUE OF CHRISTIAN FUNDAMENTALISM

Contents:

Introduction: p.3

ABSOLUTE TRUTH: FUNDAMENTALISM AND GOD
p.7

AN OUTLINE CRITIQUE THE CHRISTIAN FUNDAMENTALIST SYSTEM
p. 15

PROBLEMS WITH THE INSPIRATION AND INERRANCY OF SCRIPTURE -AN AXE LAID TO THE ROOT OF CHRISTIAN FUNDAMENTALISM
p 32

SPIRITUAL AND MORAL AUTHORITY IN THE CHRISTIAN CHURCH
p. 63

WHO DO MEN SAY THAT I AM?
A CRITICAL EXAMINATION OF THE PERSON AND TEACHING OF JESUS CHRIST
p. 142

THE VISIONS OF THE APOSTLE PAUL AND THE EARLY CHURCH TRADITION
p. 269

PSYCHOLOGY OF BELIEFS
p.288

WHY IS LEAVING FUNDAMENTALISM SO HARD?
p.297

GROUPS, CULTS, SECTS AND MIND CONTROL
p. 305

TOWARDS A 21ST CENTURY CHRISTIANITY
p. 314

THE SPIRITUAL LIFE OF A MANIC-DEPRESSIVE
p.384

Foundations of spirituality and religion may be quoted for non-commercial use in any form (written, visual, electronic or audio) up to and inclusive of 2000 words without the express permission of the author, providing that the quote does not amount to more than 25% of a complete chapter or more than 25% of the total text of the work in which they are quoted.

With regard to commercial publication, all rights reserved. No part of this manuscript may be reproduced, stored in or introduced into a retrieval system or transmitted in any form, or by any means, (electronic, mechanical, photocopying, recording or otherwise) without the prior written permission of the author. Any person who does any unauthorised act in relation to this publication may be liable to criminal prosecution and civil claims for damages.

COPYRIGHT ROBERT LAYNTON 2012
Introduction
by Pilgrim Simon (Robert Laynton)

All the essays in this collection have been published before on various blog sites and e-book sites on the web, but they have never been gathered together in this way before. They deal with key issues that are central to Christian Fundamentalism. *Christian* Fundamentalism is dealt with rather than Fundamentalism as whole, because it is Christian Fundamentalism that I am most familiar with and have most experience of. Nevertheless, certain aspects of these essays and certain principles contained within them can be applied to the wider Fundamentalist movement.

Christian fundamentalist ideology can be very powerful indeed. Once the believer accepts certain assumptions as fact, Christian fundamentalist thinking can exert an iron grip on the believer, locking them into a self-perpetuating and isolated system of thought and behaviour. Indeed, for Calvinist thinkers such as B.B. Warfield and Charles Hodge who found their theology under threat by rationalism, scientific development and evolutionary theory – this closing of the theological/ideological circle to lock believers into a certain belief system was exactly what was intended.

Many Christians are very happy within the Christian Fundamentalist system. Of course they do not call themselves Christian Fundamentalists because this is now seen as a pejorative term with negative connotations – even though the term originated within their own ranks as a sort of 'back to basics' movement within the broader and more liberal protestant church. Terms come and go, but phrases such as 'Bible believing Christian' or 'Born again Christian' mean roughly the same thing. However, if doubts begin to creep in to the believer's mind such that this theology begins to be openly, but sincerely questioned, then the believer may well find themselves subtly (or even not so subtly) threatened, excluded, isolated, ostracised, unfairly criticised, disapproved of and so on. There is the idea within Christian Fundamentalism that the 'truth' that they believe in is particular, exclusive and absolute. To question it is to question (and therefore doubt) God, to inquire into other religions is to 'go after other gods' or even to follow 'the devil and deceitful spirits'. There is only 'one way' (which happens to be their way) to God. In this way, Christian Fundamentalism in ultra-orthodox.

The author takes the position that we cannot create a fixed or an adequate conception of God. The Divine is far too Transcendent to be bound by finite conceptualisations and theologies. In his view, belief systems, theologies, conceptions of the Divine and so on serve to both reveal and mask the Transcendent – they can only point to That which cannot be known. Belief systems serve to give us finite creatures of form a relative perspective of the Infinite. But as we draw near to the Formless, these forms fall away, rendered useless by the Vastness of the Absolute. So why pick on Christian Fundamentalism? It is one of a number of approaches to the Godhead, so why critique this approach?

It is the closed absoluteness of Christian Fundamentalism (and Fundamentalism generally) that makes demands for a collection of articles such as this. There is within Christian Fundamentalism an express belief that the Bible forms a now-closed inspired or God-breathed revelation from the one God. No new revelations are to be expected – the rule-book is closed and complete. There is also a certain type of literalism present within Christian Fundamentalism: Jesus really did perform miracles and rise from the dead. God really did create the world in six literal, twenty-four hour days. Moses really did lead the Israelites through the parted waters of the Red Sea. Christian Fundamentalism constantly draws the believer back to what are perceived as literal, objective events of history. Then there is also a great emphasis on belief – on believing the right 'key' doctrines that often serve as 'proof' of one's salvation.

The author is an ex-Christian Fundamentalist – a Calvinist – who has experienced first hand the power and grip both of the theology and the group pressures involved in Christian Fundamentalism and what happens when one leaves. Following some deep spiritual experiences *within* Christian Fundamentalism (Baptism of the Spirit, Extraordinary Witness of the Spirit), his Christian Fundamentalist theology proved especially tenacious, with the result that it took over thirty years to deconstruct these now deep-rooted spiritual beliefs and to establish new ones. It is that deconstruction that we have presented here, in a series of essays and articles that have been written between 1976 and 2011. As a result of such a compilation, there is inevitably some repetition of certain sections and passages, which I hope that the reader will bear with. However, the author has not become an atheist – he embraced secular humanism only briefly before rejecting it as inadequate – rather he retains a lively interest in and engagement with spirituality and thus, it is not his intention to dismiss Christianity. There is much within Christianity that is of value and interest – but nevertheless, key orthodox ideas have to be questioned. At the end of this collection of essays, there is an attempt to present some sort of outline Christianity in the light of the comments made throughout this collection – but it is a Christianity that is quite radically different from the mainstream orthodox Christianity handed down to us through history and particularly different from the ultra-orthodoxy of Christian Fundamentalism.

The articles and essays in this collection deal with the fundamentalist idea of absolute truth, the Christian Fundamentalist system and the people that subscribe to it. The foundation of Christian Fundamentalism is looked at – the idea that the Bible is a closed revelatory book which is without major error or contradiction. A whole series of questions relating to spiritual and moral authority in the church are explored The founding figure in Christianity, Jesus Christ is looked at in order to explore what Jesus really seemed to teach and how orthodox ideas were developed and established around him as the central figure of the faith. Since the thought of the Apostle Paul makes up most of the New Testament, we explore where he obtained his ideas. There are also brief articles on the nature of belief, why leaving fundamentalism can be so hard and a look at groups sects and cults. There is also an exploration on what a 21st century might look like and the testimony/spiritual biography of the author.

Pilgrim Simon Feb 2012
ABSOLUTE TRUTH: FUNDAMENTALISM AND GOD

In discussing fundamentalism in this essay I am referring particularly to Christian fundamentalism and that from a Calvinist perspective. Even so, some of the concepts and ideas put forward here will apply to any religious fundamentalist system and so those from systems other than Christianity may be able to apply such ideas to their own framework.

Christian fundamentalism is considered to be a conservative movement – not necessarily politically, but in terms of seeking to conserve or preserve the traditional doctrines and practices of the group. In fact the more theology-based fundamentalists may even be described as ultra-conservative. Christian fundamentalists claim a line right back to the Apostles and disciples of Christ seeing themselves as preservers and inheritors of the truths which they declared. As far as they are concerned, these truths were laid down by the Apostles in the gospels and book of Acts of the Apostles and particularly by the Apostle Paul in his various letters that make up most of the New Testament of the Bible. These writings are seen by many fundamentalists as the inspired Word of God, because fundamentalists consider that God in the Person of the Holy Spirit breathed as it were these ideas, insights or revelations into these writers, withholding the effects of sin and transgression such that in their original form at least, these writings are inerrant: that is they contain no mistakes or errors. God is Perfect, has inspired these writers, withheld the corrupting effects of sin and so therefore these writings are without error. Since then, there have been through time, in one place or another, those who have conserved and maintained the purity of the teachings that these writings contain. For Protestant fundamentalists, these truths became obscured and hidden under the Roman Catholic system, which, they say, over time, became distorted and corrupt, especially by late medieval times. Nevertheless, these truths were brought back to the forefront at the reformation in Europe in 16th and 17th centuries. Religious leaders such as Martin Luther, John Calvin and others led a protest movement against what they saw as the mistakes and corruptions of the church, reforming the church so that it was based upon the Bible or Scripture alone instead of on the dictates of the Pope. Furthermore Scripture was made available to everyone by translating it into the language of the people, instead of keeping it in obscure Latin which was only understood by educated priests. So fundamentalists particularly trace their history back to this period. They will speak of the Puritans, of the heroes of the faith such as Wycliffe, Tyndale, John Knox, the Covenanters and others. These and their successors such as Hodge, Warfield, Spurgeon, Howell Harris, Jonathan Edwards, George Whitfield, Lloyd-Jones and many others are all seen as 'sound' teachers – that is they adhere to and conserve this line and tradition of teaching, refusing to compromise it in the face of 'unsound' liberals and academics within the church and unbelievers outside of it.

It is in these kinds of ways that 'sound' teaching becomes elevated: such teachings are seen as the inspired, inerrant teachings of God under the light of which every idea and practice of the believer and church is examined. From the Apostle Paul to the protestant reformers and beyond, leaders began to set out and define systematically the teachings contained in the inspired writings. After some divisions and errors within the early church in the first centuries after Christ and after some debate amongst church leaders, the writings were closed so that no other writings could be added to them. Some writings were included in the canon, some, such as the Gospel of Philip and Shepherd of Hermas, were excluded. It should be noted that the actual principles on which these decisions were made can now be seen as weak and even spurious, such that with the extra knowledge and analysis that we have benefit of today concerning these writings, some of the letters now included in the New Testament would have to be excluded on the basis of this new evidence. Nevertheless, a canon or rule of faith was defined and bordered by this set of writings and with it, an orthodoxy and orthopraxy – one belief and one practice for the church. The ideas of heresy and apostasy were put forward: failure to conform to the canon, or conversely, the suggesting alternative or new concepts concerning God which contradicted the canon or which were simply were not present in it, meant that a person holding such views was an outcast and could even suffer the penalty of death for holding such contrary ideas to those of this set of writings and the teachings they proclaimed. Indeed, some religious leaders made it their business to enforce conformity, demanding the burning of writings that were contrary to those of the canon, such as the Gnostic gospels. In this way, as they saw it, they thoroughly purged the church of impurity and corruption. Even so we should note that Protestant leaders such as Calvin, Luther and later Wesley, all excluded some of the books that we have in our New Testament. We can also note that the Roman Catholic Church included a set of books known as the Apocrypha, whilst Protestants rejected them.

With the advent and onslaught of the Age of Reason, modern science and thinkers such as Charles Darwin, these traditional ideas came under increasing scrutiny and stronger and stronger challenges. As a result, the Fundamentalist's approach to Scripture and thus the teaching contained within it, hardened and became less flexible. Certain doctrines, such as for example a literal six-day creation period and/or a young earth theory, whereby through calculating dates in the Bible, the earth was said to have been created between 6,000 and 10,000 B.C., became 'badges' of identification – 'markers' of a 'true believer' holding steadfastly to and conserving the traditions of truth held to by previous generations of born-again believers.

What this systematic, ultra-conservative orthodoxy does is, amongst other things, define and conceptualise God for believer and it does so in a way that is unquestionable. This literature is the Word of Infallible, Perfect God, written by men inspired by God in such a way that all corrupting influence which would give rise to false and mistaken ideas about God is restrained. To question this teaching therefore is to question God. To doubt it, is to doubt God. To suggest alternative or contradictory ideas to those of Scripture is to fall into error, to be self-deceived or deceived by the devil, or to oppose God.

It is recognised by fundamentalists that there are different interpretations and different degrees on emphasis on different passages of Scripture and that these in turn lead to different practices. Thus we have Congregationalists, Methodists, Baptists, Presbyterians and so on all within the protestant fundamentalist banner. This is accepted and tolerated so long as the main principles, plainly understood verses and truths of the Scripture are agreed upon.

But what the Fundamentalist has done is to elevate these writings and the ideas and concepts that they contain to an Absolute level and it is this that is one of their mistakes. Let me give an illustration. Christians call God the 'Father' – 'Our father who art in heaven...' Yet if the point is pressed, many fundamentalists will agree that God is not male and certainly not female (since fundamentalism is male orientated and patriarchal). They will acknowledge that the term 'Father' is a metaphor for a God that cannot be defined by gender: a God that transcends gender. Nevertheless, the word 'Father' is useful for describing the relationship that the believer has with God, for the way God deals with humanity. It engenders the whole Christian theology of the only begotten Son – Jesus Christ, as well as the Apostle Paul's approach whereby believers are thought of as adopted as sons of God and heirs, by reason of adoption, to the promises. But when it comes down to it, fundamentalists do not see God as a literal 'Father' or even as 'Male', but rather use the term in this 'useful metaphor' way. Fundamentalists are not always as literal in their interpretations as is usually made out. Many fundamentalists with regard to the creation account in Genesis take a similar approach. Because of the advances of science, instead of being inflexibly defensive, many fundamentalist believers find the literal interpretation too difficult to maintain, so they will talk about the six days of creation not in terms of literal twenty-four hour days but in terms of 'figurative days', that is periods of unspecified length symbolically described as 'days'. As long as the main principles and ideas of the fundamentalist faith are not compromised, such ideas may again be tolerated.

Unfortunately, the Scriptures do lend themselves to a literal interpretation. The books of the Bible are full of history – the reigns of kings, court intrigues, conquests and battles, heroic leaders, defeat and conquest, a human named Jesus living at a time of Roman occupation, claiming to be the Son of God, performing miracles as evidence, being put to death and being resurrected after three days. These fundamentalists take literally. They are quite averse to the pre-reformation approach of analogous interpretation. Thus, medieval Dominican Friar Meister Eckhart may consider the verse 'Jesus went into a house' and elaborate a doctrine concerning the mystical presence of Christ in the heart, whereby the house symbolises the Interior Castle, or heart of a person which is the proper dwelling place of Christ. For fundamentalists, Jesus just went into a house. They simply argue that using this kind of analogous interpretation can lead to any doctrine that you care to construct – that you can believe anything. So fundamentalists differentiate between scripture passages: some are historical, some biographical, some are parables, some are symbolic and metaphorical, some are concerned with practical behaviour or conduct, and some are doctrinal, though as we have seen with Genesis, some literal sounding verses may be interpreted figuratively for convenience. Either way, the Scriptures and the main teaching inherent within them are elevated to an absolute degree: Scripture and the concepts and ideas it portrays are the Final Authority for faith and conduct. The believer may be reminded of the watchwords of the reformers: 'Sola Scriptura!' – Scripture alone!

The question we have to ask is: Are such forms absolute? Are such ideas and concepts Ultimate? I suggest that they are not and we see a clue why in the approach by fundamentalists themselves to the Divine Name 'Father'. The concept, attribute, Name, quality, characteristic, relationship of 'Father' is not Absolute because God transcends gender – God is neither Male nor Female and therefore not 'Father'. I suggest that there is a higher view of the Divine than that which is encompassed and bordered by conceptual ideas and forms, whoever may advocate them – Christian, Jew or Muslim. God is transcendent of the concepts and formulations of 'Father', 'Creator', 'Love', 'Judge' and so on. These are all limited, finite, relational terms but God as Absolute is Infinite, Transcendent and Unique. God alone is Real – God alone has Self-sufficient existence – all else is dependent upon God. The Absolute is transcendent of these limited forms, names and designations. They are in fact just useful metaphors that stand between us as creatures of form and the Formless, Infinite Absolute God. We stand in relation to God and these are relational terms that reveal aspects and facets of an Absolute that we cannot comprehend or encompass with forms, ideas and concepts. God transcends any philosophy or theology.

One mistake that fundamentalists fall into then is to elevate the language and conceptual ideas of Scripture to the level of Absolute – such that these main ideas must be conserved and defended at all costs. The attention of the fundamentalist is taken away from Absolute God and instead directed to relative level of Scripture and scriptural ideas which are then falsely elevated to the level of Absolute. This focus on form and concept actually distracts the attention away from the Absolute Transcendent Divine. The eyes of the fundamentalist are often not on God, but on conformity to and agreement with a set of conceptual forms which fall short of Absolute God.

This means then that forms are Ultimately transcended, or to put it another way, as we draw close to Transcendent God in experience, these concepts and forms of the Divine may fall away and be rendered useless – inadequate to express and encompass the Vastness of the Absolute. Systems of theology and doctrine are not the Absolute but rather occupy a relational middle ground – they are useful as far as they go. In turn this means that we can be more open and tolerant of other religious systems, rather than seeking to defend our own conceptions of the Divine at all costs. This does not mean that different religious systems or schools can be merged. Though Ultimately they all point to Absolute God, yet these systems and their concepts exist in relation and thus exclude as well as enclose. What becomes important for the individual is internal consistency and coherence – an integrity and good fit of concepts whilst at the same time recognising their middle status in transcendence.

AN OUTLINE CRITIQUE THE CHRISTIAN FUNDAMENTALIST SYSTEM

This study is only an overview, in order to get something of the flavour of the major criticisms and observations concerning fundamentalist theology, the fundamentalist system and the fundamentalist believer. Having spent twenty-five years in a Calvinist fundamentalist environment I support most of the following observations. The arguments are only briefly presented here since it is not the purpose of this study to examine at large the structure of fundamentalism. I present the observations rather as a context for this study of the Calvinist's approach to spiritual gifts. Those who wish to examine the arguments and observations more fully should refer to the books listed at the end of this chapter for further reading.

FUNDAMENTALIST THEOLOGY

What sort of theology is created by a system that depends upon the inerrancy of Scripture? Fundamentalists do indeed have a theology but: -

a) It is a fossilised theology based on 18th Century revivals and the conservation of 19th Century Calvinism. But, because of discoveries and insights gained since these times, changes have taken place as regards the approach to Scripture by scholars. The reformers were not aware of these discoveries, and created an integrated system of theology which at the time was appropriate and made sense. But WE are aware of these discoveries of literature, archaeology and science. If then we still hold to certain of the reformers views, we are DIFFERENT from them, because we have knowledge that they did not possess. (1). It is like us holding to the notion that the earth is flat or that that sun goes round the earth. At one time, these seemed plausible, but new evidence has caused us to abandon or modify these ideas. If the reformers were sincere seekers after truth, I am certain that they would reappraise and modify some of their views in the light of subsequent discoveries.

b) The older theologies required a thoroughly worked out system, with interdependent parts carefully stated and worked out in detail, such as the Westminster Confession of faith. Many groups within modern fundamentalism, including Charismatic groups, merely pick out parts of these systems and have no concept of interrelatedness. Rather, adherence to vital, nodal points is required as tests of orthodoxy. (2). But the claim that the theology is orthodox must be questioned when the holistic, systematic interrelatedness of earlier systems is abandoned. It would have bean unthinkable at the tine of the composition of the Westminster Confession to merely extract certain features and leave others. Rather, the whole works together. (3). But in much fundamentalism, elements of doctrine are conserved in such a way as they have to be affirmed, even though that doctrine may not play a great role in the life of the believer, such as for example, the virgin birth of Christ. One of the functions of this doctrine is to act as a sign of the correct conservatism of the believer. This process is called formalisation.

c) Claims of orthodoxy are emphasised by fundamentalists, who trace a line of thought back to the reformation and to the early church fathers. But claims of orthodoxy must again be questioned. As with documents like the Westminster Confession, only certain parts of the theology of these people are selected. Augustine's emphasis on justification by faith for example. But other, more Catholic ideas adopted by Augustine are ignored. So when appeals are made to certain historical figures, there is a selection of ideas and doctrine, such that some aspects are emphasised and others ignored. Similarly, they may appeal a line from Athanasius and his doctrine of the incarnation and the trinity, but ignore the integrated ideas that went with it, including the priesthood, liturgy and vestments. For similar reasons, there is a break with orthodoxy when using documents like the Westminster Confession, but not only because of selective use of passages and loss of integration. There is also a different purpose. This document was drawn up to be imposed upon every person in England and Scotland by the state, but it is not used in that way by fundamentalists today. Not only is its integrated approach ignored but it is used for a different purpose than that for which it was intended.

d) It is inactive. There is no new work for theologians to do other than conservation of ideas brought out in the reformation, revivals and nineteenth century, and their reiteration. There is no progression of theology other than a reframing of it for today's world. Thus: -

e) There is no challenge to the institutions, assumptions and traditions of fundamentalism except within it's main framework of belief. Forms of church service may be changed, so that choruses are sung as well as hymns, or something similar; methods of evangelism may vary, but basic assumptions about the nature and interpretation of Scripture are not addressed. In this sense it is totally complacent and lacks self-criticism. (4)

f) Because of it's views on the authority and inspiration of Scripture, and the belief that it's interpretation is correct, preserving a long line of pure Christian thought and doctrine against the error, corruption and heresy of liberal and Roman Catholic thinkers, it has no conception of a catholic community of theological thinkers in discussion. It insists that the one question of theology is Scripture authority. (5). There is little understanding of what non-conservative theologians think and no incentive to find out. (6)

g) As regards the Lord Jesus Christ, whilst fundamentalists acknowledge that Christ is both God and man, the emphasis falls heavily on the God-ward side. He is God walking about and teaching in a man's body. Any approach that starts out seeing Jesus as a man falls under suspicion from fundamentalists and tends to be rejected, or qualified with a stronger assertion that He is God. (7). Jesus becomes more like God giving out eternally correct information through a human mouth rather than a God/man speaking under the conditions of his time and situation… he is made into a superhuman and inhuman person (8). One of the effects of this is to infer the downgrading of the suffering, pain and anguish of Jesus.

h) With regard to Pentecostalism and the Charismatic movement, there is a shift of emphasis, away from orthodoxy, intellectualism and absolute doctrinal correctness, with the coldness and formality that these imply, towards a personal experience of God. (9). There is in fact the potential for conflicts with Scripture via the 'inspired gifts' of tongues, prophecy and so on, but since there is less emphasis on the intellectual side of Scripture and the formulation of a systematic theology, such conflicts, unless very obvious, may not be noticed. Also, grading takes place, where the Scripture is seen as pre-eminent over displays of gifts in terms of authority.

i) The introduction of New Translations may force ecumenicity on fundamentalists, especially with loss of the A.V.; There is greater awareness of contradictions between sources of Biblical documents. Thus, there is a contradiction in dates as regards the Israelites time in Egypt before the Exodus between Paul quoting the Septuagint in Galatians 3 v 17 and the references in the Hebrew Old Testament, the Masoretic text. (Genesis 12 v 4, 21 v 5, 25 v 26, 47 v 9). Differences between source documents and the exact rendering of words force openness to alternative interpretations to the protestant evangelical one.

THE CONSERVATIVE EVANGELICAL SYSTEM

Having looked at problems with the foundation of fundamentalism on the idea of infallible Scripture, and having looked at some broad aspects of the theology it creates, I want to expand on some of the facets and criteria for this group as follows:
Contrary to many views fundamentalism does not rest:
in simplism.
in concreteness of approach.
or in intolerance of ambiguity. (10)

1) The fundamentalist system consists of themes of separation and alienation of believers from the surrounding world, from modern theology and from modern Bible study methods. Anything perceived as threatening to the fundamentalist ideology is to be avoided and/or criticised. In mentioning to certain fundamentalists that I was reading ' Fundamentalism' by James Barr, which is critical of fundamentalism, I was reminded by them that this was 'dangerous'. The fundamentalist position often consists in a depreciation of whatever is exterior to the Bible in their interpretation.

2) There is in fundamentalism a characterisation of the believer as chosen by God in His sovereignty, and that those who do not share this believer's worldview are not really true Christians. Fundamentalism tends to argue that fundamentalism is the one true faith, and those who

embrace other Christian systems are false Christians. But, this basis of faith in Scripture alone is not sufficiently coherent to maintain one interpretation or faith. Other fundamentalist groups also hold to inerrancy and singleness of Scripture, such as the Christadelphians. The authority of fundamentalism fails to prevent the emergence and growth of numerous and violent contradictions within it's own scheme. This is because of the vagueness and gaps present in Scripture and the variety of traditions brought to its interpretation.

3) There is fundamentalism an emphasis away from benefits and rewards in this life, and towards the life to come, when God will judge all things and complete fairness will be introduced. Thus tolerance of dissatisfaction, compliance to the status quo and lack of criticism is engendered. It is accepted that some things are not fair now, but rather than change them, an appeal to a better life to come with humble acceptance of one's lot now is made.

4) There is a negative characterisation of the individual person apart from their condition as a believer. This may serve to confirm the beliefs of those who have low self esteem that their self estimation is right, and that the gospel message is true by reason of it's accurate diagnosis of their person. Sin is a valuable intellectual resource to fundamentalism, without it, it could not get anywhere, yet fundamentalists do not have a deeper or fuller awareness of sin than other aspects of Christianity. (11).

5) The conservative approach accepts older views, though it is selective. It seeks to preserve rather than rebuild, though within Charismatic groups there are progressive elements. The Charismatic influence is by no means limited to protestant fundamentalism; it is to be found in Roman Catholicism and liberal theological groups.

6) There is today, within fundamentalism, no social gospel. One reason that there is no interest in social action is because of eschatology... the doctrine of the last things. There is an expectation of things getting worse as we enter the last days before Christ's return. Fundamentalism has departed from its fore bears in this respect. (12)

7) There is an anti clericism, such that theological scholars and academics are often not recognised, and ordinary laymen with little or no theological training may get up and speak on the Bible. The qualities

looked for by fundamentalists are conformity to fundamentalist practice, an accurate repetition of fundamentalist theology, and an absence of any scandal or overt sin such as continual thieving or overt sexual immorality. Academic qualities, if not conforming to fundamentalist ideas, are simply liberal and wrong as far as the fundamentalist is concerned.

THE MAINTENANCE OF THE INFLUENCE OF CONSERVATIVE EVANGELICALISM

How does the fundamentalist system maintain its influence? Many people like or want to believe that there is, somewhere, some book that is absolutely true and correct, and in European and American culture, that book is likely to be the Bible. But, does the Bible distinguish itself from this non-religious appetite for belief in a true book, or does it pander to those emotions? (13) We have seen that the approach to Scripture is worked out by and for the conservative position. It does not give reasons to the non conservative why Biblical inspiration should be essential, apart from a claim that the Bible says so, which is a proof only for those who already hold the fundamentalist position. It forms a tight circle around existing believers... they can escape only at the cost of a deep and traumatic shattering of their entire religious outlook. (14)

Furthermore, Conservatism is often not content to preach the gospel as a message of salvation. Rather, it may use the gospel as a weapon to attack man, undermine his security, overcome him and force him into submission to the conservative way of thinking. (15). The person who accepts such a faith soon finds that he has to live within a conservative evangelical community which also holds as essential a whole lot of other things and the personal dynamics of the group are used to enforce conformity with these opinions. (16). Conservatives present a benign persona of the Bible and of themselves as conservative evangelicals rather than fundamentalists, i.e., extremists. But there is a real danger of unbalanced and/or superficial teaching, within a system that we have already found psychologically binding.

There is also a depreciation of the world... (there is none good but God). That which is outside fundamentalism is presented as wrong, unhealthy, displeasing to God, e.t.c.. This is done partly by emphasising 'conversion' which distinguishes between 'real' and 'nominal' Christians,

17

and partly by mistrust of others arising out of a desire for purity of doctrine. Having said that, of course, it is equally true that philosophies and assumptions essential to science and social science theories in turn may and sometimes do depreciate religion. Any world-view may be prejudiced, superficial and blinkered, including evangelicalism. The Apostle Paul analysed and carefully observed other religions, (Acts 17), so, for the fundamentalist, there, should not be intellectual abandonment of religions and schemes outside their own framework. But such abandonment there is, and it may serve to protect believers from experiences that threaten their indoctrination.

There can be a danger of what Cohen calls logocide. There is a danger of not adequately defining and qualifying words from Scripture. More dangerously, there may be too many meanings assigned to one word, which effectively destroys the word, and thus false interpretations of the gospel may be offered. Thus, in problem situations with the fundamentalist scheme, believers may be told that a particular word or phrase does not mean what it appears to mean, but has other meanings, spiritual meanings, literal or allegorical meanings or subtle shades of translation, or that the word may be used in a number of different ways, such that the word 'heaven' may mean the sky, the universe, or paradise.

There is a tendency to repress any tendency to think critically about one's beliefs. (17) This may be done by becoming involved in teaching others, and thus suppressing, one's doubts whilst reiterating beliefs to others. (18) Thus there is a stifling of inner apprehensions that the believer has nothing to see, hear, touch or handle or something better in lieu of these. (19). Indeed, the only TANGIBLE evidence of God in these groups is the Bible.

There is the use of Holy terror. Much has already been written on this elsewhere. A system has been created where there is fear of judgement or apostasy or punishment for in effect not conforming to the system. Whilst Holy terror may to some extent guard the basic ideas, the believer is not necessarily in an attitude of fear, but may be quite stable, balanced and happy.

THE CONSERVATIVE EVANGELICAL BELIEVER

What then is the believer like? Contrary to a lot of views, he in fact tolerates too much ambiguity. He lets artificially induced confusion reign where he ought to throw it off. As we have seen, the Scriptures do not offer a full and comprehensive guide to life. Rather, the believer is likely to make himself dependant upon a Pastor's rendition of arcane pseudo-issues to deal with practical matters when common sense should be sufficient. (20). Cohen, looking at sub conscious and unconscious factors considers that a process of dissociation induction takes place.

By dissociation is meant a process whereby a coordinated set of activities, thoughts, attitudes, and emotions become separated and function independently. (21). So, for example, information, experiences, and impressions are gestated unconsciously. Whilst it is true that we do apply implications and principles without fully understanding, nevertheless we want to keep reworking ideas that do not fit the evidence of our senses. The believer however is obsessed with God and God's thoughts as expressed in the Bible. All other thoughts are to be avoided or else there will be a deterioration of faith. The inner man is seen as full of corruption, and desires to rework ideas may be thought of as part of this corruption, a sin of doubt and or error regarding our attitude to the inerrant Scripture.

There is often intense group loyalty. The common convictions of the group come to dominate the individual. They do not interpret the Bible individually, but rather there is a reiteration of the normal fundamentalist interpretation. If the band of doctrinal purity is drawn tight enough, freedom and spontaneity can easily be lost. The loss of contact with non-conservatives produces an in-group mentality. (22). The social and religious organism has a closed mind. (23).

There is a general tendency to accept entirely from science it's picture of natural conditions in the world and to manoeuvre the interpretation of the Bible in order to find a place for it's narratives within this picture. Fundamentalists do NOT accept science as the controlling arbiter of reality, ultimately, they go to the Bible, but for a simple account of the world and how things work, they accept the scientific picture and work within it. (24).

The life of the Christian is defined in such a way as to provide for the acceptance of the secularisation of the surrounding culture... and it's

19

economic structure. (25). This includes preponderance to the right and extreme right, a tendency to sanction the capitalist system and laissez-faire approach to society, and to look with favour on the use of military power. The system becomes the ideological guarantor of the rightness of the existing social order, and it may be a focus of nationalistic feeling. (26). Whether these characteristics are. good or bad, right or wrong is not the issue here, they are merely pointed to as observed by others a prevalent within this group.

Needless to say, Barr is not without his critics, and perhaps the most scholarly is a work by Paul Ronald Wells called 'James Barr and the Bible: Critique of a new Liberalism'. This book is hard going, and uses many long and technical words and arguments, but ultimately, in many ways, it fails to address the main issues that I have outlined above, Wells argues that fundamentalism is consistent in its argument regarding similarities between the dual nature of Christ and the dual nature of Scripture, and that it would nave to be shown to be inconsistent to be disproved. Here again, the onus is thrown upon the unbeliever to disprove the fundamentalist's position rather than the other way around. In any case, surely consistency and proof are different things. Wells argues that the fundamentalist aligns the authority of Christ and the authority of Scripture in the context of the revelation of the Father. Again, Wells argues that 'all Scripture' in II Timothy indicates an organic scriptural unity, and that they were viewed as one code, though he concedes that it is not possible to assert which books are in 'all Scripture'. He further argues that the distinction between the 'original inerrant manuscripts' and later faulty copies is a logical one, and that one can do theologians such as Warfield an injustice in implying too much calculated maintenance of Calvinism by his arguments. Wells maintains that the fundamentalist concerns about inerrancy are not to do with maintaining a series of doctrines or a system, but are rather about sin as a corrupting and God rejecting factor, however, as we have seen, too much emphasis on this leads to a position whereby all doubts and contradictory positions are sinful.

Wells argues that revelation has to be put in the context of the relationship of Divine and human elements, which are not neutral. These elements are in a context of the unity of the Spirit of God and the people of God. He argues that the real duplicity is between communion with God

20

in the Spirit and the breaking of that communion in covenant breaking disobedience.

As God communes with man, the word of God to man takes on the use of created means such as words, language and consciousness. This communion is not known to man until it enters human form, the human factor, history and created reality being necessary for this communion to be realised. The human is not an appendage to the Divine. This leads Wells to consider the problem of the letter of Scripture and it's relationship to the Spirit. He argues that Calvin recognised the problem:

Inspiration can be spoken of in a fallible sense, whilst Satan can disguise himself as an angel of light - there must be a distinguishing mark of authority. Wells argues that Calvin transcends the duality problem by stating that the Spirit is the Author of Scripture and the Spirit is consistent with Himself. However we are merely in a philosophical argument here and we still have no evidence that Scripture really is what fundamentalists claim it to be. Once again, Wells cops out by insisting that fallen reason is no judge of the truth of the Spirit. Wells argues that the Spirit takes men's words into service so that these are divinely authorised to seal the covenant communion. However, this cannot be considered in a formal way as a problem of how the divine and human are united, and that such an undertaking would be an unwarranted attempt to penetrate the mystery of the Spirit's work. In other words, Wells can't solve the problem either, and of course, to try and do so is sinful. Wells then goes on to say that Scripture is fully a work of the Spirit, and of man in restored communion with God, and that therefore, the truthfulness Scripture cannot be considered in isolation from the work of the Spirit in the new creation. He argues that it cannot be declared as having errors by taking fallen human reasoning principles and applying them to the new creation, or by looking at correspondence with certain factors accepted as true, because this sets correspondence with present human knowledge as an authority over Scripture. Here again is the 'everything outside of scripture is sin' argument, counted with the idea of insight and elitism of those in communion with God. What then are the criteria of inerrancy according to Wells?

He argues that errancy/inerrancy cannot be established or disproved by human reason but through consideration of the scope of Scripture and its ability to restore man to communion with God!! It is not that factual correspondences are eliminated, but they are not central. In other words because Scripture affects some people such that they are drawn to God, converted and so on, we should accept Scripture as inerrant. By this argument, the Koran is true also. I find Wells' argument wholly inadequate. Beliefs are supported by correspondence with perceived reality, evidence, logic and so on, and discrepancies lead to doubt, lack of commitment, conflict, dissonance and unsettlement, promoting either a change of beliefs, or, if this is too costly, attempts at denying or reinterpreting conflicting evidence, redoubling one's efforts at increasing faith, or self condemnation. If acute enough, it would lead to rejection and rebellion. Wells then addresses the issue of how Scripture is to be interpreted. He argues that if we interpret Scripture empirically, then theological connections are severed and the Bible becomes merely a human document, and it's interpreter becomes trapped in socio/cultural relativism. However, Wells suggests that we place our interpretation in the context of the renewing work of the Spirit, thus seeking the material content of the renewing work of the Spirit in the human form of the text.

Notice that Well's view has not even addressed discrepancies in Scripture, or the issue of which books are in the canon. He has rather argued for a special insight, knowledge and understanding which is a privilege gained by the believer through his renewed and restored relationship to God. Once again then, we have certain assumptions, the building up of an internal logic system linked to pleasing God. Though raising some interesting points, I think Wells fails to dismiss Barr's comments in full or to any great degree.

At best, what is supported is a softer view of inspiration, where boundaries between inspired and uninspired books are blurred and the extent of inspiration is not clearly defined.

The relational/communion perspective proposed by Wells allows for some mistakes via copying, translation and in the originals whilst still allowing for considerable unity, harmony, coherence and correlation to commonly accented truths. Human reason plays an important part in evaluating scripture: 2+2=5, is this true or false? 100 chariots or 1000? Both cannot be true. Scripture ideas are complex and human reasoning incomplete; therefore this entire issue is difficult and not absolute. This is the best that we can say.

WHAT THEN IS FUNDAMENTALISM?

Fundamentalism is a conceptual framework which structures and gives meaning to the world and Scripture in a particular way.

It centres primarily on the Scriptures, but the Scriptures, like facts, do not speak for themselves. We have to bring to Scripture concepts in order to categorise and make sense of the material that Scripture contains. Fundamentalism draws out one of many possible interpretations of Scripture for its system.

The theological meanings are created and maintained through a framework of interpretation where texts are graded, such that some are seen as more important than others, some are taken figuratively and others literally and so on. These meanings are also heavily influenced by a sense of tradition or orthodoxy that is selective in the information that it uses and which interacts with today's world, it's thoughts and experiences.

Thus for example it's strengthening of the idea of Scripture infallibility is a reaction to the rise of science and Biblical criticism. Fundamentalism is a collection of particular ideas and in that sense is an ideology, which is maintained and preserved by repetition and by avoidance of contrary ideas that are seen as dangerous and corrupting to the 'true' faith.

FURTHER READING:

BARR, J. (1977) 'Fundamentalism' SCM Press. London.
BARR, J. (1984) ' Escaping from fundamentalism' SCM Press. London.
COHEN, E.D. (1986) 'The mind of the Bible believer' Prometheus Books. Maw York.
LANE-FOX, 'R. (1992) 'The unauthorised version: Truth and fiction in the Bible'. Penguin. London.
WELLS, P.R. (1980) James Barr and the Bible: Critique of a new Liberalism. Presbyterian and reformed Publishing C o m p a n y. N e w J e r s e y.

REFERENCES

1) BARR, J. (1977) 'Fundamentalism' SC'M Press. London. p.173
2) Ibid. p.166
3) Ibid. p.163
4) Ibid. p.162
5) Ibid p. 163
6) Ibid. p.165
7) Ibid. p.160
8) Ibid. p.171
9) Ibid. p.208
10) COHEN, E.D. (1986) 'The mind of the Bible believer' Prometheus Books. 'New York.
    p.57,58.
11) BARR, J. (1977) 'Fundamentalism' SC! Press. London, pp.177-179.
12) Ibid. p.112-116
13) Ibid. p139.
14) Ibid. p.260-266.
15) Ibid. p.225.
16) Ibid. p.266.
17) COHEN E.D. (1986) The mind of the Bible Believer' Prometheus Books, New York. p.240.
18) Ibid. p.245
19) Ibid. p.244.
20) Ibid. D.244.
21) REBER, A.S. (1985) 'The Penguin dictionary of Psychology' Penguin. London, p.208.
22) BARR, J. (1977) 'Fundamentalism' SCM Press. London. p.317- 319.
23) Ibid. p. 323
24) Ibid. p.97
25) Ibid. p.99.
26) Ibid. p. 109-111.

PROBLEMS WITH THE INSPIRATION AND INERRANCY OF SCRIPTURE -

AN AXE LAID TO THE ROOT OF CHRISTIAN FUNDAMENTALISM

This essay forms Chapter Eight of a more extensive study of spiritual gifts which is available in full here: http://www.scribd.com/doc/14805101/AN-INTRODUCTION-TO-SPIRITUAL-GIFTS

I have looked at spiritual gifts from a framework adopted by fundamentalists, and Calvinists in particular, which Cohen describes as the most consistent with Biblical passages. (1) It is 'now important to stand back, and step outside this framework for a critical evaluation, and in doing so I shall look at the foundation of fundamentalism: Scripture. In doing so, we shall be looking at what fundamentalists consider to be the highest form of inspired revelation, and this has obvious implications for the gifts of inspired revelation. One of the main tenets of fundamentalist is that the Bible is inerrant and thus fully corresponds to reality. All passages of Scripture are interpreted in the light of this position. In many respects, for fundamentalists, the Scriptures are second only to God and form the supreme TANGIBLE sacred reality, because within fundamentalism there is no emphasis on relics, ceremony, ritual or art. (2). A term which often links Calvinists with Pentecostals is the phrase conservative evangelicalism. By definition, conservative evangelicals accept older views from the reformation and puritan times, which they seek to preserve. Only occasionally is the word conservative used to indicate social and political views. In other words, there is an emphasis not only on the inerrancy of Scripture, but the need to maintain the purity of doctrines in Scripture, which are seen as largely drawn out of Scripture by the reformers and other reformed orthodox leaders. There is then also a sense of tradition within fundamentalism, which goes right back to the early Christian fathers, but most overtly to the fathers of the protestant reformation. This tradition immediately frames the way in which fundamentalists interpret Scripture and leads fundamentalists to emphasise certain passages and verses and de-emphasise others, despite a belief in the total inerrancy of Scripture. I will speak more of this in a moment, but I am concerned to emphasise now that fundamentalism has its own particular tradition of interpretation of Scripture.

There are within this fundamentalist scheme, themes of separation and alienation of believers from the surrounding world, from modern theology and modern Bible study methods, which are seen as threats to the purity of the doctrines drawn out of Scripture by fundamentalists. (3). The Conservative Evangelical sees himself as a real Christian, because he upholds these views, which are considered as orthodox, plain truths from Scripture, whereas others, though they may be professing, Christians, are seen as 'nominal' Christians because they do not subscribe to these views. More will be said later, in postscript, on the system of conservative evangelicalism but the initial focus of this chapter is on these claims regarding Scripture. This is an important issue, since it forms the very foundation of this group and it's philosophy and so far has formed the basis of this study on spiritual gifts.

THE SCRIPTURES

First of all, I want to look at the Scriptures themselves. These are generally defined as the books of the Old and New Testament, beginning with Genesis, and ending with Revelation, generally referred to as the Canon of Scripture. Inspired revelation is perceived by conservative evangelicals to have ceased with the book of Revelation. The word -canon- refers to a rule, and thus this particular set of books is seen as being an authority and rule for faith. Though there may in some groups be an emphasis on tongues and prophecy, as inspired and revealed by the Holy Spirit for use today, these are generally not put on a par with Scripture, though there is an underlying source of conflict and tension here. Nevertheless, they are not considered to be a rule and authority in the same way as Scripture is. It is important to realise that this canon has not been defined by God in the Scriptures themselves. Though the last verses of Revelation are sometimes quoted to refer to an end of the canon of Scripture, these verses only refer to the book of Revelation itself, since at the time of its writing, the canon had not been formed. Cohen argues (4) that the Scriptures as a whole assume an intellectual posture as to their own interpretation and that this resides in depreciation of whatever is exterior to the Bible. Now it is a fact that the various writings may hold this view, but the scriptures as a whole do not have a view of themselves. These various writings were not gathered together fully until a few hundred years after they were written, so the writings never take a view of themselves as a whole assembled group. The exact process by which these books came to be known as authoritative is not known.

Who wrote these books and how were they preserved? For the conservative evangelical, these books were written by the declared authors:

Moses wrote the first five books. Matthew, Mark Luke and John wrote the gospels, and Paul wrote many of the New Testament letters along with Peter and John. Historians and scholars take different views. According to LANE FOX (5) the earliest known authors are from the 8th Century B.C., known E (Elohist) from the northern kingdom of Israel, and later, J, (Yahwehist) from the southern kingdom. The actual earliest surviving documents are from about a century later and shortly after this, covenant ideas were added to J. Following the fall of the northern kingdom, the work of E was brought to the southern kingdom, and following the collapse of the south, most of the Old Testament material was gathered together and/or written during the period of exile by D, (Deuteronomist). Following the return to Jerusalem after the captivity, another source was added, P (Priest) when the ceremonial and sacrificial laws were added. The other two divisions, the prophets and the writings were selected out of a larger body of literature, some of which is mentioned in the Old Testament itself: The book of the Wars of the Lord (Numbers 21 v 14), the book of Jasher, (Joshua 10 vl3), the book of the Acts of Solomon, (I Kings 11 v 31), the book of Samuel the seer, the book of Nathan the prophet, the book of Gad the seer, (I Chronicles 29 v 29). Fifteen or more such books are mentioned in the Old Testament. LANE FOX argues (6), that some material was written as late as 160 B.C. He argues that there was much forgery and a wide range of documents, but as such, no Old Testament canon. This suggests a different approach and understanding of the Scriptures by these Jews than that of fundamentalists or conservative evangelicals today. The oldest surviving list of the Old Testament canon dates from A.D.170, from a Christian scholar, Melito of Sardis, who made a trip to Palestine in order to determine the order and content of the Hebrew Bible. Neither his order nor content agrees with our modern Bibles. LANE FOX also argues that there appears to be a wide diversity of meanings and emphases between translations and particular groups, of which we see evidence in various manuscripts such as the Dead Sea Scrolls, Proto Masoretic and Masoretic texts. He argues that the debate about just which texts were holy went on well into the end of the first century.

LANE FOX (7) argues that Jesus treated the Scriptures as other Jews: the Law was most important, other texts were important but we do not know which. At this time, there were lots of debates about gaps in Scripture, and considerable freedom in their interpretation, much more freedom than the fundamentalist-s views held today. In fact, there were few if any principles of interpretation, and passages were sometimes taken out of context. Acts 1 v 20 itself gives us an indication of no known modern principles of interpretation being used in the quoting of Old Testament texts and their fulfilment in the New Testament. Nevertheless, Jesus Himself accepted Jewish Scriptures as the Word of God. They supported His work and person via prophecy but did not control it absolutely. So, for example, there is no record of Jesus planning a New Testament, or instructing his disciples to write such a document. Neither did His communication of the gospel largely rely on Scripture, but rather on His own unique teachings, His parables and so on. So the idea that Scripture is our only guide for religion does not come from Jesus. Rather, it arises from a particular interpretation and tradition of viewing Scripture.

Paul received teaching from Christian followers within a year of Christ's death, and within twenty years, the Hebrew text became the Old Testament, though it took a while for a Christian interpretation of Ecclesiastes or Esther to be formed since they had no obvious relevance. Jude quotes books other than the Old Testament canon which we now use. The use of proof texts by Christians from the Hebrew texts widened, some of which were not considered authoritative, and it is perhaps for this reason that an Old Testament canon was formed. But the debate as to which was authoritative and which was not, continued into the 16th Century. (8).

Similarly, there is debate about the scope, authorship and writing order of our New Testament. Some have been and still are considered suspect, such as the letters to Timothy and the letters of Peter. The grounds for doubt arise from their sense of history, style of writing and doctrine. The earliest list containing only the books which we use appeared in A.D. 367, in a letter of Athanasius, Bishop of Alexandria. Justin Martyr for example, argued for only the four gospels. Much discussion took place regarding the content of a canon in these early centuries. The books that we have are drawn from a larger collection of writings, such as another letter to the Corinthians, a letter to the Laodiceans, I & II Clement, and the Teachings of the Apostles. At the same time, there were a number of fraudulent documents around. However, an ecumenical council, in Carthage in 397 A.D., appears to be the first undisputed decision as to what was canonical. But even here, there was no central authority to decide the canon. The Syriac, Ethiopian, Greek Orthodox and

28

others all issued various canons, despite great care being taken in deciding which was of the canon and which was not. The Old Testament apocrypha, a collection of thirteen books have at times been rejected and accepted by various groups. The reformers rejected them, but Luther considered them profitable. The Coverdale and Geneva Bibles included them, but the British and foreign Bible society, after much debate excluded them from it's Bibles in 1827, the American branch soon following suit. (9). The point I am emphasising is that this has been a much-debated human decision. The final canon that we know is not absolutely, clearly defined by God for us. In the main, one of the criteria seemed to be that any document other than that from an Apostle, was rejected, the Apostles having been eyewitnesses to the life, death and resurrection of Jesus. Except of course Paul, who was one called out of time. For the fundamentalist, this helps to give authority to these New Testament books, but again, it must be remembered that these were human beings, prone to sin and error, (Galatians 2 v 11-21, Acts 15 v 36-40), and that the authorship of some of these books is disputed. The assumption is, certainly by modern fundamentalists, (because Scripture does not declare it), that the Apostles were, in effect, like the modern Pope, infallible in doctrine, therefore, their writings are infallible.

I am concerned to show at the moment that human beings, perhaps sincere believers in the church, have created the canon of Scripture over a period of time, with much debate, and with disagreement even amongst reformers and modern Protestants, and that there is no God defined canon. This raises the possibility that our present canon almost certainly excludes some inspired revelation, and that it may also contain some non inspired works. For this latter, one need look no farther than the end of Mark's gospel, (16 v 9-20), which though previously accepted as canonical is now prefixed by the statement '(the most reliable ancient manuscripts and other ancient witnesses do not have Mark 16 v 9-20)'.

As we look at the Reformers we find a much more flexible approach to Scripture than the identification of a hard and fast canon. Luther denied the canonicity of James, Esther, Ecclesiastes, Hebrews and Revelation, (10). It did not matter to him if some of the writings of the Old Testament have passed through revising hands. 'What would it matter if Moses did not write the Pentateuch?' (11). He called James 'a right strawny epistle'. (12). Calvin doubted the Petrine authorship of II Peter and excluded the book of Revelation (13). Calvin places Psalms 74 and 79 to the period of

Antiochus Epiphanes, far later than usually acknowledged. (14) Calvin argues, 'it is not by David... it is probable that many Psalms were composed by different authors after the death of David. (15). The point that I want to make here is that it is clear that the reformers, or some of them were ready to make some critical literary judgements on Biblical texts. The fact that these were made at all suggests that with fuller evidence, they may have gone farther along this line.

The canon then is like a room with contents of furniture and decoration from different dates to which we have agreed not to add or take away. The contents DO add up to a new whole, but they do not lose their individual natures. However, by placing them in association we alter our perception of the individual items. Nevertheless, the individual items still retain their meaning. In Scripture, whether in our particular canon or another, the Song of Songs is still a collection of erotic poetry. (16). But, by lumping the texts together there is a high chance that the community will misread them. (17) It adds another way of reading them which may quite often be wrong. Furthermore, as we have seen, scholars argue that the Bible documents are not in the main, primary sources. Rather they are an amalgam of previously written material, which are not necessarily accurate and later authors none of whom had a critical eye for accuracy or good method. They simply took earlier accounts as fact. (18)

THE INSPIRATION OF SCRIPTURE.

Now Scripture declares an inspiration of Scripture. 'All Scripture is God breathed and is useful for teaching, rebuking, correcting and training in righteousness.' (11 Timothy 3 v 16), and 'for prophecy never had it's origin in the will of man, but 'men spoke from God as they were carried along by the Holy Spirit.' (II Peter I v 21). But, as we have seen, when Scripture appears to look at itself, it does not in fact have the canon of Scripture in view as we know it. This canon, this rule of faith was not formed until some considerable time after these writings had been circulated and the authors themselves had died. As such, the Bible has no view of itself as a complete entity. Any writers commenting upon Scripture were referring to the Old Testament and possibly other documents.

The word for inspiration in the New Testament is Theopneustos, and means 'God breathed'. (19). Our question must be, what is the nature and decree of this inspiration? For example, does it extend to the very words, accents, vowels and punctuations? Some conservative evangelicals will insist that it does. They use a prophetic paradigm: As God inspired and breathed His Word into the mouths of the prophets such that they spoke God's Word without error, so in the same way. God inspired the Scripture writers. But in fact there are linguistic problems here, since in the Hebrew language, in the case of some Old Testament books, the vowels were not added until a few hundred years later as the language changed, more importantly, such a view leads to a mechanistic view of inspiration. Here the writers are not even penmen in God's hands, but merely pens. Now it does seem apparent that in some cases, God did give commands and statements by audible voice and so on, and in some cases they were written or commanded to be written down. For example, Numbers 7 v 89, Daniel 4 v 31, Exodus 3 v 4. But such a view of inspiration cannot account for the diversity of styles and accounts from Scripture writer to writer. The individual authors' style and personality can be seen to vary from person to person in the various books of the Bible. Neither is this God's normal way of working as indicated in Scripture itself. God does not dictate and dominate the person so that they are a mere puppet or automaton. God uses the individual's gifts and abilities.

STRONG, (20) outlines various views of inspiration. Some argue that it is a heightened sense of man's natural powers, knowledge and insight. The fundamentalist will argue that, while it is true that man can aspire to nobler powers and insights, as regards religion, such insights are often corrupted by mistaken affections arising from his own corrupt nature. It is especially as regards God and righteousness before Him that the Scripture speaks of our corruption. Also there is a contradiction, since by such inspiration, men are supposed to have written the Bible, the Koran and other religious works. Since these books contradict one another on basic ideas, then one man has been inspired to utter what a second man has been inspired to pronounce false. Thus, they argue, we enter a realm of subjectivism, and the end result is that there is no objective reality independent of men's opinions concerning these things. Ultimately, they argue, such a view of inspiration denies God, and elevates man to the highest intelligence. Another view, similar to the one above, argues that the religious perceptions of the believing writers were intensified and elevated by the Holy Spirit. Here, the writers, not the writings were inspired, and no objective truth beyond the believing writers ability to conceive and understand were communicated. Certainly, the fundamentalist will argue, there may be instances where the writers were illuminated in this way, but such a view is not sufficient to account for the revelation of new truths in the evolving nature of Scripture. The giving of a new truth by revelation is different not only in degree but also in kind.

If we are to propose a theory of inspiration at all, we must move to a more dynamic and interactive theory. I will suggest that firstly, we must hold that inspiration is not merely natural but a supernatural act, an immediate work of a personal God in or on a person or persons. This of course assumes the existence of such a God. Because of the way that Scripture is written, it is not as simple as God inspiring a single Scripture writer, but also those who compiled and selected the various works at various times. Secondly, the inspiration extends not only to the writers, but also to their writings. The degree and extent to which this takes place is not known. The writers themselves were sinners, and further corruptions have entered over time and through copying and translation, but taken together, if we are insisting on an idea of inspiration, such writings would constitute a more trustworthy and sufficient record of divine revelation than mere human speculation. One analogy is that Jesus is both God and man. He is not a composite, or superhuman but both God and man. If we could have physically examined Christ we would have found nothing extra in his body to make Him more than a man, yet He was also God. His divinity exists alongside His Humanity. So too, we look at Scripture and find them written by ordinary, sinful men, and it is in many ways no more than an ordinary book, yet it is inspired. It has all the weakness and variability of a human work, yet it is the Word of God through which He communicates to us. In such a work, we would expect to find a broad and main unity and agreement be they in the canon or not. Thirdly, such writings would contain a human as well as a Divine element, such that the revealed truth is shaped and adapted to ordinary human minds, customs and cultures of the time. To describe such writings as the Word of God then, is in some ways a misnomer. Rather, it is a joint work, of man and God, which would contain in some places, the literal words of God, as spoken by Him, audibly. The Bible could be seen as a collection of such writing, gathered together after much debate by various people, handed down, changed and sometimes uncertain in origin, being neither solely the work of God, nor solely the work of man, but a joint work. This view takes into account the Divine side of the Scriptures and the human side, and the customs, culture, limited knowledge and traditions of this human side in both the formulation and writing of Scripture together with the sinful nature of the writers. But this leads us on to our next theme, the inerrancy of Scripture.

THE INERRANCY OF SCRIPTURE

The over emphasis of the God ward side of Scripture by fundamentalists, to the point where it is regarded as the 'Word of God' has led to a conclusion that the Scriptures are inerrant or totally without mistake. In fact, many who believe the Bible to be inerrant have never fully read it. Rather, it is a matter of faith, and logical argument based on presupposition. This logical argument goes something like this: -

It begins with the assumption that God is perfect, infallible and true. The idea that because God has inspired books they too must be perfect is essentially an idea of Greek origin, an idea that presents perfection as the essence of God. However, in Scripture, God is represented as personal and active. He can change his mind, regret what he has done, be argued out of positions chat he has already taken up and operates in a narrative sequence and not out of static perfection. (21). But this idea of perfection is an assumption for the fundamentalist, since it's basis is also implied from Scripture itself. For the fundamentalist, God is the Author of the Bible as a whole, that is, He is the author of the canonical books by the third person of the trinity of the Godhead, the Holy Spirit. The conclusion from these two assumptions is that therefore, the Bible is perfect, infallible and true. This makes no allowance for the human element in Scripture writing, and has to be a mechanistic view of inspiration. But, it is a problem, with such detailed inspiration as inerrancy demands, to explain the variations of linguistic style of the writers, and the substantial variation between different manuscripts. For confirmation of this view however, the fundamentalist enters a circular argument: - the Bible says that God is perfect, infallible and true. If God is infallible and He inspired the Bible, then it must therefore be infallible also, and we know that this is true because the Bible says that God is infallible.

This then leads to two further conclusions: if an idea is consistent with the Bible, then the idea is true. If an idea is not consistent with the Bible, then the idea is false, because the Bible is perfect, infallible and true. But this connection between inspiration and inerrancy is a philosophical rather than a Biblical argument. Thus the Bible as inerrant frames the fundamentalist believer's worldview. It is a global, underlying philosophy that underpins their outlook. That which is outside the framework is mistaken, false, corrupt or not particularly relevant. But, there is a sense in which the framework is not complete. Because there are vagaries, and because there are areas not covered by Scripture, the framework is extended. It is extended by common sense, by self-interest, by personal philosophies and worldviews outside the scope of Scripture and so on. In the area of guidance and worship, spiritual gifts may supplement or even contradict the Biblical framework, ' especially for those with a low tolerance of ambiguity. Nevertheless, it is felt by many that if one side of this triangle of perfection, truth and inerrancy with regard to Scripture fails, then all fails, therefore, there is much attention given to interpretation and harmonisation of Scripture. Theologically however, it is a closed system. Anything which threatens this view is either avoided or attacked.

How else then it is argued that Scripture in inerrant? There are further approaches: - One is an ascending argument which states that the historical accuracy of Scripture is so great that the theology must be true. Another is a descending argument which states that the theology is so marvellous and convincing that we can be sure it contains no error of any sort. Also, important people in Scripture testified that it was so. Jesus and the Apostles said it was so. If it is not, if the Bible contains error, then these people were wrong or not trustworthy. Here, personal loyalty is used to force people into a fundamentalist position. But, if a professor of mathematics gives mistaken directions, his professorship or sincerity is not in doubt; rather he has made an error. The fundamentalist will argue that it is different when we are talking about the Son of God, and reassert the infallibility of Jesus as a person and the Apostles when it comes to doctrine. In the case of Jesus, his manhood and his context of talking to a particular generation is ignored. But the fundamentalist believes the Bible anyway: these verses merely formulate his existing belief which he comes to through the personal and moral pressure of the fundamentalist community, and through a pressure to come to terms with and develop a framework for dealing with such existential issues such as death, finiteness and meaning.

Conservative evangelical attempts to prove inerrancy make little or no contact with Biblical or textual criticism. In these approaches, texts are studied to look for differences which indicate different authors, functions and traditions. Criticisms slay be raised such as those raised by Calvin on the Psalms, and questions relating to myth, function, formulation, customs, history, discrepancy and error are asked. It is through this sort of approach that the last verses of Mark are now suspect. The basic difference is that fundamentalists see Scripture as a unified whole, to be harmonised, whereas the critics see the writings as separate texts, with the differences being of interest. Our model of -inspiration puts us between these two views... the Bible is more than human, it has an element of unity because it assumes that a single person, God, inspired it, but, because of the profusion of documents, copies and the human authors and context in which they were written, we should be carefully critical, not only of which books we include in the canon, but of the content of those books. To move from the dogmatic position to maximal conservatism where say, MOST of Deuteronomy can be attributed to Moses or the date of an apparently Davidic psalm is 'near' to David's time is LESS satisfactory, because it is less honest and more prejudiced. The dogmatic position may merely become a concealed norm and evidence may be slanted in favour of those concealed norms.

THE HISTORY OF THE FUMDAMENTALIST VIEW OF INERRANCY

Where has this particular fundamentalist view of inerrancy come from? What is its history? The establishment in the reformation of 'Scripture only' effectively cut off any philosophical theology or philosophical dialogue with the world, and it was this that made way for the birth of full fundamentalism. (22) Indeed, within this framework, people have believed that the Bible is true for many reasons, as illustrated in the Westminster Confession. Such reasons include the testimony of the Church, the heavenliness of the themes, the effectiveness of the doctrines, the majesty of the style, its harmony and scope, and the way in which reveals the way of salvation. But the Hodges and B. B. Warfield in Princeton in the nineteenth century were maintaining a high Calvinist view against a background of rising Biblical criticism. Hodge took what the Bible said about inspiration to be a doctrine. When faced with the question, 'How do we know it is true?' Hodge declared this to be beyond theology, and anything purporting to be a theology should accent this without question. However, he did not insist that inspiration was congruent with inerrancy. But Warfield did not allow this relaxed approach to stand, possibly because of perceived threats from Biblical criticism. Warfield argued that it was inerrant because it was inspired. This was a doctrine designed to prevent those who were already fundamentalists from abandoning that position. It was worked out by and for the conservative evangelical position. It does not give reasons to the non conservative why Biblical inspiration should be essential, apart from the fact that the Bible says so, which is a proof only for those who already hold the fundamentalist position. It is a circular argument because it is meant to be. The outsider can break in only by abandoning his objections and accepting entirely the worldview of those within. Equally, it forms a tight circle around existing believers... they can escape only at the cost of a deep and traumatic shattering of their entire religious framework. This is exactly what is intended. Nevertheless, it is little known among conservatives that Warfield asserted that Biblical inspiration was not an essential of Christianity. (23)

PROBLEMS WITH INERRANCY

There are a number of problems for the view of inerrancy. I have already indicated that Scripture has no view of itself as a canon, and that this view of inerrancy demands a detailed inspiration that requires a mechanical, deterministic approach contradicting the varieties of style that we have between the Scripture authors. To have suggested that a device using personal loyalty is used to persuade people of this view, and that the argument is philosophical and circular rather than Biblical. To these we may add another question. If sin is as pervasive as fundamentalists make out, does it affect the authorship and inerrancy of the Bible? According to fundamentalists, not at all. (24). Arguments are put forward to counter this suggestion, namely, that God held back the effects of sin in the writers as regards their writings. Again, this is a logical, philosophical argument, rather than a Biblical one. It is logical once one accepts certain suppositions and wishes to maintain inerrancy. But, if this modern view of inerrancy is correct then there can be no mistakes in Scripture whatsoever, whereas the view of inspiration that I have proposed earlier allows for mistakes, indeed, we would expect some mistakes. There are indeed many detailed passages which create problems of coherence for Scripture.

Compare:

I Samuel 17 with II Samuel 21 v 19 and I Chronicles 20 v 5. Just who DID kill Goliath?

Matthew 27 v 9 puts Jeremiah for Zechariah.

Was Jairus's daughter dead, or nearly dead? Matthew 9 v 18 with Mark 5 v 22,23 and Luke 8 v 42.

When did Jesus cleanse the temple of moneychangers? Was it early in His ministry as John 2 v 13, or late as Matthew 21 v 12, Matthew 11 v 15-17, Luke 19 v 45,46? To insist on two cleansings is to ridicule the gospels as literary works.

A comparison between Genesis 1 and 2 reveals two different accounts of the order of creation.

There are contradictory accounts about how Judas Iscariot died. (Acts 1 v 18, Matthew 27 v 5).

There seem to be many contradictions between Samuel/Kings and Chronicles:

Compare:

II Samuel 3 v 4: 1,700 horsemen, 20,000 foot taken by David.
I Chronicles 18 v 4: 1000 chariots, 7000 horsemen, 20,000 foot.

II Samuel 10 v 6: 20,000 + 1,000 + 12,000 mercenaries of Ammonites.
I Chronicles 19 v 7: 32,000 chariots + army of King Maacah.

II Samuel 10 v 18: 700 charioteers + 40,000 horsemen slain.
I Chronicles 19 v 18: 7,000 charioteers + 40,000 horsemen.

II Samuel 24 v 9: Israel 800,000, Judah 500,000 (census).
I Chronicles 21 v 5: Israel 1,100,000. Judah 470,000.

II Samuel 24 v 24: 50 shekels (price of threshing floor)
I Chronicles 21 v 25: 600 shekels.

I Kings 4 v 26: 40,000 stalls for chariot horses.

II Chronicles 9 v 25: 4,000.

I Kings 7 v 26: 2,000 baths (Capacity of the sea.)
II Chronicles 4 v 5: 3,000 baths.

There are problems too with fitting the stories to the facts. Even the most ardent Creationists tend to admit to some kind of gap in the genealogy of Genesis, by talking about a MINIMUM of 1655 years from Adam to Noah's flood. (25). There are problems with fitting the creation account into modern scientific knowledge. There are problems finding evidence of a major poll tax at the time of Christ's birth, or that people had to travel for such a tax. In other words, the Scriptures do not seem to fulfil the two commonly accepted definitions or requirements of truth, namely, a coherent internal system, (there are contradictions), and correspondence to facts.

Such contradictions and difficulties have long exercised the minds of believers, and, in the face of such problems, another approach was used by fundamentalists, which is that of declaring that the Scriptures were inerrant as originally given, but that through time, via copying, some corruptions have crept in. In theory, this allows for some space in the exceptionally rigid doctrine held by Warfield. In practice, Evangelicals regard that to criticise one part is to affect the whole. But some flexibility in translation means that 'we are delivered from the paralysing fear that if one single discrepancy should found in Scripture we should have to abandon all belief in it's authority.' (26). BUT, no actual instance of error is permitted. This 'flexibility' has no effect other than to avoid the psychological consequences entailed if complete inerrancy was affirmed as an absolute doctrine. (27). Other problems with this idea of Inspiration as originally given are that it excludes as far as possible any active role of church tradition in the formation and preservation of scripture. Also, in fundamentalism, there is practically no awareness of original texts at all. Finally, the original inspired documents will never be found, so the position cannot be disproved. Lane Fox (28) argues that this idea of reconstruction of the original texts is strongly present in non-historians. But the starting point for such a quest is the late Masoretic text, which itself excludes earlier alternatives and is only one arbitrary system, which has been hallowed by use, not by history. The New Testament texts do not take us beyond variants and alternatives a hundred years after the gospel's likely date of composition.

BIBLICAL SCHOLARSHIP

What then is the attitude by fundamentalists to Biblical scholarship? The believer is encouraged to read only 'sound' literature, that is literature which expounds and conforms to the conservative evangelical point of view, very often, for the Calvinist at least, older literature from the puritan period, or eighteenth century. The attitude to literature is similar to the attitude taken to speakers at meetings, who are vetted one way or another by the leadership to allow only 'sound' speakers. Thus, non-conservative books should not be read. (29), and non-conservative, speakers do not enter the pulpit. There is, of course, modern conservative literature, and this particularly, serves the function of giving assurance. It displays the fact that there are people full of erudition about Biblical matters who are yet fully reliable in their evangelical belief. Yet, though these people may write for conservative encyclopaedias and so on, and write on a conservative view, they may not themselves hold those views, though this is not made plain. In this sense, the function of the literature is propagandistic. This is confirmed by the reluctance of fundamentalists to read other non-conservative literature. (30) Fundamentalism generally has a tendency to fall back onto dogma, which is not respected by scholars. (31) Interestingly, the main area of study is not the Bible, but environing fields, like archaeology and customs. Problems of the Bible are approached from outside the Bible. Thus, a religion that depends exclusively for truth on the Bible turns increasingly to non-Biblical sources for verification. The reasons for this include unwillingness by fundamentalists to be involved in Bible Criticism. Conservatives argue that the Bible truth is betrayed into the hands of scholars who arrogate to themselves the right to decide what is truth and what is not. But there is a lack of polemic against fundamentalists because they are considered weak. (32)

The idea that archaeological findings confirm the Bible is a propagandist use of archaeology and conceals the limits of what can be demonstrated by these means. All archaeological finds have to be interpreted. Fragments of clay, and diggings in ancient cities all have to be interpreted. The archaeologist, who is interested in the Bible, interprets his findings within that framework, but it may be hopelessly wrong. Claims have been made before that findings represent Biblical locations and times, such as those made by Leonard Wooley in the 1920's regarding Ur of the Chaldees, Abraham's town, with, beneath it, evidence of the flood

39

in a large clay deposit. But qualifications and retractions had to be made with later investigation. Wooley was sympathetic to the Bible stories, and they framed his interpretation of his findings, which later had to be modified. Archaeologists today are more cautious. The approach of fundamentalists to archaeology is to stop criticism before it starts. In this controversy, HISTORICAL evidence is more important than doctrine, because history is EMPIRICAL. So too with literary matters, such as styles, discrepancies e.t.c. Therefore, if the fundamentalist can show accuracy here, then there are implications for the more philosophical, doctrinal part's. Attitudes to history work out as follows: Historical demonstration is probabilistic, but conservative evangelical historical statements are not limited on the ground of their probabilistic nature. Conservative statements are put forward as fully reliable knowledge and they cannot be disproved except by the most final, coercive proofs. (33) BUT, when it comes to critical judgements of the conservative view from a historical perspective, these are regarded at best as HYPOTHESES, requiring final coercive proofs. Thus, conservative statements have to be fully disproved, whilst criticisms have to be fully proved. Similarly, the use of parallels in other near eastern cultures to those of the Bible is a precarious area. (34). The fact is that if the interpretation of the Bible is a matter of history, then the changes of interpretation and possibilities of history must be our destiny... there is no certainty to be had. (35). In fact, on the synoptic problem, conservative evangelicals have shown a marked slide toward the Biblical Critical position. (36)

One may, on recognising the hopelessness of the fundamentalist position try to follow the broad lines of fundamentalism. Here is a test though... How far is it distinct from actual fundamentalism? How far does it make clear to fundamentalists that a quite different understanding of the Bible has to be found? How far does it lead to a fresh theological explanation? (37)

THE INTERPRETATION OF SCRIPTURE

How then do conservative evangelicals interpret Scripture and what problems are there? As we have seen, their view of the Scriptures is part of a long tradition that results in emphasis of certain texts and the ignoring of others. The basis of their approach is philosophical rather than Biblical. The Scriptures themselves are seen as harmonious and perfect, implying a close connection between God and the text. In fact, though this is often denied, as we have seen, the only connection close enough is dictation, but this does no justice to the authors, to the contents or to God, who appears to lie and contradict. Fundamentalists argue that if there appear to be contradictions, and then we have not understood correctly. They view the canon as a coherent system, bringing each book into a new relationship with its neighbours which affect the perceived meanings of the texts, such that denial of the afterlife in Ecclesiastes is reinterpreted to a meaning within the context of the canon. This gives authority to the Bible as a whole, though originally, these were separate texts, scrolls and letters. With this idea of inerrancy as a foundation of interpretation, certain questions like: - Is this a Myth? Is this mistaken in historical fact? Is this passage generated not by external events but by problems in the inner experience of the church? DO NOT OCCUR. The framework of belief PRECLUDES certain questions like this. (38). Some argue that fundamentalists take the Bible literally. This is not so. Swings occur from literal to figurative to ensure inerrancy. Sometimes this is done badly, as in certain interpretations of Genesis; it's genealogies, and the gap theory. This is just one technique used to preserve inerrancy and harmony of interpretation. The quality that distinguishes a Pastor of a fast growing conservative church..is..delving into the Bible relating one passage to another… to find consistency, unity and continuity in it. (39) This is a process called harmonisation, and because Scripture is seen as inerrant, a great deal of harmonisation is required, sometimes to the point of absurdity. It is a major activity to preserve inerrancy.

The techniques of harmonisation include:

a) Multiple events: Two cleansings of the temple for example to explain why in John's gospel, the cleansing is early on in the ministry of Jesus as opposed to later in the other gospels.
b) Literal/figurative: Switching from literal to figurative and vice versa to accommodate difficult passages.
c) Gaps/telescoping: As in the Genesis account to cope with various scientific and other difficulties.
d) Vagueness: For example the idea that the varying accounts in the gospels shows the genuineness of the authorship. Vagueness is related to the raising of critical suggestions, which are usually dismissed in a vague way as though not too important. Whereas in fact, they are very important to a position of inerrancy, and the onus is on those who hold this position to explain them in detail.

Scripture is also graded by evangelicals. Though it is all considered to be inspired, and inerrant, some parts are more important than others, say for example, Romans is more important or relevant than Ecclesiastes. However, if NON-evangelicals do grading, then it is considered to be downgrading: a scholar setting up his own judgement against God.

When it comas to teaching the bible, the only way to maintain evangelical thinking is to avoid non-evangelical thinking. As already mentioned, recommended books are essentially propaganda, and only speakers 'approved' by the leadership are permitted to speak. The teaching method is essentially didactic, that is, meant to instruct, though often, Scripture is not even opened up and explained, but rather, conservative evangelical ideas are repeated.

When it comes to miracles and the supernatural, miracles are confined to a zone identical with the Bible, except for modern displays of 'gifts'. Any 'miracles' outside this zone are depreciated as superstition. Thus, conservative evangelicals' use of the supernatural is occasionistic and opportunistic. (40). Sometimes, where scientific knowledge is used as the basic dictum, miracles are either got rid of or down graded to a naturalistic explanation. They are de-miracularised. (41). On other occasions it can be stated that anything can happen, everything is supernatural. But the problem here is that there are no rules for governing this kind of explanation. (42). If God could put Jonah in a large fish for three days, and even prepare this fish, he could give Jonah a writing desk and chair in the whale while he was there.

Critical approaches to Scripture of the kind that I have just outlined are rarely if ever entertained by Fundamentalists, and they are dismissed largely as the product of sinful minds.

Although Calvin is often quoted as having the basis of a more critical approach to Scripture, in fact he had a very high opinion of Scripture, as John Murray shows. (43). He was certainly aware of apparent contradictions in Scripture, and he was concerned with them because of his high view of Scripture. The mistakes he points out, such as the wrong name in Matthew 27 v 9, and errors of number as in Acts 7 v 14-16 with Genesis 23 v 8—18 he largely assigns to errors of transcription. (44). Calvin, as his Institutes of religion show, was certainly against the idea of the church judging Scripture in the way proposed by liberals. (45). The authority of God resides in the Scriptures rather than the church for Calvin, as one would expect of a Protestant reformer. Murray concludes that Calvin's approach was similar to that of John Owen which I outlined in an earlier chapter. Calvin distinguished between an authority that was intrinsic to Scripture and our persuasion that Scripture is authoritative. The Scriptures carry their own evidence as to their authorship, but the perception of this evidence proceeds only from the work of the Holy Spirit in the believer's heart. Therefore, says Murray, faith in the authority of Scripture is not established until we are indubitably persuaded that God is its Author. The highest proof of Scripture is always taken from the character of God, and we know that the Scriptures are from God via the internal testimony of the Spirit. There is no authority higher than God, and He appeals to no higher authority, rather He is a sufficient witness to Himself, and there is, says Calvin, Owen, Murray and other fundamentalists, ample evidence in the Scriptures themselves that God is the Author. But men will give no credit for the authority of Scripture unless it is sealed by the internal testimony of the Spirit. (46).

To state the argument again, Calvin argues that Scripture evidences itself to be from God like coloured objects evidence their colours. (47). Owen argues that Scriptures evidence themselves to be of God like light evidences itself, requiring no further proof. Murray argues that Scripture has a special, divine quality by reason of it's inspiration, (48), and faith in the authority of Scripture as God's word rests in the perfections inherent in Scripture by reason of this inspiration by God, and is elicited by the perception of these perfections (49) via the internal operation of the Holy Spirit. It is reasonable to ask then, just what are these evidences? What qualities are we to perceive that will evidence God's authorship? They are those which I have already outlined in an earlier chapter: -

    i)   The holiness, power, majesty and knowledge of God in Scripture.
    ii)   The sublimeness, mystery, scope and heavenliness of the subject matter.
    iii)   The efficacy of the doctrines to move and save people.
    iv)   It is still applicable and relevant despite it's age.
    v)   Despite it's diverse styles it has unity and authority.
    vi)   Despite its many authors and lengthy period of writing, it has a harmony, symmetry, agreement and consent.

vii) Its prophecy was accurately fulfilled.
viii) Its doctrines are confirmed by miracles and signs.
ix) It has survived attempts by men to eradicate it.

Now some of these are simple evidences. They are not of the same nature as light or colour being self-evidencing. They require examination, reason, logic selection of evidence, and balancing of argument. It is true that certain of these qualities may seem more apparent to a person at certain times more than at others and so on. But they are not simple and self-evident. Neither do they necessarily prove divine authorship. The fact that the Scriptures have been preserved does not necessarily prove that God is their Author. They may have been preserved for reasons other than this. Neither does its subject matter, or continuing relevance, or the fact that it still affects people constitute definite proof of authorship.

What then if you are not persuaded of these evidences, as many are not? According to the fundamentalist, this reveal? Your sin. According to Murray, 'when we bring a SOUND mind it compels our submission and obedience.'(50). If we are thinking rightly, we cannot but submit to and obey Scripture. The fact that we are not submitting or do not perceive these evidences as compelling does not mean that the evidence is weak, or that or that Scripture is not what it claims to be, but that we are not thinking correctly, are unwise, unsound in our thinking and sinful. This obviously has a powerful effect on the sincere fundamentalist believer who is plagued by doubt. He is directed not to examine the evidence, but to examine himself and presumably seek a stronger faith and freedom from doubt by confessing the sin of unbelief. 'The effect of sin is not only that it blinds the mind of man and makes it impervious to the evidence, out also that it renders the heart of man utterly hostile to the evidence. (51). In this way, many fundamentalists dismiss critical approaches to Scripture and doubts as regards it's authorship: they examine themselves or dismiss others who take this approach as blind, sinful and mistaken, because their minds have not been enlightened to perceive that God is the Author of Scripture.

I have sought to lay the axe to the root of the tree of fundamentalism. Fundamentalism argues for a very tight notion of inspiration, whereby every word is God breathed and as such, because God is perfect, there can be no errors in scripture, which then forms a closed authority for

44

faith. I have tried to show that there are problems with this view. The arguments have been out forward very briefly and inadequately, but I hope, give us a flavour of the sorts of problems that the worldview of fundamentalism faces. If we wish to accent the idea of inspiration for writings such as those in Scripture, then we must argue for a looser view of it, which does not demand such an absolute connection with inerrancy, but which allows for the fallibility, social historical context and uniqueness of the writers as Strong suggests. We must also recognise that the writings that make up our Bible have been ordered in a particular way and selected to form a rule of faith by a church that is itself fallible. The content of Scripture itself seems to demand this softer view of inspiration. Before I move on to other perspectives as regards gifts, I want to look a little more at the area of the fundamentalist system and then move on to a study of what some fundamentalists really believe about gifts.

REFERENCES

1) COHEN, E.D. (1986) 'The mind of the Bible believer' Prometheus Books. New York. p.10.
2) BARR, J. (1977) 'Fundamentalism' SCM Press. London. p. 36.
3) COHEN, E.D. (Ibid) p.50.
   BARR, J. (Ibid) p.1.
4) COHEN, E.D. (Ibid) on. 57,58.
5) LANE FOX, R. (1992) 'The unauthorised version. Truth and fiction in the Bible.'. Penguin. London.
6) LANE FOX, R. (Ibid) pp.88-100.
7) LANE FOX, R. (Ibid) pp.116-118).
8) LAME FOX, R. (Ibid) p.123.
9) ELWELL, W.A. (Ed) (1934) 'Evangelical dictionary of theology', Marshall Pickering. p1140.
10) STRONG, A.H. (1907) 'Systematic Theology' Pickering and Inglis, London. p.238.
11) STRONG, A.H. (Ibid.)
12) STRONG, A.H. (Ibid) p.236
13) STRONG, A.H. (Ibid) pp. 236-237.
14) BARR J. (Ibid) p.135.
15) CALVIN, J. (1847) 'Commentaries on the Psalms'. Calvin Translation Society. Edinburgh.
16) LANE FOX, R. (Ibid) pp.157, 158.

17) LANE FOX, R. (Ibid) p.155.
18) LANE FOX, R. (Ibid) pp. 161-174
19) VINE, N.E. (1940) 'An expository dictionary of New Testament words' Oliphants. London.
20) STRONG, A.H. (Ibid) pp.202-212.
21) BARR, J. (Ibid) p.277.
22) BARR, J. (Ibid) p.182.
23) BARR, J. (Ibid) pp.260-266.
24) BARR, J. (Ibid) p. 178.
25) WHITCONB, J.C. (1988) 'The world that perished'. Baker. p.55.
26) BARR, J. (Ibid) p.54.
27) BARR, J. (Ibid) p.55.
28) LANE FOX, R. (Ibid) p.156.
29) BARR, J. (Ibid) pp. 121-122.
30) Ibid. p. 23
31) Ibid. p.127
32) Ibid. pp. 128-132.
33) Ibid. p.93
34) Ibid. pp. 135-138.
35) Ibid. p.153
36) Ibid. p.143.
37) Ibid. o.157.
38) Ibid. p.51.
39) COHEN. E.D. (Ibid) p.18.
40) BARR, J. (Ibid.) p.239.
41) Ibid. p.245.
42) Ibid. p.253.
43) MURRAY, J. (1979) 'Calvin on Scripture and Divine sovereignty'. Evangelical Press.
44) Ibid. pp.28-29.
45) CALVIN, J. (1989) 'Institutes of the Christian Religion' Translated by H. Beveridge. Eerdmans. Michigan U.S.A. I vii 1. pp. 68-73
46) MURRAY, J. Ibid. pp.44-48.
   CALVIN, J. Ibid. I vii 4 p.71.
47) CALVIN, J. Ibid. I vii 2 p.69.
48) MURRAY, J. Ibid. p.49.
49) MURRAY, J. in WILLIAMSON, G.I. (1964) 'The Westminster confession of faith for study classes.'. Presbyterian and Reformed publishing Co. Ltd. p.8.
50) MURRAY, J. (1979) Ibid. p.50.

51) MURRAY, J. in WILLIAMSON, G.I. Ibid. p.8.

SPIRITUAL AND MORAL AUTHORITY IN THE CHRISTIAN CHURCH

1) From where does the church obtain its authority on spiritual and moral matters?
2) How does God reveal Himself and His will to mankind?
3) What does the word 'canon' mean?
4) Which sacred writings are in the canon of Scripture?
5) Has God told us directly which books are in the canon?
6) Are there other sacred writings in existence?
7) Were all of these genuine religious writings?
8) Who decided what books to include in the canon?
9) How was the Old Testament canon formed?

10) Was this selection accepted by all Jews?
11) How did New Testament believers form an Old Testament canon?
12) How was the New Testament canon formed?
13) Why was the New Testament canon formed?
14) What principles were used in forming the canon?
15) Did the church have any other defences against error?
16) What is a creed?
17) What is apostolic succession?
18) What is the common theme of these defences?
19) Who and what were the Apostles?
20) What did the Apostles do?
21) What is the tradition of the Apostles?
22) Who formed the Jewish church tradition?
23) What did the Jewish church tradition teach?
24) What is the foundation of the Jewish tradition?
25) What happened to the Jewish tradition?
26) Whop formed the Gentile church tradition?
27) What did the Gentile church tradition teach?
28) What is the foundation of the Gentile tradition?
29) What happened to the Gentile tradition?
30) Were these traditions of the church unified?
31) What is distinctive about the Apostolic visions and revelations?
32) Were the Apostles and their teaching without error?
33) What was the early church's view of the canon?
34) What is the position of the canon today?
35) What does inspiration mean?
36) Is inspiration limited to the Scripture writers?
37) How can we check if someone really has been Inspired?
38) If a person is inspired is what they say without error?
39) What evidence is there that Scripture is inspired?
40) What can we conclude about this evidence?
41) What can we conclude about inerrancy?
42) What can we conclude about the Bible?
43) Which books are written by the apostles?
44) Has the church altered the canon?
45) What about those people who have never had a Bible?
46) What evidence is there in creation for God's existence?
47) Who or what is the Holy Spirit?
48) How was He given in a fuller way?
49) Where is the Holy Spirit?

48

50) What does the Holy Spirit do?
51) How does the present work of the Spirit relate to His work in the apostles?
52) What does the Spirit do in Christians?
53) What does He do to both Christians and unbelievers?
54) How do we recognise His work?
55) What are the evidences of His work?
56) How does the church know what is right and wrong?
57) Is there an order to these authorities?
58) Is the church united in all that it does?
59) What lies behind the need for spiritual authority?
60) What about texts from other religions and faiths?
61) What can we conclude about spiritual and moral authority?
INTRODUCTION

I could have called this 'Questions I wish I'd asked.' or Questions I wish I'd had straight answers to.' I have been a Christian for almost thirty years, and largely been involved in that group of Christianity known as Fundamentalists, those who consider the Bible to be the Word of God, and therefore absolutely without error of any kind. Everything is examined by this group in the light of what the Bible says. The Bible is THE authority for faith and behaviour. It is regarded as a spiritual authority, because it is the Word of God on unseen, non-material matters. It is the authority on God, Angels, the Devil, unclean spirits and so on. It is regarded as a moral authority because it is the Word of God on what is right and what is wrong, and about the judgement of God because of evil and wrongdoing. But are fundamentalists right in their insistence on a collection of writings that are God inspired and without error? Following a study on spiritual gifts that I did in the 1970's nagging questions started to arise about this position. I would do a little bit of research, find some sort of answer to my question, and carry on for a while, but eventually, the answer turned out not to be an answer after all, and the nagging questions returned. There also arose an increasing dissatisfaction with fundamentalist ideas on other issues, such as politics and so on, which came to a head after reading Christian critics of fundamentalism, as well as criticisms by non believers. Fundamentalism seemed to me to be narrow stagnant, right wing, intolerant and indefensible. Once I rejected fundamentalism, the great danger was to throw the baby out with the bath water as it were, and to reject the whole of the Bible as a myth, as a fake. I lost the [false] sense of authority, everything was open to

49

question, and I know that for a good twelve months I felt adrift in a sea of conflicting religious and moral ideas. I no longer seemed to have a base from which to work in terms of spiritual and moral matters. Hence I have written this study on spiritual and moral authority. It is an attempt to deal with some of these questions, hence it's question and answer format. It is not a deep study, but it has served as a way for me to get my various strands of thought together in a more logical way, and think through a reasonable basis and authority for my faith and conduct. As such, it may be of help to others also.

SPIRITUAL AND MORAL AUTHORITY IN THE CHRISTIAN CHURCH.

1) From where does the Church obtain its authority on spiritual and moral matters?

The Church claims its authority from God in three Persons.
i) God the Father is the absolute and final authority.
ii) God the Father mediates or communicates through the middle person of Jesus Christ, God the Son.
iii) Jesus Christ, at His ascension, made way for and gave the Holy Spirit to dwell inside believers, who together make up the true Church, the Spirit being an influence towards holiness or purity and truth.

2) How does God reveal Himself, His will and thus His authority to mankind?

The Church declares that there are a number of ways in which God reveals Himself and His will to man:

i) According to the Church, God is revealed through the things He has made, like a painter is revealed by his paintings. Creation is declared by the Apostle Paul to be a universal witness to all mankind of the existence. Divine nature, might and invisible qualities of God, such that all are without excuse. This continues despite the church also declaring that man's disobedience to God affected and spoiled the whole of creation. This knowledge that each person has may be suppressed by wickedness and exchanged, in the name of wisdom, for other ideas. Similarly, God's provision of the seasons, of rain and sunshine to grow crops in their

50

season, is another witness to God and His character. Even calamities such as famine, plague and earthquake may declare God's moral character and His hatred for sin. This revelation is a universal but impersonal revelation of God. It is limited in scope in that it is not God speaking personally; neither does it reveal the way of salvation. It is categorised by theologians as Natural Theology, but Reformation theologians generally rejected the competence of fallen human reason to engage in Natural Theology. Whether this is entirely correct is open to dispute. In their zeal to emphasise the dominion of sin in every part and faculty of a person and the resulting inability of a person to earn salvation, the Reformers may have gone too far as will be suggested later. What is evident is that a person cannot live up to even this limited revelation.

Over and above this universal but limited revelation is a more personal and special revelation. Broadly speaking it has three modes or forms:

a) PHYSICAL PHENOMENON of various kinds, such as the burning bush, or pillar of fire. Also under this heading we find miraculous signs, visible symbols and theophanies, or physical appearances of God to a person, as with Moses.

b) INWARD SUGGESTION such as through dreams, visions, and voices, as when the prophets say: 'The word of the Lord came unto me.'

c) CONCURSIVE OPERATIONS. This is where the Holy Spirit works in, through and with human activities rather than superseding them. B.B. Warfield argues that there may be no consciousness of God working with us in this way.

In more detail. God is revealed in the following ways:

ii) He is revealed chiefly through Jesus Christ, who declared himself to be both God and Man in mysterious union. Jesus' claim is backed up by His ability to perform wonders and miracles as testimony and witness to His Divine qualities, especially by His death and resurrection. He is such a full expression of the Father, so like the Father in character that Jesus said, 'He who has seen me has seen the Father.' This is the fullest and most personal and most physical expression of God to man. But of course, Jesus is no longer physically present with us, and we only have the written records of His life and teaching

iii) God is revealed by the miracles and wonders performed by some of His people, such as Moses at the Red Sea, or Elijah, or the Apostles. Miracles are above nature, implying a SUPER natural cause. Their unusualness causes them to draw attention to themselves, and they often act as signposts of new eras or developments in the Church. They serve to qualify the authority and truthfulness of a person's teaching, because only God can act in this supernatural way, thus spiritual enemies of God seek to make false miracles to draw people into mistakes, or to make genuine miracles seem less unusual.

iv) God is revealed through spiritual messengers called Angels. The Church considers that there is a whole hierarchy of spiritual beings who God may use at special times to communicate with people, such as the angel visiting the Shepherds at Christ's birth. Such interventions appear to be rare. Some of these beings have rebelled against God, but they are still under God's control as their effective King and Lord.

v) Sometimes, God may reveal Himself by appearing directly to a person, as in the case of Moses on Sinai. This appears to be very rare indeed.

vi) God may communicate His will, purposes and commands to a person in an extraordinary way by the Holy Spirit, revealing hidden information or giving God breathed utterances in known or unknown tongues. This sort of communication is usually given to believers, but may be given to unbelievers as well. There are many diverse views on such influences. Some believe that they ceased shortly after the death of the Apostles, some that they continue in limited form for special reasons or at times of revival, and others believe that they continue in full form in the present day. The teaching of the Apostles and Jesus Christ usually tests such influences.

vii) God is revealed through the Church, because of the Holy Spirit dwelling in them and leading them to honour God and live Holy lives. Not that the Church is perfect, because sin still remains. Because sin is still present in each person, no single person has the completely correct view of truth about God. But as believers come together, bringing their various gifts and skills, a more balanced view comes about. However, a tradition among protestant churches is to have influential leaders, and thus it has many groups following particular interpretations of the Bible.

The groupings and gatherings of Church councils: Elders, that is spiritual leaders of the church who have evidenced suitable qualities to hold such a position, gathering together to make decisions on certain Issues, are seen as very important aspects of the Church discovering the will and purposes of God.

viii) According to the Apostle Paul, the requirements of God's law is written on people's hearts, in that:-
a) People have a moral nature, humankind being made in the image of God. They know right and wrong.

b) People have a conscience that bears witness to this even though it is affected by sin.

c) People's thoughts accuse or excuse them. Those who do not have the Law and commands of God in written form will be judged at the end of time by these factors according to the Apostle.

ix) Some churches place authority on the tradition of the Apostles, and all place authority in the writings of the Apostles. These are men chosen by Jesus Himself to preach and teach the good news. More will be said on Apostles later.

x) God is revealed through the special, sacred writings of various authors, such writings being known as the Bible or Scripture. These are considered to be very special. The Scriptures are usually considered as the main authority for many churches in these days of the absence of the physical presence of Jesus Christ and the Apostles. Certainly, this is the case in Protestant Churches, and especially in the case of fundamentalists, who consider that the Bible has no mistakes or contradictions except for minor instances due to translation or copying errors. This is because the Bible is considered to be the inspired Word of God. Very often, even in churches where spiritual gifts are practiced, it is Scripture that is appealed to in terms of deciding on which gifts may be acceptable, and/or how they should be practiced. It is important to remember that the Scriptures or Bible is not one book, but a collection of many books and letters written by different people over a long time. The position that R. M. Horn, a respected fundamentalist, takes and which other Christians may well take is that God is active in all of history. He is a sovereign God, in control of all things. However, God discloses himself in only some history. Furthermore, though God has acted, these actions are open to wide interpretations by different people who bring different world views to such events. However, Horn argues. God HAS spoken and given us His servants to interpret these events for us in the correct way. Thus:-

The Exodus is interpreted for us by Moses, but the Egyptians, who had no revelation, interpreted the events in a different way.

The Apostles interpret the Crucifixion for us and to some extent the Old Testament writers, but it has different interpretations by others who have had no revelation.

Peter interprets Pentecost for us, but the bystanders who had no revelation interpreted the events as the result of too much wine

Therefore, R. M. Horn argues, a God given interpretation must accompany facts and events. Horn is certainly right to argue that facts do not speak for themselves. All facts are perceived through the 'spectacles' of our world view, which we use to interpret facts and events, which imbues them with values and which causes us to be selective in our attention. Revelation, argues Horn is events plus God given Interpretation. Horn further argues that this is why Scripture is in the form that it is. It sometimes appears to put great emphasis on apparently trivial historical facts, whilst ignoring what we would consider to be apparently important historical events. Scripture selects and interprets events in history to bring out meaning without contradicting history. Therefore Scripture is not just a collection of catechisms or doctrinal propositions or a list of commands. God speaks in a personal way through Scripture, often using analogy to illustrate the nature and character of God. The claim that the Scriptures have no mistakes in them and are the inspired Word of God, and that they alone are to be the authoritative guide and rule for Christian faith and conduct is the particular Interest of this article I have already tried to show, using ideas drawn from the Scriptures themselves that there are a number of ways in which God may reveal His will, purposes and commands to people, quite apart from Scripture itself. This immediately puts doubt on the idea that Scripture ALONE is the authoritative rule. But I am now going to examine these ideas about Scripture a little further by asking some more questions.

3) What does the word canon mean?

The word 'canon' means 'measuring rod' or 'rule'. When applied to sacred writings, it refers to those writings which can be used as an authoritative measure in determining matters of religious conduct, issues of faith, and matters to do with God, His nature, will, commands and so on.

4) Which sacred writings are in the canon of Scripture?

There are 39 books in the Old Testament, from Genesis to Malachi. There are 27 books in the New Testament consisting of the Gospels, Acts of the Apostles, letters by the Apostle Paul, and some other books including Revelation.

5) Has God told us directly which books are to be included in the canon of Scripture?

No. Neither Jesus nor the Apostles gave us a list of books that would make up the canon of Scripture. They sometimes quoted from books included in the canon, but also from other sacred writings also, such as the book of Enoch quoted in Jude.

6) Does this mean that there were other sacred, religious writings in existence?

Yes. There are works such as the books of the Wars of the Lord, the Letter of Barnabas, I Clement, the Gospel to the Hebrews, the Shepherd of Hermas, Ecclesiasticus, the Wisdom of Solomon and Esdras. Some of these books have been lost and their existence is known of because they are quoted from in parts of Scripture. Others are still in existence. Some of them are contained in the Apocrypha, a collection of writings from between the Old Testament and New Testament writings.

7) Were all these books and letters genuine religious writings, written by people close to God or moved by the Holy Spirit?

Many were written by sincere believers and leaders of believers, but also, there were many false books and letters, especially as the New Testament age began. To make things even more complicated, both believers and unbelievers considered it quite normal to write a letter or book but sign it in the name of an Apostle or leader. This was not

55

necessarily thought of as deceitful, but rather, the work, if written by a believer, was considered to be a reflection of that leader's or Apostle's teaching. So, there were many religious writings, claiming authoritative writers, some were genuine, some were written by faithful believers, some were forgeries.

8) Who decided which books to Include in the canon of Scripture and which to leave out?

Essentially, the community of believers, especially through the guidance of its leaders, made these decisions over a long period of time.

9) How was the Hebrew or Old Testament canon formed?

No record exists of how this came about. We can only make a reconstruction that seems reasonable. The following factors seem to be involved:-
i) Sacred writings were certainly treated with respect and care. For example, the stone tablets containing the Ten Commandments were carefully placed in the Ark of the Covenant.

ii) Israel almost certainly followed other countries in its dealings with sacred literature. For example, a body of official, standardised religious literature existed in Mesopotamia 2000 years B.C.

iii) It appears that sacred documents were carefully stored in temples.

v) The Old Testament can be divided into three groups:

THE TORAH - the books of the Law- that make up the first five books of the Old Testament were treated in this way, and their canonisation probably took place in the period of the exile in Babylon, when the national identity of Israel was under threat, between 600 and 538 B.C..

THE NEVIIM - the prophets- were probably assembled and ordered during the Persian period. Israel's exile in Babylon and later restoration greatly increased the reputation of the prophets. Their canonisation probably took place somewhere between 500 and 300 B.C.

56

THE KETUVIM - the rest of the books- were debated over for some time. It seems as though the debate was finally settled at a synod, or meeting of religious leaders at Jabneh in 100 A.D. Again, the destruction of the Jewish state and a collapse of the Jewish central authority following it's overthrow by Rome, made it important to identify a canon or measure of faith, an authoritative collection of sacred writings which would not be added to.

10) Was this particular selection of books accepted by all Jews?

No. The Samaritans only accepted the first five books, the books of Moses. The Alexandrian Jews rearranged the Prophets and the rest of the books into categories of history, poetry, wisdom and prophecy. Esther and Daniel contained extra material. Other books were also mixed in, such as I Esdras, Ecclesiasticus, and the Wisdom of Solomon.

11) How did New Testament believers react to Jewish sacred writings and form an Old Testament canon of their own?

Christianity arose out of Judaism, and the Church received its Old Testament canon from Greek speaking Jews. Most converts were Hellenistic, and the Greek Bible of Alexandria became the official Bible of the Christian community. Some writings, written late in the Old Testament period and now known as the Apocrypha, (containing Ecclesiasticus, Wisdom of Solomon and Maccabees, amongst others), were part of the canon, but people were not united as to their Inclusion. Some early Christian leaders, such as Origen, only had 22 books in their canon, and Josephus, a Jewish historian also only had 22 books. Eventually, the Apocryphal books were rejected by Protestants, but Included by Roman Catholics.

12) How was the New Testament canon formed?

The 27 New Testament books are what are left of many 1st and 2nd century religious writings considered sacred by Christian groups. There was a continuous Interplay between historical and theological writings such that the church finally selected these 27 books in the 4th century. As we have seen, many books were written by different authors, and by the mid 2nd century there began to be an awareness of history by the Christian community... the Apostles had died, Christ had died and ascended, but not yet returned, and a clearer difference was becoming plain between the time of Christ and the Apostles, and the later situation that believers now found themselves in. The actual process of canonisation was long and fluid, such that some churches held certain books to be canonical, which other churches did not. In the main, the church stressed the gospels, the letters of the Apostles and their lives and the tradition of the Apostles. By the late 2nd century, canons similar to the present one were in evidence, though different churches used different canons. Some churches were quite unconcerned about canons, and Clement of Alexandria made use of the Gospel to the Hebrews, the Letter of Barnabas and others. These varieties continued through the third century A.D.. The disputes seemed to be settled at a council of leaders in Carthage in 397 and 27 books were accepted as canonical. Even so, in later documents, there is sometimes no distinction between these and other material such as the Shepherd of Hermas and I & II Clement. By the 1500's with the church in reformation and Counter Reformation, the disputes continued. The council of Trent set the canon as the Vulgate... Jerome's Latin version, whilst on the side of the reformers, Luther rejected Hebrews, James, Jude and Revelation, though he bowed to tradition, placing these at the end of his New Testament. Calvin doubted that Peter was the author of II Peter, and rejected Revelation. These reformers continued the tradition of examining documents for their qualities of authorship, to see if they were suitable for Inclusion in a set of documents used as a measuring rod and authoritative guide for faith.

13) Why was the New Testament canon formed?

The Christian communities had relied for some time on an oral tradition, accounts handed down from one to another by word of mouth, but after the Apostles had died, this began to deteriorate. By the end of the 1st Century there was also a conscious production of gospels, such as 'The sayings of Christ' which began to contradict the tradition of the Apostles being handed down by word of mouth, and these were seen as heresy: that is, contrary to normal standards. There were also claims of revelations: of people being spoken to directly by the Holy Spirit, and receiving hidden information, teachings and so on. Some of these were also suspected of being in error, and the church needed a once-and-for-all revelation. Also, a number of groups began to appear which were not considered as following normal Apostolic practice, such as the Gnostics, and charismatic Montanists who had ecstatic trances, visions and new

58

revelations, and Marcion, who set up his own canon, or set of authoritative books which rejected anything Jewish. Because of these kinds of problems, the church decided it needed an authoritative set of books that would not be added to, and which could be referred to in order to establish standard practice and truth in an authoritative way.

14) What principles were used in forming the canon?

The principles that would be used began to emerge in the 2nd century. These were:-
  i) Apostolicity.
  ii) True doctrine.
  iii) Widespread geographical use by churches.

Thus, the Shepherd of Hermas and I Clement were rejected, because though they contained true doctrine, they were not written by Apostles and/or were not widely used. In the 3rd century, Origen identified three classes of sacred writings:-

  i) Those undisputed by the church of God throughout the known world.
  ii) Those writings disputed by some in the churches:
    II Peter.
    II & III John.
    Hebrews.
    James.
    Jude.
  iii) Spurious writings - those not considered to be genuine or what they claimed to be, such as the Gospel of the Egyptians.

Eusebius in the 4th century identified matters in the following way:

  i) Some books were universally accepted:
    The 4 Gospels
    Acts
    14 letters of Paul, including Hebrews that was thought to be written by him.
    I John.
    I Peter.
  ii) Disputed writings were of two kinds:
    a) Those known and accepted by many -

foul:
        James.
        Jude.
        II Peter.
        II & III John.
    b) Those called spurious but which were not impious or foul:
        Acts of Paul.
        Shepherd of Hermas
        Apocalypse of Peter.
        Letter of Barnabas.
        Didache.
        Hebrews, possibly.
    iii) Heretically spurious:
        Gospel of Peter.
        Acts of John.

However, Eusebius felt free to make authoritative use of disputed writings. Certainly at this time, the canon and authoritative revelation are not yet considered as the same thing.

Athanasius, the 4th century Bishop of Alexandria helped settle the matter, and differences between eastern and western churches were sorted out at a council of leaders in 397 A.D.. 27 books of the New Testament were accepted. Nevertheless, in later documents there was still no distinction between these and other works such as the Letter of Barnabas.

At the protestant reformation, a protest against problems and corruptions in the Roman Catholic church, such that the church was reformed, or re organised, the Reformers again questioned the canon. Luther's principles were:
    i) Apostolicity.
    ii) That which leads to Christ.
Since he could not find this latter quality in Hebrews, James, Jude and Revelation, he rejected them, though he bowed to tradition and included them at the end of his Bible. Calvin too rejected some books. All this suggests that with more and better evidence, the reformers would have continued the refining of which books and letters should be in the canon and which excluded.

This leaves a problem for fundamentalists because fallible human councils have determined the extent of Scripture. Since Scripture alone is their only authority they are obliged to look to Scripture itself for evidence. This in itself is a circular argument, and makes an assumption that Scripture is already a unified whole and Inspired by God. Arguments put forward in 'Sword and Trowel' 1994 No.4 by Malcolm H. Watts provides the following fundamentalist argument:

i) A book is canonical if written by a prophet. But he interprets this to mean ALL OF THE OLD TESTAMENT BOOKS, based on the idea of the 'Law and the prophets.'. He argues that the historical books were either written by or originated from prophets. He similarly argues that the Apostles, though not called prophets directly by Scripture, clearly were prophets!!! I think that this whole argument stretches the definition of the word prophet and clearly does not take Scripture alone as an authority.

ii) Canonicity is confirmed by predictions and miraculous events. Fulfilment is INDISPUTABLE proof that they are divine!! However, not all fulfilled predictions, say in astrology, are divine and Watts admits that MANY not all prophecies have been fulfilled. What of the rest? What if they are not fulfilled in the end? Clearly this evidence is far from Indisputable. He further argues that MIRACLES confirm the prophet's commission. But have ALL Scripture writers performed miracles? His argument only points out key persons.

iii) The testimony of contemporary witnesses helps to establish the canon. Now we are back to fallible human beings. He appeals to Scripture verses that indicate punishments for false prophets and the fact that predictions fail which all indicate a false prophet, but this is hardly great evidence for a prophet. Consequently, he falls back for the New Testament on the gift of discerning of spirits. By this gift, a person would know INFALLIBLY whether God was speaking to another person or not. In a similar way Peter in one of his (spurious) letters affirms the inspired nature of Paul's writings. This whole argument assumes that these people were inspired and had the gift of discernment, provides no evidence to us but the word of these people as supposed authorities, and is not testable or falsifiable. That is, it cannot be shown to be false, (or true).

iv) Canonical status can be JUDGED, (Assessed, interpreted) 'TO SOME EXTENT' by internal evidence. He admits that this is not always apparent in the more difficult and obscure books. Despite these statements, he still insists that 'the Word is able to assure us of its own canonicity'. This is clearly a contradiction. Also, what appears true of parts is assumed to extend to the whole, which is a false argument.

v) He then presents another unfalsifiable argument: Inspired men of God communicated to us which books are canonical as INSPIRED AUTHORATATIVE CRITICS. For example, Joshua confirms the inspiration of Moses' books (Joshua 1 v 13). Peter confirms Paul (2 Peter 3 v 16). Problems with this are that firstly we cannot test the claims of these critics to Inspiration, thus again this is unfalsifiable. Secondly, the canon was not complete until after the Apostles deaths. Thirdly, is every writer endorsed in this way?

vi) The canon of Scripture has continuity and harmony. It has design and development. This argument will be looked at later, but suffice to say now that there is evidence of contradiction in Scripture.

vii) The canon was accepted by the New Testament church. However, as we have seen, this was over a period of time, and there was not complete agreement.

I conclude that these and other fundamentalist arguments are all weak and Inconclusive, and that we must return to the more fallible human church counsels and their theologians.

15) Did the church have any other defences against error?

Yes. Besides defining a set of sacred writings as Authoritative norms or standards for the church, they also:-
a) Had Apostolic creeds and rules.
b) Had an apostolic succession of Bishops or Elders

16) What is a creed?

It is an oral and later written Apostolic tradition of the church to serve as a defence against error. This usually consists of a brief statement of Christian teaching, such as:-
'I believe in God the Father, and His son Jesus Christ, who died and rose again on the third day..' e.t.c..

17) What is Apostolic succession?

This is making the position of Elder as leader, teacher and shepherd of believers a legitimate or lawful position. Christ appointed the original Apostles, and they in turn established churches and set up overseers, signifying the authority of these new overseers by the laying on of hands. Thus they became official successors to the Apostles. Thus this practice continues, and no one can lawfully set themselves up as an Elder on their own, under normal circumstances, without this ceremony that shows approval of the person selected, both by the church and it's leaders.

18) What is the common theme running through all these defences?

Apostolicity. All these ideas are connected to and derive from the Apostles.
These defences are:
    i) Apostolic writings.
    ii) Apostolic rules and traditions.
   iii) Apostolic successors.

19) Who and what are the Apostles?

The term 'apostle' means 'one who is sent', or more accurately, one who is given a commission: authority to carry out a specific task. The word is quite general. Church Elders could make someone an apostle by giving them authority to carry out a specific task. It is in this sense that Biblical characters like Barnabas, James, Andronicus and Junius are referred to in Scripture as apostles. (Galatians 1 v 19, Romans 16 v 7, Acts 14 v 4, 14, I Corinthians 9 v 3-6.). There are also false apostles, men who transform themselves into God's servants, but who are really no such thing. (II Corinthians 11 v 14, Revelation 2 v 2.).

But there is another, more restricted usage of this word, which is determined by who does the sending. Men, leaders of the church, sent the above apostles but some were sent by Christ Himself, to teach and deliver the message of salvation. These are the twelve Apostles, 12 disciples selected from at least 72. (Matthew 10 v 2, Luke 10 v 1, 17.). One of these, Judas Iscariot, betrayed Jesus, and was replaced by Matthias, (Acts 1). God chose him by both the disciples and through the casting of lots, (the

last example of the casting of lots before the Holy Spirit was given at Pentecost). The number here seems limited to twelve, a reminder of the twelve tribes of Israel. The qualifications for these twelve appear to be:
    i) A direct commission from Christ. (Matthew 28)
    ii) They had to have been with Jesus since His baptism by John to His ascension, and therefore be a witness of His resurrection from the dead. (Acts 1, I Corinthians 15 v 8)
    iii) They were marked out or signified by the miracles and wonders that they could perform.(II Corinthians 12 v 12).

There is one Apostle who is called extra to these, the apostle to the Gentiles or non-Jews, Paul. He too was called to be an Apostle by the command of God (I Timothy 1 v 1), but as one abnormally born. ((I Corinthians 15 v 8). He considered himself the least of the apostles because before his conversion to Christianity, he ruthlessly persecuted the church. (I Corinthians 15 v 9). His qualification was that he too had seen the risen Christ (I Corinthians 9 v 1), Christ appearing to him last of all. (I Corinthians 15 v 8). His ministry had produced true spiritual fruit, genuine converts amongst the gentiles, (I Corinthians 9 v 1) and he too was marked by signs, wonders and miracles. (II Corinthians 12 v 12). He too was called, not by men, but by Jesus Christ and the Father, (Galatians 1 v 1). Fourteen years after his conversion, he went to see the apostles and was accepted by them as an apostle to the gentiles. (Galatians 2 v 1-10).

All the apostles called by Christ received teaching from the Holy Spirit. (Acts 1 v 2, Ephesians 3 v 5, Galatians 1 v 11, 12.). It is these apostles, the ones called and taught by God, the twelve plus Paul that give apostolic authority. Robert Horn stresses the importance of these apostles receiving a revelation direct from God, and not mediated by men. Certainly the twelve apostles walked and talked with Jesus Christ and received teaching directly from Him. But Paul, received revelation from God's Spirit. Like other Scripture writers apart from the twelve, he does not appear to have seen Jesus directly. The emphasis on direct revelation is exaggerated when it comes to the Scripture writers, because most of them did not see Jesus directly.

20) What did the apostles do?

The apostles:-
    Taught.

Performed signs and wonders.
Testified to Christ's resurrection with power.
Received gifts for distribution to the poor.
Suffered trials and beatings for the faith.
Resisted ungodly civil authorities.

Ceremonially appointed deacons and elders as successors who had been chosen by the church. They did this by the laying on of hands and prayer.

They investigated claims of conversion and gave help to new believers.

They passed on the Holy Spirit and/or the gifts of the Spirit by laying on of hands.

Along with Elders they helped settle controversial matters.

Along with Elders, they selected representatives for the church on different matters.

They were entitled to financial support from believers,

Were put on display for the whole universe, (I Corinthians 4 v 9)

Were appointed as the first gifts to the Church from the Holy Spirit. They were first in time and/or importance, providing, along with prophets, the foundation of the New Testament Church. (I Corinthians 12 v 28, Revelation 21 v 14).

21) What is the tradition of the Apostles?

The tradition of the Apostles is the teaching and example that the first disciples of Jesus gave to the church. In fact, there are two main strands of this tradition:
The Jewish or Hebrew church tradition
The Gentile church tradition

22) Who formed the Jewish or Hebrew church tradition?

The Jewish or Judaic tradition is that set of ideas and practices that emerged from the disciples of Jesus. Jesus designated the twelve as Apostles: 'One of those days Jesus went out to a mountainside to pray, and spent the night praying to God. When morning came, he called his disciples to him and <u>chose twelve of them, whom he also designated apostles</u>: Simon (whom he named Peter), his brother Andrew, James, John, Philip, Bartholomew, Matthew, Thomas, James son of Alphaeus,

Simon who was called the Zealot, Judas son of James, and Judas Iscariot, who became a traitor.' Luke 6 v 12 – 16. Following the death of Jesus, and the replacement of Judas, following his death, by Matthias, this group was initially based in Jerusalem. It appears very much as a group within Judaism – a Jewish sect focussed on Jesus, founded by the eyewitnesses of Jesus' life and resurrection.

23) What did the Jewish tradition teach?

Initially their message seems to be:

Jesus was a prophet
Jesus was powerful in word and deed before God and all the people.
The chief priests and our rulers handed him over to be <u>sentenced to death</u>
<u>They crucified him</u>
We hoped that he was the one who was going to redeem Israel.

Their message developed over time and as people saw the resurrected Jesus. So later, their message included the following ideas drawn from Jewish history and tradition:

Through faith in the name of Jesus, this ill man was healed in front of you
Jesus is God's servant
Jesus is holy, righteous, the Righteous One –the Messiah
Jesus is the author of life
Whom you Jews betrayed and murdered
But God raised him from the dead, and we are witnesses of this
What you and your leaders did to Jesus was done in ignorance
God was fulfilling what all the Jewish prophets had foretold about the Messiah
Repent of your sins, have a new mind and turn to God
He will again send you Jesus, your appointed Messiah.
For he must remain in heaven until the time for the final restoration of all things
Jesus the Son of Man standing in the place of honour at God's right hand.
Starting with Samuel, every prophet spoke about what is happening today.

24) What is the foundation of the Jewish tradition?

The foundation of this tradition is the teaching and work of Jesus, and following his crucifixion and death, the disappearance of the body of Jesus from the tomb followed by a number of visionary experiences of Angels and of Jesus himself. These visions were experienced by the disciples, their women companions and other followers of Jesus.

25) What happened to the Jewish tradition?

The Jews had an uneasy relationship with the Roman government and many resented Roman occupation. There were a whole series of groups opposing Rome and eventually, in A.D. 70 there was a violent exchange in which the Jewish Temple in Jerusalem was destroyed and Jewish resistance overthrown. The Jews were scattered over the world in what is known as the Diaspora. This and other events led to the dispersal and diminishing of the Jewish tradition with the loss of its centre and as it were, headquarters, in Jerusalem.

26) Who formed the Gentile church tradition?

The Gentile tradition is a set of ideas and practices established by the Jewish Pharisee lawyer Saul of Tarsus. He was initially a strong opponent of the Jewish Christian sect, which he saw as a corruption of Judaism. He spent his time seeking out and imprisoning its followers and leaders. But while he was walking along the Damascus Road on such a mission, he had a visionary experience whereby he saw a bright light and heard the voice of Jesus. In this experience, Jesus commissions him as an Apostle to give the gospel to the non-Jews or Gentiles: 'I am Jesus, whom you are persecuting,' the Lord replied. 'Now get up and stand on your feet. I have appeared [to allow one's self to be seen, to appear] to you to appoint you as a servant and as a witness of what you have seen and will see of me. I will rescue you from your own people and from the Gentiles. I am sending you to them to open their eyes and turn them from darkness to light, and from the power of Satan to God, so that they may receive forgiveness of sins and a place among those who are sanctified by faith in me.' Acts 26 v 16 – 18. Paul (as Saul was to become known) also considered himself an eyewitness of the resurrection and co-equal with the Jerusalem Apostles: 'Am I not free? Am I not an apostle? Have I not

67

seen [to see with the eyes; to see with the mind, to perceive, know; to see, i.e. become acquainted with by experience, to experience] Jesus our Lord?' I Corinthians 9 v 1, and again: 'for [says Paul] I am not in the least inferior to the most eminent [Jerusalem] apostles' II Corinthians 12 v 11.

27) What did the Gentile church tradition teach?

Initially, immediately after the Damascus Road experience, Paul's message is:
Repent and have a new mind and turn to God
Demonstrate repentance by your deeds.
Jesus Christ is God's Son.
Christ died for our sins according to the Scriptures.
He was buried
He was raised on the third day according to the Scriptures

Paul worked out or received a theology concerning Jesus whereby he is the Messiah/Redeemer, God's supreme sacrificial offering to pay the price for the sins and transgressions of believers. Jesus is eternally co-equal with God, humbled in time and space to come to us in the likeness of flesh, but, following his crucifixion, he is raised up from the dead as a guarantee of the future resurrection of humanity to the Final Judgment and the restoration of all things. The old Jewish Law was powerless to accomplish this and in the New Covenant established by Jesus, these Laws, both ceremonial and moral, are superseded and transcended by a new relationship in Jesus and a righteousness gained not by works and obedience to the law, but imputed to us by and through faith in God. The True Israel is not the Jewish nation with its sign of circumcision, but is the spiritual Israel - those who believe and have faith in God. Thus all Israel will be redeemed, having a righteousness by faith, imputed to them and credited to their account. This exalted view of Jesus is further carried on in the tradition of John's gospel.

28) What is the foundation of the Gentile tradition?

The initial foundation of the Gentile tradition, as we have seen, in the visionary experience of Paul on the Damascus Road. A companion of Paul writes that Paul declares: 'So then, King Agrippa, I was not dis-obedient to the vision from heaven. [the act of exhibiting one's self to view; a sight, a vision, an appearance presented to one whether asleep or awake] First to those in Damascus, then to those in Jerusalem and in all Judea, and then to the Gentiles, I preached that they should repent and turn to God and demonstrate their repentance by their deeds.' Acts 26 v 9 – 20. Paul's practice was to go to synagogues on the Sabbath and to declare the good news of Jesus. As a teacher of the Law he could freely do this. Often, his message was met with anger and rejection, but some followed him and with these people, he established new churches with their own elders and so on.

It is interesting to note that Paul as a point of principle did not immediately go to the Apostles in Jerusalem following his Damascus Road experience. He did not seek their instruction, teaching or help. Rather, he retreated to Arabia. He tells us himself: 'I want you to know, brothers and sisters, that _the gospel I preached is not of human origin. I did not receive_ [to receive with the mind] _it from any man, nor was I taught it; rather, I received_ [to receive with the mind] _it by revelation [_ a disclosure of truth, instruction - concerning things before unknown; used of events by which things or states or persons hitherto withdrawn from view are made visible to all; manifestation, appearance] _from Jesus Christ_. For you have heard of my previous way of life in Judaism, how intensely I persecuted the church of God and tried to destroy it. I was advancing in Judaism beyond many of my own age among my people and was extremely zealous for the traditions of my fathers. But when God, who set me apart from my mother's womb and called me by his grace, was pleased to reveal [to uncover, lay open what has been veiled or covered up, to disclose, make bare, to make known, make manifest, disclose what before was unknown] his Son in [in, by, with] me so that I might preach him among the Gentiles, _my immediate response was not to consult any human being._ I did _not_ go up to Jerusalem to see those who were apostles before I was, but I went into Arabia. Later I returned to Damascus. Then after _three years_, I went up to Jerusalem to get acquainted with Cephas [Peter] and stayed with him fifteen days. _I saw none of the other apostles—only James_, the Lord's brother. I assure you before God that what I am writing you is no lie. Then I went to Syria and Cilicia. I was personally unknown to the churches of Judea that are in Christ. They only heard the report: "The man who formerly persecuted us is now preaching the faith he once tried to destroy." And they praised God because of me.

Then after <u>fourteen years</u>, I went up again to Jerusalem, this time with Barnabas. I took Titus along also. I went <u>in response to a revelation</u> and, meeting privately with those esteemed as leaders, I presented to them the gospel that I preach among the Gentiles. I wanted to be sure I was not running and had not been running my race in vain. Yet not even Titus, who was with me, was compelled to be circumcised, even though he was a Greek. This matter arose because some false believers had infiltrated our ranks to spy on the freedom we have in Christ Jesus and to make us slaves. [to the law and practice of circumcision]. We did not give in to them for a moment, so that the truth of the gospel might be preserved for you. As for those who were held in high esteem—whatever they were makes no difference to me; God does not show favouritism—<u>they added nothing to my message</u>. On the contrary, <u>they recognized that I had been entrusted with the task of preaching the gospel to the uncircumcised, just as Peter had been to the circumcised.</u> For God, who was at work in Peter as an apostle to the circumcised, was also at work in me as an apostle to the Gentiles. James, Cephas and John, <u>those esteemed as pillars, gave me and Barnabas the right hand of fellowship when they recognized the grace given to me. They agreed that we should go to the Gentiles, and they to the circumcised.</u> All they asked was that we should continue to remember the poor, the very thing I had been eager to do all along.
Galatians 1 v 11 – Ch 2 v 10.

The foundation of the Gentile tradition then, like that of the Jewish tradition, is based on visionary experience, in this case of Jesus to Paul, commissioning him as an Apostle and giving him direct revelatory teaching.

29) What happened to the Gentile tradition?

It is the Gentile tradition that gained ascendancy and came to dominate as the orthodox Christian view. Events such as the Jewish Diaspora diminishing the Jewish influence, coupled with the initial persecution of the church, which served to entrench serious and committed Christians, followed by not only the acceptance of Christianity by Roman emperors but its establishment as the state religion, all served to establish the Gentile tradition of Christianity as the orthodox Christian view.

30) Were these traditions the church unified?

Though as we have seen, the writer of Acts declares that there was no fundamental disharmony between the message of Paul and those at Jerusalem, Christianity itself was not static and was not totally unified. There begins to develop an anti-Jewish trend for example contributing to a further diminishing of Judaic influence in Christianity. Also, if we explore the New Testament and related non-canonical documents over time, we see that there is an increasing development with regard to the person of Jesus Christ and especially his Divinity. Ideas such as the Incarnation, miracles and post-death appearances all increase in frequency the later the document is written. Thus, the first gospel to be written, that of Mark, has little to say either of the Virgin Birth or of post resurrection experiences. By Matthew and Luke, written later on, more stories of this kind are to be found, and the last gospel to be written, that of John, which emphasises the transcendent, divine nature of Jesus, contains the most of these accounts, written 'so that people might believe that Jesus is the Son of God in the sense of being the Word of God made flesh'. There is within Christianity an aspect concerned with revelations, miracles, prophesies, discerning spirits, casting out unclean spirits and so on. So much so that there arises theological division - some say Jesus is only a man, others say he is not a man but only God while others say he is just spirit. It is in the light of these kinds of divisions and conflicts that a proto-orthodoxy begins to emerge. Those of the proto-orthodox school of thinking wanted to remain faithful to the teaching and practice of the Apostles. It is from the proto-orthodox movement that calls begin to arise for a set of reliable, authoritative teachings regarding the Christian faith. Here then we find the first calls for a canon of Scripture – for a set of writings that are agreed upon as being suitable for use as an authoritative guide and rule for faith. Other documents must be rejected as false, heretical or spurious as to their authority. Thus eventually, the leaders of the early church sought to exclude all documents and writings that were considered not to have been written by the Apostles or which were not widely used and accepted as reliable in content and led to a movement eventually extending to the confiscation and burning of unacceptable literature. But, just like Paul and the Jerusalem Apostles, there were those in the church, such as Christian Gnostics, who were declaring that they had received visions and revelations from and about Jesus, and just like the Apostles, they were basing their faith on the content of these experiences. So who was right? Does it matter?

31) What is distinctive about the Apostolic visions and revelations?

If the whole basis and foundation of the Jerusalem Apostle's theology and the Apostle Paul's theology is grounded upon visions and revelations and if the post-resurrection appearances of Jesus Christ can be explained at least in part by similar revelatory visions, then why is there an antagonism towards the mystical element brought to the church by Gnostics and the proto-orthodox Christians of the early church with emphasis on a written rule of faith? Why weren't the visions, revelations and gnosis of these esoteric believers accepted by the Apostles and Elders when such experiences lie at the very heart of the foundation of Christianity itself? If we look at some of the verses from the bible relating to the issue of Gnosticism, we can note that these are all from secondary writers – that is, they are probably not written by the Apostle Paul or the disciples of Jesus, even though they are attributed to some of them, but rather they are probably written by close followers of Paul:

'As I urged you when I went into Macedonia, stay there in Ephesus so that you may command certain people not to teach false doctrines any longer or to devote themselves to myths and endless genealogies. Such things promote controversial speculations rather than advancing God's work—which is by faith. The goal of this command is love, which comes from a pure heart and a good conscience and a sincere faith.' I Timothy 1 v 3-5

'For the time will come when people will not put up with sound doctrine. Instead, to suit their own desires, they will gather around them a great number of teachers to say what their itching ears want to hear. They will turn their ears away from the truth and turn aside to myths.' II Timothy 4 v 3 – 4.

'Do not let anyone who delights in false humility and the worship of angels disqualify you. Such a person also goes into great detail about what they have seen; they are puffed up with idle notions by their unspiritual mind. They have lost connection with the head, from whom the whole body, supported and held together by its ligaments and sinews, grows as God causes it to grow'. Colossians 2 v 18-19:

I want to suggest that the Apostle Paul and the Apostles in Jerusalem believed that in their visions and revelations they encountered an objective phenomenon - the real Jesus. In the same way, at the transfiguration of Christ, I think that the disciples thought that they saw the real Moses and Elijah as real tangible 'objects out there':

'After six days Jesus took Peter, James and John with him and led them up a high mountain, where they were all alone. There he was transfigured before them. His clothes became dazzling white, whiter than anyone in the world could bleach them. And there appeared before them Elijah and Moses, who were talking with Jesus. Peter said to Jesus, "Rabbi, it is good for us to be here. Let us put up three shelters—one for you, one for Moses and one for Elijah." (He did not know what to say, they were so frightened.) Then a cloud appeared and covered them, and a voice came from the cloud: "This is my Son, whom I love. Listen to him!" Suddenly, when they looked around, they no longer saw anyone with them except Jesus'. Mark 9 v 2 – 8.

There are two distinguishing features about Christian (and probably Hebrew) visionary experiences:
What is seen in the vision exists objectively 'out there' – it is not just a subjective, imaginary experience produced by the mind.
What is seen is a real person – like Jesus, Moses or Elijah – as opposed to a mythical or imaginary person, creature or god.
In angelic visitations, the Angels were considered to be objectively real – they were not mythical and neither were they just a subjective or symbolic creation of the mind.

I consider that in these visions, the recipients believed that they were seeing the actual, real, people – people such as Moses, Elijah and Jesus – people who had actually existed and been alive but who were now dead, or that they considered that they were seeing real, objectively existing spiritual beings. In other words, these were 'visitations' by real persons. They were not seeing fantasy figures or mythical beings or symbolic creations from their minds. Paul did not consider that he had received some kind of presentation that had arisen in his mind or imagination, or from his sub-conscious, or that his imagination and mind was stimulated in some way to present a symbolic representation of a Jesus-like figure. No, he believed that he had actually met the objectively existing, real, historical and now resurrected Jesus in his vision, as opposed to some fantasy or myth created in his mind or some mere, what we would call today, psychological/emotional/cathartic experience. Paul considered that Jesus had 'visited' him in this experience.

This is why connection with the head – Jesus – is so important to Paul. For him it is the seeing of the objectively existing real, resurrected Jesus and the faithful following of the teaching received in this (and probably other) encounter(s) that distinguishes the Christian experience as 'sound', and places it in opposition to the 'mere' 'idle notions' encountered by the Christian and Pagan Gnostics, because in Gnostic mystical encounters, they did not necessarily 'see' real historical people, but rather they may 'see' mythical spirit-beings, wise guides and demi-gods, which they may well have interpreted in symbolic, allegorical ways instead of regarding them as literally objectively existing. For Gnostics, the resurrection was a 'spiritual' event rather than a physical one, for example.

Therefore for the Apostle Paul and his devotees, such experiences as those of the Christian Gnostics had no real foundation – because the recipients had not encountered actual, real people – let alone Jesus. They had not experienced a 'visitation' but a mere product of their imagination. This is where Paul and the Apostles are: they believe that their visions are based in objective reality – in a real person, that actually existed and lived and died, objectively appearing to them to instruct them, whereas to the Apostles, the Gnostics experience and ideas are the product of an inflated imagination that has lost touch with (for the Apostles) the real foundation – Jesus.

Whether the Apostles were correct in insisting that their visions were 'objective visitations' in this way is another matter. I am sure that arguments can be brought forward to suggest that these experiences were more subjective than the Apostles suppose. We can also see the development of the idea of the deification of Jesus as time goes on – an idea possibly not originally present immediately following the death of Jesus or even immediately following these visions. Nevertheless, it is these visionary experiences that form the basis of orthodox Christianity, even though many in orthodox Christianity would later dismiss continuing revelations as 'pretended', 'demonic' 'the product of enthusiasm' and 'heretical' – insisting instead upon the documents that they had selected to form the Bible as the only rule of faith and practice.

32) Were the apostles and their teaching without any error of any kind?

No. Whilst the Apostles claim that their teaching is God breathed, making it something more than mere human invention, the sins of the apostles were not removed such that they were perfect. Paul and Peter argued over Christian practice for example. (Galatians 2 v 11-14). Jesus Christ did not leave any writings for us, but commissioned these apostles to teach the church, and it is to their authority that the church looks because, though not absolutely without mistake due to the effects of sin, they received instructions from Christ Himself and were commissioned by Him to teach. Furthermore, Jesus promised them the special assistance of the Holy Spirit to teach them and assist them, even to the point of giving them words to say in difficult circumstances. Therefore, the church considers that their writings form a good measure and authority for standards of religious conduct in the
New Testament.

33) What was the early church's view of the canon of Scripture?

It did not forget that:
    i) The Scriptures are the result of a co working of God and man.
    ii) It was the church that selected the books under the guidance of the Holy Spirit.
    iii) It was the church that fixed the canon, declaring that no more was to be added.
    iv) That this was done because of the threat from heretical writings.

The Roman Catholic church emphasises, in contrast to Protestant churches that:-
    a) The church existed prior to the canon.
    b) The church in many ways is the source and origin of Scripture.

The Protestant church emphasises that:-
    a) The truth of God and the plan of creation and salvation existed before the church.
    b) God is the source and origin of Scripture that He created through human instruments.

Though these appear to contradict each other, in fact all these statements are true, and the issue is one of balance. Protestants over emphasise the God-ward side seeing the catholic emphasis as being too glorifying to man and taking away the glory of God. But in taking this position, the danger of Protestantism is to dehumanise the Scriptures in a very subtle way. Fundamentalists will always point out the human characteristics of the Scripture writings, but the emphasis on Scripture as the pure word of God nevertheless has a kind of dehumanising effect, turning the Scriptures into something that the original church might not recognise.

34) What is the position of the canon today?

The protestant reformation was firmly based on Scripture alone as the final authority and standard for Christian faith and conduct. It was considered to be the inerrant word of God. This tradition has continued, but in the 19th century, problems began to arise with this view as sincere believers had problems with apparent contradictions. Others sought to dismiss such claims for this literature, and criticism of various kinds began to emerge. Ancient manuscripts were re examined, styles of writing and composition of the various texts were looked at and so on. Thus it is now longer considered that the Apostle Paul wrote the letter to the Hebrews. Some would cast doubt on whether he wrote the letter to the Ephesians. The authorship of II Peter is in doubt. Some Old Testament prophets are perceived to have been written by a number of authors rather than just one, and so on. On the basis of what we have seen as principles for establishing the New Testament canon, this would mean that books not written by the 12 apostles or Paul should be removed from the canon because they have been revealed not to be Apostolic, and therefore lose the qualification to be included in the canon. As a defence against these problems, some protestants argue that though these writings were not written by the apostles themselves, they were nevertheless approved by them and so should be included in the canon, though exactly how we ascertain which non apostolic writings received approval is not explained. Perhaps by apostolic tradition. This is a position that cannot be disproved or proved, and the debate concerning some non apostolic writings is therefore still open. Certain groups, particularly Reformed Calvinists, maintained that scripture was the very word of God, inspired by Him in every detail, and because God is without sin, and because an authoritative rule for faith is necessary. God withheld the effects of sin from the Biblical authors when He inspired them, their Biblical writing being without error of any kind, except for a few minor errors in translation that do not affect the main truths. In other words, there was a shift in emphasis to the God-ward side of the origin and creation of Scriptures. This was coupled with the implication that to criticise Scripture is to criticise God Himself. It has been argued that this was a deliberate move on the part of leaders such as B.B. Warfield to keep and maintain the fundamentalist type of believer in that form of belief. Some fundamental protestant leaders further argue that like creation, Scripture contains evidence within Itself that God is its Author. Since God inspired the writers, the character of God can be seen in the Bible writings themselves, just like the character and distinctive qualities of a writer can be seen in a letter or a painter in a painting. We shall examine this argument shortly. First we need to look at the nature of inspiration.

35) What does inspiration mean?

Primarily, it means God breathed. It means that inspired writings are more than mere human productions, because God has breathed the words and truths into them via human writers. Someone may be Inspired but not write anything down, rather giving speech that is God breathed.

36) Is Inspiration limited to the writers of the canon of Scripture?

No. Many fundamentalists argue that inspiration equals inerrancy, and that therefore it is limited to Scripture writers and their particular canonical writings because only these writings are without mistakes of any kind. However even some respected fundamentalists such as Dr. Martyn Lloyd-Jones recognise that people other than the Scripture writers have been Inspired. Dr. Lloyd-Jones in one of his Westminster lectures on Howell Harris, a leader of the Welsh revival in the 18th Century, argues that God through the Holy Spirit inspired Harris' preaching. ('Howell Harris and revival' Westminster Conference 1973, "Adding to the church".) Similarly, other leaders, respected by fundamentalists, such as John Knox and John Flavel, appeared to have revelations and inspirations from the Holy Spirit. Despite attempts by some fundamentalists to use the latter part of I Corinthians 13 as proof that revelation. Inspiration and gifts of the Spirit generally have ceased; such an interpretation of this text is, in my opinion doubtful, and by no means shared by all fundamentalists anyway. There is a tendency in fundamentalism to see inspiration as a black and white issue: a person is either inspired, and thus what they say largely if not fully without error, or they are not inspired at all. I think that the reality is more complex, and that inspiration should be seen not as an all or nothing event, but rather as a continuum. In other words, there are various degrees of Inspiration, the influence is brought about by the Holy Spirit to a greater or lesser degree, and is by no means limited to the Scripture writers. I consider that God is able to, and does at various times influence believers and unbelievers alike, directly by the Holy Spirit, such that they may be inspired to varying degrees, and may also receive secret, hidden Information, or revelations by the Spirit.

37) How can we check that someone who claims Inspiration or revelation really has been inspired by God or had information revealed to them by God?

This of course was the problem in the early church. Some people had emotional experiences and thought that they were Inspired, some proclaimed teaching that they claimed or thought to be inspired, and some attempted to deceive the church by saying that they were inspired. Some moved to positions of contradicting the Apostles or encouraging practices which seemed extreme after declaring that God had commanded them directly to such teaching or practices. It is for this very reason that certain writings were included in a canon or rule of faith. Any opposition to these teachings was considered to be suspect, and to be treated with caution or rejected. So, the Scriptures, (however we define them) are considered by the church to be an authoritative guide in such matters, for reasons that I have already outlined. We would expect such influences to agree then with these Scripture documents. Indications are that people who experience such events do not lose their self control, and that the emphasis is on understanding and teaching, on glorifying God and on opposing sin. The powerful emotions that may accompany such an event arise from the powerful perception of God and aspects of His character. It is not the emotional feelings themselves that are the centre of attention. They are also often accompanied by a deep sense of unworthiness and absence of pride in oneself and even one's highest and best achievements, but not in such a way that one is made to feel depressed. However, they may be anxiety about salvation and a deep sense of one's sin before one is assured of mercy. There is no standard length of experience. Some may last a few moments, some for hours, and some for days.

One may enter into a state of ecstasy, losing all sense of one's surroundings and sensations such as hunger. There appears to be no formula for creating such an experience, though often, they are preceded by deep concern over some spiritual issue, and/or by prayer or meditation. Such events cannot be announced beforehand, but are given, according to Paul, by God's own pleasure and to accomplish His purposes of which we are often ignorant. The influence itself contains its own evidence as to it's authorship in it's manner of coming, subject matter and general tendency and effects, and the Holy spirit may show very strongly the evidences of authorship to the person concerned.

Nevertheless, this area remains one in which there remain many problems, and where believers and unbelievers alike can easily be deceived. There are many psychological, group and emotional effects that can appear to be truly extraordinary, but on further Investigation, be found to have little foundation in spiritual terms. Great claims can be made, and the mind can have unusual effects upon the body, apparently causing healings, involuntary movements, shaking, and pseudo language speaking, even the speaking of foreign languages not learned by the speaker.

Thus we see again the need for some appeal to authority, and the church has agreed that the writings in the canon provide us with such an authority and guide for our faith, as being the results of high degrees of inspirations and revelations that have withstood usage, time and investigations, in many ways.

38) If a person is inspired by God, does this mean that what they say or write whilst inspired is without error?

No. This would depend on the degree or amount of inspiration. To have no errors at all would mean that every letter, word and punctuation mark would have to be given by God, and this could only be done by dictation. Robert Horn like many fundamentalists recognises that such dictation contradicts the variety of styles present in the Scripture writings, and so like most fundamentalists rejects the idea of dictation. He suggests that truths were given in units of meaning where words are symbols, and Inspiration extends to single words in the sense that these words are servants of phrases, sentences, arguments and books, and one cannot hold up a single word as inspired because it has no meaning without its context. Nevertheless, such arguments and doctrines may hinge upon single words. He concludes that '... the actual production of any part of Scripture is always to be viewed as the final stage or act in a series of processes - providential, gracious, supernatural and historical. This taken as a whole culminates in a recorded revelation in which words act as component parts of units of meaning. These words convey through their human authors and features the authentic and PURE WORD OF GOD. (pp. 54-55. My capitals). This is a very round about way of saying that a number of events and circumstances worked together under God's guidance, together with the Holy Spirit working in the author, to produce the pure word of God. There was no strict dictation, neither was it an accident, but these things working together gave us an inspired word from God to the point where the writings are totally without error.

This has a certain appeal because it does less violence to the character of the authors than direct dictation. Again however, we are in the realms of philosophical speculation, and we must look at the evidence to see if this kind of argument for inerrant revelation is sufficient. Do all these Imperfect factors somehow come together to create something perfect? Some of the problems with dictation are:

a) There were changes in the Jewish language such that accents and spellings were changed, some of which did not occur in the originals, and therefore, older manuscripts had to be interpreted.

b) Human perspectives, and limitations together with social and historical perspectives clearly shine through. The writer of Matthew is clearly different in style from that of John and both are different from Isaiah. The degree of inspiration required for dictated inerrancy is not there.

c) There is no evidence that God held back the effects of sin in the writers as regards their writings, this is a logical, philosophical argument, rather than a Biblical one. It is logical once one accepts certain suppositions and wishes to maintain the idea of no mistakes at all.

Problems with inerrancy in general are:
a) Biblical verses which indicate that all Scripture is Inspired, and therefore without errors, cannot be used as 'proof because which books and letters are in the canon and which are excluded had not been defined when these verses were written. This verse could only be used in

a more general way to say that all religious, sacred writing is God breathed and therefore helpful in Instruction.

b) With Inerrancy there can be no mistakes in Scripture whatsoever, however, there are indeed many detailed passages that create problems of unity of truth for Scripture, of which we can only look at few.

Compare:
I Samuel 17 with II Samuel 21 v 19 and I Chronicles 20 v 5. Just who DID kill Goliath?
Matthew 27 v 9 puts Jeremiah for Zechariah.
Was Jairus's daughter dead, or nearly dead? Matthew 9 v 18 with Mark 5 v 22,23 and Luke 8 v 42.
When did Jesus cleanse the temple of moneychangers? Was it early in His ministry as John 2 v 13, or late as Matthew 21 v 12, Matt 11 v 15-17, Luke 19 v 45,46? To insist on two cleansings is to ridicule the gospels as literary works.
There are contradictory accounts about how Judas Iscariot died. (Acts 1 v 18, Matthew 27 v 5).
There seem to be many contradictions between Samuel/Kings and Chronicles:
Compare:
II Samuel 8 v 4: 1,700 horsemen, 20,000 foot taken by David.
I Chronicles 18 v 4: 1000 chariots, 7000 horsemen, 20,000 foot.
II Samuel 10 v 6: 20,000 + 1,000 + 12,000 mercenaries of Ammonites.
I Chronicles 19 v 7: 32,000 chariots + army of King Maacah.
II Samuel 10 v 18: 700 charioteers + 40,000 horsemen slain. I Chronicles 19 v 18: 7,000 charioteers + 40,000 horsemen.
II Samuel 24 v 9: Israel 800,000, Judah 500,000 (census) I Chronicles 21 v 5: Israel 1,100,000. Judah 470,000.
II Samuel 24 v 24: 50 shekels (price of threshing floor) I Chronicles 21 v 25: 600 shekels.
I Kings 4 v 26: 40,000 stalls for chariot horses. II Chronicles 9 v 25: 4,000.
I Kings 7 v 26: 2,000 baths (Capacity of the sea.) II Chronicles 4 v 5: 3,000 baths.
Some, but not all of these can be ascribed to errors by copyists.

Some prophesies are not fulfilled:

Ezekiel prophesies concerning the fall of Tyre, that God declares it will be utterly destroyed by Nebuchadnezzar and never rebuilt. Ezekiel 26 v 9-14. But, sixteen years later, Ezekiel begins Chapter 29 from the evident fact that Nebuchadnezzar failed to destroy Tyre. Ezekiel 29 v 17 - 20.

II Samuel 24 v 1: The Lord incites David. I Chronicles 21 v 1: Satan incites David.

I Kings 15 v 14 with II Chronicles 14 v 5: Did Asa remove the high places or not?

Ephesians 4 v 8 with Psalm 68 v 18: Were gifts given or received by God?

Mark 6 v 7-9 with Luke 9 v 1-3: Did the disciples have to take a staff or not?

c) There are problems too with fitting the stories to the facts:
Even the most ardent Creationists tend to admit to some kind of gap in the genealogy of Genesis, by talking about a MINIMUM of 1656 years from Adam to Noah's flood. In other words, there are problems with fitting the creation account into modern scientific knowledge.

There are problems finding evidence of a major poll tax at the time of Christ's birth, or that people had to travel for such a tax. In other words, the Scriptures do not seem to fulfil the two commonly accepted definitions or requirements of truth, namely, a coherent internal system, (it fails to have complete and absolute unity of Information), and correspondence to facts, (there are difficulties in finding Independent evidence to support some of the major events described).

Of course, those who believe that the Scripture has no mistakes will often find explanations for these difficulties. One of their major tasks is harmonisation: relating together and explaining difficulties like those above. The question that has to be asked is: How believable are those explanations? How reasonable do they sound? Are their alternative explanations that sound better? Obviously, each problem has to be considered separately, as there are different difficulties with each one. But even writers like R.M Horn are forced to admit that they cannot reconcile and solve all these contradictions and problems. Many fundamentalists like Horn then shift their ground. They argue that these verses have not been proved to be untrue, and until they are, we can live with them. They shift the burden of proof to the unbeliever, requiring them to disprove the verses. Similar approaches are often used with supportive disciplines like archaeology, which are quoted and appealed to when they support the fundamentalist's position, but if they do not, the burden of proof is shifted so that archaeology has to absolutely disprove historical statements in the Bible. However, as we have seen earlier, this will never be the case because facts have to be interpreted. Fundamentalists may also argue that we live and function every day with ideas that have not been proved to be true, but which serve us well. If we all took the position that everything had to be proved before we accepted it we would get nowhere. Of course, it is true that we do accept many ideas without having proof. But it is usually because we have good reasons for doing so, and because we have not come across evidence or Indications suggesting that our position is incorrect. I have not circled the globe, and have not proved to myself that the world is round rather than flat. Nevertheless, I believe it is round because I see lots of evidence and reports to suggest that it is so, and no serious evidence to suggest that it is flat. Fundamentalists make the claim that Scripture is inerrant. The onus is upon them to show the evidence that this is indeed the case; especially in the light of the sort of problems we have just seen. Putting the onus on fundamentalists is consistent with the older arguments put forward by puritans such as John Owen in his 'Reason of faith', namely that Scripture carries within Itself its own evidence of Divine Authorship. It is quite legitimate therefore to ask: 'What exactly is this evidence?'.

39) What evidence is put forward to suggest that the writings in the canon of Scripture are inspired, or God breathed?

i) The contents are so grand and awe Inspiring, far above anything else. Their content is so full of secrets and matters that cannot be explained that they could never be just a human invention or discovery: For example, it declares a Trinity in the Deity, it describes the Person of Christ, the corruption of man, the plan of salvation, the law of God, and comprehends a universal history of the world, past, present and future.

ii) It is very old, yet still very much means something to us today, such that we can use it's ideas when other ancient writers have lost their application to us, or have been replaced by new and better ideas.

iii) They are written in a style that cannot be copied, with a style of authority, despite being written by a number of writers, over a considerable length of time.

iv) There is a character of purity in the writings, condemning sin and extolling goodness.

v) They have a harmony and balance, an agreement and consent, which are maintained despite the time span of writings and variety of authors.

vi) Its prophecies have been fulfilled accurately.

vii) It's teaching was confirmed by miracles and signs

viii) These writings have survived many attempts to eradicate them by both men and Satan.

ix) It has a tremendous range and scope of subject matter.

x) It's teaching is effective: lives are changed.

xi) The church has had a high esteem for Scripture, regarding it as inspired.

40) What can we conclude about this evidence?

That depends on who is doing the evaluating and what assumptions and beliefs they already hold. Some would say that these reasons prove beyond doubt that the Scriptures are Inspired and therefore without error. Others will say there are problems with each of these ideas. There are other books with grand, awe Inspiring ideas which do not claim to be written by God. There is other old literature still of relevance, including some of the books not included in the canon. There are other very moral and even God glorifying writings that are not in Scripture. Other religious systems often have a harmonious well worked out system. It is questionable whether all the prophesies of the Bible have been accurately fulfilled. Nevertheless, these ideas go some way to showing that the Bible is a special collection of books, highly regarded by the Christian community, and quite possibly something more than a mere human invention. Here again, fundamentalists often resort to philosophical/theological argument to maintain their position. They argue basically that Scripture is inerrant because written by God. The evidence of this is there in the Scriptures themselves. But humankind, because its nature is fallen, is blind towards God, biased against Him, and has a preference for self interest over and above interest in God. The evidence is there, but we are blinded, hardened and biased by sin. This is a circular argument that to the fundamentalist only serves to confirm the sinful state of those who do not accept the Bible as God's inerrant word.

41) What can we conclude about inerrancy then?

Some of the evidence listed may Indeed point to the fact that the Bible is a special collection of books and letters, to the point of being Inspired, having something of the influence or breath of God infused into them, but not to the point of being without error. Internal and external evidence points to contradictions and errors to a degree where the claims of fundamentalists do not seem to be proved. The onus of proof is indeed upon them, but their arguments appear merely philosophical or circular in nature, or they shift their ground attempting to put the onus on others to disprove the fundamentalist position, which is not possible.

42) What can we conclude about the Bible then?

The bible is a collection of letters and books written over a long period of time by various authors. The items which have been Included and excluded have been decided upon by the community of believers, and have been much debated and have varied to some degree. They were assembled as an authority for faith because of the collapse or threat to the Jewish nation and it's Identity, and because of mistakes and heresies coming into the new testament church following the death of the Apostles and the worsening quality of word of mouth accounts, together with the rise of false written accounts. It's qualities and preservation, together with the miracles and wonders performed by some of it's writers, indicate this collection to be something special, but not to the degree that they are without mistake or contradiction of any kind. Some of the literature excluded from the canon may also be inspired, or God breathed, though parts of them were thought to have qualities that were not quite right. The main quality for New Testament inclusion was Apostolic authorship. Scholarship and information has improved since the early church decided on the New Testament canon, and some of the New Testament is now considered not to be written by Apostles. Problems within and between the writings themselves, and in confirming some of the events recorded from other independent sources, mean that though inspired, they are not without mistakes and human limitations, reflecting certain ideas of the time, and that therefore, inspiration does not mean that they are totally without mistakes.

43) The church has defined the existing New Testament books as being inspired by God. Which of these are now considered to be written by Apostles and which by others?

To give an answer requires a very complex and long series of facts and theories well beyond the scope of this study. Needless to say, there is not agreement amongst scholars, who approach the subject from different angles. However, a typical overview of the New Testament might be something like this:

For three of the gospels, which are very similar in content, it is thought that there was firstly Mark, itself a copy from a now lost original source, and another lost original source, called by scholars Q. Matthew and Luke drew from both Mark and Q, and thus these three are very similar. Matthew and Luke add a small amount of unique material of their own. The titles, the gospel of Mark, e.t.c., were not part of the originals, and these works are not thought to be written by any of the twelve apostles. One of the gospels, John, is quite different, and many think that it is indeed and eyewitness account. Acts is written by the same author as Luke. Of the letters assigned to Paul, many are not in doubt as to their authenticity. Some express doubts about Ephesians, Colossians, Philemon and Philippians, but a really powerful case is not presented. II Thessalonians is doubted to be by Paul quite often. Most doubt that Paul wrote the pastoral letters of I Timothy, II Timothy and Titus, because of problems with style and content. Hebrews is not considered to be by Paul, but possibly by Barnabas, or Appollos. I Peter is disputed by some because of it's accomplished use of Greek, but most think it genuine. II Peter is doubted by most as being by Peter. The letter of James is thought to be by the leader of the council in Jerusalem at the time of the apostles, James the lesser. (Acts 15 v 13). A very influential and important leader, but not one of the twelve apostles. I John is considered genuine, but quite a few scholars express doubts about II John and III John. Jude is thought to have been written by Judas the apostle, or Judas the brother of the Lord, but not one of the twelve. Revelation is thought by many to be written by John, one of the twelve apostles, or by John the Presbyter, a John who is not one of the twelve.

44) Has the church altered the canon in response to these findings?

No. At the present time, the various groupings within the church have kept their particular canons.

45) Fundamentalists place a great deal of importance on Scripture as the only way of knowing salvation. If this is the case, what about those people who do not have or have never seen a Bible? Are they automatically lost, or bound for hell?

There are obviously many people who have lived and died without ever knowing of these writings, or about the Lord Jesus Christ. Obviously, the church considers it an important matter to make these writings available to as many as possible, and some Christians have been imprisoned or died trying to do just that. The position of people without the bible must be similar to early Old Testament believers. Abraham for example did not have any of our scriptures: Moses had not yet been born. Neither did people of this time have any understanding of Jesus or who he was. They could not look forward in time to see Jesus or what He would be like. Some, like Abraham were privileged to have God speak to them directly, but not all believers had this kind of communication. Nevertheless, Abraham's faith, and the faith of those like him, was reckoned to them as righteousness. Abraham was a sinner like everyone else. His works condemned him in God's sight. But Abraham, like other Old Testament believers, trusted God. God's plan was not fully revealed, the method of salvation was not clear at all, but these people trusted God for deliverance, and that faith was counted as righteousness, according to the Apostle Paul. (Romans 4 v 3, Genesis 15 v 6). Paul argues that the man who does not work, who is not in the position of earning favour or righteousness by good deeds, but rather trusts God is in a position where his faith is credited as righteousness. The details of how God can do this and maintain consistency with His pure character, and the details of how this plan is accomplished vary in their clarity. For some, these details are vague and obscure. As we have seen, it is possible to know that God exists and to know something of His character by our own moral human nature, thoughts and conscience and from evidences in creation. It may be also that God may speak to us directly, but this is rare. Nevertheless, there is a universal testimony and witness to God's character and existence in creation. What scripture does then is to refine and define in a fuller way what this God is like, making His character and plans more plain, and revealing more than creation and human nature can about God. And for this reason it is very precious. As we have already seen, people without Scripture will be judged by the standards of their thoughts and consciences and their trust in a God revealed to all through creation in such a way that all are without excuse for not trusting God. Even if such a faith may be poorly defined and not well Informed, it will be counted as righteousness and that faith revealed to others by the behaviour of that person. The one who has scripture is able to see God's plan for saving people and to understand more fully Gods dealings. With this extra knowledge comes increased accountability. The more we know of what God has revealed about Himself, the more grievous our sins are and the greater the punishment may be, because we ignore or go against such a high degree of knowledge. Those who believe God, or trust in Him, apart from any self righteousness have their faith credited to them as righteousness, and are the children of Abraham in that they are heirs to the promises made to Abraham. (Galatians 3 v 6). The object of that faith may be slightly defined through creation, or more precisely defined through the more personal and detailed inspired revelation of Scripture. The fundamentalists, in depreciating the power of natural revelation through creation because of the effects of sin are obliged to lay greater emphasis still upon the Importance of Scripture as the ONLY way of finding salvation. I suggest that this position is one of imbalance.

46) What evidence is there in creation of God' existence?

First of all it must be emphasised that we cannot point to one element or part of creation and from it conclusively prove that God exists. God cannot be proved in this way at all. Secondly, theology drawn from Scripture tells us that the earth and creation are not as God created them. They have been blighted by the result of sin and God's curse. The harmonious paradise that God created has been spoiled. Thus for every glorious flower we can find some ugly, pernicious weed: alongside lush, fertile countryside, there exist barren deserts and frozen wastelands: and with every aspect of harmony we also find violence and cruelty in the struggle of species to survive. According to Scripture we find as a result that the earth is sometimes shaken by natural calamities, storms and earthquakes, partly as a result of the curse, sometimes as specific punishments or demonstrations of wrath against sin by God. The world then is not a perfect reflection of God's character as it once was. Nevertheless, the marks of its creation as being Divine are still present to some degree. Evidence for God's existence and character is indirect in the sense that some deduction or inference is necessary, and as we have already seen, it is limited in the amount of Information it contains. Paul argues that the provision of rain, crops in season, food and hearts filled with joy are testimony to God and His kindness. He elsewhere argues that God's Invisible qualities. His power and divine nature are clearly seen, being understood from what has been made. Thus, as the Psalmist says, the heavens declare the glory of God, without words they display knowledge to all.

Of course, it is quite easy to approach the universe and the daily provision of food with another perspective, and to interpret them differently. This of course is what happens. Different peoples have created different religions based on interpretations of creation, often worshipping creation itself. This is what Paul mentions in Romans 1. In other words, though the evidence is there, says Paul, it has to be interpreted. God's character and nature has to be understood from the things that are made, and of course, fundamentalists are correct in pointing out that the bias that sin creates in human beings against God means that people tend to suppress the knowledge of God that creation and providence gives, and exchange it for something else. Unfortunately, this seems to be as specific as we can get. Scripture does not elaborate upon what it is about creation that reveals God, and philosophers have probed the question to such a depth that the arguments are way beyond the scope of this study.

Arguments tend to revolve around the size, order and complexity of creation.

47) Another source of authority claimed by the Church is the Holy Spirit. Who or what is the Holy Spirit?

The Holy Spirit is the third person of the Godhead. There is one God in three persons:- The Father, The Son and the Holy Spirit. Thus the Holy Spirit is not an impersonal force or power, but an actual person. Though these three are equal, they willingly submit to each other in the following way: The Son submits to the Father, and the Spirit submits to Son, seeking to glorify the Son and the Father. As the Father sent the Son to live, die and be resurrected, so, when the Son ascended to heaven. He gave the Spirit, in a different and fuller way than had been known before.

48) What is this different and fuller way?

The Holy Spirit was given at Pentecost, with signs that witnessed to this event. From that moment, the Holy Spirit Himself was given to Indwell or live in believers as an influence towards truth and purity and as a foretaste of promises to yet be fulfilled. Thus, when Individual believers gather together, and especially when church leaders gather together, (since they are chosen by existing Elders and church for their qualities of faith and purity), the Holy Spirit is present in a very special way, and the church has an advantage that unbelievers, however numerous or educated, do not have. This does not mean that the church is perfect or without mistake. There is still much sin present, and many mistakes can be made, and there are of course many divisions, groups and opinions in the church.

49) Is the Holy Spirit anywhere else besides living in believers?

Yes. He is God; therefore He is omnipresent, that is. He is in all places. In other words, He is not restricted to one geographical location like the angels or humans. He is at work all over the world. He deals with unbelievers as well as believers, but He has this special relationship with believers, and deals with them in ways that are unique.

50) What kind of work does the Holy Spirit do?

His works can be categorised into two types:
a) Common grace works. These are works done by the Holy Spirit that are common to all mankind and which are not limited to believers only. For example, the Spirit restrains sin in unbelievers, stopping them from becoming absolutely evil. He gives people gifts and abilities. He convicts or makes people aware of their guilt of sin.
b) Gracious or saving works. These are unique to believers, and are not shared by unbelievers. To believers, the Spirit acts as a Witness, Earnest, Sealer, Leader, Intercessor and Comforter.

All His works exist somewhere along a line between two

points:-
a) Ordinary works. That is, works that are frequent, or seemingly natural, such as the gift of being able to teach, or have a 'natural' ability to be a carpenter.

b) Extraordinary works. These are either rare, and/or unusually high in degree, for example being a genius as opposed to being clever; and/or supernatural, such as miracle working and prophecy.

51) How does this present work of the Spirit in believers relate to the work of the Spirit in the Apostles and their traditions and writings?

There is a tension between the inspiration of the Apostles and the current work of the Holy Spirit in believers. In the early church, the current work of the Spirit was emphasised, and there were many prophets for example, declaring messages from God. A typical group, in the 2nd Century were the Montanists, a prophetic movement in Turkey. Montanus was a recent convert who held no position of Elder. Eventually synods or councils of Bishops in Asia and elsewhere condemned it. Since this period, the church has favoured the authority of the Apostolic tradition, effectively recorded in their writings and creeds, over and above any new revelations or inspirations of the Spirit. Any claimed new Inspirations or revelations of the Spirit in believers are tested by the writings of the Apostles, to make sure that there are no differences in ideas or teaching.

52) In a little more detail, what sort of works does the Spirit do when indwelling the Christian?

He acts as a:
Witness. He reveals evidences of being a believer, and draws attention to Christian characteristics such as hope, joy, hatred of sin and so on, as they are present.

Earnest. His presence acts as a foretaste and guarantee of the reality of future promises of heaven.

Sealer. He establishes, by His influence, the character or likeness of God in a believer as a stamp of God's ownership.

Leader. He inclines the Christian to do the will of God and live in purity. He alters the taste or preferences of the person, such that they love the things that God loves and hate the things that He hates.

Intercessor. He steps in between the believer and the Father, pleading the believer's case before the throne of grace.

Comforter. He comes alongside believers, offering help, by energising, or causing them to remember teaching, or persuading of sin, and so on.

53) In a little more detail, what sort of works does the Spirit do to both Christians and non Christians?

The Holy Spirit:
Restrains sin. He holds back the effects and desires that are in opposition to God.
Awakens to sin. He makes people aware that they have done things that are not right.
Convicts of guilt. He persuades people that they are guilty of offending God.
Leads to repentance. He leads people to be sorry for their sins, confess them to God and turn away from them.
He gives gifts and abilities.
    These include:
    Prophets
    Evangelists
    Pastors
    Teachers
    Word of wisdom
    Word of knowledge
    Miracle working
    Faith
    Overseers
    Tongue speaking and interpretation.
Some of these gifts are people, some are qualities, they are all given for the benefit of the Church, but in some cases, extraordinary abilities may be given to unbelievers, usually in connection with God dealing with that person in a very special way, perhaps to protect them, or protect believers in some way.

54) How are each of these works recognised?

Since all these things come from God there is expected to be some sort of unity in them. Therefore they are expected to conform to the character of God revealed in creation, Jesus and the Inspired writers and especially with Apostolic writings, traditions, teachings and creeds. The more extraordinary gifts evidence themselves by their very unusualness as well as having the above qualities.

55) What are the evidences of the indwelling of the Spirit?

This has to be inferred: to be concluded reasoned and interpreted from the facts available. The Holy Spirit's influence varies in degree, such that sometimes evidences are plain but at other times difficult to make out. With some extraordinary influences there may be a strong accompanying witness of the Spirit, testifying to the authorship of the phenomenon. As such, the person concerned may have great confidence as to the divine authorship of the gift or message. This is not merely great confidence, but a confidence based upon internal evidence of the nature of the influence's coming to the person, together with a very clear perception of the marks of God in the influence itself, its content and main thrust. The content and nature of the Influence is always consistent with the character of God, has a tendency towards holiness and moral purity, and does not promote the recipient of the Influence, who may be full of humility and self abasement as a result of their perception of God. For onlookers, who do not receive such an extraordinary work, they have to look at the event and interpret what is going on, as the onlookers did at Pentecost. It may be that the Interpretation given by a person moved by the Spirit will persuade others. In the more usual cases of the normal Christian life and experience, the chief evidence is in the quality of the person's life rather than what they say or claim to believe: The indwelling of the Spirit produces the fruit of the Spirit.
This Is:
Love for God and man as opposed to hatred of God.
Joy in the Lord   as opposed to   misery.
Peace with God   as opposed to   restlessness with God
Longsuffering   as opposed to   impatience.
Gentleness   as opposed to   roughness.
Goodness   as opposed to   badness
Faith   as opposed to   unbelief.

Meekness   as opposed to   pride.
Self control   as opposed to   want of restraint.

Those not indwelt by the Spirit may have qualities in their lives such as:
    Sexual immorality.
    Impurity.
    Too much involvement in pleasure for it's own sake.
    Following other religions
    Discord.
    Jealousy.
    Anger.
    Selfish ambition.
    Being divisive.
    Being envious.
    Drunkenness

These are not just isolated qualities. Obviously Christians may get drunk sometimes, or become jealous or angry. Rather, these are settled characteristics that last a long time. If a person is continually angry, or drunk, and hardly ever has peace with God or love for Him, then we may doubt them when they say that they are a Christian, and may doubt the indwelling of the Holy Spirit in them. It is in this way that we reason and conclude the Indwelling of the Holy Spirit. Of course, since the moral qualities of the fruit of the Spirit may be present or appear to be present in those not professing Christianity, and since alternative interpretations can be placed upon the reasons for the presence of such qualities, we are left again with a variety of interpretations.

56) To return to our original question then: Where does the church get it's authority from? How does the church know what is right and wrong in spiritual matters?

The ultimate authority for these matters is God Himself.
God reveals Himself and His will by:
    i) Direct appearances, which are exceptionally rare.
    ii) Angelic appearances, which are also rare.
    iii) Through Jesus Christ: His life and His teaching.
    iv) Through miracles and wonders, which are rare.
    v) Through Apostolic tradition and customs.
    vi) Through various sacred. God breathed writings.

vii) Through the gathered church, or community of believers, each of whom is indwelt by the Holy Spirit, and especially through it's leaders and their councils.
viii) Through gifts, both ordinary and, more rarely, extraordinary gifts from the Holy Spirit.
ix) Through creation.
x) Through a moral human nature, created in God's image, such that conscience and thoughts accuse or excuse a person's deeds.

We are left with the fact that God, angels, and other heavenly beings are spiritual beings, invisible, not provable by scientific investigation. The suggestions are that:-
a) God has made himself a physical being in the form of Jesus, but He is no longer present with us in this physical form.

b) God Himself, or other spiritual beings with His permission can influence people and objects in terms of power, for example by transcending physical laws. Such events have to be interpreted, to assess their cause, and they will be interpreted by prevailing world views of the witnesses. Someone present may be influenced by God to give an interpretation, in which case see (c) below. These spiritual beings may change a person's life, and again, these changes have to be interpreted to ascertain their cause.

c) God Himself or other spiritual beings with His permission can Influence people by communication, such as revealing themselves or information via dreams, tongues e.t.c.. This is inspiration, but this does not appear to occur to a degree whereby there are absolutely no mistakes. However, since God declares Himself to be truth we would expect a high degree of truth and accuracy in inspired statements. The manner in which such Influences come, and the nature of their content have to be interpreted also, in order to assess their authorship. This Includes written revelation and Inspiration such as Scripture.

d) God has evidenced Himself to all through His work of creation and providence. The disposition of man is such that he tends to dismiss this evidence, which again has to be interpreted, and he tends to suppress it and exchange it for other world views.

e) The Judeo-Christian Church has taken certain writings and after consideration and interpretation of the evidence, considered them to be inspired to a degree that they can profitably be used for teaching and Instruction, and as an authoritative rule for Christian practice. The debate as to what should and should not be included in this rule has continued through the centuries. Further evidence and examination suggests that some of the New Testament writings are not what they claim, and perhaps not suitable for a rule of faith. The main qualification for inclusion was Apostolicity.

57) Is there any order or hierarchy to these? How do they work together?

This is difficult to express in diagram form, but a simple idea may look as follows:-

HIERARCHY OF SPIRITUAL REVELATION

GOD THE FATHER

    Revealed in CREATION... (Indirect)
    via Things that are made
    Providence.
    Human moral nature...
        via Knowledge of good and bad.
        Conscience.
    and through the CHURCH...
        because of the indwelling of the Spirit.
        via Apostles and their works.
        Sacred writings.
        Church leaders and councils.
        Gathered Believers.

JESUS CHRIST
    Direct visitations.
    No longer physically present.
    Full revelation-God made flesh.
    Life and teaching recorded via

Apostolic writings inspired by

HOLY SPIRIT
Given to believers and at work in the world.

RIGHTEOUS ANGELS - Visitations.

FALLEN ANGELS - Visitations and influences Lies and Half-truths.

HIERARCHY OF HUMAN AUTHORITY IN THE CHURCH.

JESUS CHRIST
(Ascended to heaven and no longer physically present. So He gave..)

HOLY SPIRIT
(To teach apostles and enable them to remember Jesus' teaching
and perform wonders as testimony to the truth of their message.)

ISRAEL'S
PROPHETS/ LEADERS   APOSTLES   GIFTS
(moved by Holy Spirit)

Inspired sacred writings

Hebrew canon   New Testament canon*

Teaching - writings - traditions - creeds

APOSTLES SUCCESSORS

Other sacred writings – teachings - writings - creeds and councils

97

OTHER BELIEVERS

writings - creeds - councils - traditions

* Here, the New Testament writings are considered as Apostolic writings only.
Secular knowledge and expertise is assumed to pervade all human levels.

We can see from the first diagram that God the Father is the final Authority, with the Son submitting to him and the Spirit in turn submitting to the Son. The Son has been amongst us and taught men and demonstrated proof of Who He is by His miracles, but He is no longer present. He has left us with the Holy Spirit, working in various ways and degrees. Then there are the messengers of God, created spiritual beings called angels. God is revealed in all his works, but these are in the main invisible beings, and it does not seem to be usual for God to talk to us via these messengers. God is revealed in His works of creation, and though a universal witness to God, it is in many ways limited in what it declares. It is also affected by the fall into sin, such that though man has a moral nature and a conscience, it does not work properly because sin: a preference of self over and above God, distorts it. A written revelation inspired by the Holy Spirit is more detailed in its content and has some of the effects of sin overcome. It is also less open to misinterpretation. Therefore, in the absence of the physical presence of God, and in the light of the effects of sin distorting our sense of what is right, inspired religious writings are our only record of what Jesus said and did, and the most authoritative and reliable account of what God requires. Writings by believers of repute who are not one of the twelve are also helpful in teaching and enabling the understanding, but of all the writings, those by the twelve and Paul are the most authoritative, since they were taught by Jesus and the Holy Spirit, and commissioned by God to be the founders of the New Testament church. It is for this reason that we find the writings of the apostles more relevant to us than those of the Old Testament because we live in the New Testament age. Matters of conscience and our sense of right and wrong, since distorted by sin, should therefore be examined in comparison to their writings, where those writings cover the issues involved. But other writings by believers should not be ignored. Early writings such as Didache, and I Clement, and Christian classics such as

Pilgrims Progress are all valuable for teaching, even if they do not have the same authority.

58) Is the Church united in all that it does then?

No. Different groups place different degrees of importance between tradition, creeds and writings, and even within the canon of Scripture, different groups place different degrees of importance on different passages and verses. Some passages are hard to understand, and different groups understand them differently. Some groups are more patient with sin and error than others, and so on. And of course, the church is not without sin. Ultimately, each person has to be persuaded in their own minds, having listened to teachers, read the literature and thought carefully, as to which path they think is correct. But the writings of the apostles themselves encourage us to unity and peace in God. Nevertheless, there may come a point at which a person considers that a certain type of behaviour and thought is not in line with thoughts expressed in sacred writings, and differences of opinion may occur between believers. It is especially important that at such times, each maintains humility love and peace, especially towards God before Whom one is ultimately answerable to.

59) What lies behind the need for spiritual authority?

Spiritual authority is concerned, amongst other things, with the need for consistency of form, with the need for orthodoxy. It is felt that Truth, spiritual truth about God, has been declared in one form or another by those who have reached some spiritual attainment, and that this form must be maintained and protected from the corrupting influence of other (lesser and inferior) ideas and practices that are seen as erroneous or heretical. Spiritual authority is partly about conserving and preserving received spiritual wisdom, about maintaining traditional spiritual beliefs and practices. The answer to question 13 showed that there was a profusion of sects and groups each going of at various tangents, and that this was why some rule of faith was needed. Of all these groups, Christian Fundamentalists are amongst the most conservative…it is no wonder then that they are at the forefront of maintaining what they see as the sole rule of faith…the Bible.

60) What about texts from other religions and faiths?

In the ten years that have passed since writing this study I have travelled wide in the spiritual country. It seems to me that God is Formless, but that God necessarily communicates to us in appropriate forms in order that we may understand and communicate something about God. We have already seen that God is generally revealed to all through creation, for example. The Christian faith can be more properly called the Judeo-Christian tradition. It has emerged from the culture of Judaism and has a particular interpretation concerning Jesus, (which Jews do not share). There is, in turn, within this Judeo-Christian tradition, a wide range of different interpretations, emphases, and balances giving rise to different movements and divisions within Christianity. The perspective advocated by Fundamentalists means that they cling to their particular form as the one and only authoritative form. Other perspectives take a different or wider view. I personally lean towards an approach of Mysticism, of direct communication and experience with God, as providing the best personal evidence of God's existence and as being the most authoritative. In this view, the forms of God that are presented are merely appropriate and apt symbols by which the Formless Absolute communicates to us. Ultimately, as one draws near to God in experience, our need for form and indeed the forms themselves, fall away and are rendered useless as they are swallowed up in God. In looking at and experiencing mysticism, I have seen that people from other faiths have had the same experiences, but expressed in the forms of their own culture and religious tradition.

In our normal level of functioning in this world, we need some form or other, some concept of God, some form or way of approach, some commonly held perspective in order for us to begin our approach to God, communicate our understanding and share in fellowship; some boundary that gives us a framework and structure. This form may or may not be that of Christianity. Thus there are other forms, such as Islam, Hinduism, Buddhism and so on. These too have their sacred writings and authorities and these too originate at a particular time and within a particular culture. Though they may share some ideas in common, they are at the same time too diverse to be harmonised: to diverse to create a single, authoritative world religious text. When we try to harmonise all the world's religions, this results in too much compromise and watering down of any one tradition. Rather, each tradition tends to enclose us within its own boundary and system of teaching, insight and practice...we are sheep within a particular pen. The writings of one tradition may even appear heretical, false and dangerous from the viewpoint of another tradition. One way to think of this is to regard these different religions as different schools; different disciplines and methods of approach to an Absolute that is Transcendent of any form and which cannot be grasped or encompassed by any mind or system of thought. All these schools, these religions, are partial and inadequate, and are also firmly based in an historical and cultural context. As spiritual seekers after truth, some of them will seem more adequate, more resonant, more applicable, more Godly than others. The situation would seem to be this:

ABSOLUTE / GOD

REVELATION / INSPIRATION
(within a context of time and culture)

PROPHECY
(Faithful Declaration of what is received)
(Q 24 – 29)

Some of this written down   Some lost and forgotten

May be mixed with other writings:
i)   Historical accounts
ii)   Opinions and teachings
iii)   Genealogies

Some destined for Scriptures Some destined for sacred writings
            and   but
    considered authoritative   quotes not considered authoritative
    or that tradition / school   (Q 6)   for that tradition / school
        (Canonical)
       (Q 3 – 5, 8 – 14)

101

Heretical   Apocryphal

                                        Deutero-canonical
        Dangerous
                                        Secondary
Unprofitable
                            Profitable   (Q 6, 7)

61) What can we conclude about spiritual and moral authority?

This study has mainly concerned itself with the Christian church and therefore the Christian perspective and Christian forms. But the issue is a wider one and in our latter questions we have also considered very briefly the position of other faiths and religions. The same issues apply to them: from where do they get their moral and spiritual authority? On what is it based? What evidence is there to support their claims? Other faiths follow other sacred writings or scriptures: The Vedas, the Upanishads, the Qu'ran and so on, as well as other cultural traditions. What we can say of all of these, including the Bible, is that:
  a)   They consist of interpretations of the world, society, people, God and the Universe that were made a very long time ago, without the advantage of our growth in knowledge. In some cases, these are almost stone-age interpretations.
  b)   These interpretations and perspectives of God and the Universe are bound in the time that they were written – these writers did not have insight into nuclear physics, modern medicine, biology and chemistry and so on. They are interpretations and forms that fitted well with their level of development and understanding; they were appropriate forms to them as God met them where they were.
  c)   These writings, (and I am thinking of the Bible primarily) contain a variety of material such as genealogies, interpretations of then current or recent political events, views of origins, messages from God, histories of people as they were seen at that time and metaphorical forms in relation to the Divine. The messages and encounters with God were given in forms that were appropriate to and consistent with the level of development of these people, in some cases in a high degree of 'closeness' with God (inspiration/revelation). Within this mass of literature are faithfully recorded some of the experiences and communications that some people, such as the prophets, had from God. Nevertheless, it does not seem

102

credible to hold to a view whereby every letter and syllable is inspired and therefore without error. Such a view does not seem to stand up to close examination. These scriptures are special, insightful, profitable, useful and helpful, but they are not infallible or completely without error.

d) Some of these sacred writings or scriptures became, by one means or another, to be regarded as authoritative within the circle of disciple/believers. Others faded into obscurity or were lost, and yet others achieved a secondary function: not perceived as having such a high degree of authority, yet useful and profitable if read carefully.

e) Though most faiths limit their canon or rule of authoritative scripture documents, there is no Biblical evidence at least to declare that revelation and inspiration have ceased. Limiting the canon helps to establish firm boundaries and limits to the faith concerned, and also helps avoid the problem of identifying which writings are truly inspired and which are in error or a deception. But the limiting and finalising of the canon may also stagnate the faith to forms that are increasingly outdated or irrelevant. Also, religious history suggests that various believers through the ages after Christ or Mohammed etc have had mystical encounters with God and written accounts of what they have seen and heard whilst in these states of closeness with God. The religious authorities have regarded such literature with more or less favour at different times and places.

f) Since the literature of each faith is firmly bound in different times and cultures, it is not possible to reconcile them fully. They may oppose and contradict each other as well as having elements and themes in common. They are like facets of a diamond, each facet reflecting different aspects of God. Furthermore, God cannot be encompassed by form, because all forms limit and bound the Unlimited Formless and so inevitably, forms are limited and temporal, inadequate and partial.

g) Recognising the limits of this authoritative literature as well as its strengths is one way forward: it prevents black and white 'ours is the only way' thinking; it recognises the insights of other faiths; it opens the way for further, lively communication with God instead of declaring such communications ceased; it enables us to move on past interpreting some ideas that are now proving outdated as literal facts, yet we can still maintain the essence of truth contained in them. Nevertheless, because these different traditions and scriptures are not reconcilable, we can say that it is good to have a boundary and a limit, something that orders and contains our perspective, so that we can function and communicate. Two of the strongest bindings seem to be those of culture and personality. Not many believers (of any faith) change their faith to another and the most comfortable faith is often that of our own culture: it is our background, our heritage and our context. As to which faith one chooses initially, this is more of a personal, individual matter than anything else. Even within a faith, the different denominations often reflect different personal needs, orientations and personalities. It is often said for example that the Anglican Church is the upper and middle class at prayer.

Authority in moral and spiritual matters then has proved more diverse and complex than at first thought, its borders being more permeable, more vague than fundamentalists would have us believe. But this permeability opens the door to tolerance of those of other faiths and if used wisely, does not detract from any of them. Perhaps a good model is that of different schools: each school has its own uniform, its own rules and ways of doing things, but the aim of each is education. Similarly, each faith has its own approach to the Divine, its own way of doing things, its own emphasis, but the aim of all should be increased closeness to God. Even if the schools mix, their uniform easily identifies each pupil. Separateness or rather, distinctiveness, remains. But each school is valid, and each individual may consider one school better, or more suitable than another.

Further reading:

'Fundamentalism' James Barr S.C.M. Press.
'Escaping fundamentalism' James Barr. S.C.M. Press.
'The unauthorised version' Robin Lane Fox. Penguin.
'The mind of the Bible believer' L. Cohen. Prometheus U.S.A.
Encyclopedia Britannica. References on: Early Church.
Bible Literature.
                                  Fundamentalism.
'Concise dictionary of the Christian Church' E.A. Livingstone (Ed). Oxford.
'Oxford history of Christianity'. John McManners (Ed). Oxford
'Early Christian writings'. M Staniforth (Trans.) Penguin.
'The reason of faith' John Owen. T & T Clarke.

WHO DO MEN SAY THAT I AM?
A CRITICAL EXAMINATION OF THE PERSON AND TEACHING OF JESUS CHRIST

Traditional orthodox Christianity presents Jesus as the Messiah/ Redeemer, God's supreme sacrificial offering paying the price for the sin and transgression of the believer. Jesus is declared to be eternally co-equal with God, the second Person of the Trinity of Father, Son and Holy Spirit, but humbled in time and space to come to us in the likeness of flesh, born of a virgin, and at about thirty five years of age, crucified, but raised up from the dead as a guarantee of the future resurrection of humanity to the Final Judgment and the restoration of all things. Having completed his task, he ascended to heaven from which he will return at the end of the age. Is this really what Jesus was like? Are these historical facts? Can we find out how genuine this picture of Jesus is after all these centuries?

SOURCES OF INFORMATION

If we want to explore who Jesus really is and what he taught, that is, if we want to know something of the historical Jesus, then of course we want to try and look at any writings that Jesus might have left us and at any writings of his immediate followers in order to try and gain as much first hand knowledge of the life and teachings of Jesus as we can. Unfortunately, Jesus himself did not write any letters, or any essays or dissertations explaining his teaching; and neither did he write his own biography. So straight away we are left with having to search for accounts of Jesus and his teaching by consulting any writings of his immediate followers and subsequent to them, the leaders of the early church.

THE BIBLE: DATE AND AUTHORSHIP OF NEW TESTAMENT DOCUMENTS

Of course, one source that we have to look at are the gospels and letters that make up the New Testament in our Bibles. However, this matter is not as straightforward as it may seem. Theories as to the dates of the writing of the letters and gospels that make up the New Testament, and just who their authors are, vary. So it is necessary for us to take an aside for a moment in order to explore what modern scholarship says about these issues and also to see why the Bible has come down to us in its present form and order, which means that we must also spend a little time exploring the very early history of the Christian church. Once we have done this, we may be then able to return to our main theme and have a better understanding of the views of the early church and also have a better understanding of which New Testament documents are reliable.

DIFFERENT OPINIONS OF BIBLE SCHOLARS

Once again it is unfortunate to note that not all scholars agree on these issues. Different scholars have different interests: the conservative scholar is keen to maintain the view of the Bible and the New Testament as God's Word, written by the Apostles as commissioned by Jesus and inspired by the Holy Spirit, so they want all these documents to be written in the first century. Needless to say, secular scholars have a different agenda. Various methods and approaches are used – too complex to go into here – and all together, this results in different opinions with regards to the date of writing of these documents.

DATE OF WRITING

Below are three lists of the New Testament books, arranged in order of date according to three different sources – conservative scholars writing for the N.I.V. Study Bible, then a list from the Encyclopaedia Britannica and finally a list drawn from research on the web from various sites. Thus, if we were to look again at these New Testament writings and order them according to the date of writing, we would have a New Testament that would look like this:

Date of writing - Title

N.I.V. Study Bible:

48-49 or 51-53 or 53-57 Galatians
51 I Thessalonians
51-52 II Thessalonians
50's or 60's Mark
50's 60's or 70's Matthew
53-55 or 57-59 or 61 Philippians
55 I Corinthians
55 II Corinthians
57 Romans
60 Ephesians
60 Colossians
60 Philemon
Early 60's or before 50 James
63-65 I Timothy
63-65 Titus
66-67 II Timothy
60-68 I Peter
65-68 II Peter
Prior to 70 Hebrews
70's or 80's Luke
63 or 70-> Acts

65 or 80 Jude
50's 60's or 85 John
85-95 I John
85-95 II John
85-95 III John
95 Revelation

Or like this:

Encyclopedia Britannica:

I Thessalonians.
53-54 Philemon
53-54 Galatians
53-54 I Corinthians
55 II Corinthians
circa 56 Romans
64-70 Mark
70-80 Matthew
80-85 Luke
80-90 Acts
80-90 Hebrews
80-90 Revelation
90-100 II Thessalonians spurious
90-100 John
90-100 Jude
95-105 James
100-120 Colossians
100-120 I John
100-120 II John
100-120 III John
100-125 I Peter
Possibly 2nd century I Timothy
Possibly 2nd century II Timothy
Possibly 2nd century Titus
Circa 150 II Peter
Ephesians spurious

Or like this:

From a web site on early Christian writings:

40-80 Lost sayings of Gospel Q
50-60 1 Thessalonians
50-60 Philippians
50-60 Galatians
50-60 1 Corinthians
50-60 2 Corinthians
50-60 Romans
50-60 Philemon
50-80 Colossians
50-90 Signs Gospel
50-95 Book of Hebrews
50-120 Didache
50-140 Gospel of Thomas
50-140 Oxyrhynchus 1224 Gospel
50-200 Sophia of Jesus Christ
65-80 Gospel of Mark
70-100 Epistle of James
70-120 Egerton Gospel
70-160 Gospel of Peter
70-160 Secret Mark
70-200 Fayyum Fragment
70-200 Testaments of the Twelve Patriarchs
  80-100 2 Thessalonians
80-100 Ephesians
  80-100 Gospel of Matthew
80-110 1 Peter
  80-120 Epistle of Barnabas
  80-130 Gospel of Luke
80-130 Acts of the Apostles
  80-1401 Clement
80-150 Gospel of the Egyptians
  80-150 Gospel of the Hebrews
90-95 Apocalypse of John

90-120 Gospel of John
90-120 1 John
90-120 2 John
90-120 3 John
90-120 Epistle of Jude
100-150 1 Timothy
100-150 2 Timothy
100-150 Titus
100-150 Apocalypse of Peter
100-150 Secret Book of James
100-150 Preaching of Peter
100-160 Gospel of the Ebionites
100-160 Gospel of the Nazoreans
100-160 Shepherd of Hermas
100-160 2 Peter

We can note that in the third list, I have also included other Christian documents that did not make it into the Bible, for reasons that we shall see in a moment. So the New Testament is not our only source of information about Jesus and the early church, but it is the Bible documents that we considered authoritative, as we shall see.

AUTHORSHIP OF THESE DOCUMENTS

There is also debate concerning who wrote some of these documents. So, if we average out these various dates and add some of the known authors, we end up with a list that looks something like this:

Lost sayings of Gospel Q (Hypothetical)   Circa 40 - 70
I Thessalonians (Apostle Paul)   Circa 50 A.D.
Galatians (Apostle Paul)   Circa 50-60 A.D.
I Corinthians (Apostle Paul)   Circa 50-60 A.D.
II Corinthians (Apostle Paul)   Circa 50-60 A.D.
II Thessalonians (spurious - no consensus as to authorship) Circa 50–100 A.D
Gospel of Thomas (spurious – esoteric – may include sayings of Jesus not in gospels) Circa 50 –100 or 110-150
Philemon (Apostle Paul)   Circa 55-60 A.D.
Romans (Apostle Paul)   Circa 55-60 A.D.
Philippians (Apostle Paul)   Circa 62 A.D.

110

Hebrews (not by Apostle Paul - anonymous)   Circa 63-64 A.D.
James (No consensus as to authorship)   Circa 45-100 A.D.
Mark (written by John Mark, or anonymous, based on Apostle Peter) Circa70-75
I Timothy (falsely attributed work)   Circa 63–100A.D.
Matthew (written by an anonymous Jewish Christian) Circa 70–100A.D.
Jude (No consensus as to authorship)   Circa 70–125 A.D Ephesians (spurious - no consensus as to authorship)
Circa 70–170A.D.
Colossians (No consensus as to authorship)   Circa 60–160A.D.
Gospel of Peter (spurious)   Circa 150 - 200
Revelation (No consensus as to authorship)   Circa 80–95 A.D.
Luke (written by Luke the evangelist, or an anonymous associate of Paul) Circa 80-90
Acts (written by Luke the evangelist, or an anonymous associate of Paul)Circa 80-90
I Peter (Apostle peter or Unknown author) Circa 75-112 A.D.
1 Clement (Sometime canonical – proto-orthodox) - concerns division and removal of elders by church at Corinth c. 96 A.D.
John (written by Johannine community based on John the apostle) Circa 90-100
Gospel of the Ebionites (Written to Jewish Christians)   Circa 100
Gospel of the Nazareans (Possible original document based on oral traditions) Circa 100
I John (written by John the apostle) Circa 100-110 A.D
II John (written by poss. follower of John the apostle) Circa 100-110 A.D
II Timothy (falsely attributed work, follower of Paul)   Circa 100-125 A.D.
III John (written by poss. follower of John the apostle)   Circa 100-110 A.D
Didache (Proto-orthodox – on the borders of the canon – church manual) Circa 100 – 120
Preaching of Peter (Apologetic – not canonical- proto apologetic) Circa 100 - 130
Gospel of the Egyptians (Proto- Gnostic) Circa 100 - 150
Gospel of the Hebrews (Proto- Gnostic) Circa 100 - 150
Shepherd of Hermas (Sometime canonical but not Apostolic) Circa 100-150

Gospel of Thomas (spurious – esoteric – may include sayings of Jesus not in gospels) Circa 50 –100 or 110-150
Epistle of Barnabas (Sometime canonical – proto-orthodox) Circa 130
II Peter (Spurious. No consensus as to authorship)   Circa 65 – 160 A.D.
Titus (falsely attributed work)   Circa 80-200 A.D.
Apocalypse of Peter (spurious)   Circa 110 - 150
Gospel of Truth (Gnostic/esoteric) Circa 150 - 180

Once again, scholars vary in their opinions concerning the authorship of these documents, so the above list can only be an approximation to give us a flavour of the issues and debate.

'Q' – A HYPOTHETICAL SOURCE DOCUMENT

What we have then is a gradation of writings emerging from a Jewish background and context. Jesus himself leaves no written documents, but within ten to forty years after his death there is a hypothetical document in circulation, one which is now lost to us - a document that scholars have called 'Q', for 'Quelle' meaning 'source'. This 'Q' document seems to be the source document for the synoptic gospels of Matthew, Mark and Luke. They are called synoptic because they are three gospels which are very similar in content. Nevertheless there are also some significant variations between them. The gospels are written about thirty to forty years after the death of Jesus. It would seem that Mark was written first with Matthew being written within the next decade or so and Luke about a decade later. Luke is the first of two books by the same author, the second book being the Acts of the Apostles written it would seem about fifty years after the death of Jesus at the earliest.

THE EARLY JEWISH CHRISTIAN TRADITION

Aside from 'Q' and the variants that emerge from it, there is the early Jewish Christian tradition. Initially, Christianity was a Jewish sect with the Holy Spirit being poured out on Jews at Pentecost. This sect was based in Jerusalem and was headed by the disciples of Jesus, particularly Peter. It is regarded that there are some fragments of what this group taught that can be found in the book of Acts of the Apostles. Two sections in particular are cited: Peter preaching in the temple in Acts Ch 3; and Stephen addressing the council in Acts Ch 7.

Acts Ch 3 v 12 – 26 - Peter Preaches in the Temple

Peter saw his opportunity and addressed the crowd. "People of Israel," he said, "what is so surprising about this? And why stare at us as though we had made this man walk by our own power or godliness? For it is the God of Abraham, Isaac, and Jacob—the God of all our ancestors—who has brought glory to his servant Jesus by doing this. This is the same Jesus whom you handed over and rejected before Pilate, despite Pilate's decision to release him. You rejected this holy, righteous one and instead demanded the release of a murderer. You killed the author of life, but God raised him from the dead. And we are witnesses of this fact!

"Through faith in the name of Jesus, this man was healed—and you know how crippled he was before. Faith in Jesus' name has healed him before your very eyes.

"Friends, I realize that what you and your leaders did to Jesus was done in ignorance. But God was fulfilling what all the prophets had foretold about the Messiah—that he must suffer these things. Now repent of your sins and turn to God, so that your sins may be wiped away. Then times of refreshment will come from the presence of the Lord, and he will again send you Jesus, your appointed Messiah. For he must remain in heaven until the time for the final restoration of all things, as God promised long ago through his holy prophets. Moses said, 'The Lord your God will raise up for you a Prophet like me from among your own people. Listen carefully to everything he tells you.' Then Moses said, 'Anyone who will not listen to that Prophet will be completely cut off from God's people.'

"Starting with Samuel, every prophet spoke about what is happening today. You are the children of those prophets, and you are included in the covenant God promised to your ancestors. For God said to Abraham, 'Through your descendants all the families on earth will be blessed.' When God raised up his servant, Jesus, he sent him first to you people of Israel, to bless you by turning each of you back from your sinful ways."

Acts Ch 7 v 1 – 60 - Stephen Addresses the Council

Then the high priest asked Stephen, "Are these accusations true?"

This was Stephen's reply: "Brothers and fathers, listen to me. Our glorious God appeared to our ancestor Abraham in Mesopotamia before he settled in Haran. God told him, 'Leave your native land and your relatives, and come into the land that I will show you.' So Abraham left the land of the Chaldeans and lived in Haran until his father died. Then God brought him here to the land where you now live. But God gave him no inheritance here, not even one square foot of land. God did promise, however, that eventually the whole land would belong to Abraham and his descendants—even though he had no children yet. God also told him that his descendants would live in a foreign land, where they would be oppressed as slaves for 400 years.

'But I will punish the nation that enslaves them,' God said, 'and in the end they will come out and worship me here in this place.'

"God also gave Abraham the covenant of circumcision at that time. So when Abraham became the father of Isaac, he circumcised him on the eighth day. And the practice was continued when Isaac became the father of Jacob, and when Jacob became the father of the twelve patriarchs of the Israelite nation. These patriarchs were jealous of their brother Joseph, and they sold him to be a slave in Egypt. But God was with him and rescued him from all his troubles. And God gave him favour before Pharaoh, king of Egypt. God also gave Joseph unusual wisdom, so that Pharaoh appointed him governor over all of Egypt and put him in charge of the palace. But a famine came upon Egypt and Canaan. There was great misery, and our ancestors ran out of food. Jacob heard that there was still grain in Egypt, so he sent his sons—our ancestors—to buy some. The second time they went, Joseph revealed his identity to his brothers, and they were introduced to Pharaoh. Then Joseph sent for his father, Jacob, and all his relatives to come to Egypt, seventy-five persons in all. So Jacob went to Egypt. He died there, as did our ancestors. Their bodies were taken to Shechem and buried in the tomb Abraham had bought for a certain price from Hamor's sons in Shechem. As the time drew near when God would fulfil his promise to Abraham, the number of our people in Egypt greatly increased. But then a new king came to the throne of Egypt who knew nothing about Joseph. This king exploited our people and oppressed them, forcing parents to abandon their newborn babies so they would die.

At that time Moses was born—a beautiful child in God's eyes. His parents cared for him at home for three months. When they had to abandon him, Pharaoh's daughter adopted him and raised him as her own

114

son. Moses was taught all the wisdom of the Egyptians, and he was powerful in both speech and action.

One day when Moses was forty years old, he decided to visit his relatives, the people of Israel. He saw an Egyptian mistreating an Israelite. So Moses came to the man's defence and avenged him, killing the Egyptian. Moses assumed his fellow Israelites would realize that God had sent him to rescue them, but they didn't. The next day he visited them again and saw two men of Israel fighting. He tried to be a peacemaker. 'Men,' he said, 'you are brothers. Why are you fighting each other?'

But the man in the wrong pushed Moses aside.

'Who made you a ruler and judge over us?' he asked. 'Are you going to kill me as you killed that Egyptian yesterday?'

When Moses heard that, he fled the country and lived as a foreigner in the land of Midian. There his two sons were born. Forty years later, in the desert near Mount Sinai, an angel appeared to Moses in the flame of a burning bush. When Moses saw it, he was amazed at the sight. As he went to take a closer look, the voice of the Lord called out to him,

'I am the God of your ancestors—the God of Abraham, Isaac, and Jacob.'

Moses shook with terror and did not dare to look. Then the Lord said to him,

'Take off your sandals, for you are standing on holy ground. I have certainly seen the oppression of my people in Egypt. I have heard their groans and have come down to rescue them. Now go, for I am sending you back to Egypt.'

So God sent back the same man his people had previously rejected when they demanded, 'Who made you a ruler and judge over us?' Through the angel who appeared to him in the burning bush, God sent Moses to be their ruler and saviour. And by means of many wonders and miraculous signs, he led them out of Egypt, through the Red Sea, and through the wilderness for forty years. Moses himself told the people of Israel,

'God will raise up for you a Prophet like me from among your own people.'

Moses was with our ancestors, the assembly of God's people in the wilderness, when the angel spoke to him at Mount Sinai. And there Moses received life-giving words to pass on to us. But our ancestors refused to listen to Moses. They rejected him and wanted to return to Egypt. They told Aaron,

'Make us some gods who can lead us, for we don't know what has become of this Moses, who brought us out of Egypt.'

So they made an idol shaped like a calf, and they sacrificed to it and celebrated over this thing they had made. Then God turned away from them and abandoned them to serve the stars of heaven as their gods! In the book of the prophets it is written,

'Was it to me you were bringing sacrifices and offerings during those forty years in the wilderness, Israel? No, you carried your pagan gods—the shrine of Molech, the star of your god Rephan, and the images you made to worship them. So I will send you into exile as far away as Babylon.'

Our ancestors carried the Tabernacle with them through the wilderness. It was constructed according to the plan God had shown to Moses. Years later, when Joshua led our ancestors in battle against the nations that God drove out of this land, the Tabernacle was taken with them into their new territory. And it stayed there until the time of King David. David found favour with God and asked for the privilege of building a permanent Temple for the God of Jacob. But it was Solomon who actually built it. However, the Most High doesn't live in temples made by human hands. As the prophet says,

'Heaven is my throne, and the earth is my footstool. Could you build me a temple as good as that?' asks the Lord. 'Could you build me such a resting place? Didn't my hands make both heaven and earth?'

You stubborn people! You are heathen at heart and deaf to the truth. Must you forever resist the Holy Spirit? That's what your ancestors did, and so do you! Name one prophet your ancestors didn't persecute! They even killed the ones who predicted the coming of the Righteous One—the Messiah whom you betrayed and murdered. You deliberately disobeyed God's law, even though you received it from the hands of angels."

The Jewish leaders were infuriated by Stephen's accusation, and they shook their fists at him in rage. But Stephen, full of the Holy Spirit, gazed steadily into heaven and saw the glory of God, and he saw Jesus standing in the place of honour at God's right hand. And he told them,

"Look, I see the heavens opened and the Son of Man standing in the place of honour at God's right hand!"

Then they put their hands over their ears and began shouting. They rushed at him and dragged him out of the city and began to stone him. His accusers took off their coats and laid them at the feet of a young man named Saul. As they stoned him, Stephen prayed,

"Lord Jesus, receive my spirit."
He fell to his knees, shouting,
"Lord, don't charge them with this sin!"
And with that, he died.

THE EARLY GENTILE CHRISTIAN TRADITION

I will look a little at the content of these passages with regard to Jesus in a moment. But before I do, I want to note the establishment of the Gentile or non-Jewish Christian tradition, which is established by the Apostle Paul, or Saul as he was initially known.

JEWISH PERSECUTION OF THE JEWISH/CHRISTIAN SECT - SAUL

It is the upstart, troublesome Jewish Christian sect that Saul, a Jewish Pharisee and purist trained in Jewish religious law, begins to persecute in an attempt to stamp it out, because it is what he sees as a deviant, heretical, troublesome group within Judaism.

SAUL'S DAMSACUS ROAD EXPERIENCE

Even as Saul is busy on this mission to purge Judaism of this troublesome group, he is stopped in his tracks on one particular day. Three times we have an account of this event in Acts of the Apostles. So we should note that this is not Paul speaking or writing here in Acts, but someone else in the early church. The passages in Acts are as follows:

Acts 9 v 1 – 12

Saul was still breathing out murderous threats against the Lord's disciples. He went to the high priest and asked him for letters to the synagogues in Damascus, so that if he found any there who belonged to the Way, whether men or women, he might take them as prisoners to Jerusalem. As he neared Damascus on his journey, suddenly a light from heaven [the vaulted expanse of the sky with all things visible in it] flashed around him. He fell to the ground and heard a voice say to him,
"Saul, Saul, why do you persecute me?"
"Who are you, Lord?" Saul asked.
"I am Jesus, whom you are persecuting," he replied. "Now get up and go into the city, and you will be told what you must do."

The men travelling with Saul stood there speechless; they heard the sound but did not see anyone. Saul got up from the ground, but when he opened his eyes he could see nothing. So they led him by the hand into Damascus. For three days he was blind, and did not eat or drink anything.

In Damascus there was a disciple named Ananias. The Lord called to him in a vision, [a sight divinely granted in an ecstasy or in a sleep, a vision]

"Ananias!"

"Yes, Lord," he answered.

The Lord told him, "Go to the house of Judas on Straight Street and ask for a man from Tarsus named Saul, for he is praying. In a vision he has seen a man named Ananias come and place his hands on him to restore his sight."

And again in Acts 22 v 2 - 13

Paul said: "I am a Jew, born in Tarsus of Cilicia, but brought up in this city. I studied under Gamaliel and was thoroughly trained in the law of our ancestors. I was just as zealous for God as any of you are today. I persecuted the followers of this Way to their death, arresting both men and women and throwing them into prison, as the high priest and all the Council can themselves testify. I even obtained letters from them to their associates in Damascus, and went there to bring these people as prisoners to Jerusalem to be punished. About noon as I came near Damascus, suddenly a bright light from heaven flashed around me. I fell to the ground and heard a voice say to me, 'Saul! Saul! Why do you persecute me?'

'Who are you, Lord?' I asked.

'I am Jesus of Nazareth, whom you are persecuting,' he replied.

My companions saw the light, but they did not understand the voice of him who was speaking to me.

'What shall I do, Lord?' I asked.

'Get up,' the Lord said, 'and go into Damascus. There you will be told all that you have been assigned to do.'

My companions led me by the hand into Damascus, because the brilliance of the light had blinded me. A man named Ananias came to see me. He was a devout observer of the law and highly respected by all the Jews living there. He stood beside me and said, 'Brother Saul, receive your sight!'

118

and at that very moment I was able to see him.

And finally in Acts 26 v 9 - 20

"I too was convinced that I ought to do all that was possible to oppose the name of Jesus of Nazareth. And that is just what I did in Jerusalem. On the authority of the chief priests I put many of the Lord's people in prison, and when they were put to death, I cast my vote against them. Many a time I went from one synagogue to another to have them punished, and I tried to force them to blaspheme. I was so obsessed with persecuting them that I even hunted them down in foreign cities. On one of these journeys I was going to Damascus with the authority and commission of the chief priests. About noon, King Agrippa, as I was on the road, I saw a light from heaven, brighter than the sun, blazing around me and my companions. We all fell to the ground, and I heard a voice saying to me in Aramaic,

'Saul, Saul, why do you persecute me? It is hard for you to kick against the goads.'

Then I asked, 'Who are you, Lord?'

'I am Jesus, whom you are persecuting,' the Lord replied. 'Now get up and stand on your feet. I have appeared [to allow one's self to be seen, to appear] to you to appoint you as a servant and as a witness of what you have seen and will see of me. I will rescue you from your own people and from the Gentiles. I am sending you to them to open their eyes and turn them from darkness to light, and from the power of Satan to God, so that they may receive forgiveness of sins and a place among those who are sanctified by faith in me.'

So then, King Agrippa, I was not disobedient to the vision from heaven. [the act of exhibiting one's self to view; a sight, a vision, an appearance presented to one whether asleep or awake] First to those in Damascus, then to those in Jerusalem and in all Judea, and then to the Gentiles, I preached that they should repent and turn to God and demonstrate their repentance by their deeds.

SAUL'S RESPONSE TO THE DAMASCUS ROAD EXPERIENCE

So what did Saul do in the period immediately following the Damascus Road experience? He tells us in one of the earliest New Testament documents, his own account in his letter to the Galatians:

Galatians 1 v 11 – Ch 2 v 10

Paul says: 'I want you to know, brothers and sisters, that the gospel I preached is not of human origin. I did not receive [to receive with the mind] it from any man, nor was I taught it; rather, I received [to receive with the mind] it by revelation [a disclosure of truth, instruction concerning things before unknown; used of events by which things or states or persons hitherto withdrawn from view are made visible to all; manifestation, appearance] from Jesus Christ. For you have heard of my previous way of life in Judaism, how intensely I persecuted the church of God and tried to destroy it. I was advancing in Judaism beyond many of my own age among my people and was extremely zealous for the traditions of my fathers. But when God, who set me apart from my mother's womb and called me by his grace, was pleased to reveal [to uncover, lay open what has been veiled or covered up, to disclose, make bare, to make known, make manifest, disclose what before was unknown] his Son in [in, by, with] me so that I might preach him among the Gentiles, my immediate response was not to consult any human being. I did not go up to Jerusalem to see those who were apostles before I was, but I went into Arabia. Later I returned to Damascus. Then after **three years**, I went up to Jerusalem to get acquainted with Cephas [Peter] and stayed with him fifteen days. I saw none of the other apostles—only James, the Lord's brother. I assure you before God that what I am writing you is no lie. Then I went to Syria and Cilicia. I was personally unknown to the churches of Judea that are in Christ. They only heard the report: "The man who formerly persecuted us is now preaching the faith he once tried to destroy." And they praised God because of me.

Then after **fourteen years**, I went up again to Jerusalem, this time with Barnabas. I took Titus along also. I went in response to a revelation and, meeting privately with those esteemed as leaders, I presented to them the gospel that I preach among the Gentiles. I wanted to be sure I was not running and had not been running my race in vain. Yet not even Titus, who was with me, was compelled to be circumcised, even though he was a Greek. This matter arose because some false believers had infiltrated our ranks to spy on the freedom we have in Christ Jesus and to make us slaves. [to the law and practice of circumcision]. We did not give in to them for a moment, so that the truth of the gospel might be preserved for you. As for those who were held in high esteem—whatever they were makes no difference to me; God does not

120

show favouritism—<u>they added nothing to my message</u>. On the contrary, <u>they recognized that I had been entrusted with the task of preaching the gospel to the uncircumcised, just as Peter had been to the circumcised.</u> For God, who was at work in Peter as an apostle to the circumcised, was also at work in me as an apostle to the Gentiles. James, Cephas and John, <u>those esteemed as pillars, gave me and Barnabas the right hand of fellowship when they recognized the grace given to me. They agreed that we should go to the Gentiles, and they to the circumcised.</u> All they asked was that we should continue to remember the poor, the very thing I had been eager to do all along.

The Council of Jerusalem (or Apostolic Conference) is a name applied by historians to this early Christian council that was held in Jerusalem and it is dated to around the year 50 AD. The council decided that Gentile converts to Christianity were not obligated to keep most of the Mosaic law, including the rules concerning circumcision of males, however, the Council did retain the prohibitions against eating blood, or eating meat containing blood, or meat of animals not properly slain and against fornication and idolatry. Descriptions of the council are found in Acts of the Apostles chapter 15 (in two different forms, the Alexandrian and Western versions) and also possibly in Paul's letter to the Galatians chapter 2. Some scholars dispute that Galatians 2 is about the *Council of Jerusalem* (notably because Galatians 2 describes a private meeting) while other scholars dispute the historical reliability of the Acts of the Apostles. Paul was likely an eyewitness, a major person in attendance, whereas Luke, the writer of Luke-Acts, who was a later follower of Paul, may not have been in attendance, and thus may have written second-hand, about the meeting he described in Acts 15.

APOSTLES

Paul uses the word 'apostle' to describe himself – as an 'apostle to the Gentiles', as well as the leaders of the Jerusalem Jewish/Christian church and particularly Peter, as 'apostles to the circumcised', that is apostles to Jewish Christians. At its highest expression, an apostle is one called by God to be a messenger, specifically a messenger of the gospel.

Qualifications in order to be an Apostle appear to be: -

1) A direct call from God for the person to be an Apostle.

Romans 1 v 1:

Paul, a servant of Christ Jesus, called to be an apostle [a delegate, messenger, one sent forth with orders
specifically applied to the twelve apostles of Christ
in a broader sense applied to other eminent Christian teachers
of Barnabas
of Timothy and Silvanus]
and set apart for the gospel of God

I Corinthians 1 v 1:

Paul, called to be an apostle of Christ Jesus by the will of God.

Ephesians 1 v 1:

Paul, an apostle of Christ Jesus by the will of God.

Luke 6 v 12 – 16:

One of those days Jesus went out to a mountainside to pray, and spent the night praying to God. When morning came, he called his disciples to him and chose twelve of them, whom he also designated apostles: Simon (whom he named Peter), his brother Andrew, James, John, Philip, Bartholomew, Matthew, Thomas, James son of Alphaeus, Simon who was called the Zealot, Judas son of James, and Judas Iscariot, who became a traitor.

Acts 26 v 16 – 18 – To Paul on the Damascus Road:

'I am Jesus, whom you are persecuting,' the Lord replied. 'Now get up and stand on your feet. I have appeared [to allow one's self to be seen, to appear] to you to appoint you as a servant and as a witness of what you have seen and will see of me. I will rescue you from your own people and from the Gentiles. I am sending you to them to open their eyes and turn them from darkness to light, and from the power of Satan to God, so that they may receive forgiveness of sins and a place among those who are sanctified by faith in me.'

2) They had to see the Lord Jesus Christ and be an eyewitness to His resurrection.

John 15 v 27:

"When the Advocate comes, whom I will send to you from the Father—the Spirit of truth who goes out from the Father—he will testify about me. And <u>you also must testify, for you have been with me from the beginning</u>.

Luke 24 v 44 – 48:

He said to them, "This is what I told you while I was still with you: Everything must be fulfilled that is written about me in the Law of Moses, the Prophets and the Psalms." Then he opened their minds so they could understand the Scriptures. He told them, "This is what is written: The Messiah will suffer and rise from the dead on the third day and repentance for the forgiveness of sins will be preached in his name to all nations, beginning at Jerusalem. <u>You are witnesses of these things</u>.",

Acts 1 v 8:

But you will receive power when the Holy Spirit comes on you; and <u>you will be my witnesses</u> in Jerusalem, and in all Judea and Samaria, and to the ends of the earth.

Acts 1 v 21-26:

Therefore it is necessary to choose one of the men who have been with us the whole time the Lord Jesus was living among us, beginning from John's baptism to the time when Jesus was taken up from us. For <u>one of these must become a witness</u> [one who is a spectator] <u>with us of his resurrection</u> [rising from the dead]." So they nominated two men: Joseph called Barsabbas (also known as Justus) and Matthias. Then they prayed, "Lord, you know everyone's heart. Show us which of these two you have chosen to take over this apostolic ministry, which Judas left to go where he belongs." Then they cast lots, and the lot fell to Matthias; so he was added to the eleven apostles.

I Corinthians 9 v 1:

Am I not free? Am I not an apostle? Have I not seen [to see with the eyes; to see with the mind, to perceive, know; to see, i.e. become acquainted with by experience, to experience] Jesus our Lord? Are you not the result of my work in the Lord?

Now with regard to the Apostle Paul, these first two Apostolic qualifications are interesting because there is no evidence to suggest that Paul was a witness to the crucifixion itself or that he ever met Jesus prior to the crucifixion. His encounter(s) with Jesus are of a revelatory and visionary nature, like that in the Damascus Road experience: 'This is what we speak, not in words taught us by human wisdom but in words taught by the Spirit, explaining spiritual realities with Spirit-taught words'. I Corinthians 2 v 12 – 13. Paul does appear to have a mystical frame of mind: It is generally accepted that Paul is talking about himself when he says: 'Although there is nothing to be gained, I will go on to visions and revelations from the Lord. I know a man in Christ who fourteen years ago was caught up to the third heaven. Whether it was in the body or out of the body I do not know—God knows. And I know that this man—whether in the body or apart from the body I do not know, but God knows—was caught up to paradise and heard inexpressible things, things that no one is permitted to tell.' II Corinthians 12 v 1-5. For Paul, the visions and revelations of Jesus to him are the same as if he had met Jesus physically, face-to-face after his resurrection. Thus he says: 'Have I not seen Jesus our Lord?' I Corinthians 9 v 1. He sees no difference between his visionary, revelatory experiences of Jesus such as that in the Damascus Road experience and the experiences of the other eminent Apostles, that is, those who were in Jerusalem and who were with Jesus when he was alive and saw him after the resurrection: 'for [says Paul] I am not in the least inferior to the most eminent apostles' II Corinthians 12 v 11. His commission to be an Apostle is given by Jesus in the Damascus Road vision/revelation: 'I am Jesus, whom you are persecuting,' the Lord replied. 'Now get up and stand on your feet. I have appeared [to allow one's self to be seen, to appear] to you to appoint you as a servant and as a witness of what you have seen and will see of me. I will rescue you from your own people and from the Gentiles. I am sending you to them [the Gentiles] to open their eyes and turn them from darkness to light, and from the power of Satan to God, so that they may receive

124

forgiveness of sins and a place among those who are sanctified by faith in me.' Acts 26 v 16 – 18.

3) It would appear that the Apostles had an ability to pass on gifts to others by laying on hands.

Acts 8 v 6 with Acts 8 v 14-18:

When the crowds heard Philip and saw the signs he performed, they all paid close attention to what he said…..When the apostles in Jerusalem heard that Samaria had accepted the word of God, they sent Peter and John to Samaria. When they arrived, they prayed for the new believers there that they might receive the Holy Spirit, because the Holy Spirit had not yet come on any of them; they had simply been baptized in the name of the Lord Jesus. Then Peter and John placed their hands on them, and they received the Holy Spirit. When Simon saw that the Spirit was given at the laying on of the apostles' hands, he offered them money. (Philip can not pass on the gifts, but Peter and John do).

Romans 1 v 11:

Paul says: 'I long to see you so that I may impart to you some spiritual gift to make you strong.'

4) The task of the Apostles was to lay the foundation of the New Testament Church by God's Word which they could distinguish from their own.

This idea of being able to separate and distinguish 'God's Word' from a person's own theorising and philosophising will not be strange at all to anyone who has experienced an immediate encounter with the Divine. Mystical encounters are indeed 'received' as the Apostle Paul says, as opposed to being rationally worked out and actively formulated. The receiving of concepts in mystical experience form the basis on which theological and doctrinal ideas are subsequently worked out.
Ephesians 2 v 19-20:

'Consequently, you are no longer foreigners and strangers, but fellow citizens with God's people and also members of his household, built on the foundation of the apostles and prophets, with Christ Jesus himself as the chief cornerstone.'

I Corinthians 2 v 12 – 13:

'What we have received is not the spirit of the world, but the Spirit who is from God, so that we may understand what God has freely given us. This is what we speak, not in words taught us by human wisdom but in words taught by the Spirit, explaining spiritual realities with Spirit-taught words.'

I Corinthians 3 v 10 – 11:

By the grace God has given me, I laid a foundation as a wise builder and someone else is building on it. But each one should build with care. For no one can lay any foundation other than the one already laid, which is Jesus Christ.

I Corinthians 7 v 10 –12:

To the married I give this command (not I, but the Lord): A wife must not separate from her husband. But if she does, she must remain unmarried or else be reconciled to her husband. And a husband must not divorce his wife. To the rest I say this (I, not the Lord): If any brother has a wife who is not a believer and she is willing to live with him, he must not divorce her.

DATING THE DAMASCUS ROAD EXPERIENCE

Paul's Galatian letter was written about 50 – 55 AD, just twenty to twenty five years after the death of Jesus Christ. If we include the time scales mentioned in this letter – three years in Arabia and a further fourteen years in Syria and Cilicia, then we have a time span of seventeen years. This would indicate that the events on the Damascus Road occurred just a few years after the death of Christ, which is generally considered to be about 33 A.D. The Damascus Road experience seems to be in the period 34 – 40 A.D.

126

THE SOURCE AND AUTHORITY OF PAUL'S TEACHING - REVELATION

So Saul, or Paul as he was to be known, did not go to the Jerusalem Jewish Christian sect in order to obtain teaching and instruction from Peter and the disciples/Apostles. He did not want to consult human teachers at all and instead went to Arabia for three years where he received his understanding of Jesus and the gospel by immediate revelation from God. He then spends fifteen days seeing Peter in Jerusalem and then spends fourteen years in Syria during which his gospel mission is established, not with the Jews, but with the non-Jews or Gentiles. In order to make sure that he is not in error, he returns, to the Jewish Christians in Jerusalem, with Barnabus and Titus. The esteemed Jewish Christian leaders add nothing to Paul's message and formally recognise his apostolic mission to the non-Jews or Gentiles.

Paul confirms that his teaching and understanding is received immediate revelation from Jesus Christ in his letter to the Corinthians and the letter to the Ephesians, though this second letter is considered spurious by some scholars:

1 Corinthians 15 v 2-4:

By this gospel you are saved, if you hold firmly to the word I preached to you. Otherwise, you have believed in vain. For what I <u>received</u> [to receive something transmitted] I passed on to you as of first importance: that Christ died for our sins according to the Scriptures, that he was buried, that he was raised on the third day according to the Scriptures.

Ephesians 3 v 3

'…the mystery [hidden thing, secret, not obvious to the understanding] made known to me by <u>revelation</u>,' [a disclosure of truth, instruction: concerning things before unknown used of events by which things or states or persons hitherto withdrawn from view are made visible to all; manifestation, appearance]

JEWISH CHRISTIANS AND GENTILE CHRISTIANS – TWO TRADITIONS

a) The Jewish Christian tradition

In effect, by the time of Paul's second meeting at Jerusalem, the Christian church has two branches or aspects: Peter, James, John and the other disciple/Apostles continue to declare the gospel as a Jewish sect, focussing on the Jews as heirs and inheritors of the prophets and promises – just as we have seen in the quotes from Acts concerning Peter and Stephen earlier, with Christ as the promised messiah/Deliverer. They draw on the history and tradition of the Jews, on the prophets and their messages to show that Jesus Christ was the Messiah. Their message includes the following ideas drawn from Jewish history and tradition:

Through faith in the name of Jesus, this ill man was healed in front of you
Jesus is God's servant
Jesus is holy, righteous, the Righteous One—the Messiah
Jesus is the author of life
Whom you Jews betrayed and murdered
But God raised him from the dead, and we are witnesses of this
What you and your leaders did to Jesus was done in ignorance
God was fulfilling what all the Jewish prophets had foretold about the Messiah
Repent of your sins, have a new mind and turn to God
He will again send you Jesus, your appointed Messiah.
For he must remain in heaven until the time for the final restoration of all things
Jesus the Son of Man standing in the place of honour at God's right hand.
Starting with Samuel, every prophet spoke about what is happening today.

b) The Gentile Christian tradition

Paul and his co-workers head the branch or aspect of the church that is concerned with the Gentiles or non-Jews. Initially, immediately after the Damascus Road experience, Paul's message is:

Repent and have a new mind and turn to God
Demonstrate repentance by your deeds.

Jesus Christ is God's Son.
Christ died for our sins according to the Scriptures.
He was buried
He was raised on the third day according to the Scriptures

Following the period of further immediate teaching by revelation given to Paul from Jesus Christ and following confirmation by the leaders at Jerusalem of his message and mission, according to the book of Acts of the Apostles, Paul and his co-workers go from place to place, tending to speak to those who were interested in spiritual matters. By this time, their method of approach is established and the ideas of the message more elaborated. The book of Acts is written circa 70 – 90 AD, a good forty to sixty years after the death of Jesus Christ, which is about twenty five to forty five years after Paul was given approval by the Jerusalem leaders. It records that their main practice was to speak to those who already believed the Old Testament which they did by speaking to these people on the Sabbath in the synagogues. This was the method by which they spoke to both Jews and Gentiles. (Compare Acts 26 v 20, with Acts 5 v 42, Acts 9 v 20, Acts 13 v 5, 14,15, Acts 14 v 1, Acts 17 v 1,2,10,17, Acts 18 v 4,19, Acts 19 v 8.) Though they went to synagogues, they did not limit themselves to synagogues only, but they would go wherever believers in the Old Testament gathered for worship. (Acts 16 v 3). As a Jew himself, this was quite a natural thing for Paul to do and he had freedom to share his applications of the Old Testament, though often of course, the Jews resented his teaching and reacted violently.

When it came to those people who did not attend synagogues, or who did not gather for worship, we find that Paul and his co-workers did not seek them out. They did not seek to preach the gospel to everyone that they encountered and so they did not seek such people out in out in order to preach the gospel them. As we have seen, when dealing with people who claimed to believe the Old Testament, the approach was to skilfully use the Old Testament to show that Jesus Christ was the promised Messiah, showing His ancestry, how He fulfilled prophecy, types, e.t.c. (Acts 2 v 14-38, Acts 3 v 12-26, Acts 7 v 2-53, Acts 3 v 30-38, Acts 13 v 14-41, Acts 17 v 1-3, Acts 23 v 23.). Having shown from Hebrew scripture that Jesus Christ is the Messiah, they then called for repentance and belief on Him, together with a call for baptism and a warning of future judgment. (Acts 2 v 38, Acts 3 v 26, Acts 13 v 38-41, Acts 20 v 21).

However, when dealing with people who were ignorant of the Hebrew scripture, or not familiar with it, or who did not claim to believe it, they did not use the Hebrew Scripture at all in their approach. A prime example of the approach that they did take is given in Acts 17 v 16-Ch 18 v 1. (See also Acts 14 v 15-18).

In their approach:
i) The Apostle acknowledges religious interest in his hearers and uses it to his advantage as common ground to start with. (Acts 17 v 22, 23) This would not extend to being called a god or being identified as anything but ordinary men. (Acts 14 v 14). Any vagaries in the prevalent religion would be used to declare the character of God as Paul understood it. (Acts 17 v 23).

ii) Religious or secular writers who were respected by the hearers would be quoted where they support the message Paul was giving. Thus Paul quotes the Greeks own poets. (Acts 17 v 22). This has a double edge: it secures common ground and it may put the person being spoken to into a corner in logical argument. Thus, for example, in dealing with a person who follows Islam, we could quote the Koran passages that refer to Christ as a prophet. This would mean that the person is now forced to be inconsistent if they deny that Christ is a prophet, for they must then deny the Koran. This is an approach particularly used by Paul with rulers and those in authority, whose loyalties are put on the line. Thus Aggrippa in Acts 26 is forced to acknowledge respect for Old Testament prophets out of respect for the Jews whom he did not want to upset.

iii) The gospel is proclaimed, not debated. (Acts 17 v 23- 31)

iv) Though no reference is made to the Old Testament or Hebrew scriptures to those who have no familiarity or belief in it, doctrines concerning God are not ignored. Remember, these hearers wanted to hear and were curious about the message being presented... they were not insolent. Analysing the two main passages in Acts where the Apostles deal exclusively with non-synagogue attending Gentile unbelievers, (Acts 14 v 8-18, Acts 17 v 16-18 v 1) the following components of the Apostles message can be drawn out:-

Concerning God:

i) He is the Creator -
a) of all things

                    b) of heaven
                    c) of Earth
                    d) of every nation
                    e) of the sea
                        f) of man... therefore we are God's offspring.

                ii) He is Lord, Sovereign.-
                    a) of heaven
                    b) of Earth
                    c) of nations
                    d) of time
                    e) of the boundaries of nations
                    f) of Christ

                iii) He is alive

                iv) He transcends man-
                    a) He does not live in temples made by man
                    b) He is not like a silver or gold image or idol
                    c) He is self sufficient, not needing human help.

                v) He is omnipresent

    vi) He is merciful and forbearing in the past he overlooked ignorance of idolatry

                vii) He is not without a witness as to His existence.
   a)   God's provision of rain, crops, food and joy is a witness.
                    b) creation is a witness. (Romans 1 v 20)

                viii) He is Just

                ix) He is a moral judge
                    a) of the whole world

                    b) He will judge the world by a man
                    c) He has appointed a time for judgement
    d) He has given proof of the coming judgement to all men or nations
                    e) Christ's resurrection from the dead is the proof

                    x) He is kind. This kindness is shown in His provision.

                    xi) He is a provider- God gives-
                        a) to all men
                        b) He gives life
                        c) He gives breath
                        d) He gives everything
                        e) He gives rain from heaven
                        f) He gives crops in their seasons
                        g) He gives plenty of food

    xii)   God's purpose in creating man was for him to fill the whole earth.

                  xiii) God's desire for us is that-
                      a) we should seek Him
                      b) We should reach out for Him
                      c) We should find Him.

                  xiv) God commands all men, everywhere, all nations
                    a) To repent
                    b) To turn from worthless idols
                    c) To turn to the living God.

DIFFERENT TRADITIONS – SAME MESSAGE – REPENT AND BELIEVE

So we can see by that by comparing the message given to the Jews in Acts Chapters 3 and 7 with given to the Gentiles in Acts Chapter 17 that the approach of presenting the message of Jesus to the Jews was quite different from the approach of presenting the message of Jesus to non-

Jews or Gentiles - but the actual message itself was the same. We have seen that Paul deliberately went to the Elders at Jerusalem and his message was not added to or modified, he was not accused of being in error but rather given the right hand of fellowship by the Jewish Christian Apostles. Despite these differing branches within early Christianity, the message was the same.

PROBLEMS IN THE EARLY BRANCHES OF THE CHURCH

We can also note that the Jerusalem church was having problems with traditional Jews who were insisting on obedience to the old laws and commandments and rituals – threatening to take away the freedom of the Jewish Christians by enslaving them again to the law, symbolised particularly by the need for circumcision and also by what foods should or should not be eaten. This is why Paul talks about circumcision in his second visit with Barnabus and Titus: there was pressure being exerted by these Jews that Christians should undergo circumcision. But these Jewish traditionalists are branded as false believers by Paul and indeed, much of Paul's letter to Galatians is about this issue of the Christians relationship to the old laws and commandments given under Moses.

Acts 15 v 1:
'And certain men came down from Judea and taught the brethren: "Unless you are circumcised according to the custom of Moses, you cannot be saved." Therefore…. Paul and Barnabas had no small dissension and dispute with them.'

And of course there were other problems and difficulties in the early Gentile churches too and the Letters or Epistles of Paul often deal with these matters, for example the imposition of religious law on Christians in the letter to the Galatians and immoral Christians in the letters to the Corinthians, as well as doctrinal matters such as a belief that the resurrection had already occurred.

WRITINGS NOT INCLUDED IN THE NEW TESTAMENT

Also, though difficult to date exactly, it would seem that from about twenty years after the death of Jesus, in other words at about the same time as Paul beginning to write his letters, (if not before), we also find Christian writings that are not penned by the Apostles. I have placed some of these writings in the list at the start of this study. There is nothing unusual in this: church leaders would have communicated to one another by letter giving advice, instruction and teaching. Authorship becomes important though when we try to establish an authoritative set of writings that can be used as a 'rule' or authoritative guide for Christian faith and conduct. However, worse than this, we also have the rise of spurious gospels and writings: works that claim to be by or about one of the Apostles, but which are fakes. Some groups wanted to gain authority and influence by declaring that such gospels were authoritative. By the end of the first century A.D. these spurious writings were starting to become a real problem, because it was considered by some church leaders that these writings were leading Christians astray from the original teaching and tradition of the Apostles concerning Jesus.

DIVERSE EARLY CHRISTIAN GROUPS

1) Esoteric and mystical groups - Gnosticism

Christianity was not one simple group then, but soon consisted of a wide variety of groups emphasising different traditions and aspects. One such group were the Gnostics – themselves a diverse group who had esoteric beliefs with origins in paganism – but who began to adopt some of the Christian ideas with their own, creating a strand of Christian Gnosticism. Valentinus (also spelled Valentinius) (c.100 - c.160) was the best known, and for a time most successful, early Christian Gnostic theologian. He founded his school in Rome and according to Tertullian, Valentinus was a candidate for the bishop of Rome, but started his own group when another person was chosen. Valentinus produced a variety of writings, but only fragments survive, largely those embedded in refuted quotations in the works of his opponents and there is not enough here to reconstruct his system except in broad outline. He taught that there were three kinds of people, the spiritual, psychical, and material and that only those of a spiritual nature received the *gnosis* (knowledge) that allowed them to return to the divine Pleroma, while those of a psychic nature (ordinary Christians) would attain a lesser form of salvation and that those of a material nature (pagans and Jews) were doomed to perish. A new field in Valentinian studies opened when the Nag Hammadi library was discovered in Egypt in 1945. Among the very mixed bag of works classified as Gnostic was a series of writings which could be associated with Valentinus, particularly the Coptic text called the

Gospel of Truth which bears the same title reported by Irenaeus as belonging to a text by Valentinus. It is a declaration of the unknown name of the Father, possession of which enables the knower to penetrate the veil of ignorance that has separated all created beings from the Father. It declares Jesus Christ as Saviour has revealed that name but it does so through a variety of modes laden with a language of abstract elements. Besides the Gospel of Truth, there were the proto-Christian Gnostic Gospel of the Egyptians, The Gospel of the Hebrews and also the Gospel of Thomas. By definition, these documents were for the initiated – for those who had sufficiently grown in knowledge and understanding to be able to receive them. Thus, these documents were not in popular usage in the church but reserved for an elite group of esoterically minded Christians within the church. It may be easy to condemn this approach as elitist and divisive, but there is a strong tradition in many spiritual disciplines of such a practice. Even in mainstream Christianity, it was only with the invention of the printing press and the rise of a reformation against perceived corruption in the church that brought the Bible itself both literally into the hands of the layman as well as into their own language. Previously, the Bible was in the hands of priests and in Latin rather than the vernacular language of the people. The gospel phrase: 'Do not give that which is holy to dogs', as well as the whole idea of Elders ruling the church (it is not democratic), support this idea of hierarchy and to some degree elitism.

It is arguable then that there is another aspect or trend in early Christianity – that which involves mysticism or esoteric beliefs, such as that in the development of Christian Gnosticism. Esoteric means 'pertaining to the more inward'; mystical, and the dictionary defines esoteric as information that is understood by a small group or those specially initiated, or of rare or unusual interest. Esotericism refers to the holding of secret doctrines, the practice of limiting knowledge to a small group, or an interest in items of a special, rare, novel, or unusual quality. Mysticism is the pursuit of communion with, identity with, or conscious awareness of God through direct experience, intuition, instinct or insight. Mysticism usually centres on a practice or practices intended to nurture such experiences or awareness. Mysticism may be dualistic - maintaining a distinction between the self and the divine, or may be non-dualistic – where all things are an expression of God. Mystical and esoteric beliefs are by no means limited to Christianity. They are present in Judaism, in the Kabala, and in Sufism in Islam for example.

The gospel of John is sometimes closely associated with this trend, although, as we have seen, the Apostle Paul also talks about mystical experience. The authorship of the Gospel of John is anonymous. John 21 states it derives its authorship from the testimony of the 'disciple whom Jesus loved'. Along with Peter, the unnamed disciple is especially close to Jesus and early-church tradition identified him as John the Apostle, one of Jesus' Twelve Apostles. The gospel is closely related in style and content to the three surviving Epistles of John such that some commentators treat the four books together. According to the majority of modern scholars, John was not the author of any of these books, although some prominent scholars believe that the community that it was written in could have been founded or influenced by him. Some scholars today believe that parts of John represent an independent historical tradition from the synoptic gospels, of Matthew Mark and Luke, while other parts represent later traditions. The Gospel of John was probably shaped in part by increasing tensions between synagogue and church, or between those who believed Jesus was the Messiah and those who did not. By the 2nd century, the two main, conflicting expressions of Christology were John's Logos theology, according to which Jesus was the incarnation of God's eternal Word, and adoptionism, according to which Jesus was 'adopted' as God's Son, this usually being seen as taking place at Jesus' baptism. Logos Christology won out over adoptionism in the orthodox church.

The discourses of John seem to be concerned with the actual issues of the church-and-synagogue debate at the time when the Gospel was written c. 90 AD. It is notable that in the gospel of John, the community still appears to define itself primarily against Judaism, rather than as part of a wider Christian church. Though Christianity started as a movement within Judaism, gradually Christians and Jews became bitterly opposed.

John presents a higher Christology than Matthew, Mark and Luke, describing Jesus as the incarnation of the divine Logos through whom all things were made, as the object of veneration and more explicitly as God incarnate. Only in John does Jesus talk at length about himself and his divine role, conversations that are often shared with the disciples only. Against the other gospels of the canon, the gospel of John focuses largely on different miracles, given as signs that are meant to engender faith. Synoptic elements such as parables and exorcisms are not found in the gospel of John. John's gospel presents a realized eschatology in which salvation is already present for the believer and the gospel includes Gnostic elements. As such the Gospel of John was the favourite gospel of Valentinus, a 2nd-century Gnostic leader. A student of Valentinius claims that Theudas was a student of the Apostle Paul, and in turn taught Valentinius, which would put Theudas in the late 1st century if true. His student Heracleon wrote a commentary on the gospel, the first gospel commentary in Christian history.

According to the majority viewpoint, the differences between the teaching in John and in the synoptic gospels is so great that only one of the two accounts can be historical, and scholars choose the Synoptics over John. Some however, maintain that the gospel was indeed written by the disciple John and that it, like the synoptic gospels, is historically reliable. Like the previous gospels, it circulated separately until Irenaeus proclaimed all four gospels to be scripture. The Church Fathers Polycarp, Ignatius of Antioch, and Justin Martyr did not mention this gospel, either because they did not know it or did not approve of it.

Gnosticism (Greek: γνῶσις *gnōsis*, knowledge) refers to a form of mystic, revealed, esoteric knowledge and this notion of immediate revelation through divine knowledge seeks to find absolute transcendence in a Supreme Deity. This concept is very important in identifying what evidence there is pertaining to Gnosticism in the New Testament, which would influence orthodox teaching.

Main Gnostic beliefs that differ from Biblical teachings include:
The creator as a lower being ['Demiurge'] and not a Supreme Deity;
Scripture has a deep, hidden meaning whose true message can only be understood through 'secret wisdom'.
Jesus is a spirit that 'seemed' to be human,
Belief in the incarnation (Docetism).

At its core, Gnosticism formed a speculative interest in the relationship of the Oneness of God to the 'triplicity' of his manifestations. It seems to have taken Neoplatonic metaphysics of substance and hypostases ['being'] as a departure point for interpreting the relationship of the 'Father' to the 'Son' in its attempt to define a new theology. This would point to the theological controversies by Arius against followers of the Greek Alexandrian school, headed by Athanasius.

The ancient Nag Hammadi Library, discovered in Egypt in the 1940s, revealed how varied the Gnostic movement was. The writers of these manuscripts considered themselves 'Christians', but their syncretistic beliefs borrowed heavily from the Greek philosopher Plato. The find included the hotly debated Gospel of Thomas, which parallels some of Jesus' sayings in the Synoptic Gospels. This may point to the existence of a postulated lost textual source for the Gospels of Luke and Matthew, known as the 'Q' document. Thus, modern debate is split between those who see Gnosticism as a pre Christian form of 'theosophy' and those who see it as a post-Christian counter-movement.

In the New Testament the best known origin story of Gnosticism comes in the person of Simon Magus [Acts 8 v 9-24]. Although little is known historically about him, his first disciple is said to have been Basilides. The epistles to Timothy, written by an unknown author, contain refutations of 'false doctrine and myths' [1 Timothy 1 v 3-5]. The importance placed here, as in most New Testament scripture, is to uphold the truth since through such knowledge God hopes for 'all men' to be saved [1 Tim 2 v 4]. Paul's letters to the Corinthians have much to say regarding false teachers (2 Corinthians 11 v 4), 'spiritualists' [pneumatikos]—1 Corinthians Ch 2 v 14-15: 'The person without the Spirit does not accept the things that come from the Spirit of God but considers them foolishness, and cannot understand them because they are discerned only through the Spirit. The person with the Spirit makes judgments about all things, but such a person is not subject to merely human judgments, for, "Who has known the mind of the Lord so as to instruct him?",' and their gnosis. They warn against the 'wisdom of the wise' and their 'hollow and deceptive philosophy' 1 Corinthians 1 v 19; 2 v 5. The book of Jude also contains scripture exhorting believers to seek the true faith (Jude 3).

The writings attributed to the Apostle John contain the most significant amount of content directed at combating the progenitors of what came to be seen as so called heresies. Most Bible scholars agree that these were some of the last parts of the New Testament written and as such, can offer the most insights into a 1st century perspective. The writer's repeated adherence to true knowledge ('hereby we know') - inherent in Jesus' ministry and nature seem to challenge other speculative and opposing beliefs.

It is hard to sift through what actual evidence there is regarding Gnosticism in the New Testament due to their historical synchronicity. The Hammadi library find contains Pagan, Jewish, Greek and early Gnostic influences, further reinforcing the need to tread lightly. The antiquity of the find being of utmost importance since it shows primary evidence of texts that may also have influenced the process of NT canonization.

In addition Gnosticism, as time went on, other so-called 'heresies' began to arise – in other words, more leaders in the church began to teach doctrines that did not fit or conform to the teaching of the Apostles as it was perceived by other leaders. For example, in the early second century, Marcion held Jesus Christ to be the son of the Heavenly Father but understood the incarnation in a docetic manner, i.e. that Christ's body was only an imitation of a material body. He held that Christ in his crucifixion paid the debt of sin that humanity owed, absolving humanity and allowing it to inherit eternal life. Yet paradoxically, despite being considered heretical, it was Marcion who was the first to propose a scripture canon: an authoritative set of scriptures that could be used as a rule of faith and conduct.

PROTO-ORTHODOXY, THE QUALIFICATIONS OF DOCUMENTS FOR INCLUSION IN THE CANON AND THE ESTABLISHMENT OF ORTHODOXY

These kinds of problems meant that there was also a proto-orthodox movement within the church[1]: a group of leaders and believers who wanted to maintain what they considered to be the tradition and teaching of Jesus Christ and the first Apostles and who wanted to establish one, authoritative, uniform teaching and practice for all the Christian churches. They too produced their own literature such as Didache, The Epistle of Barnabas, I Clement and The Shepherd of Hermas. So with all these different documents and factions within the church, the question became more urgent: which documents were reliable to use as an authority and guide for faith? The debate was to prove to be an ongoing one.

The principles that would be used for the selection of writings for inclusion in such a canon began to emerge in the 2nd century. These were:-

i) Apostolicity – they were written by Apostles.

ii) True doctrine – they reflected the ideas of the Apostles.
iii) Widespread geographical use by the churches.

Thus, the Shepherd of Hermas and I Clement were rejected, because though they contained true doctrine, they were not written by Apostles and/or were not widely used.

By the 3rd century, Origen, another of the Church Fathers, identified three classes of sacred writings:-

i) Those undisputed by the church of God throughout the known world. Origen included in these the Letter of Barnabas, Didache and Shepherd of Hermas.
ii) Those writings disputed by some in the churches:
II Peter.
II & III John.
Hebrews.
James.
Jude.
iii) Spurious writings - those not considered to be genuine or what they claimed to
be, such as the Gospel of the Egyptians.

Eusebius in the 4th century identified matters in the following way:
i) Some books were universally accepted:

The 4 Gospels of Matthew, Mark, Luke and John
Acts of the Apostles
14 letters of Paul, including Hebrews which at that time was thought to be
    written by him.
I John.
I Peter.

ii) Disputed writings were of two kinds:

a) Those known and accepted by many, such as –

James.
Jude.

II Peter.
II & III John.

b) Those which were called spurious but which were not impious or foul, such as:

Acts of Paul.
Shepherd of Hermas
Apocalypse of Peter.
Letter of Barnabas.
Didache.
Hebrews, possibly.

iii) Finally there were the heretically spurious writings which were rejected, such as:

Gospel of Peter.
Acts of John.

Even so, Eusebius felt free to make authoritative use of disputed writings. Certainly at this time, even three hundred years after Christ, the idea of a canon or authoritative measure of sacred writings and the idea of God's Word of inspired revelation are not yet considered as the same thing, and even in the 4th century, churches were still using the Shepherd of Hermas, I Clement and II Clement.

Athanasius, the 4th century Bishop of Alexandria helped settle the matter and differences between eastern and western churches were sorted out at a council of leaders in 397 C.E.. The 27 books of the New Testament as we know them were accepted at this time. Nevertheless, in later documents there was still no distinction between these and other works such as the Letter of Barnabas.

Even at the Protestant Reformation in the 16th and 17th centuries, which was a protest against problems and corruptions present in the then Roman Catholic Church, the Reformers again questioned the canon. Martin Luther's principles were:

i) Apostolicity.

ii) That which leads to Christ.

But since he could not find this latter quality in Hebrews, James, Jude and Revelation, he rejected them, although he bowed to tradition and included them at the end of his Bible. Calvin too rejected some books. All this evaluation and editing of which works were included in the canon suggests that with more and better evidence, the Protestant reformers would have continued the refining of which books and letters should be in the canon and which of them should be excluded.

ERRORS IN THE SELECTION OF DOCUMENTS

Today we know that errors were made in the selection criteria: modern linguistic analytic techniques have shown that letters that were thought to be written by Paul were not written by him after all, and so on. 'But these critical questions of the authority of Scripture have dealt less with the canon as such than with the genuineness of literature – the canon is seen as an historical record of church opinion. On the other hand, those who accept inspiration of the New Testament do not connect this closely with such critical questions, thus for them, the canon is not affected. Thus doubts, say about the authorship of II Peter does not lead to moves to have it, and similar books removed from the canon. The canon rests mainly on tradition and usage.' (W. F. Adeney in Dictionary of the Bible (Hastings, J. (Ed)) (1936) T&T Clark Edinburgh. P.117). The canon of Scripture as we know it, in the form of the Bible, has been further entrenched and established by its translation into the common tongue and the invention of printing. 'The translation of the Bible into the vernacular of various languages laid the question of the canon to rest again, by familiarizing readers with the same series of books in all variations and editions'. (W. F. Adeney in Dictionary of the Bible (Hastings, J. (Ed)) (1936) T&T Clark Edinburgh. p.117).

REVISING THE CANON

Of course, we should note that these qualifications of Apostolicity, usage and disputed and undisputed writings are not compound qualities....a piece of writing did not have to fit all these qualities. Apostolicity of authorship was prime but other writings are allowed through their popular usage and through their contents not being disputed. We have then a graded canon, beginning with those documents that are known to

142

be written by Apostles. Today this would work out as something like this:

I Thessalonians (Apostle Paul) Circa 50 A.D.
Galatians (Apostle Paul) Circa 50-60 A.D.
I Corinthians (Apostle Paul) Circa 50-60 A.D.
II Corinthians (Apostle Paul) Circa 50-60 A.D.
Philemon (Apostle Paul) Circa 55-60 A.D.
Romans (Apostle Paul) Circa 55-60 A.D.
Philippians (Apostle Paul)   Circa 62 A.D.
I John (written by John the apostle) Circa 100-110 A.D

Then we would have writings of disputed authorship but being used by the churches. This would look something like this:

? Lost sayings of Gospel Q (Hypothetical)   Circa 40 – 70 A.D.
? Mark (written by John Mark, or anonymous, based on Apostle Peter) Circa70-75 A.D.
? Luke (written by Luke the evangelist, or an anonymous associate of Paul) Circa 80-90 A.D.
? Acts (written by Luke the evangelist, or an anonymous associate of Paul) Circa 80-90 A.D.
? I Peter   (Apostle peter or Unknown author) Circa 75-112 A.D.

Then we would have writings almost certainly or definitely not written by any Apostles, but rather written by their associates or close followers, and which are used widely in the churches. This would look something like this:

II Thessalonians (spurious - no consensus as to authorship) Circa 50–100 A.D
Hebrews (not by Apostle Paul - anonymous)   Circa 63-64 A.D.
James (No consensus as to authorship) Circa 45-100 A.D.
I Timothy (falsely attributed work)   Circa 63–100A.D.
Matthew (written by an anonymous Jewish Christian)   Circa 70–100A.D.
Jude (No consensus as to authorship) Circa 70–125 A.D
Ephesians (spurious - no consensus as to authorship) Circa 70–170A.D.
Colossians (No consensus as to authorship)   Circa 60–160A.D.

143

II Peter (Spurious. No consensus as to authorship)　　Circa 65 – 160 A.D.

Revelation (No consensus as to authorship)　　Circa 80–95 A.D.

Luke (written by Luke the evangelist, or an anonymous associate of Paul) Circa 80-90

Acts (written by Luke the evangelist, or an anonymous associate of Paul) Circa 80-90

Titus (falsely attributed work) Circa 80-200 A.D.

1 Clement (Sometime canonical – proto-orthodox) - concerns division and removal of elders by church at Corinth c. 96 A.D.

John (written by Johannine community based on John the apostle) Circa 90-100

Gospel of the Ebionites (Written to Jewish Christians)　　Circa 100

Gospel of the Nazareans (Possible original document based on oral traditions)　　Circa 100

II John (written by poss. follower of John the apostle) Circa 100-110 A.D

II Timothy (falsely attributed work, follower of Paul)　　Circa 100-125 A.D.

III John (written by poss. follower of John the apostle) Circa 100-110 A.D

Didache (Proto-orthodox – on the borders of the canon – church manual) Circa 100 – 120

Shepherd of Hermas (Sometime canonical but not Apostolic) Circa 100-150

Epistle of Barnabas (Sometime canonical – proto-orthodox) Circa 130

Then we have esoteric/mystical documents. By definition, these are reserved for Christians 'in the know' as it were, for those attaining insights into higher mysteries of spirituality. By definition, some of these documents are not widely and popularly used in the church and are branded as heresies by proto-orthodox believers. This list would include the Gospel of John and possibly the book of Revelation as well as those below:

Gospel of Thomas (spurious – esoteric – may include sayings of Jesus not in gospels) Circa 50 –100 or 110-150

Gospel of the Egyptians (Proto- Gnostic) Circa 100 - 150

Gospel of the Hebrews (Proto- Gnostic) Circa 100 - 150

144

Gospel of Truth (Gnostic/esoteric) Circa 150 - 180

Then we have spurious documents both in terms of authorship and content, which are rejected as forming any sort of orthodox Apostolic tradition:

Preaching of Peter (Apologetic – not canonical- proto apologetic) Circa 100 – 130
Apocalypse of Peter (spurious)   Circa 110 – 150
Gospel of Peter (spurious) Circa 150 - 200
And others such as:
Gospel of Philip
The Acts of John
The acts of Thecla
III Corinthians
Paul's letter to the Laodicians

This certainly begins to give us a quite different version of the Bible from that which Christian Fundamentalists insist on as the Word of God.

BACK TO EARLY WRITINGS

We can notice that in scheme of dates of the writing of the New Testament letters and gospels at the start of this study, there is the suggestion of a proto-gospel, a now lost document which is referred to by scholars as 'Q' from the word 'Quelle' - Source. It is suggested that this document, 'Q', forms the basis of the three synoptic gospels of Matthew, Mark and Luke - the three gospels that are very similar in content. But I want us to note first of all the wide margin of the date of composition of this document, which is anywhere between 40 – 80 AD. If we go for the early date then it is in effect the earliest source document of what we now call the New Testament. If it is later, then it is a document written at the same time or even later than Paul's letters.

PAUL AND THE GOSPELS

What we can note is that nowhere in his letters does the Apostle Paul quote from any of the four gospels and neither does he refer to any earlier gospel that precedes them. This may be because the gospels were not yet written or at least not in any sort of wide circulation in the churches.

But similarly, the gospels do not mention Paul's writings, ending at the death and resurrection of Jesus Christ. It is true to say that Acts of the Apostles, written by the writer of Luke's gospel, does indeed have a lot to say about the Apostle Paul's activities. This places the writing of Acts (and probably Luke's gospel) sometime after Paul's Damasacus Road experience and his three-year stay in Arabia and his fourteen year period in Cilicia. It also puts the date of its writing sometime after Paul's subsequent so called missionary journeys with Acts culminating in Paul's ultimate arrest and transportation to Rome. This must bring us to the period of about 65 AD. So this suggests that Luke and Acts were written sometime around or after this period If Luke is written about 65 A.D, then the proto-gospel 'Q' is in existence by this time. This suggests a number of ideas:

a) The writings of Paul are possibly contemporaneous with and in some cases precede the proto-gospel Q

b) They are possibly written for different audiences: Paul's letters are written for the new branch of the Christian church – that made up mainly of Gentiles of non-Jews. Whereas the proto-gospel 'Q' and the synoptic gospels that follow it - especially Matthew -may be more directed at the Jerusalem church – the Jewish Christians.

c) It is not clear that Paul was aware of the proto-gospel 'Q'. If the Apostle Paul knew of such a gospel, he does not quote it or refer to it at all.

d) If the writer Luke is contemporary of Paul, then it may be that Luke has written his gospel, based on 'Q' to be used by Paul in his endeavours of establishing churches.

DIFFERENT STYLES OF WRITING

Another quality that we can note is the quite different styles between the Apostle Paul's writing and that of the gospels and Acts. Both the gospels and Acts are a mixture of narratives of events and quotes or sayings. They are like biographies recording what happened and some of the things that were said. Paul's writings on the other hand have a legal/philosophical quality about them. They have a similar structure: greetings/introduction, pertinent theological/philosophical statements, practical application of those statements, concluding salutations. The Apostle became aware of problems and issues in a particular church, such as the division and immorality at Corinth and addressed these problems firstly by stating formally a theological doctrine and then practically applying this doctrine to the problem at hand. This is not surprising because Paul is an expert in religious law - he has a legal frame of mind. Also he is writing to Gentiles and not to those steeped in Old Testament or Hebrew tradition. Only when he is dealing with Jews, such as those trying to re-introduce circumcision, does he venture into the traditional Jewish scriptures to explain his position. But in the gospels and presumably the proto-gospel 'Q', we do not find such formal statements and logical setting out of philosophy or doctrine. What teaching there is tends to be scattered in brief quotes and especially in parables. Indeed, in the gospels, there is a holding back of teaching from the Jews which is why parables are used in the first place – the explanation of the meaning of parables is given only to a select few close followers – the disciples. We will come to gospel teaching a little later in this study. But for now, let's note that one area of commonality is the Lord's supper. It appears in the gospels like this:

Luke 22 v 19 – 20:

And he took bread, gave thanks and broke it, and gave it to them, saying, "This is my body [given for you]; do this in remembrance of me." In the same way, after the supper he took the cup, saying, "This cup is the new covenant in my blood, [which is poured out for you].

Mark 14 v 22 – 24:

While they were eating, Jesus took bread, and when he had given thanks, he broke it and gave it to his disciples, saying, "Take it; this is my body." Then he took a cup, and when he had given thanks, he gave it to them, and they all drank from it. "This is my blood of the [new] covenant, which is poured out for many," he said to them. "Truly I tell you, I will not drink again from the fruit of the vine until that day when I drink it new in the kingdom of God."

Matthew 26 v 26 – 28:

While they were eating, Jesus took bread, and when he had given thanks, he broke it and gave it to his disciples, saying, "Take and eat; this is my body." Then he took a cup, and when he had given thanks, he gave it to them, saying, "Drink from it, all of you. This is my blood of the

[new] covenant, which is poured out for many for the forgiveness of sins. I tell you, I will not drink from this fruit of the vine from now on until that day when I drink it new with you in my Father's kingdom."

In the Apostle Paul's writings, it looks like this:

I Corinthians 11 v 23 – 26:

For I received from the Lord what I also passed on to you: The Lord Jesus, on the night he was betrayed, took bread, and when he had given thanks, he broke it and said, "This is my body, which is for you; do this in remembrance of me." In the same way, after supper he took the cup, saying, "This cup is the new covenant in my blood; do this, whenever you drink it, in remembrance of me." For whenever you eat this bread and drink this cup, you proclaim the Lord's death until he comes.

For our purposes we can note that Paul says he 'received [this] from the Lord' Paul does not seem to be quoting the gospels or the proto-gospel 'Q'. The intimation again is that he received this by immediate teaching from God, since he uses the same terminology as he does in his letter to the Galatians where he stresses that he did not consult with the other disciples.

THE VICTORY OF PROTO-ORTHODOXY AND SUPRESSION OF DISSENTING VOICES

So we are left with a canon of scripture that is at least somewhat selective and blinkered; and which ignores or negates alternative opinions of the time. It is a canon that we now know contains spurious documents. If the proto-orthodox group had not won the victory in this battle, and say, the Gnostics had won – which at one point they nearly did – then what a different Christianity we would have and what a different set of scripture writings we would have. The picture of Jesus that we have is the picture filtered down through orthodoxy, excommunications and the punishment of heresy or deviation from this orthodoxy. So what can we say about the person of Jesus. What might modern scholarship tell us in these times where religious inquisitions are a thing of the past?

A QUICK SUMMARY

It does appear that the whole basis of the Apostle Paul's teaching and calling to be an Apostle is based on his mystical or immediate experiences of the Divine. His skills and background as a Jewish religious lawyer and as a Roman citizen make him uniquely placed to present this Judeo-Christian message to the Gentiles. We have some authentic letters and documents written by him so that his received teaching is set out in a lawyer-like formal way as a systematic, interrelated set of propositions and principles that have practical applications. With regard to his message, he checked with his Jewish contemporaries, the disciples who knew Jesus and who had founded the Jewish branch of the Christian church, that he was not hopelessly mistaken or in error. They approved of his message and mission to the Gentiles. What we get from Paul then is a particular aspect or perspective concerning Jesus Christ, where, following Paul's dramatic experience on the Damascus Road and further immediate revelations, Jesus and his life, death and resurrection are incorporated into the grand scheme of Judaic thought, practice and tradition in a formal, philosophical way, which includes the transcending and the leaving wholesale of the Jewish legal traditions. There is no evidence that Paul ever met Jesus prior to his crucifixion and as he says himself, he did not obtain his ideas by consulting with the Jewish Christian leaders. In this, he follows a tradition of mysticism whereby it is the content of the mystical experience itself that generates and frames a subsequent religious philosophy or theology. This theology is one of a number of different Christian viewpoints existing at the time and it happens to be the one, along with the same basic message of the Jewish Christians at Jerusalem that becomes established over the centuries as the one, right belief. A strong and militant proto-orthodox group within the newly emerging Christianity embarks upon extinguishing any alternative theologies and philosophies, such that these alternatives are driven underground and/or die out – their followers being charged with heresy and possibly being excommunicated or even martyred; and their writings confiscated and burned.

SOME KEY ASPECTS OF THE COMMON MESSAGE OF THE APOSTLES IN THE ORTHODOX CANONICAL DOCUMENTS

Jesus is God's servant, the Righteous One – (for the Jews) - the promised Messiah
Jesus Christ is God's Son. – (for the Gentiles)
Christ died for our sins according to the Scriptures (for the Jews)

Jesus died and he was buried.

He was raised on the third day according to the Scriptures (for the Jews)

But God raised him from the dead and we are witnesses of this (for the gentiles)

Repent of your sins, have a new mind and turn to God

Demonstrate repentance by your deeds.

He will again send you Jesus who must remain in heaven until the time for the final restoration of all things.

God is a judge of the whole world and he will judge the world by a man

He has appointed a time for judgement

He has given proof of the coming judgement to all men or nations

Jesus Christ's resurrection from the dead is the proof and we are witnesses of this

Certainly the resurrection of Jesus is absolutely vital to the tradition of the apostles. The resurrection is central to Paul's philosophy and faith. He says himself: 'If there is no resurrection of the dead, then not even Christ has been raised. And if Christ has not been raised, our preaching is useless and so is your faith. More than that, we are then found to be false witnesses about God, for we have testified about God that he raised Christ from the dead. But he did not raise him if in fact the dead are not raised. For if the dead are not raised, then Christ has not been raised either. And if Christ has not been raised, your faith is futile; you are still in your sins. Then those also who have fallen asleep in Christ are lost. If only for this life we have hope in Christ, we are of all people most to be pitied. (I Corinthians 15 v 14 -19). Why does Paul stand in jeopardy every hour if there is no resurrection? What advantage does he have in fighting beasts at Ephesus if there is no resurrection? Paul says, if there is no resurrection, then let us eat drink and be merry, for tomorrow we die. If there is no resurrection, let us get the most enjoyment and pleasure out of life that we can, while we can, because tomorrow we die, and have nothing. (I Corinthians 15 v 30-32).

The person of Jesus is central in both the Jewish and Gentile early church. Jesus is not portrayed as just a religious teacher or spiritual philosopher, but as a special, righteous person, favoured by God who by his death has obtained deliverance from sin. More than this he was raised from the dead and will return as the Judge of all people.

150

Extraordinary claims that mean that we have to go back in time a little further to consider Jesus himself and his ministry.

INFORMATION ABOUT JESUS CHRIST

We can see from the modified list of Scripture documents that we made earlier that:
a) Jesus himself did not write any documents outlining his life or teaching
b) It is at best dubious whether many of his immediate disciples/ Apostles wrote anything concerning the life and teaching of Jesus
c) The documents that we do have are written thirty or forty years after his death at least, probably either by the disciples or more likely by their followers.
d) Some of these documents may be based on oral traditions – on teaching and descriptions handed down by word of mouth.
e) Some of these documents may be based on a source document (Q): an idea which is purely hypothetical as no proof of its existence has been found.

So, it is from these kinds of sources and from scholarly research, that we can build up some kind of description of what Jesus did and taught. Again, we should note that this is quite a different kind of approach to that of Christian Fundamentalists, who would say that Mark, a follower of Jesus wrote Mark's gospel, and that Matthew, a follower and witness of Jesus, called to be an Apostle, wrote Matthew's Gospel and so on.

JESUS - THE MESSIAH

Jesus of Nazareth was born in what in effect 5 BC due to inadequacies and errors in the construction of the calendar that we use today. He lived for about thirty five years or until *c.* 30 AD. Commonly known as Jesus Christ or simply Jesus, he is the central figure of Christianity. Christians view him as the Messiah, which means "anointed". Messiah is a term used in Judaism, Christianity and Islam for the redeemer figure expected in one form or another by each religion. More loosely, the term messiah denotes any redeemer figure and the adjective messianic is used in a broad sense to refer to beliefs or theories about an eschatological improvement of the state of humanity or the world, that is a figure concerned with what are believed to be the final events in history, or the ultimate destiny of humanity. The word Messiah is used in the Old Testament to describe priests and kings, who were traditionally anointed with holy anointing oil as described in Exodus 30 v 22-25. For example, Cyrus the Great, the king of Persia, though not a Hebrew, is referred to as "God's anointed" (messiah). To anoint is to pour onto or smear a person with perfumed oil, milk, water, melted butter or other substances, a process employed ritually by many religions. People and things are anointed to symbolize the introduction of a sacramental or divine influence, a holy emanation, spirit, power or god. In later Jewish messianic tradition and eschatology, messiah refers to a leader anointed by God, and in some cases, a future King of Israel, physically descended from the Davidic line, who will rule the people of the united tribes of Israel and herald the Messianic Age of global peace. In Judaism, the Messiah is not considered to be God or a Son of God. The translation of the Hebrew word *Mašíaḥ* as Χριστός (*Khristós*) in the Greek Septuagint, the oldest of several ancient translations of the Hebrew Bible into Greek, became the accepted Christian designation and title of Jesus of Nazareth, indicative of the principal character and function of his ministry, thus Jesus 'Christ', or Jesus 'messiah'. Christians view Jesus as the Messiah foretold in the Old Testament and as the Son of God who provides salvation and reconciliation with God to humankind by dying for their sins, then rising from the dead.

CANONICAL AND NON-CANONICAL SOURCES OF INFORMATION

The principal sources of information regarding Jesus' life and teachings are the four canonical gospels, especially the Synoptic Gospels, though some scholars believe non-canonical texts such as the Gospel of Thomas are also very valuable. *The Gospel of Thomas* is very different in tone and structure from the synoptic Gospels of Matthew, Mark and Luke and from the fourth gospel of John. Unlike the canonical Gospels, it is not a narrative account of the life of Jesus; but instead it consists of sayings attributed to Jesus, sometimes stand-alone sayings, sometimes sayings embedded in short dialogues or parables. The text contains a possible allusion to the death of Jesus in saying 65, but doesn't mention crucifixion, resurrection, or Final Judgment; nor does it mention a messianic understanding of Jesus. Since its discovery, many scholars see it as a proof for the existence of the so-called hypothetical 'Q' proto-gospel, which might have been very similar in its form - as a collection of sayings of Jesus without any accounts of his deeds or his life and death, a so-called "sayings gospel". The Gospel according to the Hebrews is also relevant. The Gospel according to the Hebrews commonly shortened to the *Gospel of the Hebrews*, or simply the *Hebrew Gospel* is a lost gospel preserved in fragments within the writings of the early Church Fathers. This non-Canonical Gospel gives an account of the life and ministry of Jesus of Nazareth. It details his story from the events of his baptism to his resurrection. It is controversial because it casts doubt upon the virgin birth and other teachings of the orthodox and Catholic churches. It is also said to be written by Matthew and is the only one of the Jewish Gospels to be included in the Early Church Catalogues. It is subject to heated and ongoing scholarly debate.

A BIBLICAL OUTLINE OF JESUS

Most critical scholars in biblical studies believe that other parts of the New Testament are also useful for reconstructing Jesus' life, agreeing that:
Jesus was a Jew
Regarded as a teacher and healer,
Baptized by John the Baptist
Was crucified in Jerusalem on the orders of the Roman Prefect of Judaea, Pontius Pilate, on the charge of sedition against the Roman Empire.

A BIBLE SCHOLAR OUTLINE OF JESUS

Critical Biblical scholars and historians have offered competing descriptions of Jesus as:
A self-described messiah
The leader of an apocalyptic movement
An itinerant sage
A charismatic healer
The founder of an independent religious movement.

THE HISTORICAL JESUS

Most contemporary scholars of the historical Jesus consider him to have been an independent, charismatic founder of a Jewish restoration movement, anticipating an imminent apocalypse. The term 'historical

153

Jesus' refers to scholarly reconstructions of the 1st-century figure Jesus of Nazareth. These reconstructions are based upon historical methods including critical analysis of gospel texts as the primary source for his biography, along with consideration of the historical and cultural context in which he lived. The quest for the historical Jesus operates under the premise that the New Testament does not necessarily give a historical picture of the life of Jesus. The biblical description of Jesus is sometimes referred to as the Christ of Faith in this context. The *Historical Jesus* is thus based on the ancient evidence for his life, supplemented by materials uncovered more recently, such as fragments of the Gospels. Therefore the historical Jesus is constantly evolving as new evidence is being uncovered. The purpose of research into the Historical Jesus is to examine the evidence from diverse sources and critically bring it together in order to create a composite picture of Jesus. Use of the term the *Historical Jesus* implies that the figure thus reconstructed will differ from that presented in the teaching of church councils ("the dogmatic Christ"). It will also sometimes differ from representations of Jesus in other Christian traditions, or in Jewish, Muslim or Hindu beliefs.

THE HISTORICAL JESUS

Historical Jesus scholars typically contend that:
He was a Galilean Jew
He lived in a time of messianic and apocalyptic expectations
He was baptized by John the Baptist
He followed the example of John the Baptist
After John was executed, Jesus began his own preaching in Galilee for only about two to three years prior to his death.
He preached
salvation,
everlasting life,
cleansing from sins,
and the Kingdom of God, with some scholars crediting the apocalyptic
    declarations of the Gospels to Jesus, while other scholars
portray the
    Kingdom of God as a moral one, and not apocalyptic in nature,
    contending that Jesus' 'Kingdom of God' meant radical personal and
    social transformation instead of a future apocalypse.
He taught using parables with startling imagery
He was a teacher

154

He was a faith healer.
He sent his disciples out to heal and to preach the Kingdom of God.
Later, he travelled to Jerusalem in Judea
He caused a disturbance at the Temple at the time of Passover, when political and
    religious tensions were high in Jerusalem.
The temple guards (believed to be Sadducees) arrested him
He was turned over to Pontius Pilate for execution.
The movement that Jesus had started survived his death
It was carried on by his brother James the Just and also by
  the disciples/apostles
The apostles proclaimed the resurrection of Jesus.

According to the New Testament:
After the Romans crucified Jesus, he was buried in a new tomb but he rose from the dead
Jesus then appeared to many people over a span of forty days
Jesus then returned to heaven (Ascension).

THE RESURRECTION OF JESUS

In Christianity the resurrection of Jesus refers to the return to bodily life of Jesus three days after his death by crucifixion. As we have already seen, it is a key element of Christian faith and theology and absolutely central to the thinking of the Apostle Paul. Christians understand that in several episodes in the canonical Gospels, Jesus foretells of his coming death and resurrection and states that it was based on the plan of God the Father. Christians view the resurrection of Jesus as part of the plan of salvation: that is of delivering people from the penalties incurred by our sin and transgression against a morally pure God. The English word redemption means to 'repurchase' or 'buy back' and in the Old Testament referred to the ransom of slaves (Exodus 21 v 8). In the New Testament the redemption word group is used to refer both to deliverance from sin and freedom from captivity. Therefore for Christians, the death of Jesus pays the price of a ransom, releasing Christians from bondage to sin and death.

However, scholars debate the origin of the resurrection narratives. Some contemporary scholars consider the accounts of Jesus' resurrection to have derived from the experiences of Jesus' followers and of the Apostle Paul.

JEWISH AND GENTILE CHRISTIANITY

The ideas of the virgin birth and the resurrection developed into the Christianity of the first and second centuries. As we have already seen, this appears to start as a Judaic/Christian movement and then, under the Apostle Paul, incorporates non-Jews or Gentiles, and these two aspects of the church eventually split. The split between Pharisaic/Rabbinic Judaism and Early/Proto-orthodox Christianity is commonly attributed to: the Rejection of Jesus c.30 AD; the Council of Jerusalem c.50 AD; the Destruction of the Second Temple in 70AD; the postulated Council of Jamnia c.90AD; and/or the Bar Kokhba revolt of 132–135 AD. However, rather than a sudden split, there was a slowly growing chasm between Gentile Christians and Jewish Christians in the first centuries of the Christian church. Even though it is commonly accepted that the Apostle Paul established the Gentile church, it took centuries for a complete break to manifest.

For centuries, the traditional understanding has been that Judaism came before Christianity and that Christianity separated from Judaism some time after the destruction of the Second Temple. Recently, scholars have begun to recognize that the historical picture is quite a bit more complicated than that. In the first century, many Jewish sects existed in competition with each other. The sects which eventually became Rabbinic Judaism and Proto-orthodox Christianity were but two of these. Some scholars have begun to propose a model which envisions a twin birth of Proto-Orthodox Christianity and Rabbinic Judaism rather than a separation of the former from the latter. For example, Robert Goldenberg asserts that it is increasingly accepted among scholars that 'at the end of the 1st century AD there were not yet two separate religions called 'Judaism' and 'Christianity'.'.

Daniel Boyarin proposes a revised understanding of the interactions between nascent Christianity and nascent Judaism in late antiquity which views the two 'new' religions as intensely and complexly intertwined throughout this period. Boyarin writes: 'for at least the first three centuries of their common lives, Judaism in all of its forms and Christianity in all of its forms were part of one complex religious family, twins in a womb, contending with each other for identity and precedence, but sharing with each other the same spiritual food, as well'.

Without the power of the orthodox church or the Rabbis within this aspect of Judaism who could declare people to be 'heretics' and thus outside the system, it remained impossible to declare in experience who was a Jew and who was a Christian. At least as interesting and significant, it seems more and more clear that it is frequently impossible to tell a Jewish scriptural text from a Christian one. The borders are fuzzy, and this has consequences: religious ideas and innovations can cross borders in both directions.'

TRADITIONAL IDEAS ABOUT JESUS

Christians traditionally believe that Jesus (the Jesus of faith) was born of a virgin, performed miracles, founded the Church, rose from the dead, and ascended into heaven, from which he will return. Most Christian scholars today present Jesus as the awaited Messiah and as God, arguing that he fulfilled many Messianic prophecies of the Old Testament. The majority of Christians worship Jesus as the incarnation of God the Son, of the divine Trinity.

A) THE INCARNATION AND VIRGIN BIRTH

The Incarnation is the belief that Jesus is the second person in the three-person Christian Godhead, so that Jesus is also known as 'God the Son' or the 'Logos' (Word), which 'became flesh' when he was miraculously conceived in the womb of the Virgin Mary. This is something certainly portrayed in the canonical gospels and in the writings of Paul.

References to the virgin birth are found in:

Matthew 1 v 22-24:

All this took place to fulfil what the Lord had said through the prophet: "The <u>virgin</u> [a virgin
  1. a marriageable maiden
  2. a woman who has never had sexual intercourse with a man
  3. one's marriageable daughter]

157

will conceive and give birth to a son, and they will call him Immanuel" (which means 'God with us'). When Joseph woke up, he did what the angel of the Lord had commanded him and took Mary home as his wife.
Luke 1 v 30-35:

But the angel said to her, "Do not be afraid, Mary; you have found favour with God. You will conceive and give birth to a son, and you are to call him Jesus. He will be great and will be called the Son of the Most High. The Lord God will give him the throne of his father David, and he will reign over Jacob's descendants forever; his kingdom will never end."
"How will this be," Mary asked the angel, "since I am a virgin?" [I know not a man - Jewish idiom for sexual intercourse between a man and a woman]
The angel answered, "The Holy Spirit will come on you, and the power of the Most High will overshadow you. So the holy one to be born will be called the Son of God.

The earliest gospel, Mark, makes no reference to the virgin birth at all but begins with the baptism of Jesus. (Mark 1), and neither does John's gospel. As we have seen, the virgin birth is denied in the Gospel of Thomas.

With regards to incarnation, we find:

Matthew 1 v 23:

'and they will call him Immanuel" (which means 'God with us')'. So this is not really a statement about incarnation but rather about God being 'with' a person, in this case, being with Jesus.

Luke 1 v 30-35:

'He will be great and will be called the Son of the Most High.... The Holy Spirit will come on you, and the power of the Most High will overshadow you. So the holy one to be born will be called the Son of God.' Here, Jesus is called the Son of God because of the virgin birth and that therefore the child is the result of the 'overshadowing' and power of the Holy Spirit of God.

158

By the later time of John's more transcendent gospel we have:

John 1 v 14:

The <u>Word became flesh</u> and made his dwelling among us.

The Apostle Paul also makes reference to the Incarnation:

Romans 8 v 3:

For what the law was powerless to do because it was weakened by the flesh, God did by <u>sending his own Son in the likeness</u> [that which has been made after the likeness of something, a figure, image, likeness, representation, likeness i.e. resemblance, such as amounts almost to equality or identity] <u>of sinful flesh</u> to be a sin offering.

And again:
Philippians 2 v 6-8:
<u>Who, being in very nature God</u>, did not consider equality with God something to be used to his own advantage; rather, he made himself nothing by taking the very nature of a servant, <u>being made</u> [to become, i.e. to come into existence, begin to be, receive being
   1. to become, i.e. to come to pass, happen
      1. of events
   2. to arise, appear in history, come upon the stage
      1. of men appearing in public
   3. to be made, finished
      1. of miracles, to be performed, wrought
   4. to become, be made]
<u>in human likeness</u>. [that which has been made after the likeness of something
   1. a figure, image, likeness, representation
   2. likeness i.e. resemblance, such as amounts almost to equality or identity]
And being <u>found in appearance</u> [Schema: fashion, appearance, the habitus, as comprising everything in a person which strikes the senses, the figure, bearing, discourse, actions, manner of life etc.] <u>as a man</u>, he humbled himself by becoming obedient to death…

The word Incarnate derives from (in=in or into, caro, carnis=flesh) meaning 'to make into flesh' or 'to become flesh'. The incarnation later becomes a fundamental theological teaching of orthodox (Nicene) Christianity, based on its understanding of the New Testament. The incarnation represents the belief that Jesus, who is the non-created second hypostasis of a triune God, took on a human body and nature and became both man and God. In the Incarnation, as traditionally defined, the divine nature of the Son was joined but not mixed with human nature in one divine Person, Jesus Christ, who was both 'truly God and truly man'.

The incarnation and virgin birth are important to the Apostle Paul because sin is far more than just a failing to reach a standard set by the commandments and law of a morally pure God: sin is a law, or better, a principle, or as the Apostle Paul put it, a craving in our very physical nature, in our bodies, in our flesh. This craving, this inclination or disposition of our flesh leads to desires, passions and thoughts that are in error, that miss the standard or mark of thought and behaviour for which we were created and which lead us to be in opposition to God. Thus, says Paul, we are slaves to our sinful nature: to physical flesh that has a law or principle of desire and craving that leads us to miss the mark (sin) and to disobedience of God's commands and law (transgression). Because this principle or law is present in our flesh, every part of us is affected and we are slaves to it. Thus we have totally pervasive sin because:

a) The law or principle of sin is in our physical flesh, it affects our whole body; but it is not absolute as regards degree: we are not as totally wicked and depraved as we can be.
b) The law or principle of sin affects every person – all have sinned and fallen short of the mark.

For Paul and certain other Christians, the virgin Incarnation means that, Jesus Christ does not inherit this sinful, human nature, thus enabling him to be God's acceptable sacrifice for sin. This is central to the traditional, orthodox faith held by most Christians.

NON-ORTHODOX VIEWS OF THE BIRTH OF JESUS

There are alternative views on the subject of both the Incarnation and the Trinity. It has been claimed that the rivalry that developed between Gentile Christians and Jewish Christians brought about the intentional destruction of Hebrew texts. The doctrinal or theological reason for this centred on a view called Adoptionism. This adoptionist theology was a minority Hebrew Christian belief that:
a) Jesus was merely human, being born of a physical union between Joseph and Mary.
b) He only became divine, by adoption at his baptism, being chosen because of his sinless devotion to the will of God.

The Adoptionist view may date back almost to the time of Jesus and the reconciling of the the claims that Jesus was the Son of God with the radical monotheism of Judaism. Both the primary gospels i.e. (the *Gospel of the Hebrews* and the *Gospel of Mark*) had similar adoptionist views of the incarnation, but the *Gospel of the Hebrews* was the most radical. Jesus was seen to be 'adopted' at his baptism when the voice from heaven declared: "You are my beloved Son, *this day* have I begotten you".

Adoptionism then, (sometimes called dynamic monarchianism), is a minority Christian belief that Jesus was born of Joseph and Mary in the normal way. Jesus was adopted as God's son (Son of God) at his baptism. By Jewish-Christian accounts, Jesus was chosen because of his sinless devotion to the will of God. Early Jewish Christians understood Jesus as the Messiah and the Son of God in terms of the anointing at his baptism which some see as in line with the radical monotheism of 1st century Judaism. The Jewish-Christian Gospels make no mention of a supernatural birth, but rather, they detail his experience in the River Jordan. Some scholars see Adoptionist concepts in the Gospel of Mark and in the writings of the Apostle Paul. Mark has Jesus as the Son of God, occurring at the strategic points of Mark 1 v 1 ('The beginning of the gospel about Jesus Christ, the Son of God'), but not in all versions, and Mark 15 v 39 ('Surely this man was the Son of God!'), but the virgin birth of Jesus has not been developed. By the time the Gospels of Luke and Matthew were written however, Jesus is portrayed as being the Son of God from the time of birth, and finally the Gospel of John portrays the Son as existing 'in the beginning'.

Adoptionism (or dynamic monarchianism) holds that God is one being, above all else, wholly indivisible and of one nature. It reconciles the problem of the Trinity (or at least Jesus) by holding that the Son was not co-eternal with the Father, and that Jesus the Christ was essentially granted godhood (adopted) for the plans of God and for his own perfect life and works. Different flavours of adoptionism hold that Jesus was 'adopted' either at the time of his baptism or at his ascension. An early exponent of this belief was Theodotus of Byzantium.

By the end of the 2nd century however, Adoptionism was declared a heresy and was formally rejected by the First Council of Nicaea (325 AD), where the orthodox doctrine of the Trinity was written and which also identified Jesus as eternally begotten of God. The Roman Emperor Constantine fostered the faith as an imperial religion.

Modalism (or modalistic monarchianism) considers God to be one person appearing and working in the different 'modes' of the Father, the Son, and the Holy Spirit. The chief proponent of modalism was Sabellius, hence the view is commonly called Sabellianism. It has also been labeled *Patripassianism* by its opponents, because it purports that the Person of God the Heavenly Father suffered on the cross.

B) THE TRINITY

As we can see, orthodox views of the incarnation are closely related to the idea of the Trinity: that God exists as one God in Three Person – Father, Son and Holy Spirit. The Christian doctrine of the Trinity is considered as one of the most important in the Christian faith. It declares the unity of Father, Son, and Holy Spirit as three persons (Greek: hypostases) in one divine Being (Greek: Ousia), called the Godhead. Saying that God exists as three persons but is one God means that God the Son and God the Holy Spirit have exactly the same nature or being as God the Father in every way. Whatever attributes and power God the Father has, God the Son and God the Holy Spirit have as well. Thus, God the Son and God the Holy Spirit are also eternal, omnipresent, omnipotent, infinitely wise, infinitely holy, infinitely loving, omniscient.

NON-ORTHODOX VIEWS OF GOD

As already indicated however, a few Christian groups reject Trinitarianism wholly or partly, believing it to be non-scriptural. Non-Trinitarian persons and groups do not generally use the term *non-Trinitarian* to describe themselves. Unitarians have adopted a name that speaks of their belief in God as subsisting in a theological or cosmic unity. Modern non-trinitarian views differ widely on the nature of God, Jesus, and the Holy Spirit. Various non-trinitarian views, such as Adoptionism, Monarchianism, and Arianism, existed prior to the formal definition of the Trinity doctrine in AD 325.

Arianism is the theological teaching attributed to Arius (c. 250–336 AD), a Christian Elder from Alexandria, Egypt, which concerns the relationship of the entities of the Trinity ('God the Father', 'God the Son' and 'God the Holy Spirit') and the precise nature of the Son of God. Deemed a 'heretic' by the First Council of Nicaea of 325, Arius was later exonerated in 335 at the First Synod of Tyre, and then, after his death, pronounced a 'heretic' again at the First Council of Constantinople of 381. The Roman Emperors Constantius II (337–361) and Valens (364–378) were Arians or Semi-Arians. The Arian concept of Jesus Christ is that the Son of God did not always exist, but was created by—and is therefore distinct from and inferior to—God the Father. This belief is grounded in John 14 v 28 'Ye have heard how I said unto you, I go away, and come again unto you. If ye loved me, ye would rejoice, because I said, I go unto the Father: for my Father is greater than I.'

Arianism is also often used to refer to other theological systems of the 4th century, which regarded Jesus Christ—the Son of God, the Logos—as either a created being (as in Arianism proper and Anomoeanism), or as neither uncreated nor created in the sense other beings are created (as in Semi-Arianism).

Non-trinitarianism was later renewed in the Gnosticism of the Cathars in the 11th through to the 13th centuries, and in the Age of Enlightenment of the 18th century, and in some groups arising during the Second Great Awakening of the 19th century. In recent decades, an alternative doctrine known as 'Oneness' has been espoused among various Pentecostal groups, but has been rejected by the remainder of Christendom. Oneness Pentecostalism (also known as Jesus' Name or Apostolic Pentecostalism) refers to a grouping of denominations and believers within Pentecostal Christianity, all of whom subscribe to the theological doctrine of Oneness. This movement first emerged around 1914 as the result of doctrinal disputes within the nascent Pentecostal movement and claims an estimated 24 million adherents today. Oneness Pentecostalism derives its distinctive name from its teaching on the Godhead, which is popularly referred to as the *Oneness doctrine*. This doctrine states that there is one God, a singular spirit who manifests himself in many different ways, including as Father, Son and Holy Spirit. This stands in sharp contrast to the doctrine of three distinct and eternal 'persons' posited by Trinitarian theology. Oneness believers baptize in the name of Jesus Christ, commonly referred to as Jesus-name baptism, rather than using the Trinitarian formula.

However, by the fourth century an orthodox view was established. These alternative viewpoints on the virgin birth, incarnation and trinity were eliminated or driven underground by a mixture of polemical treatises which came from all sides but which the proto-orthodox camp won. Orthodox Christian leaders ordered that writings that were considered spurious or heretical were to be burned and those people not conforming to the emerging orthodoxy or 'one belief' were deprived of church office and/or excommunicated. The new orthodoxy or one belief is summed up in the creeds that began to emerge at this time – succinct statements outlining the main beliefs.

ORTHODOX CREED

We believe in one God, the Father Almighty, the maker of heaven and earth, of things visible and invisible.

And in one Lord Jesus Christ, the Son of God, the begotten of God the Father, the Only-begotten, that is of the essence of the Father.

God of God, Light of Light, true God of true God, begotten and not made; of the very same nature of the Father, by Whom all things came into being, in heaven and on earth, visible and invisible.

Who for us humanity and for our salvation came down from heaven, was incarnate, was made human, was born perfectly of the holy virgin Mary by the Holy Spirit.

By whom He took body, soul, and mind, and everything that is in man, truly and not in semblance.

He suffered, was crucified, was buried, rose again on the third day, ascended into heaven with the same body, [and] sat at the right hand of the Father.

He is to come with the same body and with the glory of the Father, to judge the living and the dead; of His kingdom there is no end.

We believe in the Holy Spirit, in the uncreated and the perfect; Who spoke through the Law, prophets, and Gospels; Who came down upon the Jordan, preached through the apostles, and lived in the saints.

We believe also in only One, Universal, Apostolic, and [Holy] Church; in one baptism in repentance, for the remission, and forgiveness of sins; and in the resurrection of the dead, in the everlasting judgement of souls and bodies, and the Kingdom of Heaven and in the everlasting life.

THE VIEWS OF OTHER RELIGIONS ABOUT JESUS

However, other religions took different views of Jesus:

Judaism rejects assertions that Jesus was the awaited Messiah, arguing that he did not fulfil the Messianic prophecies in the Tanakh.

The Qur'an, considered by Muslims to be God's final and authoritative revelation to humankind, mentions Jesus twenty-five times. In Islam, Jesus (Arabic: ????, commonly transliterated as Isa) is considered one of God's important prophets: a bringer of scripture, a Messenger of God who was sent to guide the Children of Israel. To aid in his ministry to the Jewish people, Jesus was given the ability to perform miracles, all by the permission of God rather than of his own power. For Muslims, Jesus is the product of a virgin birth; but did not experience a crucifixion but rather he was ascended to heaven. Islam and the Baha'i Faith both use the title 'Messiah' for Jesus, although this particular term does not correspond with the meaning given to it by Christians. Islam rejects the Christian view that Jesus was God incarnate or the son of God, that he was ever crucified or resurrected, or that he ever atoned for the sins of mankind. The Qur'an emphasizes that Jesus himself never claimed any of these things, and it furthermore indicates that Jesus will deny having ever claimed divinity at the Last Judgment, and Allah will vindicate him. Rather, the Qur'an emphasizes that Jesus was a mortal human being who, like all other prophets, had been divinely chosen to spread God's message. Islamic texts forbid the association of partners with God (*shirk*), emphasizing a strict notion of monotheism; i.e., God's divine oneness (*tawhīd*). Islamic tradition holds the view that Jesus will again return to Earth in end times after the arrival of Imam Mahdi to defeat the 'great deceiver' i.e. Dajjal (false messiah). Jesus is considered honoured in this world and in the Hereafter, and he is one of those brought nearest to God. As a result, Islam teaches Muslims to love Jesus, honour him, and believe in him. Like all prophets in Islam, Jesus is considered to have been a Muslim by the term's definition; i.e., one who submits to the will of God, as he preached that his followers should adopt the 'straight path' as commanded by God.

Hinduism and Buddhism see Jesus as an Avatar of god. In Hinduism, Avatar or Avatāra refers to a deliberate descent of a deity (an incarnation of a deva (god) from heaven to earth, or a descent of the Supreme Being and is mostly translated into English as 'incarnation', but more accurately as 'appearance' or 'manifestation'.

Traditionally, Buddhists as a group take no particular view on Jesus. However, some scholars have noted similarities between the life and teachings of Gautama Buddha and Jesus. These similarities might be attributed to Buddhist missionaries sent as early as Emperor Ashoka around 250 BC in many of the Greek Seleucid kingdoms that existed then and then later became the same regions that Christianity began. To the extent that Buddhists and Christians were exposed to each other, individual Buddhists may have had positive or negative impressions of Jesus depending on their individual inclinations.

WHAT DID JESUS TEACH?

Can we glean any clues about Jesus in what records we have about Jesus' teachings?

What did Jesus teach about himself? Again, we must remember that these accounts are almost certainly second or third hand at least – Jesus did not write any documents himself and the gospels are not written by his immediate disciples, but are written by followers thirty to forty years after his death.

As well as more general sermons, such as the Sermons on the Mount and on the Plain, which touch briefly on several different topics, the Biblical narrative portrays Jesus as having concentrated on particular themes and topics. The biblical narrative of the Synoptic Gospels mentions and gives details of several instances in which these subjects are more specifically discussed; the Gospel of John appears less interested in the teachings, concentrating instead more on Jesus' life and attributing various miracles to him. These themes include:

166

a) Ethics and morality

When asked what is the greatest commandment, Jesus is portrayed by Mark 12 v 2 and Matthew 22 v 34-40 as stating that the first two commandments and the greatest, are:
1. One should *love* God with one's entire heart, soul, mind, and strength
2. One should *love* one's neighbour as one would *love* oneself

Though it isn't clear what the word 'commandment' refers to, the latter part of the first of these two statements is a quotation from the Ritual Decalogue in Deuteronomy. The second, however, does not appear as one of either set of Ten Commandments, instead appearing in the Holiness Code, (Leviticus 19 v 18) and therefore it is likely that the word 'commandment' is a reference to the 613 mitzvot: 613 commandments, statements and principles of law and ethics contained in the Torah or Five Books of Moses. The first part of the first 'commandment' given by Jesus is from the Shema, the most important prayer in Judaism: ('Hear, [O] Israel'), the first two words of a section of the Torah that is a centrepiece of the morning and evening Jewish prayer services. The first verse encapsulates the monotheistic essence of Judaism: 'Hear, O Israel: the Lord our God, the Lord is one', Deuteronomy 6 v 4. This suggests to several scholars that when the earliest of the Synoptic Gospels was written the Christian groups still retained Jewish prayer formats. The second 'commandment', the 'Great Commandment', is essentially a formulation of the 'Golden Rule', and is also present in the writings of the Apostle Paul where it is portrayed as the summary of Jewish Law (i.e., as the most important command, not the second most important), and textual critics argue that this is likely where Mark ultimately derived the passage from.

The Gospel of Mark, but not that of Matthew, states that the man who posed the question responds that these commands are wise teachings, and so Jesus replies that the man is 'not far from the kingdom of God'. While being *not far* from God can be seen in the sense of close to knowledge of God, and this is the usual interpretation, more literal minded Christians have argued that the word *'far'* here refers to a spatial distance from God, i.e., that Jesus is categorically stating that he is God.

The Gospel of John only has one commandment, often called 'The New Commandment': 'A new commandment I give unto you, that you love one another.' John 13 v 31 – 35.

b) The establishment: Secular governments and so on

In both Mark 12 v 13-17 and the Gnostic Gospel of Thomas, when presented with a coin and questioned about taxation, Jesus is stated to have said that one should give to Caesar what is Caesar's and to God what is God's. This passage has often been used in arguments on the nature of the relationship between church and state.

In Mark's gospel, this saying is framed as the response of Jesus to a clever trap laid by the Sadducees, who had sent the Pharisees together with supporters of Herod Antipas to him. The supporters of Herod favoured Rome and hence the payment of taxes to it, while the Pharisees (in particular the Zealot faction) opposed such taxes and regarded them as a form of oppression, hence the favouring one option above the other by Jesus would have insulted the other side. In the Gnostic gospel of Thomas there is no such framing, as is the case with most sayings in Thomas and its presence in Thomas as well as Mark makes it plausible that the saying originated in the hypothetical 'Q' document, which also is a collection of sayings without any narrative context.

Mark also specifies that the coin in question is a *denarius*; a coin marked with the image of the Caesar, signifying ownership. The coin thus is technically Rome's anyway and so giving it back by paying it as tax could be logically argued as changing nothing. On the other hand, the instruction to give to God could be argued to imply that one ought to fulfil religious obligations as strongly as secular ones. In Thomas, the saying has the additional instruction to *give [Jesus] what is [his]*, raising questions about the nature of Jesus since Jesus is presented as a distinct third division apart from God and apart from Secular Authority, as well as more obvious questions of what exactly is meant by it. Further interpretations of this passage allude to the statement in Genesis 1 v 26-27 that man and woman were created 'in the image of God.' Therefore, the coin, which bore Caesar's image, was rightly to be rendered to Caesar, and people who are bearing God's image, were rightly to render their obedience to God.

c) Ritual cleanliness

The Gospel of Mark and the Gospel of Thomas present Jesus as making a significant statement downplaying the Pharisaical laws about ritual cleanliness: 'Nothing outside a man can make him ritually unclean by going into him. Rather, it is what comes out of a man that makes him ritually unclean'. Mark 7 v 15.

Unlike Thomas, Mark's biblical gospel adds an explanation stating that it is the evils of sexual immorality, theft, murder, adultery, greed, malice, deceit, lewdness, envy, slander, arrogance, and folly, which make someone ritually unclean, not what they eat. The Gospel of Thomas has a simpler implication, since rather than stating that it is what comes out of a man that makes him unclean, Thomas states that it is what comes <u>out of a man's mouth</u>, i.e., his words are what condemn him. Since the Thomas version of the saying about ritual cleanliness directly contrasts that which goes into the mouth with that which comes out of it, rather than the weaker contrast between what one eats and what one produces, many scholars think it is the Thomas version of the saying that is more original than that present in Mark.

As is common in sayings like this, the point of the latter part of the passage is frequently ignored and much more literature is devoted to considering the implications of the former section. The passage has been considered by most Christians over the centuries to imply that Christians are not bound by the laws of unclean food that apply in Judaism and that what food a person eats matters not to God. The passage also played a central role in the arguments in the early church between the Christianity developed by the Apostle Paul and the Jewish Christianity largely present at Jerusalem, as to how much of Old Testament law one ought obey.

In Mark 7 1-8, the saying is framed as a response by Jesus to the Pharisees who were criticising how some of the followers of Jesus did not follow the ritual Jewish practice of washing their hands before eating. Mark also has Jesus refer to a quote from the Book of Isaiah about superficial adherence to the law, Isaiah 29 v 13, and instead following rules laid by men. Mark more specifically portrays Jesus as condemning the Pharisees as hypocrites for letting people give money to the priests (theoretically an offering to God), in order to be excused from helping their own parents, violating one of the commands of the Ritual Decalogue. Similar, but more general, criticism also appears in the introduction to the saying in Thomas, where Jesus is presented as sarcastically complaining that it is sinful to fast, prayer leads to condemnation, and charity harms one's spirit. Mark's claim about the Pharisees allowing people to buy their way out of the Ritual Decalogue is not, however, found in other sources of the period, although there are hints of the possibility in some rabbinic texts and it may simply be the case that Mark has refined the more general introduction present also in Thomas into a more specific case.

d) Innocence and children

The Synoptic Gospels portray Jesus as asserting very strongly that innocence ought to be preserved, arguing that it is better for someone to be cast into the sea with a millstone around one's neck, than to destroy the innocence of children. Mark 9 v 42. Furthermore, it is asserted that one should dispose of other things which bring sin, even to the extreme of cutting off one's own hands and plucking out one's eyes, if their action results in sinfulness, arguing that it is better to be maimed in heaven than to be fully functional in hell. Mark 9 v 43 – 49.

The Synoptics describe Jesus as insisting that whoever welcomes children in his name also welcomes him. (Mark 10 v 13 – 16). When the disciples question which of them would be the greatest, Jesus rebukes them saying that he who wishes to be first must be last, and the least shall be the greatest, emphasising that unless they receive the kingdom of God like a child they will never enter. (Mark 9 v 33 – 37). While some argue that the children are metaphorical in this saying, being a reference to childlike dependence and unquestioning acceptance of God, the ancient Gnostics argued that it referred instead to reclaiming innocence and curiosity about the world.

Insistence on the innocence of children seems to contradict the message of the Apostle Paul concerning our inherited sinful nature as outlined earlier.

e) Divorce, Marriage and adultery

In Jewish law, men were permitted to divorce their wives simply by writing out a formal certificate of divorce, but Jesus is portrayed by the

Gospels of Mark and of Matthew as arguing that divorce is invalid, essentially arguing that any marriage subsequent to a divorce, whether by the man or by the woman, constitutes adultery. In Mark, Jesus is described as attempting to justify his stance by combining two parts of Genesis: 1 v 27; 2 v 24, referring to the creation of the sexes, and how the two become one flesh by marriage (or perhaps by the procreation of children). According to the Documentary Hypothesis, however, these two passages originally came from quite separate sources. In Matthew, but not in Mark, there is an explicit exception to this prohibition, namely that divorce is permitted if adultery has been committed by one or more of the spouses.

Historically, orthodox Christian leaders upheld the teaching and there remains a general prohibition of divorce in the Roman Catholic Church, and the Eastern Orthodox Church, although the exception is retained in the case of adultery. In the time of Jesus, the view of divorce as an evil was shared primarily with the Essenes, a group with which Jesus is often considered by scholars to have had significant connections. Amongst Gnostic groups, who generally had what would now be considered 'liberal' stances, divorce was also frequently rejected, since it was argued to be a thing whose purpose could only be related to carnal desires; and hence logically inappropriate for people who are trying to escape the carnal world. Many Gnostics also argued that the Bible supported their interpretation since there is also, in Matthew's gospel and in the biblical writing of the apostle Paul, an emphasis on celibacy being the best choice, which also was a rejection of carnal desire.

f) Poverty and wealth

During his journey to Jerusalem, Jesus is described by the Gospel of Mark as meeting a rich man, who addresses him as Good Teacher. However, Mark 10 v 17–31 states that Jesus responds by saying none is good but God alone, seemingly rejecting the form of address, but in a way which also appears to exclude Jesus from being God, and hence forming one of the main issues in defining who Jesus is. The rich man is described as explaining that he has always kept the commandments, presumably the ten commandments or the 613 mitzvot, Jesus stating that he is aware that the man knows them.

171

The narrative goes on to portray Jesus as arguing that the man should give up everything, giving it to the poor, and only then follow Jesus, since it is easier for a camel to go through the eye of a needle than for a rich man to enter the kingdom of God.

Though quite radical to the Pharisees and Sadduccees, non-ownership was the normal way of life for Essenes, who lived at varying levels of asceticism and this is one of the reasons that many scholars suspect that Jesus was originally part of an Essene group.

g) Resurrection of the dead

Jesus preached the resurrection of the dead. His parable of Lazarus and Dives portrays the common Jewish belief of the time that the righteous and unrighteous await Judgment Day in peace (in the bosom of Abraham) or in torment, respectively.

The belief in the resurrection of the dead was largely a late innovation in ancient Jewish thought, and the Sadducees, who only considered the Pentateuch to be divinely inspired, considered it to be a false teaching. Since Deuteronomy decrees the obligation of Levirate marriage, Deuteronomy 25 v 5, i.e., the brother of a dead man must marry the dead man's wife if the wife is childless, the logical conclusion is that if there are seven brothers, each dying for some reason, the wife could potentially have been married seven times, and hence if the dead were resurrected she would find herself in a highly polygamous situation. According to Mark 12 v 18 – 27, the Sadducees used this logical conundrum to challenge the idea of the resurrection of the dead, but Jesus argues that the resolution is simple—there will be no marriage after the resurrection and the people will be like the angels in heaven. Jesus is described by Mark as going on to justify the doctrine of resurrection, by referring to the story of the burning bush, in which God is described as stating, at one moment in time, that he is the God of each of the three Patriarchs—Abraham, Isaac, and Jacob, using the present tense—*I am* ... not *I was*. Mark portrays Jesus as stating that, since God is God of the Living and not of the dead, Abraham, Isaac and Jacob are still living, i.e., resurrection.

h) The Kingdom of God

The Kingdom of God (Greek: βασιλεία τοῦ θεοῦ, *Basileia tou Theou*) or Kingdom of Heaven (Hebrew: ????? ?????, *Malkuth haShamayim*; Greek: Βασιλεία τῶν Ουρανῶν, *Basileia tōn Ouranōn*) is a foundational concept in the Abrahamic religions of Judaism, Christianity and Islam. According to Jesus, the Kingdom of God is within (or among) people, Luke 17 v 20 –21; it is approached through understanding Mark 12 v 34; and is entered through acceptance like a child, Mark 10 v 15; by spiritual rebirth, John 3 v 5; and by doing the will of God, Matthew 7 v 21. It is a kingdom that will be inherited by the righteous I Corinthians 6 v 9, and is not the only kingdom. Luke Ch 11 v 18: 'If Satan is divided against himself, how can his kingdom stand? I say this because you claim that I drive out demons by Beelzebul.'.

The phrase, 'Kingdom of God,' is found in the Gospel of Mark, the Gospel of Luke, and the Gospel of John, with echoes in Paul, despite the fact that the 'Kingdom of God' is not Paul's preferred way of speaking. The phrase is also found in various writing styles such as parable, beatitude, prayer, miracle story and aphorism. The Gospel of Matthew usually does not use the phrase 'Kingdom of God,' but uses 'kingdom of heaven,' perhaps because the author of the Gospel of Matthew did not wish to offend Jewish people in the Jesus Movement of the early church.

i) Person and Divinity of Jesus

Jesus asked his disciples: 'Who do you say I am?' Simon Peter answered, 'You are the Christ, (the Messiah), the Son of the living God.' Jesus replied, 'Blessed are you, Simon son of Jonah, for this was not revealed to you by man, but by my Father in heaven. And I tell you that you are Peter, and on this rock I will build my church, and the gates of Hades will not overcome it. I will give you the keys of the kingdom of heaven; whatever you bind on earth will be bound in heaven, and whatever you loose on earth will be loosed in heaven.' Matthew16 v 15 – 19. As we have seen, according to the predominant orthodox Christian interpretation, the title 'Son of God' is understood as an expression of Jesus' divinity, specifically his unique divine sonship as the Second Person of the Trinity. The title is applied often in the Gospels, notably at the Baptism and the Transfiguration (Matthew 3 v 17, Matthew 17 v 5). Jesus applies the title 'the only Son of God' to himself in John 3 v 16 - 'For God so loved the world that he gave his one and only Son', and John 10 v 22-36: Then came the Festival of Dedication at Jerusalem. It was winter, and Jesus was in the temple courts walking in Solomon's Colonnade. Following some comments by Jesus, Jewish opponents of Jesus pick up stones to stone him... "We are not stoning you for any good work," they replied, "but for blasphemy, because you, a mere man, claim to be God." Jesus answered them, "Is it not written in your Law, 'I have said you are "gods"? If he called them 'gods,' to whom the word of God came—and Scripture cannot be set aside—what about the one whom the Father set apart as his very own and sent into the world? Why then do you accuse me of blasphemy because I said, '<u>I am God's Son</u>'?. This is a quote from Psalm 82 v 1-10 and particularly verse 6:

God presides in the great assembly;
he renders judgment among the "gods":
"How long will you defend the unjust
and show partiality to the wicked?
Defend the weak and the fatherless;
uphold the cause of the poor and the oppressed.
Rescue the weak and the needy;
deliver them from the hand of the wicked.
"The 'gods' know nothing, they understand nothing.
They walk about in darkness;
all the foundations of the earth are shaken.
"<u>I said, 'You are "gods";</u>
<u>you are all sons of the Most High</u>'
But you will die like mere mortals;
you will fall like every other ruler."
Rise up, O God, judge the earth,
for all the nations are your inheritance.

This psalm is aimed at princes' courts and courts of justice, not in Israel only, but in other nations; yet it was probably penned primarily for the use of the magistrates of Israel, the great Sanhedrim and their other elders who were in places of power. God's supreme presidency and power in all councils and courts is asserted and laid down, as a great truth necessary to be believed both by princes and subjects. The magistrates and Judges are in authority, for the public good (it is a great power that they are entrusted with), and they ought to be carry out their work in wisdom and courage. They are, in the Hebrew dialect, called *gods*; the same word is used for these subordinate governors and magistrates that is used for the sovereign ruler of the world. They are *elohim*. Angels are so called both because they are great in power and might and because God is pleased to make use of their service in the government of this lower world; and magistrates in an inferior capacity are likewise the ministers of his providence in general, for the keeping up of order and peace in human societies, and particularly of his justice and goodness in punishing evil-doers and protecting those that do well. Good magistrates, who answer the ends of magistracy, are as God; some of his honour is put upon them; they are his vicegerents, and great blessings to any people. The dignity of their character is acknowledged (Psalms 82:6): *I have said, You are gods*. They have been honoured with the name and title of gods. God himself called them so in the statute against treasonable words Exodus 22:28: 'Thou shalt not revile the gods, nor curse the ruler of thy people'. And, if they have this style from the fountain of honour, God Himself, then who can dispute it? But what is man, that he should be thus magnified? He called them *gods* because *unto them the word of God came*; they had a commission from God, and were delegated and appointed by him to be the shields of the earth, the conservators of the public peace, and revengers to execute wrath upon those that disturb it, Romans 13 v 1-6: 'Let everyone be subject to the governing authorities, for there is no authority except that which God has established. The authorities that exist have been established by God. Consequently, whoever rebels against the authority is rebelling against what God has instituted, and those who do so will bring judgment on themselves. For rulers hold no terror for those who do right, but for those who do wrong. Do you want to be free from fear of the one in authority? Then do what is right and you will be commended. For the one in authority is God's servant for your good. But if you do wrong, be afraid, for rulers do not bear the sword for no reason. They are God's servants, agents of wrath to bring punishment on the wrongdoer. Therefore, it is necessary to submit to the authorities, not only because of possible punishment but also as a matter of conscience. This is also why you pay taxes, for the authorities are God's servants, who give their full time to governing.'. All of them are in this sense *children of the Most High*. God has put some of his honour upon them, and employs them in his providential government of the world, as David made his sons chief rulers. But there follows a mortifying consideration: *You shall die like men.*

John's gospel uses the title as a short formula for expressing his divinity: 'We have beheld his glory, glory as of the only Son from the Father, full of grace and truth'. (John 1:14).' I and the Father are one' John 10 v 30

NON-ORTHODOX VIEWS ABOUT DIVINITY OF JESUS

Non-orthodox groups do not accept the theology of the canonical epistles and reject the historicity of the specific events in the Gospels. Thus, because in the Old Testament the title 'a son of God' was given to various creatures (e.g., angels, the children of Israel, Jewish kings and specifically the promised Messiah), they understand it as nothing more than belief in Jesus' Messiahship, if that. Some of these groups teach that Jesus is not, or at least was not always, God. Others see Jesus as God, but not distinct from the Father or Spirit, often describing those as merely changes in appearance, or modes of existence. Some Christians generally consider Jesus to have been an ordinary man only. They generally believe that miraculous and prophetic events in Jesus' life were not historical. They sometimes find a metaphorical meaning in what they consider fictitious accounts of his life. Jesus' relationship with God is described in widely diverse views within these groups. Some Christians in the emerging church believed Jesus was an example only; and not divine. This view is looked down upon by orthodox branches of Christianity.

There are differing views within Christian groups as to whether or not Jesus himself ever claimed to be God. The majority of Christians hold that the Bible shows Jesus both as divine and claiming divinity. Many modern scholars however, argue that Jesus did not in fact, make any such claims, either directly or indirectly; John Hick contends that there is general agreement among scholars today that Jesus did not claim to be God: 'such evidence as there is has led the historians of the period to conclude, with an impressive degree of unanimity, that Jesus did not claim to be God incarnate.'. As we have seen, this dispute is also sometimes reflected in the rejection of the common Christian doctrine of the trinity. Unitarianism is Christian belief in only one God, not in the differing persons of God represented by the trinity.

A QUICK SUMMARY

During the period following the Apostles, there was both diversity and unifying characteristics that emerged simultaneously. Both gentile and some Jewish groups believed in the resurrection of Jesus. But there was an increasingly harsh rejection of Judaism and Jewish practices within Christianity and early Christianity gradually grew apart from Judaism during the first two centuries and established itself as a predominantly gentile religion in the Roman Empire.

176

There was also a mystical trend within Christianity, as seen in Christian Gnosticism and to some extent the Gospel of John as well as the Apostle Paul's own foundation for faith and authority. But the orthodox position on mysticism is maintaining conformity to and contact with Jesus Christ: if we lose sight of Christ as head/foundation then we are in error. Thus Gnosticism, Sufism e.t.c. are heresies - they have become empty myths.

For the first Christians, New Testament scripture was largely unwritten, at least in the form of canon, but there was a tradition existing in the practices, customs and teachings of the early Christian community. What was largely communicated generation to generation was an oral tradition passed from the apostles to the Elders and from Elders to the faithful through their preaching and way of life.

THE RESURRECTION OF JESUS

As we have seen, the resurrection of Jesus is absolutely central and vital to the Apostle Paul's theology. But so far I have only considered Paul's writings concerning this matter, so now I want to look at the other writings of the New Testament concerning this issue. We should remember of course that these other writings are not written by eyewitnesses to these events, but by their associates and followers a good thirty to forty years after the death of Jesus. Let's take the gospels first:

Firstly we have an account of the discovery of the empty tomb. In Mark we have no definite statement regarding the presence of an angel, but just of a man in a white robe but by Matthew and Luke we have references to angels and by the time of Luke's writing, this seems to become two angels. Similarly, in John's gospel, the last to be written, we have two angels. In Mark, Matthew and Luke we have a group of women going to the tomb, but in John, it is Mary who goes alone and also in John's account, Jesus himself appears to Mary outside the tomb.

Mark 16 v 1-7:

When the Sabbath was over, Mary Magdalene, Mary the mother of James, and Salome bought spices so that they might go to anoint Jesus' body. Very early on the first day of the week, just after sunrise, they were on their way to the tomb and they asked each other, "Who will roll the stone away from the entrance of the tomb?" But when they looked up, they saw that the stone, which was very large, had been rolled away. As they entered the tomb, they saw a young man dressed in a white robe sitting on the right side, and they were alarmed.

"Don't be alarmed," he said. "You are looking for Jesus the Nazarene, who was crucified. <u>He has risen</u>! He is not here. See the place where they laid him. But go, tell his disciples and Peter, '<u>He is going ahead of you</u> into <u>Galilee</u>. There you will <u>see him</u>, just as he told you.'"

Trembling and bewildered, the women went out and fled from the tomb. They said nothing to anyone, because they were afraid.

Matt 28 v 5 – 10:

The <u>angel</u> said to the women, "Do not be afraid, for I know that you are looking for <u>Jesus, who was crucified</u>. He is not here; <u>he has risen</u>, just as he said. Come and see the place where he lay. Then go quickly and tell his disciples: '<u>He has risen from the dead and is going ahead of you into Galilee</u>. There you will <u>see him</u>.' Now I have told you."

So the women hurried away from the tomb, afraid yet filled with joy, and ran to tell his disciples. <u>Suddenly Jesus met them</u>. "Greetings," he <u>said</u>. They came to him, <u>clasped his feet</u> and <u>worshiped him</u>. Then Jesus said to them, "Do not be afraid. Go and tell my brothers to go to Galilee; there they will see me."

Luke 24 v 1 – 6.

On the first day of the week, very early in the morning, the women took the spices they had prepared and went to the tomb. They found the stone rolled away from the tomb, but when they entered, they did not find the body of the Lord Jesus….While they were wondering about this, <u>suddenly *two* men in clothes that gleamed like lightning stood beside them.</u> In their fright the women bowed down with their faces to the ground, but the men said to them, "Why do you look for the living among the dead? <u>He is not here; he has risen</u>!….

John 20 v 1 – 16:

Early on the first day of the week, while it was still dark, Mary Magdalene went to the tomb and saw that the stone had been removed from

178

the entrance. So she came running to Simon Peter and the other disciple, the one Jesus loved, and said, "They have taken the Lord out of the tomb, and we don't know where they have put him!".... Now Mary stood outside the tomb crying. As she wept, she bent over to look into the tomb and saw <u>two angels</u> in white, seated where Jesus' body had been, one at the head and the other at the foot.

They asked her, "Woman, why are you crying?"

"They have taken my Lord away," she said, "and I don't know where they have put him."

At this, <u>she turned around and saw Jesus</u> standing there, but she <u>did not realize that it was Jesus</u>. He asked her, "Woman, why are you crying? Who is it you are looking for?" Thinking he was the gardener, she said, "Sir, if you have carried him away, tell me where you have put him, and I will get him."

Jesus said to her, "Mary."

She turned toward him and cried out in Aramaic, "Rabboni!" (which means "Teacher").

The oldest surviving gospel: that of Mark, says nothing more concerning the resurrection of Jesus. There are some extra verses in some later manuscripts but it seems that this is where the original gospel of Mark ends. The other, later gospels continue their narrative, firstly with the women returning to the disciples:

Luke 24 v 9 – 11:

When they came back from the tomb, they told all these things to the Eleven and to all the others. It was Mary Magdalene, Joanna, Mary the mother of James, and the others with them who told this to the apostles. <u>But they did not believe the women, because their words seemed to them like nonsense.</u>

And later, the account of this incident is repeated:

Luke 24 v 22 – 23:

In addition, some of our women amazed us. <u>They went to the tomb early this morning but didn't find his body</u>. They came and told us that they had <u>seen a vision of angels</u>, [o)ptasiða: the act of exhibiting one's

179

self to view; a sight, a vision, an appearance presented to one whether asleep or awake] who said he was alive.

Here is the first mention of the idea of a vision: that these women had seen a vision of angels. We may tend to think in terms of an actual angel or angels being present in the tomb but it would seem that this is not so. Rather, this is a vision that these women have and like Paul's Damascus Road experience, the vision is not limited to one person.

John 20 v 18:

Mary Magdalene went to the disciples with the news: "I have seen the Lord!" And she told them that he had said these things to her.

In John's gospel, it is Mary Magdalene only who goes to the tomb, sees two angels and also sees and speaks to Jesus, though not recognising him until he speaks and returns to the disciples to tell the news.

Then we have the reaction of the disciples to this news, and the confirmation of the empty tomb, recorded only in the gospels of Luke and John:

Luke 24 v 12:

Peter, however, got up and ran to the tomb. Bending over, he saw the strips of linen lying by themselves, and he went away, wondering to himself what had happened

And again in Luke 24 v 24:

Then some of our companions went to the tomb and found it just as the women had said, but they did not see Jesus."

John 20 v 3 – 10:

So Peter and the other disciple started for the tomb. Both were running, but the other disciple outran Peter and reached the tomb first. He bent over and looked in at the strips of linen lying there but did not go in. Then Simon Peter came along behind him and went straight into the

180

tomb. He saw the strips of linen lying there, as well as the cloth that had been wrapped around Jesus' head. The cloth was still lying in its place, separate from the linen. Finally the other disciple, who had reached the tomb first, also went inside. He saw and believed. (They still did not understand from Scripture that Jesus had to rise from the dead.) Then the disciples went back to where they were staying.

This seems to be a reference to general verses in the Old Testament that refer generally to victory over death and which can be interpreted as talking about resurrection in general. The reaction of the elders and priests when they hear about the empty tomb was to bribe the soldiers who were supposed to be guarding it….

Matt 28 v 12-16:

When the chief priests had met with the elders and devised a plan, they gave the soldiers a large sum of money, telling them, "You are to say, 'His disciples came during the night and stole him away while we were asleep.' If this report gets to the governor, we will satisfy him and keep you out of trouble." So the soldiers took the money and did as they were instructed. And this story has been widely circulated among the Jews to this very day. Then the eleven disciples went to Galilee, to the mountain where Jesus had told them to go.

POST RESURRECTION APPEARANCES

A)	The Emmaus Road

Then we have an account in Luke only of an encounter with Jesus on the Emmaus Road:

Luke 24 v 13 – 32:

Now that same day [as the women went to tomb] two of them [the disciples] were going to a village called Emmaus, about seven miles from Jerusalem. They were talking with each other about everything that had happened. [the death of Jesus] As they talked and discussed these things with each other, Jesus himself came up and walked along with them; but they were kept from recognizing him.

He asked them, "What are you discussing together as you walk along?"

They stood still, their faces downcast. One of them, named Cleopas, asked him, "Are you the only one visiting Jerusalem who does not know the things that have happened there in these days?"

"What things?" he asked.

"About Jesus of Nazareth," they replied. "He was a prophet, powerful in word and deed before God and all the people. The chief priests and our rulers handed him over to be sentenced to death, and they crucified him; but we had hoped that he was the one who was going to redeem Israel. And what is more, it is the third day since all this took place....

He said to them, "How foolish you are, and how slow to believe all that the prophets have spoken! Did not the Messiah have to suffer these things and then enter his glory?" And beginning with Moses and all the Prophets, he explained to them what was said in all the Scriptures concerning himself.

As they approached the village to which they were going, Jesus continued on as if he were going farther. But they urged him strongly, "Stay with us, for it is nearly evening; the day is almost over." So he went in to stay with them.

When he was at the table with them, he took bread, gave thanks, broke it and began to give it to them. Then their eyes were opened [dianoiðgw - to open by dividing or drawing asunder, to open thoroughly (what had been closed)
1. a male opening the womb (the closed matrix), i.e. the first-born
2. of the eyes and the ears
3. to open the mind of one, i.e. to cause to understand a thing
    1. to open one's soul, i.e. to rouse in one the faculty of understanding or the desire of learning]

and they recognized him, and he disappeared from their sight. [Aphantos: taken out of sight, made invisible] They asked each other, "Were not our hearts burning within us while he talked with us on the road and opened the Scriptures to us?"

We can note again the visionary quality of this experience in the fact that Jesus just disappears. Many of these 'appearances' of Jesus have the mixed quality of physical presence but also, for want of a better word, a ghostly or non-physical aspect. Nowhere is this more evident than in the following incident and the incident concerning Thomas.

182

B) In the upper room

Luke 24 v 33 - 49

They [the two disciples who had met Jesus on the Emmaus Road] got up and returned at once to Jerusalem. There they found the Eleven and those with them, assembled together and saying, "It is true! The Lord has risen and has appeared [Optanomai: to look at, behold; to allow one's self to be seen, to appear] to Simon." Then the two told what had happened on the way, and how Jesus was recognized [Ginosko: to learn to know, come to know, get a knowledge of perceive, feel; to become known; to know, understand, perceive, have knowledge of: to understand: to know] by them when he broke the bread.
While they were still talking about this, Jesus himself stood among them and said to them, "Peace be with you."
They were startled and frightened, thinking they saw a ghost. [Pneuma: a spirit, i.e. a simple essence, devoid of all or at least all grosser matter, and possessed of the power of knowing, desiring, deciding, and acting] He said to them, "Why are you troubled, and why do doubts rise in your minds? Look at my hands and my feet. It is I myself! Touch me and see; a ghost does not have flesh and bones, as you see I have."
When he had said this, he showed them his hands and feet. And while they still did not believe it because of joy and amazement, he asked them, "Do you have anything here to eat?" They gave him a piece of broiled fish, and he took it and ate it in their presence.
He said to them, "This is what I told you while I was still with you: Everything must be fulfilled that is written about me in the Law of Moses, the Prophets and the Psalms."
Then he opened their minds so they could understand the Scriptures. He told them, "This is what is written: The Messiah will suffer and rise from the dead on the third day, and repentance for the forgiveness of sins will be preached in his name to all nations, beginning at Jerusalem. You are witnesses of these things. I am going to send you what my Father has promised; but stay in the city until you have been clothed with power from on high."

John 20 v 19 – 29:

On the evening of that first day of the week, when the disciples were together, with the doors locked for fear of the Jewish leaders, Jesus came

183

<u>and stood among them</u> and said, "Peace be with you!" After he said this, he showed them his hands and side. The disciples were overjoyed when they saw the Lord.

Again Jesus said, "Peace be with you! As the Father has sent me, I am sending you." And with that he breathed on them and said, "Receive the Holy Spirit. If you forgive anyone's sins, their sins are forgiven; if you do not forgive them, they are not forgiven."

Now <u>Thomas</u> (also known as Didymus), one of the Twelve, was not with the disciples when Jesus came. So the other disciples told him, "We have <u>seen</u> the Lord!"

But <u>he said to them</u>, "Unless I see the nail marks in his hands and put my finger where the nails were, and put my hand into his side, <u>I will not believe</u>."

A week later his disciples were in the house again, and Thomas was with them. <u>Though the doors were locked, Jesus came and stood among them</u> and <u>said</u>, "Peace be with you!" Then he said to Thomas, "<u>Put your finger here; see my hands. Reach out your hand and put it into my side.</u> Stop doubting and believe."

Thomas said to him, "My Lord and my God!"

Then Jesus told him, "Because you have seen me, you have believed; blessed are those who have not seen and yet have believed."

We cannot escape in these accounts the visionary quality of these experiences: Jesus appears in locked rooms, Jesus disappears or vanishes and so on. Thus it is that some doubted....

Matt 28 v 17, 18:

When they saw him, they <u>worshiped him</u>; but <u>some doubted</u>. Then Jesus came to them and <u>said</u>, "All authority in heaven and on earth has been given to me......

C) By the Sea of Galilee

It is the gospel of John, the last of the canonical gospels to be written, that has most of the accounts of these post resurrection appearances. This is in keeping with its transcendent view of Jesus and his divinity.

184

John 21 v 1 – 14:

Afterward Jesus <u>appeared</u> [Phaneroo: to make manifest or visible or known what has been hidden or unknown, to manifest, whether by words, or deeds, or in any other way
1. make actual and visible, realised
2. to make known by teaching
3. to become manifest, be made known
4. of a person
    1. expose to view, make manifest, to show one's self, appear
5. to become known, to be plainly recognised, thoroughly understood
    1. who and what one is]
again to his disciples, by the Sea of Galilee. It happened this way: Simon Peter, Thomas (also known as Didymus), Nathanael from Cana in Galilee, the sons of Zebedee, and two other disciples were together. "I'm going out to fish," Simon Peter told them, and they said, "We'll go with you." So they went out and got into the boat, but that night they caught nothing. Early in the morning, Jesus stood on the shore, but the disciples did not realize that it was Jesus.

He called out to them, "Friends, haven't you any fish?"

"No," they answered.

He said, "Throw your net on the right side of the boat and you will find some." When they did, they were unable to haul the net in because of the large number of fish.

Then the disciple whom Jesus loved said to Peter, "It is the Lord!" As soon as Simon Peter heard him say, "It is the Lord," he wrapped his outer garment around him (for he had taken it off) and jumped into the water. The other disciples followed in the boat, towing the net full of fish, for they were not far from shore, about a hundred yards. When they landed, they saw a fire of burning coals there with fish on it, and some bread.

Jesus said to them, "Bring some of the fish you have just caught." So Simon Peter climbed back into the boat and dragged the net ashore. It was full of large fish, 153, but even with so many the net was not torn. Jesus said to them, "Come and have breakfast." None of the disciples dared ask him, "Who are you?" They knew it was the Lord. Jesus came, took the bread and gave it to them, and did the same with the fish. This

185

was now the third time Jesus appeared to his disciples after he was raised from the dead.

D) Other appearances

John 20 v 30-31:

Jesus performed many other signs in the presence of his disciples, which are not recorded in this book. But these are written that you may believe that Jesus is the Messiah, the Son of God, and that by believing you may have life in his name.

John Ch 21 v 25

Jesus did many other things as well. If every one of them were written down, I suppose that even the whole world would not have room for the books that would be written.

THE ASCENSION

Finally, Jesus ascends to the heavens:

John 20 v 17:

Jesus said, "Do not hold on to me, for I have not yet ascended [to go up, to rise, mount, be borne up, spring up] to the Father. Go instead to my brothers and tell them, 'I am ascending to my Father and your Father, to my God and your God.'"

Luke 24 v 50 – 53:

When he had led them out to the vicinity of Bethany, he lifted up his hands and blessed them. While he was blessing them, he left them and was taken up into heaven. [the vaulted expanse of the sky with all things visible in it, the region above the sidereal heavens, the seat of order of things eternal and consummately perfect where God dwells and other heavenly beings] Then they worshiped him and returned to Jerusalem with great joy. And they stayed continually at the temple, praising God.

Acts 1 v 1 – 11:

In my former book, Theophilus, I wrote about all that Jesus began to do and to teach until the day he was taken up to heaven, after giving instructions through the Holy Spirit to the apostles he had chosen. After his suffering, he presented himself to them and gave many convincing proofs that he was alive. He *appeared* [to stand beside, stand by or near, to be at hand, be present, to appear] to them over a period of forty days and spoke about the kingdom of God. On one occasion, while he was eating with them, he gave them this command: "Do not leave Jerusalem, but wait for the gift my Father promised, which you have heard me speak about. For John baptized with water, but in a few days you will be baptized with the Holy Spirit."

Then they gathered around him and asked him, "Lord, are you at this time going to restore the kingdom to Israel?"

He said to them: "It is not for you to know the times or dates the Father has set by his own authority. But you will receive power when the Holy Spirit comes on you; and you will be my witnesses in Jerusalem, and in all Judea and Samaria, and to the ends of the earth."

After he said this, he was taken up [to lift up, raise up, raise on high] before their very eyes, and a cloud hid him from their sight. They were looking intently up into the sky as he was going, when suddenly two men dressed in white stood beside them. "Men of Galilee," they said, "why do you stand here looking into the sky? This same Jesus, who has been taken from you into heaven, will come back in the same way you have seen him go into heaven."

The Apostle Paul summarises these encounters recording one last appearance of the resurrected Jesus after his ascension:

1 Corinthians 15 v 4-10

that he was buried, that he was raised on the third day according to the Scriptures, and that he appeared [to look at, behold, to allow one's self to be seen, to appear] to Cephas, and then to the Twelve. After that, he appeared [to look at, behold, to allow one's self to be seen, to appear] to more than five hundred of the brothers and sisters at the same time, most of whom are still living, though some have fallen asleep. Then he appeared [to look at, behold, to allow one's self to be seen, to appear] to

James, then to all the apostles, and last of all he appeared [to look at, behold, to allow one's self to be seen, to appear] to me also, as to one abnormally born. For I am the least of the apostles and do not even deserve to be called an apostle, because I persecuted the church of God. But by the grace of God I am what I am, and his grace to me was not without effect.

Concerning these post resurrection appearances, we can note that
a) Paul seems to class all these appearances as being like his own on the Damascus Road – as visions, appearances.
b) These visions are often seen and or heard by more than one person at a time.
c) The distinction between the physical and material on the one hand and the spiritual, ethereal or ghostly on the other hand seems blurred and uncertain. Jesus appears and disappears, ascends to the sky, appears in locked rooms, yet also eats, drinks and Thomas places his hands in Jesus' wounds.
d) With regard to the gospels, the later they are written, the more stories they have about the resurrection appearances, with Mark having the least accounts and the writer of John, who emphasises the transcendent divinity of Christ, having the most. His purpose in writing? - But these are written that you may believe that Jesus is the Messiah, the Son of God.

SUMMARY OVERVIEW

As we look at the Christian church we may initially see a fairly united organisation that appears to have a set of authoritative documents in the Bible that are used to establish its faith and conduct. It may even appear that these documents are God's Word – and therefore without error or mistake, and that anything outside of these documents, outside of the Bible, are necessarily suspect and not to be trusted. The church appears to have a hierarchy of authority where its leaders are educated and skilled in understanding and interpreting what these various documents in the Bible say. It may appear that the person, work and nature of the founder, Jesus Christ, has been clearly declared and worked out in various councils and meetings of elders over the years. Yes, there are divisions and differences of opinion and interpretation, but the essentials seem to be agreed upon.

In fact of course this is not the case. The church is not and never has been fully united, and the selection process and criteria for the documents that it uses as a basis for faith and conduct are suspect such that the process is vague, the boundaries indistinct and some documents should not really be there at all. Their portrayed status as the Word of God is an exaggeration which gives the Bible a false authority. The exclusion of some documents has relegated and downgraded their importance. Some church leaders have been sectarian, divisive and antagonistic. In the name of the faith they have branded people who think differently from themselves as 'heretics' and even excommunicated or executed them, and in similar acts of intolerance to alternative interpretations to their own, they have issued polemical condemnations of these people and their written works. Through these sorts of means, a particular opinion and interpretation of Christian belief and doctrine gained ascendancy – what we now call the proto-orthodox position – because it resulted in the orthodox Christianity handed down to us. Orthodoxy means 'one right belief, and along with it came orthopraxy – 'one right practice'. Thus one particular view of the person, work and nature of Jesus came to prominence over the first centuries of Christianity, a view that became established by orthodoxy and by the eventual acceptance of Christianity by the Roman State, together with the decline and dispersion of the Hebrew Christian tradition beginning particularly at the fall of Jerusalem in 70 AD. Running parallel with both the Hebrew and Gentile Christian aspects of the church is a current of mysticism and gnosticism – an esoteric Christianity that focuses on allegory, symbolism and myth as intermediate forms that stand between the material world and the ultimately Unknowable world of Absolute Spirit. Nevertheless, some form of immediate knowledge and experience of the Divine was seen as possible, even to the point of union with the One. In many ways this was an elitist movement – something reserved for the advanced spiritual seeker and for those who had these immediate experiences or gnosis – something for those in the know, where more literal and concrete interpretations were looked down as inferior and veiled. This elitist, secret and exclusive quality of some aspects of mystical Christianity such as Gnosticism, meant that this view and approach never achieved the widespread usage of the more literal Hebrew and gentile traditions.

Even so, this mystical, visionary element is present within orthodox Christianity itself: it forms the basis of the Apostle Paul's theology and calling as an Apostle to the Gentiles. It even seems to play a major part in encounters with the post-resurrection Jesus that are experienced by Jesus' immediate followers. We can see an evolution and development of these transcendent, post resurrection encounters in the writings of the gospels. The first gospel to be written, that of Mark, has little to say either of the Virgin Birth or of post resurrection experiences. By Matthew and Luke, written later, more stories of this kind are to be found, and the last gospel to be written, that of John, which emphasises the transcendent, divine nature of Jesus, contains the most of these accounts, written so that people might believe that Jesus is the Son of God in the sense of being the Word of God made flesh.

Of these three traditions – Hebrew, gentile and mystical, it is the later Gentile Christian tradition that gained ascendancy, with its view of Jesus that is derived from the visions and subsequent theology of the Apostle Paul.

Repent and have a new mind and turn to God
Demonstrate repentance by your deeds.
Jesus Christ is God's Son.
Christ died for our sins according to the Scriptures.
He was buried
He was raised on the third day according to the Scriptures

This was later developed to:

God is Creator of all things and Sovereign
God is alive
God is transcendent of created things and Self-sufficient
God is present everywhere
God is not without a witness as to His existence.
a)　God's provision of rain, crops, food and joy is a witness.
b)　Creation is a witness.
God is Just
God is a moral judge:
a)　Of the whole world
b)　He will judge the world by a man
c)　He has appointed a time for judgement
d)　He has given proof of the coming judgement to all men or nations
e)　Christ's resurrection from the dead is the proof

God is kind – His kindness is shown in His provision of life and food
God's desire for us is that-
a) We should seek Him
b) We should reach out for Him
c) We should find Him.
God commands all men, everywhere, all nations
        a) To repent
        b) To turn from worthless idols
        c) To turn to the living God.

Paul worked out or received a theology concerning Jesus whereby he is the Messiah/Redeemer, God's supreme sacrificial offering to pay the price for the sins and transgressions of believers. Jesus is eternally co-equal with God, humbled in time and space to come to us in the likeness of flesh, but, following his crucifixion, he is raised up from the dead as a guarantee of the future resurrection of humanity to the Final Judgment and the restoration of all things. The old Jewish Law was powerless to accomplish this and in the New Covenant established by Jesus, these Laws, both ceremonial and moral, are superseded and transcended by a new relationship in Jesus and a righteousness gained not by works and obedience to the law, but imputed to us by and through faith in God. The True Israel is not the Jewish nation with its sign of circumcision, but is the spiritual Israel – those who believe and have faith in God. Thus all Israel will be redeemed, having a righteousness by faith, imputed to them and credited to their account. This exalted view of Jesus is further carried on in the tradition of John's gospel.

Prior to this Gentile tradition established by Paul, we have the Hebrew Tradition of Christianity centred around the original Jewish followers of Jesus in Jerusalem. This group remained as a sect within Judaism and there view of Jesus seems more moderate:

Pre resurrection/ascension:

Jesus was a prophet
Jesus was powerful in word and deed before God and all the people.
   The chief priests and our rulers handed him over to be <u>sentenced to death</u>
   <u>They crucified him</u>
We hoped that he was the one who was going to redeem Israel.

Post resurrection/ascension, this was modified to:

Jesus is God's servant
Jesus is holy and righteous - the Righteous One—the Messiah
Jesus is the author of life
Jews betrayed and murdered him
But God raised him from the dead
We are witnesses of this (possibly in terms of visions)
What was done to Jesus was done in ignorance
God was fulfilling what all the Jewish prophets had foretold about the Messiah
Repent of your sins, have a new mind and turn to God
He will again send you Jesus, your appointed Messiah.
Jesus must remain in heaven until the time for the final restoration of all things
Jesus the Son of Man stands in the place of honour at God's right hand.
Starting with Samuel, every prophet spoke about this.

Here, Jesus is seen as the Messiah – the Redeemer of Israel anointed by God. This was only seen dimly by the disciples when they were with him and he was teaching and working miracles. Their minds had to be constantly opened so that they could see how Jesus fulfilled the prophesies contained in the Hebrew religious literature concerning the promised anointed one. Now It is revealed who the anointed one is, who the redeemer is, so that we know who to expect when he is finally sent by God from heaven to redeem Israel. There is less emphasis here on the divinity of Jesus and the Virgin birth, though the resurrection and ascension is still central. But as we have seen, these experiences of the resurrection and ascension have a quality of the visionary about them, with appearances and disappearances and so on. Certainly, as we move to the older, Hebrew Christian tradition, which saw itself as a group within Judaism, Jesus tends to be seen more as a prophet, one who reveals things about God, as one who is powerful in the things he says and does, as a servant of God and as morally pure and spiritually minded – as righteous, even as the author of life in the sense of being the chosen redeemer, anointed by God, who was going to liberate the nation of Israel and lead it into a glorious period of blessing and prosperity.

It could be argued that the whole resurrection idea is one based upon visions following the disappointment, confusion and fear that the disciples felt following the death of their spiritual leader. That they are less grounded in physical manifestations and material events but rather grounded in mystical, visionary spiritual experience.

Jesus then may well have been originally regarded as God's anointed servant, a righteous prophet sent to reveal things about God to Israel, powerful in what he said and did. His death and subsequent visionary encounters of him led his followers to regard him and identify him as the revealed Messiah – the anointed of God who will redeem Israel when God sends him to usher in this glorious period for Israel.

Subsequent literalisations and embellishments concerning equality with God, virgin birth and redeemer of humanity grew up in subsequent years and decades, particularly as the result of visions experienced by Paul who took his message to non-Jews. This aspect of the early church became dominant and established as alternative interpretations were suppressed and extinguished and certain documents elevated to the status of the infallible Word of God, and as this aspect of the church became part of the establishment.

VISIONS AND REVELATIONS – CHRISTIANITY AND GNOSTICISM

If the whole basis and foundation of the Apostle Paul's theology is grounded upon visions and revelations and if the post resurrection appearances of Jesus Christ can be explained at least in part by similar revelatory visions, then why is there an antagonism towards the mystical element brought to the church by Gnostics and the Christians of the early church? Why weren't the visions, revelations and gnosis of these esoteric believers accepted by the Apostles and Elders when such experiences lie at the very heart of the foundation of Christianity itself? If we look at some of the verses from the bible relating to Gnosticism, we can note that these are all from secondary writers – that is, they are probably not written by the Apostle Paul even though they are attributed to him, but rather probably written by close followers of Paul:

I Timothy 1 v 3-5:

193

As I urged you when I went into Macedonia, stay there in Ephesus so that you may command certain people not to teach false doctrines any longer or to devote themselves to myths and endless genealogies. Such things promote controversial speculations rather than advancing God's work which is by faith. The goal of this command is love, which comes from a pure heart and a good conscience and a sincere faith.

II Timothy 4 v 3 – 4:

For the time will come when people will not put up with sound doctrine. Instead, to suit their own desires, they will gather around them a great number of teachers to say what their itching ears want to hear. They will turn their ears away from the truth and turn aside to myths.

Colossians 2 v 18-19:

Do not let anyone who delights in false humility and the worship of angels disqualify you. Such a person also goes into great detail about what they have seen; they are puffed up with idle notions by their unspiritual mind. They have lost connection with the head, from whom the whole body, supported and held together by its ligaments and sinews, grows as God causes it to grow.

OBJECTIVE AND SUBJECTIVE

I want to suggest that the Apostle Paul and the Apostles in Jerusalem believed that in their visions and revelations they encountered an objective phenomenon - the real Jesus. In the same way, at the transfiguration of Christ, I think that the disciples thought that they saw the real Moses and Elijah as real tangible 'objects out there':

Mark 9 v 2 – 8:

After six days Jesus took Peter, James and John with him and led them up a high mountain, where they were all alone. There he was transfigured before them. His clothes became dazzling white, whiter than anyone in the world could bleach them. And there appeared before them Elijah and Moses, who were talking with Jesus. Peter said to Jesus, "Rabbi, it is good for us to be here. Let us put up three shelters—one for you, one for Moses and one for Elijah." (He did not know what to say,

194

they were so frightened.) Then a cloud appeared and covered them, and a voice came from the cloud: "This is my Son, whom I love. Listen to him!" Suddenly, when they looked around, they no longer saw anyone with them except Jesus.

There are two distinguishing features about Christian (and probably Hebrew) visionary experiences:
a) What is seen in the vision exists objectively 'out there' – it is not just a subjective, imaginary experience produced by the mind.
b) What is seen is a real person – like Jesus, Moses or Elijah – as opposed to mythical or imaginary person.
c) In angelic visitations, the Angels were considered to be objectively real – they were not mythical and neither were they just a subjective or symbolic creation of the mind.

I consider that in these visions, the recipients believed that they were seeing the actual, real, people – people such as Moses, Elijah and Jesus – people who had actually existed and been alive but who were now dead, or they were seeing real, objectively existing spiritual beings. They were not seeing fantasy figures or mythical beings or symbolic creations from their minds. Paul did not consider that he had received some kind of presentation that had arisen in his mind or imagination, or from his subconscious, or that his imagination and mind was stimulated in some way to present a symbolic representation of a Jesus-like figure. No, he believed that he had actually met the objectively existing, real, historical and now resurrected Jesus in his vision, as opposed to some fantasy or myth created in his mind or some mere, what we would call today, psychological/emotional/cathartic experience.

This is why connection with the head – Jesus – is so important to Paul. For him it is the seeing of the objectively existing real, resurrected Jesus and the faithful following of the teaching received in this (and probably other) encounter(s) that distinguishes the Christian experience as 'sound', and places it in opposition to the 'mere' 'idle notions' encountered by the Gnostics, because in Gnostic mystical encounters, they did not necessarily 'see' real historical people, but rather they may 'see' spirit-beings, wise guides and demi-gods, which they may well have interpreted in symbolic, allegorical ways instead of regarding them as literally objectively existing. For Gnostics, the resurrection was a 'spiritual' event rather than a physical one, for example.

Therefore for the Apostle Paul and his devotees, such experiences as those of the Gnostics had no real foundation – because the recipients had not encountered actual, real people – let alone Jesus. To put this in modern parlance we might think about the phenomenon of past life regression. Imagine this scenario: a person is regressed to a past life and they imagine that they are Alexander the Great, or Napoleon or some such famous figure from history. Or, more realistically, they may imagine that they are an ordinary working class person in Victorian England and may give details of their name, where they live and what they do. They may even reveal some hitherto secret information, such as the location of a hidden artefact. What is our reaction? Well, we may be sceptically amused that the person believes that they were Alexander the Great or Napoleon. Like the Apostle Paul, we may consider this to be an 'idle notion'. We may be more interested in the working class Victorian – and may decide to try and follow up the information that they have given us by looking in public records, census returns, birth registrations and so on. If we find nothing to back up the existence of such a person, we may again regard the whole thing as an 'idle notion'. However, if we find that such a person did indeed exist and then follow up the secret hiding place and discover the described artefact, then we may be more impressed, believing the regression process to have some basis in objective reality. This is where Paul and the Apostles are: they believe that their visions are based in objective reality – in a real person, that actually existed and lived and died, objectively appearing to them to instruct them, whereas to the Apostles, the Gnostics are like those who think that they were Napoleon in a past life – their ideas are the product of an inflated imagination that has lost touch with (for the Apostles) the real foundation – Jesus.

THEOMORPHISM

In fact, I would argue here that the Apostle is mistaken. I would suggest that the experience is a subjective rather than an objective one and that the imagery and symbolism that is presented to the imagination often arises within the context and experience of the recipient. Insights are gained and changes of perspective are made – Paul changes from opposing Jesus to serving Jesus, yet he does so in a way that he sees as totally consistent with his Jewish context and background, which is re-interpreted in an innovative and novel way – a way severely disliked and opposed by the orthodox Jews of his time. Certain other things remain the same – Paul remains quite a 'black and white' or all or 'nothing thinker' – remaining quite dogmatic in his beliefs and intolerant - at first he was intolerant of Christians: a sect that he sought to eliminate – then he was intolerant of Jews who would try and insist on bringing back obedience to the Law. Also typical of such mystical/revelatory/visionary experience, Paul regards his approach as the only way – all other approaches to God are in ignorance, or false: anything not based on Jesus is false teaching and to be opposed. This certainty and assurance of the content of his message arises from the unmediated nature of mystical experience. But what the Apostle Paul did not learn was the lesson that some higher stage mystics have learned – that God is theomorphic – that God changes in form in order to meet people where they are in a personally relevant and significant way. No delimiting form can encapsulate the Infinite Divine and because of the Divine Infinity, such delimited forms as God presents are non-repeatable. The forms, the symbols, the figures in mystical encounters are metaphorical and allegorical – they stand between the delimited, bounded world of material form and the Boundless, Formless Empty, Infinite Spirit. They are known personal symbols that reveal aspects of the Unknowable Absolute. The Apostle Paul did not realise that every believer has their own unique personal Lord – but such delimiting forms and beliefs merely bind and tie the believer, limiting and obscuring as well as revealing the Infinite Spirit. Nevertheless, in serving their delimited personal Lord, their intention, their 'objective', is the Unknowable, Infinite, Formless Essence.

FORMS OF BELIEF

But of course, the Gnostics had little in the way of a single belief. Tertullian noted of the Christian Gnostics that they had: 'no unity, only diversity....most of them disagree with one another, since they are willing to say – and even sincerely – of certain points, 'This is not so.'.' In other words, they emphasising their individual, personal Lord. This lack of a core, unified set of symbols for the group as whole meant that even if it had not been so elitist, it would not have gained popular, unified widespread support in the same way that Christian orthodoxy eventually did. Because believers in orthodox Christianity has a focussed and increasingly clearly defined set of ideas that identified and distinguished it from other groups. They had clearly defined ideals and aims and shared symbols and ideas.

HOW WAS THE EARLY CHURCH PROBLEM OF GNOSTICISM DEALT WITH?

How did the early church Apostles and leaders deal with the perceived problem of Gnosticism? What did they appeal to as a foundation and authority for the Christian faith and for avoiding error?

Let's just look at Gnosticism itself for a moment. Gnosticism was a form of direct mystical encounter with the Divine and like the Apostle Paul himself, Gnostics took their authority and foundation from these kinds of encounters/visions/revelations. Gnosticism took a number of forms, including Christian mysticism. It contended that human perfection and salvation was found in the immediate knowledge and experience of the fullness of the Divine: gnosis. A resurrection out of the realm of ignorance and the material occurred during the attaining of this knowledge, whereby the evil material or physical world was transcended. For some Gnostics, Jesus was seen as a spirit and the resurrection of Jesus was seen as a spiritual resurrection and these people saw the idea of a physical resurrection as ridiculous. Sin was either irrelevant or transcended in this experience of unity with the Divine. The transcendent God may speak or manifest to us through angels, spirit-guides or by all manner of symbols and metaphors. In Christian Gnosticism, these kinds of ideas were expressed using Christian terminology and symbolism.

It was countered using the following arguments:

Perfection is found in Christ, not in knowledge or the experience of gnosis. Colossians 1 v 28
Knowledge and wisdom is found in Christ, not in mystical or Gnostic experience. Colossians 2 v 2 - 4
The fullness of the deity is found in Christ, not in anything or anyone else. Colossians 2 v 8-10
Contact with Christ is vital. Losing contact with Christ leads to a puffed up and empty imagination. Colossians 2 v 18, 19
Christ is true knowledge. Ideas that oppose this are false knowledge. 1 Timothy 6 v 20
The resurrection is yet to occur in the future. The notion that we are already being resurrected is false and is an idea that spreads like gangrene. 2 Timothy 2 v 18

God is not a liar: we do sin and miss the mark. To say that we do not sin makes God out to be a liar. 1 John 1 v 10
Knowledge of God is evidenced by our obedient submission. Continuing to behave immorally is to be in error. 1 John 2 v 3
True spirits testify that Jesus is the Son of God. Therefore, test the spirits. 1 John 4 v 1-3
Jesus came in physical flesh. Jesus was not just a spirit e.t.c. (Docetism) 2 John 7

Gnostic ideas were simply counteracted or opposed with Christian ones: of these ten arguments, seven of them refer to the chief cornerstone of the Christian faith: Jesus Christ. Of the other three, one refers to God as True, one to the resurrection as being in the future, and the last to submission to a righteous God as being the evidence of the knowledge of God. This really reflects what we have been saying: the focus of the foundation and authority for the Christian faith is Jesus Christ: His Person, life and work; and Jesus is real – an actual person who lived and died – and was physically resurrected and appeared objectively to the Apostles, giving teaching. For the orthodox Christian, the Gnostic view on the other hand is based on myths (where it uses pagan or non-Christian ideas, or where it allegorises Christian ideas to mean something new) and on an inflated subjective imagination as opposed to objective reality – it is not based on the life and work of a real person and when it interprets Christian theology, Gnosticism draws out false teaching – such as the idea that Jesus is just a spirit, that we do not sin and that the resurrection is spiritual and not physical.

Orthodox Christianity then, continually returns to and is anchored in what is seen as an objective foundation of the real resurrected person – Jesus Christ who himself lived and taught within a Jewish context and background and objectively appeared post resurrection to teach and instruct the founders of the church. Thus, the Apostles declare:

Jesus is God's servant
Jesus is holy and righteous - the Messiah – God's annointed
Jesus is the author of life
Jews betrayed and murdered him
But God raised him from the dead
We are witnesses of this (possibly in terms of visions)
What was done to Jesus was done in ignorance

God was fulfilling what all the Jewish prophets had foretold about the Messiah

He will again send you Jesus, your appointed Messiah.

Jesus must remain in heaven until the time for the final restoration of all things

God will Judge the world by Jesus Christ

Jesus the Son of Man now stands in the place of honour at God's right hand.

The resurrection of Jesus from the dead is the proof of this coming judgment

Repent of your sins, have a new mind and turn to God

Orthodox Christianity cannot step out of what it perceives as this real, objective framework and therefore has a tendency to reject all other approaches to God, whether they are alternative external religious systems or esoteric, inward spiritual approaches. It rejects the use of non-Christian myth, allegory and symbolism as alternative pathways to the Divine and insists that Jesus is the only way to God – all else is false doctrine.

FINAL PERSONAL CONCLUSIONS

I suppose that at the end of this investigation I conclude that the original and more tenable view of Jesus is that of an itinerant teacher/prophet, a servant of God, blessed by God and who was considered by some Jews as a fulfilment of prophecy concerning the Messiah, and therefore a person anointed by God. His untimely death at the hands of the Jews and Romans left his followers in confusion and dismay. But they seemed to have a number of visionary experiences that persuaded them that Jesus had risen from the dead – because their view of such experiences was that they were objectively real in their content. Such a vision also happened to a strict Jewish Pharisee who was determined to stamp out this new cult and sect. The result was that this Pharisee became a Christian, and following more visionary/revelatory teaching, he took the message of the resurrection, which was viewed as objectively, physically, real, to the Gentiles or non-Jews. The view of Jesus gradually changed then to one where Jesus was considered equal with God: God incarnated in the likeness of human flesh – and who was a sacrificial offering from God for sin and transgression, consistent with Jewish thought, whereby those with faith could be redeemed and all humanity would overcome death and live forever, but having to face a Final

Judgment – the resurrection of Jesus being the proof. The subsequent demise of the Hebrew aspect of the church because of events such as the destruction of the Temple in 70 AD meant that this more transcendent view of Jesus gained in strength. False and spurious writings and alternative views of Jesus, such as those of Gnostics were suppressed in the following centuries as the need for one authoritative faith and tradition arose in the face of competing ideas. This orthodoxy stressed the tradition of the Apostles in using the literal, objective Jesus Christ, now risen from the dead, and imbued with a cosmic mission, as its sole foundation – any other imagery or interpretation being seen as being based on an inflated imagination, myths and false doctrines. The leaders and founders of the early church mistakenly I think, did not see their visions as subjective and did not recognise the infinite non-repeatability of God's manifestations and therefore God's theomorphism. Subsequent emphasis on the belief and especially the right sort of belief – orthodox belief – meant that Christians bound and tied themselves to certain delimiting ideas concerning the Infinite Spirit and more than this, they imposed such ideas onto others insisting on conformity to them. In these sorts of ways, the picture of Jesus as the Son of God and Redeemer of mankind became enshrined as the orthodox, but I think, mistaken, picture of Jesus.

THE VISIONS OF THE APOSTLE PAUL
AND THE EARLY CHRISTIAN TRADITION

REFICIATION

Reification refers to the projecting of the contents of a subjective experience to some sort of external existence, such that these contents are considered to have an objective, independent existence 'out there'. It is to transfer something subjectively perceived and imagined into something that has an independent, concrete, objective existence. In spirituality it is a danger that we have to be constantly aware of. With the reification of an experience there arises a whole raft of burden of proof: If we say something like, for example, an angel, exists 'out there' then it is quite right that people ask should ask for proof, for evidence of it's objective existence and it is reasonable for people to want to observe, measure and have such proof or evidence for the existence of this angel. However, not all mystics or those who have spiritual experiences claim such objectivity to their perceptions and experiences – they do not all insist that their experiences have an objective, independent existence 'out there'. The Hindu teacher Shankara, for example, argued that such notions of objectivity are a mere projection on our part and that the contents of these experiences have no substance.

REIFICATION AND THE JUDEO/CHRISTIAN TRADITION

However, reification *is* the tradition within early Judaic/Christian thought. Thus, if a person had some sort of unusual, subjective experience whereby they had an unusual, transcendent experience whereby they saw, let us say, an angel, then this experience became interpreted as being an objective occurrence – it was considered that an angel literally appeared to them in objectively real, physical space 'out there' and communicated to them - as opposed to any idea of the person concerned having an internal, subjective image and sound arising in their minds. When Jewish people in the Old and New Testaments had unusual dreams or had visions or heard voices, the tradition was that they were often understood as objective visitations. The Judaic tradition did not merely say 'I had an unusual dream' or 'I had an ecstatic experience whereby I went into a trance and heard a voice or saw certain images'. On the contrary, their traditional interpretation of such experiences was to reify the contents of these experiences to concrete objective reality. Thus, they would say: 'God appeared and spoke to me in a dream', or 'When I was praying the Temple, an Angel appeared to me and gave me a command from God' and so on.

REFICIATION AND TRANSCENDENT EXPERIENCE

Indeed, it must be said that some mystical or transcendent spiritual experiences do appear very Real. This is because when we experience them, we operate in a different and non-usual mode of awareness. Normally, we are active in the way that we interpret our experiences and perceptions of the world – we actively categorise, conceptualise, label, systematise, synthesise and place values on our experiences in order to make sense of our world so that we can make effective predictions concerning outcomes and thus function and survive in the world. This means that to a great degree our experiences and perceptions are mediated through our conceptual, linguistic and value categories that we have created throughout our life – we assimilate experiences through a hierarchical web of meaning and value. Mystical experiences however are often described as Immediate or Non-meditated, and we are often Passive rather than active such that we feel that they are Received rather than actively created by us. Transcendent spiritual experiences, whether arising spontaneously, or through the practice of meditation or through the taking of drugs, tend to various degrees, to by-pass our usual, active-rational mode of being and functioning. Indeed, the taking of drugs or the practice of meditation or contemplative prayer serves to quieten and subdue our active-rational mind. It is this temporary bypassing of the active/rational mode that gives the sense of Directness, Immediacy and Transcendence and thus the contents of such experiences appear very Real and True.

REIFICATION AND ASSURANCE

The cultural tradition that the contents of such unusual experiences have an objective existence 'out there', when taken together with the Immediacy, Directness and sense of Truth and Reality of this non-usual mode of being, can produce a very great certainty, assurance and confidence and may on later reflection lead to deep theological insights. It is common with mystical experience that afterwards, the powers and functions of the rational mind are brought to bear on it in order to evaluate and understand it. Such an insightful doctrinal scheme together with the confidence with which it is held may well carry on in those that become followers or advocates of the person who had the original experience and indeed, a new form of religious orthodoxy may well be established as a result.

PAUL AND THE DAMASCUS ROAD EXPERIENCE

I suggest that this exactly what happened with the disciples and the Apostle Paul after the death of Jesus. Their culture and tradition did not incline them to say: 'I had a vision, dream or subjective experience where it seemed to me that I saw Jesus risen from the dead'. Rather, their tradition and culture inclined them to say: 'The risen Jesus appeared to me in a dream or vision – therefore, he is literally alive and risen from the dead! I know that that this is true because Jesus has appeared not only to me but to others as well!' Paul, after his Damascus Road experience, went into effectual retreat for a number of years during which time he had more immediate experiences, the contents of which informed and shaped the theology which he established and formulated in the light of his experiences, background and culture. He avoided communicating with the disciples of Jesus for quite some time, eventually meeting with them to verify his understanding and become an associate with them. It is this theology that dominates the New Testament literature and also makes up its oldest texts, written about 18 – 20 years after the death of Jesus. Three of the gospels, though seemingly based on an older narrative of the life of Jesus, were not to be written for another thirty or forty years. The fourth Gospel attributed to John is written last of all and takes a more mystical strand.

Returning to the Apostle Paul, the writer of the Gospel attributed to Luke, potentially an associate of Paul, gives three accounts of Paul's Damascus Road experience in the book of Acts in Chapters 9, 22 and 26. They stand together reasonably well in agreement:

Saul as he was then known, was a strict traditional Jew – a Pharisee, one skilled in Judaic law, and he was ardently and obsessively opposed to this disruptive and upstart sect of Christianity that had emerged within Judaism. Saul went around issuing murderous threats and persecuting Christians, arresting them and having them put to death, approving for example of the stoning of Stephen. He went from synagogue to synagogue preaching against them, having them punished and forcing them to blaspheme. He obtained letters of authority from the High Priest to give authority for his actions and he even went to foreign cities to hunt Christians down.

It was on one such journey, to Damascus, that about noon, a bright light in the sky blazed around Saul and his companions and they fell down. Saul heard a voice in Aramaic saying:
"Saul, Saul, why do you persecute me?"
Saul asked: Who are you, Lord?"
"I am Jesus, whom you are persecuting," the voice replied. "Now get up and go into the city and you will be told what you must do."

The men travelling with Saul were speechless; they saw the light and they heard the sound but did not see anyone and they did not understand the sound.

Saul got up from the ground, but when he opened his eyes he could see nothing. So Saul's companions led him by the hand into Damascus, because the brilliance of the light had blinded him. He was blind for three days and did not eat or drink anything. Eventually Saul's sight was restored by Ananias. Saul spent several days with the disciples in Damascus. At once he began to preach in the synagogues that Jesus is the Son of God. All those who heard him were astonished and asked, "Isn't he the man who raised havoc in Jerusalem among the Christians there?" Yet Saul grew more and more powerful and baffled the Jews living in Damascus by showing from Scripture that Jesus is the Messiah.

Saul then seems to return to Jerusalem and while praying in the temple there fell into a trance and saw the Lord speaking:
'Quick! Leave Jerusalem immediately, because the people here will not accept your testimony about me.'
"'Lord,' he replied, 'these people know that I went from one synagogue to another to imprison and beat those who believe in you. And when the blood of your martyr Stephen was shed, I stood there giving my approval and guarding the clothes of those who were killing him.'
Then the Lord said, 'Go; I will send you far away to the Gentiles.' "

In his letter to the Galatians, Paul gives us his own account of what followed:

'The gospel I preached is not of human origin. I did not receive it from any man, nor was I taught it; rather, I received it by revelation from Jesus Christ. You have heard of my previous way of life in Judaism, how intensely I persecuted the church of God and tried to destroy it. I was advancing in Judaism beyond many of my own age among my people and was extremely zealous for the traditions of my fathers. But when God, was pleased to reveal his Son in me so that I might preach him among the Gentiles, my immediate response was not to consult any human being. I did not go up to Jerusalem to see those who were apostles before I was, but I went into Arabia. Later I returned to Damascus. Then after three years, I went up to Jerusalem to get acquainted with Peter and stayed with him fifteen days. I saw none of the other apostles—only James, the Lord's brother. I assure you before God that what I am writing you is no lie. Then I went to Syria and Cilicia. I was personally unknown to the churches of Judea that are in Christ. They only heard the report: "The man who formerly persecuted us is now preaching the faith he once tried to destroy." And they praised God because of me. Then after fourteen years, I went up again to Jerusalem, this time with Barnabas. I took Titus along also. I went in response to a revelation and, meeting privately with those esteemed as leaders, I presented to them the gospel that I preach among the Gentiles. I wanted to be sure I was not running and had not been running my race in vain. As for those who were held in high esteem—whatever they were makes no difference to me; God does not show favouritism—they added nothing to my message. On the contrary, they recognized that I had been entrusted with the task of preaching the gospel to the Gentiles, just as Peter had been to the

Jews. For God, who was at work in Peter as an apostle to the Jews, was also at work in me as an apostle to the Gentiles. James, Peter and John, those esteemed as pillars, gave Barnabas and me the right hand of fellowship when they recognized the grace given to me. They agreed that we should go to the Gentiles, and they to the Jews.

Now I am not qualified to comment on Saul's state of mind as he persecuted the early Christians and indeed after all these centuries, any such assessment can only be speculative. Luke seems to quote Saul himself in the strong descriptions of his obsessive opposition to Christianity. Certainly, on the Damascus Road, *something* external happened -- a flash of very bright light from the sky that one way or another seemed to blind Saul for three days – they all seemed to see this light and they all heard a sound – but only Saul made sense of this sound in terms of a voice speaking to him. This puts some considerable doubt on the external objectivity of this voice – though perhaps not on the fact that there was a sound – because only Saul heard it in this way. Typically and consistent with his Jewish tradition, this whole episode was reified into an external appearance and communication from Jesus. That Saul was the one most affected may say more about his mental and emotional state at this time than about the nature of any of these external events. Saul certainly seemed to have a predisposition to trances and ecstatic experiences, because on his return to Jerusalem, he has another trance experience, reified again as God speaking to him and telling him to leave Jerusalem. According to his letter to the Galatians, he relied on further visions and trances, because he says quite plainly – '…the gospel I preached is not of human origin. I did not receive it from any man, nor was I taught it; rather, I received it by revelation from Jesus Christ'…that is, in and through a set of reified experiences. It was quite a few years before he actually met the disciples in order to verify his message. The gospel that he preached was approved of by the Jewish disciples in Jerusalem and he was regarded as one sent to the Gentiles or non-Jews, just as Peter had been sent to the Jews – both of them declaring Jesus as the Messiah.

This reified view is how these events are presented to us in the narratives – as though some external event occurred – as though Jesus literally appeared in the objective external space 'out there'- in front of the disciples or Saul, just as if you or I might stand in front of someone. Thus we read that Jesus appeared to hundreds of followers following his death. It does not read that hundreds of followers had subjective impressions in their minds concerning Jesus. This second interpretation also sounds far less impressive in terms of any miraculous event. This way of presenting these events in the New Testament narrative – that Jesus actually and objectively appeared – often gives further weight and bias in our own interpretation of these events, a bias towards an objective event occurring instead of a subjective one, thus reinforcing and continuing the more miraculous-sounding reified view. I am not suggesting in any way that the disciples or the Apostle Paul for example were in any way duplicitous or dishonest in this. I consider that this is the traditional, cultural way of interpreting these kinds of events for those within Judaism. I think that Paul firmly believed that he had met with Jesus on the Damascus Road, not in terms of a subjective experience, but in terms of an objective encounter. In the light of this understanding of the experience and in the light of Paul's cultural background and learning in Judaism, he applied his Pharisaic Judaic theology and extended it to accommodate this new situation and the Pauline theology of Justification by Faith emerged as a result. What Paul considered to be the objective appearance of Jesus after his death on the cross was accommodated and assimilated within Paul's Judaic understanding as a Pharisee, which in turn, was extended and developed to what we know as the predominant New Testament theology, since the bulk of the New Testament is either written by the Apostle Paul or by his close followers or assistants – though there still remain in some writings – in the Gospel of John in particular – a more mystical interpretation.

By the time that what we now know as New Testament accounts were put in writing, anything between twenty to seventy years had passed since the death of Jesus – and more and more fantastic stories and claims about him were being made. The view of Jesus changed from him being an influential itinerant preacher and healer to being the Word of God Incarnate, born of a virgin, resurrected from the dead and ascended to heaven, surrounded in his earthly life with miracles and extraordinary powers. This was becoming the new orthodoxy and soon, those holding alternative interpretations and views, such as the Gnostics, would be classed as heretics and systematic attempts to burn and destroy their writings and silence their teachers and advocates would follow. In the end, only a few documents would make it into the canon, or rule of faith known as the New Testament and these would those documents thought have been written by first-hand witnesses of the resurrection – namely some of the disciples and Paul. Through this sort of process, the reified view held by Paul and the disciples, gained almost total supremacy as the orthodox Christian view.

If we consider that Paul and the disciples were mistaken in taking a reified view of these experiences, then we end up with a much more subjective spirituality – a spirituality of it's time in the sense that we could say that God met Saul just where he was – full of anger and venom concerning Christianity – and led him to deeper insights using the forms, symbols, types and figures that he was trained and educated in. Instead of opposing Jesus, he embraced Jesus – but still accommodated Jesus within his Judaic tradition. Paul did not stop being a Jew – he came to see that to be a Christian was to be a True Jew – not to be one circumcised outwardly only, but rather, inwardly, in the heart. He did not leave his Jewish heritage but extended and applied it to accommodate Jesus as the Promised Messiah.

THE ASSIMILATION OF TRANSCENDENT EXPERIENCE

This is true for all of us – God meets us where we are – and though there may be some radical change in our understanding and insight as a result of a mystical or transcendent spiritual experience - there usually also remains a continuum and extension of what we have learned. We absorb the insights gained according to our capacity. Sometimes our existing system of faith may become more established, more firmly held, with a deeper conviction. Sometimes we may appear to take on novel and new interpretations that make those of an orthodox persuasion feel uncomfortable – or make them feel that in some way we are becoming unorthodox or heretical. Nevertheless, sometimes, we may even change our belief system, say by moving from Christianity to Islamic Sufism or to Hinduism. In this present age of trans-cultural global knowledge via the Internet and so on, such outcomes as these may be more common. But whatever theological scheme seems best suited to our experience our cognitive scheme is nevertheless a delimited and bounded form that ultimately cannot embrace the Formless Infinite.

But the worst thing that we can do with regard to transcendent, mystical experience is to reify the contents of the experience as Paul and the disciples did, because then the contents are presented to others as objective facts. I have already said that this then results in a burden of proof being laid upon those who follow such reified ideas. A fine example is the six-day creation story in Genesis. This is not necessarily an example of reification, but it is a passage that can be read metaphorically or literally – as though it were a series of objective facts. When this passage is read literally, as though it were an objective series of facts, then people naturally look for evidence to substantiate the narrative. Thus we have had more than one archaeologist claiming to find evidence for a worldwide flood in Noah's time, only to be subsequently proved wrong. In the same way we have the Creation Research groups who constantly seek to show scientific evidence for a young earth and a literal six-day creation. Arguments and debates like these can soon become burdensome and distracting to true spirituality. A similar process and similar set of problems arise when we reify the content of a transcendent experience. But in addition to this, reification also brings in the danger of ultraorthodoxy. Since the contents of the transcendent experience are portrayed as actually happening 'out there' then these events become enshrined as THE objective truth. Paul in particular constantly refers to the fact that he and others were witnesses of the resurrection (via his reified understanding of the Damascus Road experience and others like it) and that he had received teaching from God and in turn had faithfully declared to others what he had received. These followers in turn, must remain faithful to this teaching, received it is believed through a literal, concrete, objective appearance of Jesus. Thus to deviate from this teaching and tradition is to fall into error, or worse still, to hold to ideas that are false and deceitful. Those who persistently hold on to such erroneous ideas may be classed as guilty slanderers who hold forth a lie – as heretics who deserve to be cast out in case their deceit and lies corrupt the true disciples and lead them astray. Before long the leaders of the church itself persecute them, with bishops ordering that their studies and written works should be burned. The end result of this imposition of orthodoxy – of one belief and practice – are of course organisations such as the Spanish Inquisition, or events like the Crusades and witch hunts. There is little room in theologies arising from reified experiences for tolerance, the use of metaphor, or for mutually existing but different theologies. At stake, in Christian terms at least, is an eternity in a literal heaven or hell.

IMPLICATIONS FOR CHRISTIANITY

If we acknowledge that these experiences are subjective rather than a perception of objective phenomena, then the whole view changes. For a start, in the example we have been considering, we see this very much as Saul's personal spirituality – an individual having a transcendent experience that is interpreted within his own personal world-view. When we compare the Apostle's teaching with that of Jesus and the Disciples – Paul adds to and enriches their theology with his own insights that he has gained through this subjective experience. But it is nevertheless a very powerful theology – as attested to by its prominence and survival down to this very day. It speaks to people's needs and desires in many ways. But it is also a theology that is less and less tenable in the light of the scientific discoveries that have been made in the last century or so. Part of its power has been in the fact that many of the statements in Paul's writings and in the Bible as a whole, could not be disproved or seriously questioned. But these days, in the light of our scientific discoveries, it is difficult to hold to the six-day creation story in Genesis for example. The reified, supposed 'facts' of Genesis contradict and oppose discoveries made in geology, archaeology, astronomy and physics – and this has a knock on effect in Paul's theology, as we shall see in a moment.

The Gnostics sought a more metaphorical view of ideas such as the resurrection – they thought in terms of Jesus being spiritually resurrected or raised from the dead and indeed, had a whole range of different metaphors referring for example to the creation. But early Christian teachers like the Apostle Paul criticised these teachings as phantasms and as mere empty imagination in contrast to the basis of his faith and practice which was based on what was for him a literal physical, objective occurrence – the bodily resurrection of Jesus, of which he, through his reified mystical experiences, was a witness. For Paul, his theology was not based in metaphors, symbols, figures, types and empty imagination, but in real, concrete, objective facts. But this theology of Paul's integrates within it the entire Judaic system. Paul refers to characters such as Abraham and Moses to show how their lives and teaching foreshadowed the message that Paul is preaching. In his explanation of the Headship of Christ, Jesus is referred to as the Second Adam and Paul makes comparisons between the first Adam as the head of all humanity and Jesus as the Second Adam as the Head of all who have faith. Paul's exposition seems to demand a literal view of the Genesis account: 'Therefore, just as sin entered the world through *one man*, and death through sin…if the many died by the trespass of the *one man*, how much more did God's grace and the gift that came by the grace of the *one man, Jesus Christ*, overflow to the many!.' [Romans 5 v 12, 15. My italics]. If we embrace Paul's theology properly, then we are obliged to embrace his view of a literal Genesis account and much more of the Old Testament in a similarly literal fashion too.

But I have already said that the Judaic culture had a tradition of reifying transcendent experiences and indeed, the whole of the Old Testament mixes the reified content of such experiences with literal events such as battles, the reign of kings and the general history of Israel. This is why it is so difficult to take a metaphorical view when using the Bible as a spiritual guide: the writings of the Bible constantly bring us to what seem to be concrete, historical events, (however they are debated and interpreted by historians) – we have biographies, journeys, rivalries, love affairs, battles and wars, temples being built, people being taken into slavery and captivity and so on – all mixed in with the reified contents of transcendent experiences – so that amongst these events and narratives, we have the world created in six days, God appearing, Angels appearing, the devil deceiving, commandments written in stone by the finger of God, bushes burning without being consumed, the waters of a sea being parted, people wrestling with God and so on – all described as actual, objective events. And this is before we consider how these writings may have been written in such a way that myths and magic stories became added and infused into them for one reason or another. As soon as we try to adopt a metaphorical view of these Judeo/Christian narratives, we seem to be brought back down to the objective, everyday events within which these magical and metaphorical images are reified and embedded, making it difficult to take a purely symbolic and metaphorical interpretation as the early Gnostics sought to do.

The embracing of these Judeo/Christian ideas and concepts is no longer a tenable option for me. Even as symbols and metaphors they just no longer work for me and I find that the Bible constantly draws me back into a more literal view which in turn generates a reified view of God – usually as 'Big-Stern-Old-Man-in-the-sky'. But modern discoveries have also rendered many of these narratives as questionable in content and historical accuracy. Of course, this is not the case for many believers, who still sincerely hold to beliefs and loyalty with regard to their view of Jesus.

212

Where then can we go with this? Is there any way that we can find a spiritual path through these varying, conflicting, contradictory spiritual beliefs and loyalties without finding ourselves either intolerantly dismissing or condemning a whole swathe of sincere, spiritually minded people to the dustbin of heresy and hellfire? Can we make any sense of all this or do we have to consign all spirituality to the drawer marked 'Irrelevant nonsense'?

FORMS OF THE FORMLESS

Some mystical traditions refer to the Divine Absolute as being Formless – no form, concept or object can adequately encapsulate Divine Spirit. But, we are creatures of form – we have a bounded form ourselves by having a physical body, and we live in a material universe that is made up of different bounded forms. To try and relate to an Absolute Spirit that is Unmanifest and Formless is therefore actually quite difficult for us and though it is a spiritual path that is sometimes followed by a few, the formless, iconoclastic nature of such a path makes it seem very arid and dry indeed. We are creatures of form and used to relating to forms and concepts. Even within Christianity, there is a large section of the Christian community that makes use of altar pieces, paintings and statues of Jesus, angels, the virgin Mary and so on as objects and forms that assist worship by giving us some *thing* or form to focus on. In other Christian circles, the use of such statues and paintings is regarded as idolatry. Indeed, in the Old Testament, carved images of the Divine are forbidden because such forms cannot encapsulate the Divine and may even be seen as demeaning of the Divine Spirit. Of course, similarly in Islam, there is a prohibition on depicting Allah and even the prophet, for similar reasons. The Apostle Paul contrasts his own faith with that of idol worship, which on occasion greatly distressed him. He felt that such worshippers were giving adoration to lifeless blocks of wood and stone whereas in contrast, he served an objectively existing, living, resurrected Son of God as opposed to these lifeless carvings or mere figments of the imagination. Whatever our approach to such paintings and carvings, it is clear that we all tend to have *some* form or image before us when we worship. With the more austere Calvinist Christians, they may well strip away all these church ornaments such as stained glass windows, altar pieces, statues, candles and crosses in order to not be distracted and to have a

213

minimalist environment, but nevertheless, you can be sure that they will have an image of Jesus at the forefront of their minds and imaginations.

In all of this, to whatever degree images and concepts of God are used, whether our worship environment be very minimalist or very ornate, whatever the object or image, however different, diverse and even contradictory these various forms of the Divine may be, the intention of the worshipper/believer/disciple is Transcendent Absolute. The forms of the Divine may vary and contradict, the systems and organisations may vary, but the intention of all is the same – Transcendent, Formless, Absolute. The Christian, the Jew, the Muslim, the Hindu and so on all vary and differ in their approaches to and forms of the Absolute. These different schools of thought cannot be harmonised without losing some of the essential qualities that distinguish each approach. In places they contradict one another. But the intention of all sincere disciples is Absolute Formless Spirit – That which has no form – which Transcends the limitations and boundaries of all forms. Problems arise when we fail to recognise this Divine Transcendence and try to limit the Divine exclusively to one set of forms, concepts, systems or images. Rather, at all times, the transience and limitations of all forms of the Divine should be borne in mind – such forms can only point to but never encapsulate Absolute Spirit. Indeed, some thinkers argue that Absolute Spirit is always presenting or manifesting to us in different and new forms that reveal or point to different aspects of the Infinite Spirit – a position known as Perpetual Transformation. Whether this is so or not, different, even contradictory religious or spiritual forms of the Divine, point to different aspects and perspectives of Absolute Spirit, but all such forms and conceptual systems ultimately fall far short of describing what they point to.

This therefore should lead us to humility at the paucity of our understanding of Absolute Spirit and a tolerance for others who seek Absolute Spirit but come from a different pathway – a different culture and background, a different context and perspective.

It may well be that Christian forms of understanding are suitable and acceptable to you. You may find them very useful and helpful in your spiritual journey. But we have seen that Christian ideas and theology are by no means infallible – one of its foundations – the Bible – is increasingly open to question with regard to its historical accuracy – even though it continually draws us back to what appear to be objective historical events. Even the core foundation of an objective, physical resurrection of Jesus is open to doubt because of the tendency of the Judaic culture to reify subjective experiences into objective reality.

BUILDING A CONTEMPORARY CHRISTIAN FAITH

In many ways I have been deconstructing the influence of the Apostle Paul in this essay. Over the centuries, a Christian theological edifice has been created – much of it based of the Apostle Paul's thinking - but now this building is very much under threat and this threat is right at the very foundations of the construction, with the Apostle Paul and the other Apostles. I have indicated some of the potential fault-lines running through these foundations and some of it may make uncomfortable reading for sincere Christians. But this has to be done – we cannot paper over the cracks any more. In order to make the building sound, we have to make sure that the foundation is sound. But it is not my intention to demolish the Christian faith – the word 'demolish' implies random destruction. Rather, I have deliberately used the word 'deconstruction' – we are examining the building carefully, doing a structural survey if you like – and our attention has been drawn to the foundations that urgently need attention. I am trying to be systematic rather than random and I am seeing if we can remedy the situation before the building collapses. In other words, I am trying to remove those aspects of the building that are causing it to be unsafe or in danger of collapse. Only when the foundations are right can we begin to build a new structure.

In order to build a twentieth century Christian faith we have to try and get back to who Jesus really was and what he taught. To be a Christian means to follow the teaching of Jesus - but getting to the essence of who Jesus was and what he taught means getting not only beyond the Apostle Paul and prior to the Apostle Paul's experiences and theological interpretations and applications, but also getting to grips with exactly what sort of documents the gospels are, when they were written and who actually wrote them rather than who they were attributed to. It means trying to get to their core content before the more magical and miraculous embellishments were added and gained orthodox acceptance.

PSYCHOLOGY OF BELIEFS

DEFINITION OF BELIEFS: - inferences, propositions, or hypotheses where there is insufficient evidence to prove them as correct. They exist along a CONTINUUM OF CERTAINTY that includes such positions as conviction, assurance, opinion, persuasion, inclination and sentiment.

OBJECTIVE REALITY has some inherent structure or pattern to it, e.g., grass is green, so this partly structures our perception of reality. But reality is SELECTIVELY PERCEIVED via our selective ATTENTION. Our perception of reality is not a passive reception but an ACTIVE SEEKING OUT of information FROM A PARTICULAR VIEWPOINT. Our particular perspective is a PHYSICAL, COGNITIVE, EMOTIONAL, MOTIVATIONAL viewpoint in the light of MEMORY. Thus, REALITY is INTERPRETED with a particular BIAS. Our perception of reality is a mixture of TOP DOWN/BOTTOM UP processing and is imbued with MEANING. It is top down because it is interpreted and categorised within our framework and selectively attended to. It is bottom up because raw information enters our senses. In addition, this information is often processed automatically. These beliefs about reality are shared with others in a particular SOCIETY and CULTURE at a particular TIME. It is shared by PARALLEL EXPERIENCE, COMMUNICATION using SHARED SYMBOLS (language, pictures) which are CULTURAL TOOLS. This gives a CULTURAL OR GROUP BIAS.

WHY DON'T WE WAIT FOR CONVINCING PROOF OF EVERYTHING?

We would not be able to FUNCTION. Based on what evidence we have, together with other related factors, we make INFERENCES:
    in order to make PREDICTIONS
    in order to FUNCTION, to behave appropriately in the world.
    in order to SURVIVE
    and in order to MAKE SENSE of the world.

MAKING SENSE OF THE WORLD INVOLVES using:

CONCEPTS, CATEGORIES AND SCHEMAS - REPRESENTATIONS of the world involving beliefs and interpretations about reality.

Events, people and objects are:

>LABELLED, via a language
>CATEGORISED according to features and prototypes
>SORTED with related concepts in memory.

We use SCRIPTS - stored ROUTINES in memory which give us EXPECTATIONS.

Such representations are not isolated chunks of information but are HIGHLY INTERCONNECTED with:

>OTHER BELIEFS
>OTHER KNOWLEDGE
>EMOTIONS
>BEHAVIOURS
>MOTIVES
>MEMORY
>EXPECTATIONS
>VALUES

to form a COMPLEX NETWORK.

Since all these factors are related to our beliefs, we INVEST varying amounts of ourselves in our beliefs. For example, if we believe it is important to help those less fortunate than ourselves we may invest our time, energy and money or other skills into various pursuits to this end.

Therefore:

BELIEFS ARE LOADED WITH INVESTMENTS AND COMMITMENTS which VARY IN TYPE according to the particular belief and it's strength.

As we embrace beliefs, CONSEQUENCES follow for other beliefs via the interconnected network we form. These beliefs in turn involve commitments and consequences.

In the main, we do not entertain CONTRADICTORY BELIEFS:

A person does not hold belief in God and at the same time not believe in God, this would be the opposite of the order and structure that we seek. However, FALSE BELIEFS MAY BE HELD ON TO because they may enable us to function reasonably well, even better than understanding the truth.

SUMMARY 1

In order to make sense of a partially structured or patterned world, and to function and survive in it, we interpret and categorise our biased perceptions via the cultural tool of language. Since we cannot investigate all the evidence, we make inferences, which form highly complex beliefs about our world. These interact with other beliefs, our emotions, motives, behaviour, memory and expectations to produce a complex interrelated system. These beliefs carry with them varying degrees and types of investment of our time, energy and behaviour e.t.c., and have logical and other consequences for other beliefs in the system. Because we are trying to make sense of our world, we do not tend to hold on to explicitly contradictory beliefs.

The effect of holding particular beliefs, or the function of beliefs, which affect us in these complex ways may be to give us:

IDENTITY: A sense of the qualities that make us who we are.

PURPOSE: an arousing of short and long term goals and directions.

COHESIVENESS: a sense of personal integrity and unity.

BELONGING: a sense of unity with others - of sharedness, connectedness that inevitably also means division and separateness from some other groups. For example if you are a Christian, you are divided from and separate from Muslims.

REDUCTION IN ANXIETY: a calming of fear and uncertainty, though some beliefs will increase fear and anxiety, e.g. the belief that the world is going to end tomorrow.

These effects will follow REGARDLESS of whether the belief is TRUE or NOT, so long as the person concerned considers them to be true. The above qualities may override considerations of truth/falsity. It may be more important to belong to a group than become separate from them by considering the group's beliefs to be false. Thus there may be an UNWILLINGNESS to examine the truth or otherwise of beliefs because of the investment/commitment/reward of these other factors.

Beliefs are NOT STATIC and RIGID but often FLUID and the processes of ACCOMODATION and ASSIMILATION usually apply:

ASSIMILATION: As new information is received, it is assimilated into various categories, concepts, schemas and scripts.

ACCOMMODATION: Sometimes, new information does not fit into the categories, concepts, schemas and scripts that have been formed, e.g. the world did not end as predicted, so the schema and scripts may have to be modified to accommodate the new information.

BUT, DIFFEENT BELIEFS OFFER DIFFERENT RESISTANCES TO CHANGE:-

Some beliefs are PERIPHERAL, and their alteration has hardly any effect on the network. Peripheral beliefs have not involved much in the way of investment or commitment. The average person may not believe that there is water on the Moon. Assimilation of the discovery that there is water on Mars is probably quite easy. It has little real effect on day-to-day living.

Other beliefs are CORE, well established and deeply interconnected with our orientation, identity, purpose, integrity, sense of belonging and ability to keep anxiety at bay. To change these beliefs may have GREAT COST. We may have to accept that our investment in such beliefs are misplaced. Our sense of understanding the world and ourselves may be threatened. Other beliefs may be affected as a consequence of changing this one. Our emotions, behaviours, motives, expectations, and even our memory may be affected. Our sense of orientation, identity, purpose, integration and social belonging may all be threatened. Anxiety, fragmentation and aloneness may increase. In short, challenging beliefs that have become core beliefs will cause a person to feel threatened, and thus defensive measures such as physical threats, shouting people down denial, refusal to listen and avoidance may follow. The continuation of such dissonance may lead to psychological problems.

Sometimes, new information is REFRAMED to fit in with the existing belief system. Thus when the 'Aliens will destroy the world tomorrow' prophecy fails, rather than admit failure, the believer may say that the aliens changed their minds as a result of the prophet's efforts at warning the world, even when no such efforts have been made, because it is too costly to personal integrity and cohesiveness to declare that the whole thing was a mistake. Time, effort and money had been invested in the belief that the world would end... perhaps homes and jobs were given up, and preparations made...

Beliefs are VALIDATED by reference to others, (SOCIAL REFERENTS) the world itself and our internal system. We constantly MONITOR and REVIEW our position by earning new information and via SOCIAL COMPARISON with: AUTHORITY FIGURES WE RESPECT: Scientists, religious leaders, experts. PEERS: Friends in and out of the groups to which we belong. RELATIVES.

The PRESSURES that such people can exert on our beliefs is very high, and hence they can affect our behaviour, emotions and sense of identity. (See; Zimbardo, Milgram).

Our beliefs are imbued with VALUES _ e.g. good, bad, right, wrong or worthy. We have our own INTERNAL VALUE SYSTEM - what WE think is good, right e.t.c., which though to a great degree learned from others, is nevertheless our own. Such values are linked to our sensations of pleasant/unpleasant, and are thus linked to our motives.

However, society in general has values, as do the groups to which a person belongs. This there may be DISSONANCE between our own beliefs/values and those of the society/group. To some degree this is overcome by presenting oneself to the group in such a way as is acceptable to them, and thus one is accepted by them. However, too much dissonance will result in pressure. Refusal to present oneself in an acceptable manner may maintain integrity but create the anxiety of rejection. The more important the acceptance of others is to us, the" more pressure we feel to conform.

SUMMARY 2

Our interrelated beliefs, which affect so many aspects of ourselves, help to give us orientation, identity, purpose, cohesiveness, a sense of security and understanding. New information is slotted into our schemes and/or our schemes may be changed to accommodate new information. Core beliefs, closely related to our integrated sense of self, may be difficult to change, such change making us feel threatened and vulnerable. We often validate our beliefs by comparing ourselves with others, some of whom may exert considerable pressure on us to modify or maintain existing beliefs, and the values linked with them, in order to maintain their acceptance of us and the coherence and identity of the group.

Because our beliefs are so intimately connected to our emotions, behaviours, motives, expectations, integrity, identity and belonging, we are NOT LOGICAL BEINGS, because all the above factors intrude on our logic.

Typical examples of non-logical thinking include magical or mythical thinking. Thus for example we may interpret events occurring closely in time as causal, e.g. 'I was just thinking about Joe and the 'phone rings and it's Joe on the line... ' We may infer that our thought somehow induced him to ring. So we may consider that there are special powers or an interconnectedness that we cannot explain. Thus, autistic people have no sense of the fact that other people have intentions, or are capable of deceit by saying one thing and meaning another. One autistic person on seeing the ability of someone to infer another person's thoughts by their body-language, ascribed this to special powers. Our use of magical thinking is affected by context. Though amazed by an illusionist's tricks at a magic show, we ascribe it to sleight of hand. The same trick carried out a fortune-teller, or prophet, or person claiming special powers, may induce magical thinking.

Mythical thinking occurs at a different level. It is more concerned with grand schemes, issues of destiny, salvation of mankind and so on. It is an attempt to answer these grand questions and may involve fundamentalist religion, New Age beliefs, cults and so on. These ideas usually involve gods, spirits, saviours, heroes, fate, destiny, grand purposes of the universe, the battle between good and evil and such like.

Magical and mythical thinking are regressive forms of belief that offer us a return to child-like security and comfort in the face of a harsh existential reality. In this case, the feelings of comfort and safety offered by such beliefs, together with a sense of belonging when such ideas are shared in a like-minded group, override considerations of truth and logic.

1996

WHY CAN LEAVING FUNDAMENTALISM BE SO HARD?

Why is leaving so very hard? People join and leave groups all the time. Well, a Christian fundamentalist group is not like a youth group, or camera club or amateur dramatics group. Although all groups share certain characteristics in common, they are taken to a higher level in a fundamentalist group and there are extra considerations too. I was involved in Christian Fundamentalism actively for about fifteen years and after that, on and off for about ten years. Leaving was one of the most difficult things I ever did. What sort of factors created the difficulties?

a) COMMITMENT. We all commit to any group that we belong to varying degrees, but fundamentalist church groups may engender a very deep level of commitment over time. The more your commitment and investment into the group, the more difficult it is to leave. A member of a fundamentalist group may be a lay preacher, or Sunday school teacher, or Youth leader. They may be a deacon, serving in the church. Even an ordinary member may commit and invest a vast amount of time and energy into the group and its activities. They may commit their money via tithes and gifts. When this has been done over a number of years, it is difficult to say 'Gee, it was all a mistake, a waste of time, money and effort.'

b) FELLOWSHIP. Christian fundamentalist groups often provide a terrific sense of unity, a sense of common purpose engendering intense friendships. There can be a real sense of community and belonging, a closeness and connection sometimes polarizing us (the elect, the people of God) with them (the unbeliever, the world). This unity is based on an orthodox identity and purpose – Christian fundamentalism is highly orthodox, tracing a line and tradition back to the Apostles and disciples. This sense of fellowship is something that I miss to this day. I have only seen indications of such a level of connectedness in certain sports teams and in the armed services, both of which function at a level of development called mythic – the same as Christian fundamentalism. This camaraderie works really well when all its members are singing from the same hymn sheet. But once one questions the wisdom of the orthodoxy, once one questions say the nature of the Bible, or Divinity of Christ, then the cohesion and identity of the group is threatened, and the dissenting person may be seen as divisive, schismatic, deluded, oppressed by evil spirits, backsliding, apostate, heretical e.t.c. If the dissenting opinion is persisted in, the dissenting person faces rejection, Loss of friendships, Distancing from the group, Isolation, Criticism, Judgmental attitudes, being outcast/excommunicated, increasing attempts by group members to manipulate the dissenter to conformity to group norms. The Christian Fundamentalist group is a semi-closed community. It has a certain withdrawal from the world and from unbelievers. Thus standards and norms of behaviour and belief are defined by the group and by authoritative group members such as teachers and elders. Christians may have unbelievers in their social circle as work colleagues or as neighbours and acquaintances, but they are not usually trusted friends. Thus values, meaning, purpose, significance, reward, and identity; all core personal issues, become partly or mainly defined by the group in its teaching and practice and cemented by cohesive activities such as outreach programs, painting the church e.t.c.

c) CONNECTION WITH THE ULTIMATE Christian fundamentalism is about connection with the Ultimate: with the Ultimate Person (God) and with Ultimate Endings (Heaven, Hell, Judgement). Therefore, falling out of favour with this group raises the possibility of putting at stake one's relationship with God and one's future eternal state. Christian fundamentalism gives a sense of ultimate meaning, purpose and ful fillment. An ultimate sense of place and reason for existence in the Universe. An ultimate set of moral and philosophical/theological values. An ultimate personal identity as a son and heir of God. To leave or be excluded is to feel cut adrift, aimless, uncertain and empty. Worse, it is to be accused of or to feel a betrayer of God, a Judas. Because conduct, sentiments and beliefs which do not conform to group orthodoxy – to the 'right way' – are condemned, such condemnation is also linked to the Ultimate – thus by expressing doubts about fundamentalism, a dissenter is portrayed as betraying God, letting God down, incurring God's providential judgement. Thus, though a person may have doubts about aspects of fundamentalism, they may nevertheless still believe in God and find themselves threatened with God's wrath, a threat which would remain very real to them.

d) BELIEFS, PRACTICE, IDENTITY AND GUILT. If a person expresses doubts about some basic aspect of fundamentalist belief then they, as a person, are identified as a sinner, backslider, apostate, and rebel e.t.c. There is not usually any halfway point – it is usually black and white: sheep and goats, saved and damned. This is as opposed to saying something like: 'He is a sincere seeker after truth who is expressing doubt about an aspect of our shared faith.' or 'He is a pilgrim walking along a path with ever-changing scenery as he discovers the infinity of God'. Thus, because of this black and white thinking, it is difficult to leave with honour and respect when moving to a new theological position not embraced by the group's orthodoxy. Healthy psychology separates what a person thinks, believes and does from who they are in essence. Thus a misbehaving child is not bad, or stupid child, but a loved child who did a bad or stupid thing. Even so, Christian fundamentalism may emphasize the doctrine of Total Depravity – the idea that we are, by nature, by reason of our very existence, sinners, corrupt, rebellious, ignorant, deluded and opposed to God. Though common in a number of religious approaches, it can be used to engender conformity – if you disagree with us, you must be sinning and therefore wrong and therefore in danger of God's Judgement - sort of thing. Thus dissenting opinion is

224

stifled by threat of disapproval, both of the group and its leaders and God, with all that implies.

e) SECURE WORLDVIEW. Christian Fundamentalism offers a bounded, ordered and therefore secure worldview. A Bible based worldview offers a set of boundaries – do this and you will live, do that and you will be blessed e.t.c. More than this it is an ordered Universe, with god overseeing everything with a special eye on his favoured children such that all things are working together for good. More than this, some Christian Fundamentalist schemes, such as Calvinism, are seductively coherent. Once certain assumptions are accepted, the scheme makes a lot of sense, systematically interrelating the various Bible passages. All this offers a comfortable, secure world perspective, reinforced by the mutual acceptance of this view by fellow believers and by authority figures and experts within the group such as teachers and Elders.

f) INTENSE SPIRITUAL EXPERIENCE. One of the greatest barriers preventing me from leaving fundamentalism was the experience on a number of occasions, within fundamentalism, of intense spiritual transcendence and closeness with God; what is known as the Baptism/Fullness/Extraordinary Witness of the Spirit, sometimes experienced by whole communities in awakenings or revivals. These were experiences of being 'caught up' to God; of an immediate and powerful assurance; of being fully persuaded; of one's mind being opened to the Reality of Divine Things. (Blessed Assurance! Jesus is mine! Oh! What a foretaste of glory divine!'....'Visions of rapture burst on my sight'.) With these experiences, Calvinist Christian Fundamentalist ideas and notions were indelibly impressed on my mind and heart by transcendent experience. They were difficult or impossible to shake off. During those experiences I never felt so clear headed. So how can this be reconciled to leaving fundamentalism and fundamentalist theology? This question has to do with the nature of Ultimate Reality, the Infinite One Formless God expressed in an infinity of multiple forms. It is an aspect of theology called Theomorphism.

g) RELATIONSHIP WITH THE LEADER/ELDER. For me this was more of a personal issue than one necessarily linked to Christian fundamentalism per se. In other words, I would have had problems with this guy in whatever circumstance we met. But this can be a wider problem engendered by a distortion of the shepherd/sheep syndrome where the shepherd, the leader, is too authoritarian: manipulating and controlling those they oversee, and the sheep, the church member, too sheepish: too inclined to follow rather than thinking for themselves. Such blind following of authority can lead to a dependency relationship where the member is always trying to please the father-figure of the leader/elder – trying to be a good child. Indeed, those familiar with Transactional Analysis may recognise a pattern. In my case, the pastor was operating from Critical Parent ego state – dispensing disapproval in the name of God and high standards and had a patronizing attitude using words like 'should, must, ought, sinful, bad' e.t.c., with disapproving looks and frowns. This mode of operating tries to put the other person into (obedient) Child ego state. Thus instead of two adults reasoning together, we have a patronizing Critical Parent making the other person feel like a disobedient child. There are two Child ego states however: Submissive Child – the sheep – always trying to please and be good, over keen to show their 'superiors' respect; or the Rebellious Child – the person refusing to be pigeonholed, kicking against the rules, being a non conformist, probably trying to restore their Adult ego state. (That was me). This is a dysfunctional transaction pattern. As I say, this would have happened in the workplace, or anywhere with me and this guy, but it is an element to be aware of. The teacher pupil relationship is not necessarily a bad one, and generally does involve a certain inequality – expert versus learner, professor versus student, but it does not have to dysfunctional.

Positively, for me, Christian fundamentalism also engendered:
I) An awakening to and an awareness of spirituality and the Divine.
II) A sense of personal integrity – being honest and true to myself and God – being authentic
III) A desire for Truth – wherever that takes me.
IV) A courage to stand by my principles and by truth as I see it – without feeling the need to impose my Ideas and values on others.
These are the very qualities that led me out of Christian Fundamentalism. Why is it difficult to leave? Take all the points I have raised in this article and a few more, in complex interplay, and you have some idea.

To leave is to
a) Say one's past full commitment of time, energy and money was a mistake
b) Be rejected and isolated from a close community of friends – social severance and loss with no real friends amongst unbelievers to replace and make up for that loss.

226

c) Lose one's sense of identity, meaning and purpose.
d) Feel that one may incurring the wrath of an angry God and be in danger of everlasting punishment.
e) Be adrift and alone in an unbelieving world - which may be perceived as chaotic, hostile and immoral.
f) Lose one's sense of order and certainty
g) Feel guilty and in conflict
h) Feel vulnerable and fearful
i) Feel frustrated and angry
j) Lose one's sense of orientation.
k) Be possibly isolated and alone

Leaving Fundamentalism may be the most difficult, courageous and honest thing you ever do.It requires careful thought and a gradual establishing of another, alternative social support network which may initially be seen as fellowship with the world. It may be risky to your health and psychological well-being.

GROUPS, SECTS AND CULTS

Some broad definitions.

Groups. There are many religious groupings for example within Christianity, such as Roman Catholics, Methodists, and Anglicans. All these are seen as legitimate groups, with different emphases, accents and traditions within the broad spectrum of Christianity. They may not always see eye to eye, but generally recognise each other's legitimate existence.

Sects. These are usually short lived, small groups or factions. They may arise as the result of a charismatic leader, or out of disaffection with the status quo. They may be small or large in number and may be quite active and vocal. They may decay on the death of the leader or be re absorbed into a mainstream group. Examples of this include Primitive Methodism or Puritanism. Sometimes they go on to achieve legitimacy, becoming a group in their own right. Christianity was originally a Jewish sect.

Cults. This is a negative term. It generally refers to a group or sect that has sinister aspects to it, such as attempts at coercion. In various ways they are dysfunctional, unhealthy groups.

CULTS

There are four main types: Religious, Political, Therapy/educational, and Commercial.

They do not carry out brainwashing. Brainwashing is overt, coercive and it is plain who the enemy is. Rather they carry out mind control or thought reform. Here, the perpetrators are

a) regarded as friends or peers making the candidate less defensive.
b) The candidate participates unwittingly with their controllers, for example by giving private information.
c) The new belief system is internalised into a new identity structure.
d) The group may use hypnotic processes and group dynamics.

THE COMPONENTS OF MIND CONTROL

1)   BEHAVIOUR CONTROL

By regulating the environment:
a)   Where you live
b)   What clothing you wear
c)   What food you eat
d)   How much sleep you have
e)   What jobs and goals you have.
f)   Rituals and indoctrination
g)   Restriction of free time – sometimes an apocalyptic sense of urgency
h)   Financial dependency
i)   Permission required to do things, i.e. phone relative
j)   Suppression of individuality to group conformity
k)   Pyramidical authoritarian command structure
l)   Use of punishment and reward, often keeping members off balance – praised one day, punished the next.
m)   Use of mannerisms of speech and posture
n)   Regulation of interpersonal relationships – emotional allegiance to leader – no real friends because if the person leaves they may take others with them.
o)   Group activities which creates privacy deprivation and thwarts reflection.

2)   **THOUGHT CONTROL**

By indoctrination, such that beliefs are internalised.

a)   Group has the Truth – the only map of reality. This moulds and filters incoming data. The doctrine is reality, the most effective being those which are unverifiable – global yet vague but apparently consistent. Reality is externally referenced via an authority figure and other members who are looked to for direction and meaning.
b)   Black and white thinking – Group is good, outsiders bad. Thus good vs evil, Us vs them, Spiritual vs physical. No pluralism or multi perspective taking.
c)   Group beliefs are scientifically proven and explain everything
d)   Loaded language. E.g. A Cain and Abel problem
e)   Blocking out critical thoughts by:
i)   Denial: "What you say is not happening at all"

ii) Rationalisation: "It is happening for a good reason"
iii) Justification: "It is happening because it ought to"
iv) Wishful thinking: "I would like it to be true so maybe it is"
v) Demonising: "Lies put about by Satan/Persecution that we would expect".
vi) Thought stopping: By chanting/ tongue speaking
vii) Punishment: Being given the silent treatment or transfer to another group e.t.c.

3) **EMOTIONAL CONTROL**

Emotions are controlled by the use of:

a) Guilt: in order to produce conformity and compliance. Guilt takes a number of aspects:
i) Historical guilt. – We dropped the bomb on Hiroshima
ii) Identity guilt – "I'm not living up to my potential"
iii) Past guilt – "I cheated on a test" A persons past is rewritten: everything is dark
iv) Social guilt – People are dying of starvation
v) Quality guilt- not meeting standards

b) Fear: By creating an outside enemy – unbelievers, Satan, therapists.
Of discovery and punishment by leaders
A major motivator.
c) Happiness: As defined by the group. Obtained by good performance and/or confession
d) Loyalty and devotion.
e) Confession of past sins – this is often used against the person.
f) Phobia indoctrination. Induced panic reaction at the thought of leaving. Dark stories are told of those who have left both in lectures and informal gossip. The idea of the Devil waiting to seduce and tempt, kill or drive insane. The more vivid and tangible, the more intense the cohesiveness it fosters.

4) **INFORMATION CONTROL**

The control of destabilising information by:

a) Denial of information so that sound judgements cannot be made. E.g. minimal access to T.V., non-group magazines, newspapers or radio. Partially achieved through busyness.
b) Criticism of the leader with peers not allowed
c) Members report improper activities to leader.
d) New converts do not talk to one another without a chaperone
e) Contact with ex members and critics avoided.
f) Compartmentalisation of information so that members do not know the 'big picture'.
g) Multi levelled truth- the higher you are, the more is revealed.
   i) For outsiders
   ii) For members
   iii) For leaders
   iv) For high leaders

THE PROCESSES OF MIND CONTROL

There are three steps:
1) Unfreezing
2) Changing
3) Refreezing

1) **UNFREEZING.**

This is a shaking up and disorientation. A breaking up of the frames of reference used by the person for understanding themselves and their surroundings. This disarms the person's defences against concepts that challenge reality.

Approaches include:
a) Physiological disorientation via sleep deprivation, new diets and eating schedules. Often best accomplished in a totally controlled environment such as a retreat at a country estate.

231

b) Hypnotic processes such as the deliberate use of confusion via contradictory information.
c) Sensory overload – being bombarded with material faster than it can be digested.
d) Use of double binds – "I am putting doubts in your mind".
e) Group exercises –
1) Guided meditation.
2) Personal confession
3) Prayer sessions
4) Group singing
5) Vigorous callisthenics
Group activities enforce privacy deprivation and reflection.
f) As people weaken – A bombardment with the idea that the person is badly flawed, mentally ill, incompetent or spiritually fallen. Any identified problems are blown out of all proportion. There may be humiliation in front of the group.

2) **CHANGING**

The imposition of a new identity, a new set of thoughts, emotions and behaviours to fill the void of unfreezing. This takes place:

a) Formally in lectures, seminars and rituals
b) Informally –in spending time with members, reading, listening to tapes, watching videos.

The approaches to change include:
a) Repetition, monotony and rhythm – the hypnotic cadences in which formal indoctrination is delivered
b) A focus on central themes:
1) The world is bad.
2) The unenlightened do not know how to fix it
3) The old self keeps you from experiencing the new truth fully.
4) Old concepts drag you down.
5) The rational mind holds you back – let go.
c) The material for the new identity is given out gradually – "Tell him only what he can accept." "Milk for the baby, meat for the adult"
d) Artificially induced spiritual experience. Private information is secretly passed and revealed at the appropriate time as an 'insight'.

e) Asking for God's will for them. Via prayer and study. The implication is that joining the group is God's will, leaving is not.
f) Group processes:
1) Being surrounded by people who are convinced that they know what is best for you.
2) Via cells or small groups- questioners and doubters may be isolated into their own group.
3) Sharing sessions with ordinary members, where past evils are confessed, present successes told and a sense of community fostered.

3) REFREEZING.

This is the building up of the new person, giving them a new purpose and new activities to solidify the new identity. New beliefs are internalised by the person.

Approaches include

a) Denigration of the old self, maximising sins, failings, hurt and guilt.
b) Modelling. The new member is paired with an older member whom they should emulate.
c) The group is the member's new family.
d) Possible giving of a new name.
e) Turning over the bank account – subsequently it may be too painful to admit this mistake.
f) Sleep deprivation, lack of privacy, diet changes continued.
g) New location – no links with the past – only the new identity here.
h) Evangelising/prosteletizing – selling one's own beliefs to others to firm up one's own beliefs.
i) Difficult and humiliating fund raising. Can provoke a sense of glorious martyrdom.

General comments

There is no **legitimate** way to leave a cult.

233

The result of these processes is a dual identity - the old self does not disappear, but occasionally surfaces in humour, and greater emotional range and spontaneity. But it is clothed in the new cult self such that the person is more robot-like, rigid and cold-eyed. But the real identity holds the key to escape and to the inner desires. These emerge via psychosomatic illness, requiring outside treatment, dreams of being trapped, concentration camps e.t.c. and spiritual experiences, of voices telling them to leave e.t.c..

Problems in the group are always the fault of the member, due to:
a)   His weakness
b)   His lack of understanding
c)   Bad ancestors
d)   Evil spirits
e)   His inadequacies.

ANALYSING AND ASSESSING GROUPS

Look at what the group does, not at what it believes. They have the right to believe what they want, but they do not have an automatic licence to act on those beliefs, else white supremacy groups would kill all blacks for example. Destructive groups undermine individual choice and liberty.

TOWARDS A TWENTY FIRST CENTURY CHRISTIANITY

INTRODUCTION

For a number of years I was a Christian Fundamentalist. I wholeheartedly accepted a Calvinistic framework of Christian theology and led Bible studies and preached in my local church, serving there as a deacon. However, the advent of bi-polar disorder which caused severe mood changes from acute anxiety to acute depression coupled with a fear for my very sanity and other issues from my upbringing all served to put a severe stress on my Christian Fundamentalist conceptual framework of the Divine. In many respects, my Christian faith proved to be a firm rock and foundation during those very uncertain and unstable years, providing me with an anchor and stability when all else seemed to be collapsing. Furthermore, personal mystical experiences served to strengthen and establish this framework of belief. But, my trauma and vulnerability during these years, coupled with an insistent questioning of the nature of revelation and inspiration as a result of my mystical spiritual experiences brought me to question the whole foundation of Christian Fundamentalism – the Bible - and therefore its view of Jesus. For thirty-five years, the impact of Christian Fundamentalism and its views, strengthened and deepened by my heightened spiritual experiences, could not be fully let go of. It is only recently that I have finally got somewhere near the foundation of my study on revelation, inspiration and the Bible – a Bible claimed by Christian fundamentalists to be the inspired revelation of God – to be God's very Word. Only as the result of a tenacious and determined exploration of theology and psychology in order to get at the root of these things has the pathway finally opened up for me to be able to reappraise the founding teacher of the Christian faith – Jesus.

I miss the camaraderie and fellowship of those 'heady' days in the 1970's. I had a sense of direction, purpose, identity, meaning, value and friendship that I have not recovered or improved on since. I guess other institutions such as the armed forces may provide similar experiences and certainly I do not think that such sentiments are limited to religious experience. So of course, there is part of me that would love to go back to such a sense of meaningful spiritual community but I cannot do so by embracing the ideas that I once did. I have moved on and cannot return to that philosophy. Perhaps though I could cut through the Christian Fundamentalist mentality to embrace a more realistic set of ideas about Jesus, - who he was and what he taught - and to use this revised theology, this new theology, this neo-orthodoxy as a new spiritual conceptual framework that has enough commonality with conventional Christian fellowship to enable me to join a Christian community again. Hence this study – an attempt to get to the roots and foundation of who Jesus was and what he taught – an attempt to strip away the layers of institutionalised theology and centuries of assumptions and presumptions – an attempt by a spiritual minded pilgrim to get back to the basics and foundation of Christianity.

THE HEBREW CHISTIAN SECT

When we look at Christianity, we see that Jesus Christ, the founder of the movement, had been an itinerant preacher, teacher and faith healer and had pursued this ministry for about three years after being baptized by John the Baptist. Though popular with the people he was nearly always at odds with the religious establishment and he caused quite a stir amongst them. They eventually found him guilty of blasphemy, handed him over the governor of the province who sentenced him to death by crucifixion. However, the body of Jesus was soon missing from the tomb and there were claims that he had risen from the dead. The Jews who followed Jesus, his disciples, were initially full of fear and anxiety, but following some experiences whereby they see Jesus after his death, a Jewish Christian sect becomes established in Jerusalem where they remain. They meet in the temple for worship – and become one of a number of Jewish groups or sects.

PAUL – HIS CONVERSION, CALLING AND TEACHING

However, these Jewish Christians were not always readily accepted by mainstream orthodox Jews, with one Jew in particular, a Jewish Pharisee and expert in Jewish law, named Saul, taking particular exception to what he saw as a corrupting group within Judaism. He decided to make it his business to eradicate this troublesome deviant group within Judaism and thus keep the purity of the Jewish religion and practice. He obtained authority to arrest and punish any Jewish Christians that he found and whilst on this purifying mission he too had a vision of Jesus while he was walking on the Damascus Road. In the vision, Saul (later known as Paul) is called by God to be an Apostle to the gentiles or non-Jews. This visionary event occurred about two to three years after Jesus had been crucified. Paul himself tells us that in response to this vision: 'my immediate response was not to consult any human being. I did not go up to Jerusalem to see those who were apostles before I was, but I went into Arabia. Later I returned to Damascus. Then after three years, I went up to Jerusalem to get acquainted with Peter and stayed with him fifteen days. I saw none of the other apostles—only James, the Lord's brother. I assure you before God that what I am writing you is no lie. Then I went to Syria and Cilicia. I was personally unknown to the churches of Judea that are in Christ. They only heard the report: 'The man who formerly persecuted us is now preaching the faith he once tried to destroy.' And they praised God because of me.

Then after fourteen years, I went up again to Jerusalem, this time with Barnabas. I took Titus along also. I went in response to a revelation and, meeting privately with those esteemed as leaders, I presented to them the gospel that I preach among the Gentiles. I wanted to be sure I was not running and had not been running my race in vain. Yet not even Titus, who was with me, was compelled to be circumcised, even though he was a Greek. This matter arose because some false believers had infiltrated our ranks to spy on the freedom we have in Christ Jesus and to make us slaves [to the Hebrew Law and practice of circumcision]. We did not give in to them for a moment, so that the truth of the gospel might be preserved for you. As for those who were held in high esteem—whatever they were makes no difference to me; God does not show favouritism—they added nothing to my message. On the contrary, they recognized that I had been entrusted with the task of preaching the gospel to the uncircumcised, just as Peter had been to the circumcised, or

237

Jews. For God, who was at work in Peter as an apostle to the circumcised, was also at work in me as an apostle to the Gentiles. James, Cephas and John, those esteemed as pillars, gave me and Barnabas the right hand of fellowship when they recognized the grace given to me. They agreed that we should go to the Gentiles, and they to the circumcised. All they asked was that we should continue to remember the poor, the very thing I had been eager to do all along.
(Paul's letter to the Galatians Ch1 v 11 – Ch 2 v 10)

PAUL AND THE HEBREW CHRISTIAN APOSTLES

The Council of Jerusalem (or Apostolic Conference) is a name applied by historians to this early Christian council that was held in Jerusalem and it is dated to around the year 50 AD. The council decided that Gentile converts to Christianity were not obligated to keep most of the Mosaic law, including the rules concerning circumcision of males, however, the Council did retain the prohibitions against eating blood, or eating meat containing blood, or meat of animals not properly slain and against fornication and idolatry. Descriptions of the council are found in Acts of the Apostles chapter 15 (in two different forms, the Alexandrian and Western versions) and also possibly in Paul's letter to the Galatians chapter 2 which I have just quoted. Some scholars dispute that Galatians 2 is about the *Council of Jerusalem* (notably because Galatians 2 describes a private meeting) while other scholars dispute the historical reliability of the Acts of the Apostles. Paul was most likely an eyewitness, a major person in attendance, whereas Luke, the writer of Luke-Acts, who was a later follower of Paul, may not have been in attendance and thus may have written second-hand, about the meeting he described Acts 15.

PAUL'S MESSAGE AND THEOLOGY

Paul says that the Jewish Christians did not add anything to his message, which, after the Damascus Road experience can be summarised as something like:

Repent and have a new mind and turn to God
Demonstrate repentance by your deeds.
Jesus Christ is God's Son.

Christ died for our sins according to the Scriptures.
He was buried
He was raised on the third day according to the Scriptures

But over seventeen years, Paul receives more visions – more teaching – and elaborates on his initial theology to produce a more complex theology and to a basic message that declares:

God is Creator of all things and Sovereign
God is alive
God is transcendent of created things and Self-sufficient
God is present everywhere
God is not without a witness as to His existence.
f)   God's provision of rain, crops, food and joy is a witness.
g)   Creation is a witness.
God is Just
God is a moral judge:
c)   Of the whole world
d)   He will judge the world by a man
h)   He has appointed a time for judgement
i)   He has given proof of the coming judgement to all men or nations
j)   Christ's resurrection from the dead is the proof and we are witnesses of this
God is kind – His kindness is shown in His provision of life and food
God's desire for us is that-
d)   We should seek Him
e)   We should reach out for Him
f)   We should find Him.
God commands all men, everywhere, all nations
a)   To repent
b)   To turn from worthless idols
c)   To turn to the living God.
Demonstrate repentance by your deeds.
Jesus Christ is God's Son.
Christ died for our sins.
He was buried
He was raised on the third day

239

CHRISTIAN WRITINGS AND THEIR DEVELOPMENT

It is at about the time of this Jerusalem Council in A.D. 50 that we find the oldest Christian writings – which are in fact the writings of Paul – a series of letters and epistles written from A.D. 50 to A.D. 62 – seventeen to thirty years after the death of Jesus. It is a theology that has developed and matured over this time. From his visions and revelations, Paul elaborated a theology concerning Jesus whereby he is the Messiah/Redeemer and God's supreme sacrificial offering to pay the price for the sins and transgressions of believers. Jesus is presented as eternally co-equal with God, humbled in time and space to come to us in the likeness of flesh, but, following his crucifixion, he is raised up from the dead as a guarantee of the future resurrection of humanity to the Final Judgment and the restoration of all things. Whereas the old Jewish Law was powerless to accomplish this, in the New Covenant established by Jesus, these Laws, both ceremonial and moral, are superseded and transcended by a new relationship to God through Jesus and a righteousness gained not by our works and obedience to the law, but rather imputed to us by and through faith in God. The True Israel is not the Jewish nation with its sign of circumcision, but rather it is the spiritual Israel – those who have faith in God. Thus all Israel will be redeemed, having a righteousness by faith, imputed to them and credited to their account. This exalted view of Jesus is further developed and elaborated in the tradition of John's later gospel.

We should remember that none of the gospels present in our Bible had been written when Paul was writing his own epistles which is why he does not refer to them. Indeed, they will not be written for another ten to twenty years. There is possibly a 'sayings' gospel – a book of the words of Jesus – but not a gospel describing his life and works. Also, the different groups within Judaism and the newly emergent Christianity mean that writings with different emphases begin to emerge – some emphasising the Jewishness of Jesus and his adherence to the Law for example, others emphasising views of his Divinity and his miraculous works and yet others claiming to be written by the Apostles out of reverence for them and following their particular teaching, though they were actually written by their followers. All the time, the idea of the Divinity of Jesus is growing and thus as a general trend we may speculate that the later the gospel is written, the more references they tend to have to events such as the virgin birth, miracles and so on – until we end up with the gospel attributed to John written about A.D. 90-100 – containing the most of these kinds of references – where Jesus is the pre-existent Word of God made incarnate flesh for example. John presents a higher Christology than Matthew, Mark or Luke, describing Jesus as the incarnation of the divine Logos through whom all things were made. Only in John does Jesus talk at length about himself and his divine role, conversations that are often shared with the disciples only. Against the other gospels of the canon, the gospel attributed to John focuses largely on different miracles, given as signs that are meant to engender faith. Synoptic elements such as parables and exorcisms are not found in the gospel attributed to John. The gospel attributed to John presents a more realized eschatology in which salvation is already present for the believer.

VISIONS, REVELATION AND GNOSTICISM

What is important for us to consider here is the foundation of this early Christian teaching. The original foundation in both the cases of the disciples of Jesus and the Apostle Paul is *visions*. It is through visions and appearances that Paul and the other Disciples/Apostles are persuaded that Jesus has risen from the dead. It is through visions and appearances that they have further teaching/revelation. It is through an appearance that Jesus is seen as ascending to the clouds. Paul describes his Damascus Road experience as such himself: 'So then, King Agrippa, I was not disobedient to the vision from heaven.' (Acts 26). In these accounts, Jesus appears and disappears, enters locked rooms such that they think they have seen a ghost and so on. We can discover what the Apostles themselves understood concerning the nature of these visions and appearances by looking at one of the groups within the early church – the Christian Gnostics.

Early Christianity was not one simple group but very quickly consisted of a wide variety of groups emphasising different traditions and aspects. One such group within Christianity was the Gnostics – themselves a diverse group who had esoteric beliefs with origins in paganism – but who began to adopt and merge some Christian ideas with their own, creating a strand of Christian Gnosticism. Valentinus (also spelled Valentinius) (c.100 - c.160) was the best known Christian Gnostic and for a time the most successful early Christian Gnostic theologian. He founded his school in Rome and according to Tertullian, Valentinus was a candidate for the bishop of Rome, but started his own group when another person was chosen for this role.

The word 'esoteric' means 'pertaining to the more inward': mystical. The dictionary defines 'esoteric' as information that is understood by a small group or those specially initiated, or of rare or unusual interest. Esotericism therefore refers to the holding of secret doctrines, the practice of limiting knowledge to a small group, or an interest in items of a special, rare, novel, or unusual quality. 'Mysticism' is 'the pursuit of communion with, identity with, or conscious awareness of God through direct experience, intuition, instinct or insight'. Mysticism usually centres on a practice or practices that are intended to nurture such spiritual experiences or awareness. 'Gnosticism' (Greek: γνῶσις *gnōsis*, knowledge) refers to a form of mystical, revealed, esoteric knowledge and this notion of immediate revelation through divine knowledge seeks to find absolute transcendence in a Supreme Deity. The ancient Nag Hammadi Library, discovered in Egypt in the 1940s, revealed how varied the Gnostic movement was. The writers of these manuscripts considered themselves 'Christians', but their syncretistic beliefs borrowed heavily from the Greek philosopher Plato.

PAUL'S CHRISTIANITY AND CHRISTIAN GNOSTICISM

If the whole basis and foundation of the Apostle Paul's theology is grounded upon visions and revelations and if the post-resurrection appearances of Jesus can be explained at least in part by similar revelatory visions experienced by the disciples, then why was there an antagonism towards the mystical element brought to the church by Gnostics and the Christian teachers in the early church? Why weren't the visions, revelations and gnosis of these esoteric believers accepted by the Apostles and Elders when such experiences appear to lie at the very heart of the foundation of Christianity itself? If we look at some of the verses from the Bible relating to Gnosticism, we can note that these are all from secondary writers – that is, they are probably not written by the Apostle Paul even though they are attributed to him, but rather probably written by close followers of Paul:

'As I urged you when I went into Macedonia, stay there in Ephesus so that you may command certain people not to teach false doctrines any longer or to devote themselves to myths and endless genealogies. Such things promote controversial speculations rather than advancing God's work—which is by faith. The goal of this command is love, which comes from a pure heart and a good conscience and a sincere faith'. (I Timothy 1 v 3-5)

'For the time will come when people will not put up with sound doctrine. Instead, to suit their own desires, they will gather around them a great number of teachers to say what their itching ears want to hear. They will turn their ears away from the truth and turn aside to myths'. (II Timothy 4 v 3 – 4)

'Do not let anyone who delights in false humility and the worship of angels disqualify you. Such a person also goes into great detail about what they have seen; they are puffed up with idle notions by their unspiritual mind. They have lost connection with the head, from whom the whole body, supported and held together by its ligaments and sinews, grows as God causes it to grow'. (Colossians 2 v 18-19)

I want to suggest that the Apostle Paul together with the Apostles in Jerusalem believed that in their visions and revelations they encountered an *objective* phenomenon, namely the real Jesus literally appearing 'out there'. In the same way, at the transfiguration of Jesus, I think that the disciples thought that they saw the real Moses and Elijah as real tangible 'objects out there':

'After six days Jesus took Peter, James and John with him and led them up a high mountain, where they were all alone. There he was transfigured before them. His clothes became dazzling white, whiter than anyone in the world could bleach them. And there appeared before them Elijah and Moses, who were talking with Jesus. Peter said to Jesus, "Rabbi, it is good for us to be here. Let us put up three shelters—one for you, one for Moses and one for Elijah." (He did not know what to say, they were so frightened.) Then a cloud appeared and covered them, and a voice came from the cloud: "This is my Son, whom I love. Listen to him!" Suddenly, when they looked around, they no longer saw anyone with them except Jesus.' (Mark 9 v 2 – 8)

THE NATURE OF VISIONS AND APPEARANCES

There are two distinguishing features about Christian (and probably Hebrew) visionary experiences:

d) What is seen in the vision is considered as existing objectively 'out there' – it is not just a subjective, imaginary experience produced by and in the mind.

e) What is seen is a real person – like Jesus, Moses or Elijah – as opposed to mythical or imaginary persons or deities like Zeus.

f) In angelic visitations, the Angels were considered to be objectively real – they were not mythical fantasies and neither were they just a subjective or symbolic creation of the mind and imagination. They were real, objectively existing spirit-beings.

It would seem then that in these visions, the recipients believed that they were seeing the actual, real, people – people such as Moses, Elijah and Jesus – people who had actually existed and been alive but who were now dead; or they believed that they were seeing real, objectively existing spirit-beings. They were not seeing fantasy figures or mythical beings or symbolic creations from their minds and imaginations. Paul did not consider that he had received some kind of presentation that had arisen solely in his mind or imagination, or from his sub-conscious, or that his imagination and mind had been stimulated in some way to present to his mind a subjective, symbolic representation of a Jesus-like figure. No, he believed that he had actually met the objectively existing, real, historical, once-dead and now-resurrected Jesus in his vision, as opposed to some fantasy or myth created in his mind or some mere, what we would call today, psychological/emotional/cathartic experience. This is why Paul says, 'Have I not seen Jesus our Lord?' even though there is no evidence that he ever met Jesus prior to his crucifixion. (I Corinthians 9 v 1). Paul sees *no difference* between his visionary, revelatory experiences of Jesus such as that in his Damascus Road experience and the experiences of the other eminent Apostles, that is, those who were in Jerusalem and who were with Jesus when he was alive: 'for [says Paul] I am not in the least inferior to the most eminent apostles' (II Corinthians 12 v 11).

This is why connection with the head – Jesus – is so important to Paul and his followers. For them it is the seeing of the objectively existing real, once-dead and now-resurrected Jesus coupled with the faithful following of the teaching received in this (and probably other) encounter(s) that distinguishes the Christian experience as 'sound', placing it in opposition to the 'mere' 'idle notions' encountered by the Christian Gnostics, because in Gnostic mystical encounters, they did not necessarily 'see' real historical people, but rather they may 'see' spirit-beings, wise guides and demi-gods, which they may well have interpreted in symbolic, allegorical ways instead of regarding them as literally and objectively existing. For Gnostics, the resurrection was a 'spiritual' event rather than a physical one, for example.

Therefore for the Apostle Paul and his devotees, such experiences as those of the Gnostics and Christian Gnostics literally had no 'real' foundation – because the recipients had not encountered actual, objective real people – let alone Jesus. Paul and the Apostles believed that their visions were the perception of an objective, empirical reality – and the perception of a real person, that actually existed and lived and died, appearing to them in an empirical fashion to instruct them, whereas in contrast, the Gnostic's ideas are seen as being the product of an inflated imagination that has lost touch with (for the Apostles) the real foundation – Jesus.

ARE THE APOSTLES CORRECT IN THEIR VIEW OF VISIONS?

The point is, is this Apostolic interpretation correct? I would argue that they are mistaken. I would suggest that the experience is a subjective rather than an objective one and that the imagery and symbolism that is presented to the imagination in these experiences often arises within the context, personality and historical experience of the recipient. Insights are gained and changes of perspective are made – Paul changes from opposing Jesus to serving Jesus, yet he does so in a way that he sees as totally consistent with his deeper Jewish context and background, which is re-interpreted in an innovative and novel way – a way often severely disliked and opposed by many of the orthodox Jews of his time. But certain other things remain the same also – Paul remains quite a 'black and white' or 'all or nothing thinker' – remaining quite dogmatic in his beliefs and even intolerant - at first he was intolerant of Christians: a sect that he sought to eliminate – then he was intolerant of those Jews who would try and insist on bringing back and imposing obedience to the Law. Also typical of such mystical/revelatory/visionary experience, Paul regards his approach as the only way – all other approaches to God are approaches made in the darkness of ignorance, or they are false:

anything not based on Jesus is false teaching and to be opposed. This certainty and assurance of the content of his message arises from the unmediated nature of mystical experience.

On the other hand because of their acceptance of the imagination as a medium for Divine communication and because of the near limitless scope of the imagination, the Gnostics had little in the way of a single belief, or common set of symbols for the Divine. Tertullian noted of the Christian Gnostics that they had: 'no unity, only diversity....most of them disagree with one another, since they are willing to say – and even sincerely – of certain points, 'This is not so.'.' This lack of a core, unified set of symbols for the group as whole meant that even if they had not had a tendency to elitism, (although Jesus had this too), it would still not have gained popular, unified widespread support in the same way that Christian orthodoxy eventually did, because orthodox Christian believers created a focussed and increasingly clearly defined set of ideas and symbols that identified and distinguished it from other groups. They had clearly defined ideals and aims and shared symbols and ideas.

HOW CHRISTIANITY DEALT WITH 'FALSE' CHRISTIAN GNOSTIC VISIONS

The view that I am proposing is confirmed by the way in which the early church Apostles and leaders dealt with the perceived problem of Gnosticism. Let's just look again at Gnosticism itself for a moment. Gnosticism involved a direct mystical encounter with the Divine and like the Jewish Apostles and the Apostle Paul himself, Gnostics took their spiritual authority and foundation from these kinds of encounters/visions/revelations. Gnosticism took a number of forms, including Christian mysticism. It contended that human perfection and salvation was found in the immediate knowledge and experience of the fullness of the Divine, that is, gnosis. A resurrection out of the realms of ignorance and the material occurred during the attaining of this knowledge, whereby the evil physical world and ignorance were transcended. For some Gnostics, Jesus was seen as a spirit and the resurrection of Jesus was seen as a spiritual resurrection and some of these Gnostics considered the idea of a physical resurrection as being ridiculous. Sin and transgression was either irrelevant or transcended in this experience of unity with the Divine. The transcendent God may speak or manifest to us through angels, spirit-guides or by all manner of symbols and metaphors. In Christian Gnosticism, these kinds of ideas were expressed using Christian terminology and symbolism.

It was countered in the early orthodox church by using the following arguments:

Perfection is found in Christ, not in knowledge or the experience of gnosis. (Colossians 1 v 28)
Knowledge and wisdom is found in Christ, not in mystical or Gnostic experience. (Colossians 2 v 2 – 4)
The fullness of the deity is found in Christ, not in anything or anyone else. (Colossians 2 v 8-10)
Contact with Christ is vital. Losing contact with Christ leads to a puffed up and empty imagination. (Colossians 2 v 18, 19)
Christ is true knowledge. Ideas that oppose this are false knowledge. (1 Timothy 6 v 20)
The resurrection is yet to occur in the future. The notion that we are already being resurrected is false and is an idea that spreads like gangrene. (2 Timothy 2 v 18)
God is not a liar: we do sin and miss the mark. To say that we do not sin makes God out to be a liar. (1 John 1 v 10)
Knowledge of God is evidenced by our obedient submission. Continuing to behave immorally is to be in error. (1 John 2 v 3)
True spirits testify that Jesus is the Son of God. Therefore, test the spirits. (1 John 4 v 1-3)
Jesus came in physical flesh. Jesus was not just a spirit e.t.c. (Docetism) (2 John 7)

Christian Gnostic ideas were simply counteracted by or opposed with orthodox Christian ones: of these ten arguments, seven of them simply refer to 'facts' concerning the chief cornerstone of the Christian faith: Jesus Christ. Of the other three, one refers to God as True, one to the resurrection as being in the future and the last to submission to a righteous God as being the evidence of the knowledge of God. This really reflects what we have been saying: the focus of the foundation and authority for the Christian faith is Jesus Christ: His Person, life and work; and Jesus is real – an actual person who lived and died – and as far as the Apostles were concerned, was physically resurrected and appeared objectively and empirically to the Apostles in visions, giving them teaching and making them witnesses of the resurrection. For such Christians the Gnostic view on the other hand is based on myths (where it uses pagan or non-Christian ideas, or where it allegorises Christian ideas to mean something new) and on an inflated subjective imagination as opposed to an objective reality. Neither is it based on the life and work and objective, empirical resurrection of a real person and thus when it interprets Christian theology, Christian Gnosticism draws out false teaching – such as the idea that Jesus is just a spirit, or that we do not sin and that the resurrection is spiritual and not physical.

Orthodox Christianity then, continually returns to and remains anchored in what is seen as the objective foundation of the real resurrected person – Jesus Christ - who himself lived and taught within a Jewish context and background and (it is claimed) objectively appeared post-resurrection to teach and instruct the founders of the church as witnesses of this fact. Orthodox Christianity cannot step out of what it perceives as this real, objective framework and therefore has a tendency to reject all other approaches to God, whether they are alternative external religious systems or esoteric, inward spiritual approaches. It rejects the use of non-Christian myth, allegory and symbolism as alternative pathways to the Divine and insists that Jesus is the only way to God – all else is false doctrine and has lost contact with the head.

But I am suggesting that there a real doubts concerning this view. I am suggesting that this emphasis on the real, the literal, the objective and the empirical content of visions and appearances is a mistake. When Paul was on the Damascus road, he was accompanied by his companions, but they *did not* experience what Paul experienced – thus casting doubt on the objectivity of the vision. 'The men travelling with Saul stood there speechless; they heard the sound but did not see anyone'. (Acts 9). 'My companions saw the light, but they did not understand the voice of him who was speaking to me'. (Acts 22). The way in which Jesus appears and disappears, or the way people change as in the transfiguration all suggest a more subjective experience.

THE DEVELOPMENT AND OUTLINE OF CHRISTIAN ORTHODOXY

Nevertheless, the proto-orthodox view of Paul and the Hebrew Apostles was maintained and through numerous disputes, divisions and so-called 'heresies' this proto-orthodox view grew and developed into the orthodox view – a view elaborated by church leaders in the fourth century together with a 'canon' or set of gospels and epistles that were considered suitable to be used as a rule of faith and conduct – thus eliminating or marginalizing other Christian writings, such as for example those by the Christian Gnostics. Alternative viewpoints on the virgin birth, incarnation and trinity were eliminated or driven underground by a mixture of polemical treatises which came from all sides but which the proto-orthodox camp won. Orthodox Christian leaders ordered that writings that were considered spurious or heretical were to be burned and those people not conforming to the emerging orthodoxy or 'one belief' were deprived of church office and/or excommunicated. The new orthodoxy or one belief is summed up in the creeds that began to emerge at this time – succinct statements outlining the main beliefs:

We believe in one God, the Father Almighty, the maker of heaven and earth, of things visible and invisible.
And in one Lord Jesus Christ, the Son of God, the begotten of God the Father, the Only-begotten, that is of the essence of the Father.
God of God, Light of Light, true God of true God, begotten and not made; of the very same nature of the Father, by Whom all things came into being, in heaven and on earth, visible and invisible.
Who for us humanity and for our salvation came down from heaven, was incarnate, was made human, was born perfectly of the holy virgin Mary by the Holy Spirit.
By whom He took body, soul, and mind, and everything that is in man, truly and not in semblance.
He suffered, was crucified, was buried, rose again on the third day, ascended into heaven with the same body, [and] sat at the right hand of the Father.
He is to come with the same body and with the glory of the Father, to judge the living and the dead; of His kingdom there is no end.
We believe in the Holy Spirit, in the uncreated and the perfect; Who spoke through the Law, prophets, and Gospels; Who came down upon the Jordan, preached through the apostles, and lived in the saints.
We believe also in only One, Universal, Apostolic, and [Holy] Church; in one baptism in repentance, for the remission, and forgiveness of sins;

and in the resurrection of the dead, in the everlasting judgement of souls and bodies, and the Kingdom of Heaven and in the everlasting life.

VISIONS: A PERCEPTION OF THE OBJECTIVE OR THE SUBJECTIVE?

But I am suggesting that these ideas are built on a mistake – a mistake based on the idea that the visions of the Apostles and some other early Christians were literal, objective, empirical events-out-there. I am suggesting that the truth is that these visions were subjective.

There can only be these two understandings of these experiences of the Disciples and Apostles – in their visions they either:
a) Witnessed objective, real, empirical phenomena, or
b) Had a non-usual subjective experience.

As we have seen, Christian orthodoxy took the first view, as did the Disciples and Apostles themselves in what seems to be a traditional Hebrew understanding of these phenomena. If they are correct, then indeed, the events surrounding Jesus are the most momentous in history and Jesus himself is the most unique person in history being the Word of God Incarnate. More than this, our relationship to Jesus – our trust and commitment to him - or otherwise – has, according to Paul especially, eternal consequences, because our relationship to Jesus determines our standing on the coming Day of Judgment. According to Paul the death and resurrection of Jesus has secured the physical resurrection of all humanity together with the securing of a new, uncorrupted creation. Following the resurrection comes the Judgment where all moral imbalance is corrected and either Jesus takes the penalty for our transgressions and failures upon himself, or, if we have rejected Jesus, then it is we who take the penalty upon ourselves. Those who entrust themselves to Jesus are adopted as sons of God and if sons, then heirs to a great inheritance. All this is perceived as real, tangible, objective reality. It is for this reason that everything: our behaviour, spirituality, thoughts, passions and so on – has to be founded on the real, objective resurrected Jesus Christ. It is for this reason that orthodox leaders of the early church were critical of those who lost contact with Jesus Christ – the Head and Foundation – the chief cornerstone of the faith. It is the understanding that these events are real and objective that motivates much present day Christian

Fundamentalism and it is the desire to give people the opportunity to entrust themselves to Jesus that motivates certain aspects of missionary work and evangelism – because unless people hear the good news about Jesus they are doomed to a lesser resurrection – a resurrection of anguish and sorrow as they bear the just penalty for their own transgressions and failings in their new resurrected body. This is the heart of orthodox Christianity. The resurrection is central to Paul's philosophy and faith. If there is no resurrection, he says of all people, Christians are most to be pitied. (I Corinthians 15 v 19).

The second view is that the Disciples and Apostles did not experience a literal, objective event. Rather, what they saw and heard was an internal, subjective event. This does not mean however that the experience is to be dismissed or that it is a mere product of the mind. Today, in our predominantly materialistic world-view, many would tend to reduce these experiences, these visions, to a mere unusual activity of the brain – in other words – they would reduce it to a mere material event caused by the interaction of neurones, impulses and other activity in the brain that are then experienced by the individual as visions. A similar sort of reductionism goes on with regard to any modern day claims to mystical experiences such that they are often dismissed or marginalized as some sort of unusual brain state or activity, or even as mental 'illness'. When some of these objectors are then able to reproduce in some form or another such states in the laboratory, they think that they have proved their point, but this is by no means so. Also in a similar way, those who would call themselves rationalists – those who pride themselves on the use of logic and reason often dismiss such experiences by using the pejorative term 'enthusiasm', by which they mean someone who is governed by their emotions and feelings to the detriment of their reason and logic. However, if we look at Paul's writings, we can see a legal mind at work – where he tends to state a doctrine, then anticipate objections and answer them before drawing out the practical implications of his doctrine. Paul was no mere 'enthusiast'.

THE FOCAL POINT OF REVELATION

Where then do the images, sounds and sensations contained in these spiritual visions come from? Like philosophy, other religions and branches of psychology, Christianity and Judaism uses subjective

251

abstract terms to describe subjective experience. The word 'mind' is a simple example. We cannot put a person in a laboratory and surgically operate on them and open their skull to reveal the mind. We can reveal the brain – but not the mind. Terms like 'mind', 'ego', 'heart', 'intellect' all describe subjective qualities that emerge from our objective, empirical, physical being. This is why a person cannot be 'mentally ill'. The concept 'mental' is an abstract concept and not a concrete one which 'brain' is. 'Illness' is a concrete concept and therefore the phrase 'mental illness' is a conceptual mis-match, or mixed concept. The 'brain' can suffer disease and illness but the 'mind' cannot. Using these abstract terms then, Christians and some other religions talk in terms of these images arising in the 'ground' of our being, in the 'essence' of who we are, in our 'soul' and 'heart', in our 'True Self'. Also such experiences, as we have seen, have the sense of being received – the person does not *actively* speculate and construct such ideas and forms of the Divine or spiritual themes using reason and logic, but rather there is an arising and emerging, manifesting as concepts in our imagination and intellect and as feelings and emotions in our heart. The subjective locus or central focus of this experience is our 'True Self' or 'soul' or 'essence' with the forms becoming manifest in our mind or imagination, in our emotions and in our inclinations.

Thus it is then that those on the spiritual path are encouraged to listen to the 'Still Small Voice', in Christian terms, the 'Spirit of God' within, the 'Inner Light'. I want to further suggest that the 'Still Small Voice' is present in everyone as part of our 'ground of being': it is the Voice that is niggling and insistent, always asking questions about Existence, Meaning and Ultimate Things. This is the point or locus where Spirit meets the material, the locus or focal point of personal inspiration and revelation. The Spirit of God within is quiet and cannot be seen with physical eyes because Spirit is Subtle. The Source of these images, Divine representations and teachings then, is what Christians would call God: the Transcendent Spirit *Essence*, but these images and teachings, these *revelations*, are *expressed* from the 'soul' or 'individual essence' to our minds, imaginations and hearts in meaningful, personal, individual forms that fit our temperament, background and circumstances. Many spiritual masters argue that they are given to us in the degree and capacity to which we can accommodate them. They are personally tailored image forms to suit us as particular individuals in a particular place and time. Just as with the Apostle Paul, as we later contemplate, reflect and study the content

252

of these received encounters, teachings and forms and apply our rational, analytical faculties to them, we, as individuals may then begin to rationally, logically, through the means of analysis, construct a personal web of meaning and orientation with regard to our relationship to the Divine. In other words we begin to construct a personal theology, a personal religious philosophy, which others may or may not find useful and relevant. So there is not only the Godly aspect to the Still Small Voice arising from the Spirit of God, but also an individual, personalised quality of mind in the forms presented to, used and interpreted by the individual. However, such forms of theology and God remain closer to our natural ignorance than they do to Infinite Spirit. Such ideologies, philosophies and theologies are to a great degree still a human construction and they ultimately become just one partial, flawed perspective, often set against other flawed perspectives, sometimes in violent warfare.

Furthermore, though the Inner Voice of the Spirit of God is quiet and cannot be seen with physical eyes because Spirit is Subtle, the spectacular declaration of the existence of God is already done in the material realm through the very existence of the Universe. The whole Universe declares the power of Spirit. But because of our natural ignorance, or in Christian terms, our sinful blindness, people do not see this. Rather, they tend to reduce the Universe to the material level and to material terms. All the spectacular power of God is displayed in the Universe for those who can see: nothing more can be displayed in the material realm. Even so, despite the ignorance and blindness that we naturally have concerning God, it is to be understood that the Spirit of God is in all people as fully as anyone or anything else. But our natural ignorance, blindness and our natural inclination - the state of our heart and mind nevertheless takes us away from God by making the darkness of our ignorance even thicker. Thus we do not hear the 'Voice' of God, neither are we usually aware of God's presence. It is as if we are in a room with two doors and the Still Small Voice is present between the doors. One of the doors we can open easily: the door of Ignorance. We can open it wide and certainly the spiritual seeker may feel an unwelcome coldness. The other we can barely open at all: so intense is the blinding light behind it that we can only open the door a little way. Material existence and the expressions or manifestations of forms in the imagination concerning God are much closer to and more tolerant of Ignorance than of Light and our natural ignorance drowns out the Still Small Voice almost completely, though it does not extinguish its subtle persistence.

REIFICATION: THE OBJECTIFYING OF SUBJECTIVE EXPERIENCE

The locus of Divine forms arise then from our 'True Ground' and Nature: from 'Essence within' manifest in us as the Still Small Voice arising from our 'Innermost Self'. We are not saying that saying that God is just in the imagination: this would be a reductionist stance whereby the Divine is reduced to mere brain activity and the configuration of neuronal pathways. God is not perceived by the recipient of such experiences merely as a fantasy of the imagination. Rather, we are saying that saying that it is *in* the imagination and *in* the heart that delimited forms of and inclinations towards Infinite Transcendent God emerge from the Source or Essence in our True Nature and Ground – in Christian terms, our 'soul'. The Divine forms in revelatory visions and experiences then are not just a figment of imagination or a fantasy, but neither is the Divine form a reified abstract idea turned by us into a perceived 'objective reality'.

However, the tendency to turn these forms and revelations into a concrete objective reality 'out there' is a strong one. This is known as the process of reification: turning metaphors and symbols into an objectively existing concrete object: into something that exists 'out there'. It is to transfer something that is subjectively and internally perceived in the imagination and intellect and then to transpose it into a literally existing, empirical object 'out-there'. For example we may turn metaphorical, symbolic manifestations of a Christian saint like Saint Christopher into an external spirit/soul/entity which is seen as independently existing 'out there' or 'up there' and which is also seen as being capable of acting upon us, the subject, as well as on the world and universe around us, thus, in this case, keeping us safe in our travels. This process of reification happens for a number of reasons. Firstly, it happens because as creatures of form, we are nearly always operating in a rational/active/logical mode that uses forms. We are always making reference to 'things out there' in order to successfully navigate and operate in the material world. Secondly, because many of the images and concepts that we have concerning God are anthropomorphic, or human-like, there is then a tendency to reify these anthropomorphic images and concepts so that we tend to think of God as 'Big-Person-in-the-sky-out-there'. Thirdly, because these experiences take place at such a deep level within us, at the 'ground' of our being or 'soul', they may appear very real and certain. There is an immediacy or unmediated quality about the revelatory/mystical/Gnostic experience that makes it seem vitally real and certain. The experience is not initially mediated by reason and logic or transmitted through external stimuli, but it is internal, subjective and to a great extent non-mediated by reason, analysis and logic.

Reification is a danger that those who receive these experiences have to be constantly aware of. If reification takes place then there follow a whole raft of burdens of proof – of the need to prove that what we experienced does indeed exist 'out-there'. If we say something exists 'out there', then it is quite right that people ask for proof, for evidence. If we are saying in effect that Saint Christopher is a 'spirit/soul entity-out-there', then it is reasonable for people to want to observe St Christopher, measure St Christopher and have proof or evidence of St Christopher and any effects he may have. This is not the position that I am taking.

Reification seems common in religion generally however, restricting ourselves to Christianity, believers may reify particular saints – such as St. Christopher as we have seen. They may invoke other saints for particular areas of their life – especially the Virgin Mary, the mother of God. They may even invoke angels as guides or protectors. In each case, the object of veneration or appeal is considered as something that really exists 'out-there', a 'spirit/soul entity-out-there' that is capable of acting upon us and our circumstances. On the darker side they may believe that evil spirits and the devil exist 'out-there', ready to oppose them in their faith or to hinder or malign them in some way. The Apostle Paul, or one of his followers expresses this view in the letter to the Ephesians: 'Put on the whole armour of God, that you may be able to stand against the craftiness of the devil. For we wrestle not against flesh and blood, but against principalities, against powers, against the rulers of the darkness of this world, against spiritual wickedness in high places'. (Ephesians 6 v 11,12). But here, in each of these cases, the 'spirit/soul entity-out-there' that is appealed to has some sort of 'scope' or 'purview' or 'domain'. St. Christopher is appealed to with regard to journeys and travelling and other saints too have their specific areas. Even the devil is curtailed and limited by the sovereign power of God – let loose on a leash as it were in order to accomplish the higher purposes of God. However, many Christians reify the Spirit of God and none more so today perhaps than Christian fundamentalists. It is Christian fundamentalists who take this process of reification to its near-absolute conclusion. The difference here is that this is no lesser spirit or saint that is being reified, but God's Spirit which has the widest and fullest domain or scope of all as Almighty God.

THE RISE OF REASON, SCIENCE AND FUNDAMENTALISM

With the advent and onslaught of the Age of Reason and the development of modern science grounded firmly in a materialistic perspective, traditional religious ideas came under increasing scrutiny and stronger and stronger challenges. As a defence reflex within Christianity, some Christians hardened their approach and became less flexible with regard to Scripture and the teaching it contained. Certain doctrines, such as for example a literal six-day creation period and/or a young earth theory, whereby through calculating dates in the Bible, the earth was said to have been created between 6,000 and 10,000 B.C., became 'badges' of identification – 'markers' of a 'true believer' conserving and holding steadfastly to the traditions of truth held to by previous generations of Christians. Such believers hold tenaciously to what they understand to be the fundamentals of Christianity, to the traditional orthodox forms of God. What this systematic, ultra-conservative orthodoxy does amongst other things is to define and conceptualise God in a way that seems unquestionable. This view sees the Bible as the Word of Infallible, Perfect God, written by men inspired by God in such a way that all corrupting influence which would give rise to false and mistaken ideas about God is restrained and withheld. To question the orthodox teaching arising from the Bible therefore is to do no less than to question God, to doubt it, is to doubt God, to suggest alternative or contradictory ideas to those of Scripture is to fall into error, to be self-deceived or deceived by the devil, or to oppose God.

Despite this, Christian fundamentalists know that the Bible will sustain different interpretations and different degrees of emphasis on different passages of Scripture and that these in turn lead to different practices. Thus even within fundamentalist Christianity, we have Congregationalists, Methodists, Baptists, Presbyterians and so on all within the Christian protestant fundamentalist banner. This is accepted and tolerated - so long as the main principles: plainly understood verses and truths of the Scripture that conceptualise particular forms of God are agreed upon.

But what the Christian fundamentalist has done is to elevate these writings and the ideas and concepts that they contain to an Absolute level and it is this that is one of their mistakes. Let me give an illustration. Christians call God the 'Father' – 'Our Father who is in heaven...' Yet if the point is pressed, many Christian fundamentalists will agree that God is not male and certainly not female (since Christian fundamentalism is male orientated and patriarchal). They will acknowledge that the term 'Father' is a metaphor for a God that cannot be defined by gender: a God that transcends gender. Nevertheless, the word 'Father' is useful for describing the relationship that the believer has with God and for the way in which God deals with humanity. It engenders the whole Judaic-Christian theology of the only begotten Son, Jesus Christ, as well as the Apostle Paul's approach whereby believers are thought of as being adopted as sons of God and therefore heirs to the inheritance of God. But when it comes down to it, at a certain level, many Christian fundamentalists do not see God as a literal 'Father' or even as 'Male', but rather use the term in this 'useful metaphor' way. Christian Fundamentalists are not always as literal in their interpretations as is usually made out. With regard to the creation account in Genesis many Christian fundamentalists take a similar approach. Because of the advances of science many fundamentalist believers find the literal interpretation too difficult to maintain, so instead of being inflexibly defensive they will talk about the six days of creation not in terms of literal twenty-four hour days but in terms of 'figurative days', that is periods of unspecified length symbolically described as 'days' or adopt some similar technique to avoid the difficulty. As long as the main principles and ideas of the Christian fundamentalist faith are not compromised, such ideas may again be tolerated.

The question we have to ask is: Are such forms of God absolute and final? Are such ideas and concepts of the Divine Ultimate? I suggest that they are not and we see a clue why in the approach by Christian fundamentalists themselves to the Divine Name 'Father' as I have just outlined above. The concept, attribute, Name, quality, characteristic, relationship of 'Father' is not Absolute because God transcends gender – God is neither Male nor Female and therefore not 'Father'. I want to suggest that there is a higher view of God than that which is encompassed and bordered by conceptual ideas and forms, whoever may advocate them –

Christian, Jew or Muslim – and whatever forms they may be. God is transcendent of the concepts and formulations of 'Father', 'Creator', 'Love', 'Judge' and so on. These descriptive terms and forms are all limited, finite, relational terms but God as Absolute is Infinite, Transcendent and Unique. Essence alone is Real – Essence alone has Primary Self-sufficient existence – all else is manifestation of Essence and thus dependent upon Essence for its secondary existence. The Absolute is transcendent of all these limited forms, names and designations. These forms, names and descriptors, these concepts of God are in fact just useful metaphors that stand between us as creatures of form and the Formless, Infinite Absolute. We, as temporal, spatial, finite forms stand in relation to Transcendent Infinite Formless God and these are relational terms that reveal *aspects* and *facets* of our *finite relationship* with an Absolute that we cannot comprehend or encompass with forms, ideas and concepts. Essence transcends *any* philosophy or theology or conceptualisation.

One mistake that Christian fundamentalists fall into then is to elevate the language and conceptual ideas portrayed in Scripture to the level of Absolute – such that these main ideas become inseparable from the Divine and thus have to be conserved and defended at all costs. The Bible and the ideas it contains are seen as inseparable from God: attack the ideas and it is God that is being attacked. The attention of the Christian fundamentalist is taken away from Transcendent Absolute Spirit and instead directed to the relative level of Scripture and scriptural ideas which are then falsely elevated to the level of Absolute Spirit. This reification of and focus on form and concept actually distracts the attention away from Absolute Transcendent Divine because the eyes of the Christian fundamentalist are often not on Spirit, but on conformity to and agreement with a set of conceptual forms which actually fall short of Absolute Spirit and are merely pointers to That which cannot be known. We start to have big problems when we mistake these relational symbols, metaphors and allegories for absolute concrete realities through the process of reification, or delimit Spirit solely to one absolute set of symbols to the exclusion of others, not allowing for the infinity, transcendence and paradox of Infinite, Timeless, Formless Spirit. It is by these processes that we might soon find ourselves thinking of God as some old, grey-bearded Man-in-the-sky, or as a stern Judge-looking-down-on-us who is taking account of all that we do, or as a compassionate, merciful Father ready to heal and forgive.

258

THEOMORPHISM

Because the Apostle Paul and the other disciples all believed that what they had encountered in their visions was an objective reality – namely that they had really seen the physically existing resurrection body of Jesus it meant, as we have seen, that they remained fixed to this foundation. The resurrection was a real, objective event and to stray from the objective, real, resurrection of Jesus was to lose touch with the foundation of the faith. This notion of Jesus as the resurrected Messiah and therefore the only way of salvation becomes a fixed form of the Divine. However, I am casting doubt on the objectivity of these visions and suggesting rather that they are subjective experiences. And we can go further: what the Apostle Paul and the disciples did not learn because of their insistence on this objectivity of their visions, was the lesson that some higher stage mystics have learned – namely that God is theomorphic – that is, God changes in form in order to meet people where they are in a personally relevant and significant way. No delimited form can encapsulate the Infinite Divine and because of the Divine Infinity, such delimited forms as God does present to us are non-repeatable. The forms, the symbols, the figures in mystical encounters are metaphorical and allegorical – they stand between the delimited, bounded world of material form and the Boundless, Formless Empty, Infinite Spirit. They are known, meaningful, personal symbols that reveal aspects of the Unknowable Absolute. The Apostle Paul did not realise or move to the position that every believer has their own unique personal Lord or recognise that such delimiting forms and beliefs merely bind and tie the believer, limiting and obscuring as much as revealing Infinite Spirit. Nevertheless, in serving their delimited personal Lord, the pilgrim's intention, their 'objective', is the Unknowable, Infinite, Formless Essence.

METAPHOR AND ALLEGORY

Those who have experienced transcendence should be able to extract a reasonably coherent and systematic philosophy or theology from their experiences, and indeed, this is what the Apostle Paul and the disciples did. But the important thing to remember, and something which should distinguish those who experience transcendence from fundamentalists, is that these forms of belief are limited, metaphorical, and liable to change. They do not form a complete explanation – the mind cannot encompass God – they are not literal and concrete and should not be reified as such – they are transient and not permanent or eternal, but relative to our personality and contexts of our education, geographical and temporal location. They are finite formulations created in some degree of Ignorance of the Formless Unknowable Infinite. Different backgrounds, contexts, personalities and different depths of transcendent experience mean that different, contradictory, paradoxical systems of theology arise. Such systems are not only different from person to person but also within a person over time. This means that different people have different perspectives on:

Aspects and facets of God and the spiritual realm.
How God should be approached
The nature of Unity and interconnectedness
How Divine Truth is communicated
The nature of Guidance (if any) from the Divine
The role, (if any), of providence, fate and destiny
The nature of the post death state
The nature and usefulness (if any) of Prayer
The importance and relevance of sin, guilt or moral failure before the Divine
The need (if any) for Forgiveness.
The value and method of seeking to walk a righteous path
The role, (if any), of Ritual and Ceremony

In other words, this seems to take us closer to a Gnostic perspective than the more inflexible and literal approach taken by the Disciples and Paul.

CHRISTIAN WRITINGS AND THEIR DEVELOPMENT

We need to get to the situation before Paul's visions and his particular interpretation of their content, which later developed into Christian orthodoxy. What we would like to do is to go back to the fledgling Christianity that existed when Jesus was teaching and that existed shortly after his death before these visions of resurrection and ascension occurred to try and get to the heart of the ministry of Jesus. Of course it is here that we hit a near impenetrable problem: Jesus himself left no writings or record of his teaching and life and the earliest Christian writings that we do have are those by Paul himself, written between 50 – 65 A.D., and as we have seen, the very foundation of Paul's Christianity and his writings are these very visions and appearances. The gospels that we have in our Bibles are written later and none of them seem to be written by the Disciples themselves, so we have no actual eyewitness accounts of the ministry and teaching of Jesus. It has long been noted that the three gospels attributed to Matthew, Mark and Luke contain very similar accounts and for this reason they are known as the 'synoptic gospels'. It would appear that these three gospels may have drawn on an earlier document – an earlier gospel which is thought to be a 'sayings gospel' – that is, a record of statements and sayings by Jesus rather than an account of his life and ministry. This hypothetical gospel is referred to by scholars as Gospel 'Q' which is a reference to this gospel being 'source' material for the gospels that we do have. It is thought that this lost gospel could have been written any time between 40 to 70 A.D., but Paul himself makes no reference to any gospel. There seems to be no way of knowing whether Paul used such a proto-gospel document in any way. His own writings seem to be a reasonably systematic and developing theology based on the consequences and implications of his 'objective' visions in the light and context of his Jewish upbringing, Jewish history and tradition. Certainly his writings seem to indicate a preference to rely on 'what he received from Jesus Christ' (in his visions) rather than any reliance on other testimonies.

It is considered by scholars that the author of Luke's gospel and of the Acts of the Apostles was a companion of Paul's. Paul's last letter, to the Philippians, was written about 62 A.D. The Acts of the Apostles does not record the death of Paul so it may be that the Acts of the Apostles and the Gospel attributed to Luke were written sometime after 62 A.D. but before the death of Paul, since one would assume that his death would have been mentioned in Acts if this event had occurred when the document was written. But dates for the authorship of nearly all the New Testament documents have a wide range and vary according the different theories of different scholars and I do not think that it is profitable for us to go too far down this speculative route. It is however generally agreed that the first Gospel to be written was that which is known to us as the Gospel attributed to Mark and it is believed by some scholars that it is based on the teaching of Peter. Again, the dates of authorship for this document are wide, but it is generally attributed to about 70 – 75 A.D., that is, forty to forty-five years after the crucifixion and some twenty to twenty-five years since the meeting of Paul with the Council in Jerusalem – and therefore twenty to twenty-five years into the ministry of Paul to the Gentiles. Nevertheless, since the author seems to be following the tradition of the Hebrew Christians as opposed to the Pauline tradition, it may be less affected by the theology that Paul was developing as a result of his visions. We can also note that the Gospels are quite different in style from the writings of Paul. The Gospels are not systematic philosophical or theological documents. They do not make theological propositions and then anticipate and seek to answer any objections before outlining practical consequences of the doctrine. They are not set out in this formal, legalistic or philosophical way at all. Rather, they contain sayings attributed to Jesus and portray events in his life and ministry that sometimes serve to illustrate or reinforce either the sayings themselves or the portrayal of the character and nature of Jesus that the author wishes to declare.

Thus for example, the Gospel attributed to Matthew upholds the Jewishness of Jesus, written as it is by a Jewish Christian. It is in the gospel attributed to Matthew that we read that 'not one jot or tittle shall pass from the law' (moral or ceremonial) and this is quite a different sentiment from that expressed by Paul to the Gentiles. There was pressure being exerted by some Jews that Gentile Christians should undergo circumcision. But these Jewish traditionalists are branded as false believers by Paul and indeed, much of Paul's letter to the Galatians is about this issue of the Christian's relationship to the old Mosaic laws and commandments: 'And certain men came down from Judea and taught the brethren: "Unless you are circumcised according to the custom of Moses, you cannot be saved." Therefore.... Paul and Barnabas had no small dissension and dispute with them.' (Acts 15 v 1). So we can see that even at this stage, there are differences of emphasis, different nuances and different balances of ideas within the broad movement of Christianity.

THE PERSON, LIFE AND TEACHING OF JESUS AS PORTRAYED IN THE OLDEST GOSPEL

Given that it is the Gospel attributed to Mark that appears to be the first that is written, and that like The Gospels attributed to Matthew and Luke, it may be using an older but now lost Gospel as source material, all we can do in our search for a more contemporary picture of Jesus and his ministry is look a little more closely at the Gospel attributed to Mark to see what it does and does not say about Jesus. In overview we find this:

The Gospel attributed to Mark makes no reference to the virgin birth at all but it is the baptism of Jesus by John the Baptist that begins the gospel attributed to Mark. Right away we need to take an aside to look at the major groups within Judaism at this time so that we get some idea of the context and background of Jesus.

BACKGROUND AND CONTEXT OF THE TIMES

John the Baptist was an itinerant preacher and a major religious figure who led a movement of baptism at the Jordan River. Some scholars maintain that he was influenced by the Essenes, although there is no direct evidence to substantiate this.

ESSENES

The Essenes were a Jewish religious group that flourished from the 2nd century BCE to the 1st century CE that some scholars claim seceded from the Zadokite priests. Being much fewer in number than the Pharisees and the Sadducees (the other two major sects at the time) the Essenes lived in various cities but congregated in communal life dedicated to asceticism, voluntary poverty, daily immersion, and abstinence from worldly pleasures, including marriage. Many separate but related religious groups of that era shared similar mystic, eschatological, messianic, and ascetic beliefs. These groups are collectively referred to by various scholars as the 'Essenes.' Josephus records that Essenes existed in large numbers, and thousands lived throughout Judæa. The Essenes believed they were the *last generation of the last generations* and anticipated Teacher of Righteousness, Aaronic High Priest, and High Guard Messiah, similar to the Prophet, Priest and King expectations of the Pharisees. The Essenes have gained fame in modern times as a result of the discovery of an extensive group of religious documents known as the Dead Sea Scrolls, commonly believed to be their library. These documents include preserved multiple copies of the Hebrew Bible untouched from as early as 300 BCE until their discovery in 1946. Some scholars, however, dispute the notion that the Essenes wrote the Dead Sea Scrolls.

Roman writer Pliny the Elder (died c. 79 A.D.) in his *Natural History* (N'H,V,XV). relates in a few lines that the Essenes do not marry, possess no money, and had existed for thousands of generations. Unlike Philo, who did not mention any particular geographical location of the Essenes other than the whole land of Israel, Pliny places them in Ein Gedi, next to the Dead Sea. A little later Josephus gave a detailed account of the Essenes in *The Jewish War* (c. 75 A.D.) with a shorter description in *Antiquities of the Jews* (c. 94 A.D.) and The Life of Flavius Josephus (c. 97 A.D.). Claiming first hand knowledge, he lists the *Essenoi* as one of the three sects of Jewish philosophy alongside the Pharisees and the Sadducees. He relates the same information concerning piety, celibacy, the absence of personal property and of money, the belief in communality and commitment to a strict observance of the Sabbath. He further adds that the Essenes ritually immersed in water every morning, ate together after prayer, devoted themselves to charity and benevolence, forbade the expression of anger, studied the books of the elders, preserved secrets, and were very mindful of the names of the angels kept in their sacred writings.

The accounts by Josephus and Philo show that the Essenes led a strictly celibate and communal life – often compared by scholars to later Christian monastic living – although Josephus speaks also of another 'order of Essenes' that observed being engaged for three years and then being married. According to Josephus, they had customs and observances such as collective ownership, elected a leader to attend to the interests of them all whose orders they obeyed, were forbidden from swearing oaths and sacrificing animals, controlled their temper and served as channels of peace, carried weapons only as protection against robbers, had no slaves but served each other and, as a result of communal ownership, did not engage in trading. Both Josephus and Philo have lengthy accounts of their communal meetings, meals and religious celebrations. After a total of three years' probation, newly joining members would take an oath that included the commitment to practice piety towards 'the Deity' and righteousness towards humanity, to maintain a pure lifestyle, to abstain from criminal and immoral activities, to transmit their rules uncorrupted and to preserve the books of the Essenes and the names of the Angels. Their theology included belief in the immortality of the soul and that they would receive their souls back after death. Part of their activities included purification by water rituals, which was supported by rainwater catchment and storage.

THE PHARISEES

Two other major groups within Judaism were the Pharisees and Saducees. The Pharisees were at various times a political party, a social movement, and a school of thought among Jews during the Second Temple period under the Hasmonean dynasty (140–37 BCE) in the wake of the Maccabean Revolt. Conflicts between the Pharisees and the Sadducees took place in the context of much broader and longstanding social and religious conflicts among Jews dating back to the Babylonian captivity and exacerbated by the Roman conquest. One conflict was class, between the wealthy and the poor, as the Sadducees included mainly the priestly and aristocratic families. Another conflict was cultural, between those who favoured hellenization and those who resisted it. A third was juridico-religious, between those who emphasized the importance of the Temple, and those who emphasized the importance of other Mosaic laws and prophetic values. A fourth, specifically religious, involved different interpretations of the Scriptures and how to apply the Torah to Jewish life, with the Sadducees recognizing only the written letter of the Torah and rejecting life after death, while the Pharisees held to Rabbinic interpretations additional to the written texts. Josephus indicates that the Pharisees received the backing and goodwill of the common people, apparently in contrast to the more elite Sadducees. Pharisees claimed prophetic or Mosaic authority for their interpretation of Jewish laws, while the Sadducees represented the authority of the priestly privileges and prerogatives established since the days of Solomon, when Zadok, their ancestor, officiated as High Priest. After the destruction of the Second Temple in 70 CE Pharisaic beliefs became the basis for Rabbinic Judaism, which ultimately produced the normative traditional Judaism which is the basis for nearly all contemporary forms of Judaism.

Pharisaic views were non-creedal and non-dogmatic, and heterogenous. Not one tractate of the key Rabbinic texts, the Mishnah and the Talmud, is devoted to theological issues; these texts are concerned primarily with interpretations of Jewish law, and anecdotes about the sages and their values. Only one chapter of the Mishnah deals with theological issues; it asserts that three kinds of people will have no share in 'the world to come:' those who deny the resurrection of the dead, those who deny the divinity of the Torah, and Epicureans (who deny divine supervision of human affairs). Another passage suggests a different set of core principles: normally, a Jew may violate *any* law to save a life, but in Sanhedrin 74a, a ruling orders Jews to accept martyrdom rather than violate the laws against idolatry, murder, or adultery. (Judah haNasi, however, said that Jews must 'be meticulous in small religious duties as well as large ones, because you do not know what sort of reward is coming for any of the religious duties,' suggesting that all laws are of equal importance). In comparison with Christianity, the Rabbis were not especially concerned with the messiah or claims about the messiah.

One belief central to the Pharisees was shared by all Jews of the time: monotheism. This is evident in the practice of reciting the *Shema*, a prayer composed of select verses from the Torah, at the Temple and in synagogues; the *Shema* begins with the verses, 'Hear O Israel, the Lord is our God; the Lord is one.' According to the Mishna, these passages were recited in the Temple along with the twice-daily *Tamid* offering.

Pharisaic wisdom was compiled in one book of the Mishna, *Pirke Avot*. The Pharisaic attitude is perhaps best exemplified by a story about Hillel the Elder, who lived at the end of the 1st century BCE. A man once challenged the sage to explain the law while standing on one foot. Hillel replied, 'That which is hateful to you, do not do to your friend. That is the whole Torah, the rest is the explanation — go and study it.'

According to Josephus, whereas the Sadducees believed that people have total free will and the Essenes believed that all of a person's life is predestined, the Pharisees believed that people have free will but that God also has foreknowledge of human destiny. According to Josephus, Pharisees were further distinguished from the Sadducees in that Pharisees believed in the resurrection of the dead.

It is likely that Josephus highlighted these differences because he was writing for a Gentile audience, and questions concerning fate and a life after death were important in Hellenic philosophy. In fact, it is difficult, or impossible, to reconstruct a Second Temple Pharisaic theology, because Judaism itself is non-creedal; that is, there is no dogma or set of orthodox beliefs that Jews believed were required of Jews. Josephus himself emphasized laws rather than beliefs when he described the characteristics of an apostate (a Jew who does not follow traditional customs) and the requirements for conversion to Judaism (circumcision, and adherence to traditional customs). In fact, the most important divisions among different Jewish sects had to do with debates over three areas of law: marriage, the Sabbath and religious festivals, and the Temple and purity. Debates over these and other matters of law continue to define Judaism more than any particular dogma or creed.

Unlike the Sadducees, the Pharisees also believed in the resurrection of the dead in a future, messianic age. The Pharisees believed in a literal resurrection of the body.

Fundamentally, the Pharisees continued a form of Judaism that extended beyond the Temple, applying Jewish law to mundane activities in order to sanctify the every-day world. This was a more participatory (or 'democratic') form of Judaism, in which rituals were not monopolized by an inherited priesthood but rather could be performed by all adult Jews individually or collectively; whose leaders were not determined by birth but by scholarly achievement. In general, the Pharisees emphasized a commitment to social justice, belief in the brotherhood of mankind, and a faith in the redemption of the Jewish nation and, ultimately, humanity. Moreover, they believed that these ends would be achieved through halakha ('the way,' or 'the way things are done'), a corpus of laws derived from a close reading of sacred texts. This belief entailed both a commitment to relate religion to ordinary concerns and daily life, and a commitment to study and scholarly debate.

The Pharisees believed that all Jews in their ordinary life, and not just the Temple priesthood or Jews visiting the Temple, should observe rules and rituals concerning purification. The Pharisees believed that in addition to the written Torah recognized by both the Sadducees and Pharisees and believed to have been written by Moses, there exists another Torah, consisting of the corpus of oral laws and traditions transmitted by God to Moses orally, and then memorized and passed down by Moses and his successors over the generations. The Oral Torah functioned to elaborate and explicate what was written, and the Pharisees asserted that the sacred scriptures were not complete on their own terms and could therefore not be understood.

The sages of the Talmud believed that the Oral law was simultaneously revealed to Moses at Sinai, *and* the product of debates among rabbis. Thus, one may conceive of the 'Oral Torah' not as a fixed text but as an ongoing process of analysis and argument in which God is actively involved; it was this ongoing process that was revealed at Sinai, and by participating in this ongoing process rabbis and their students are actively participating in God's ongoing act of revelation.

The commitment to relate religion to daily life through the law has led some (notably, the Apostle Paul and Martin Luther) to infer that the Pharisees were more legalistic than other sects in the Second Temple Era. Jesus also spoke harshly against the Pharisaic Law. In some cases Pharisaic values led to an extension of the law.

Just as important as (if not more important than) any particular law was the value the rabbis placed on legal study and debate. The sages of the Talmud believed that when they taught the Oral Torah to their students, they were imitating Moses, who taught the law to the children of Israel. Moreover, the rabbis believed that 'the heavenly court studies Torah precisely as does the earthly one, even arguing about the same questions.' Thus, in debating and disagreeing over the meaning of the Torah or how best to put it into practice, no rabbi felt that he (or his opponent) were in some way rejecting God or threatening Judaism; on the contrary, it was precisely through such arguments that the rabbis imitated and honoured God.

THE SADUCEES

The other main Jewish group, the Sadducees, were a sect or group of Jews that were active in Ancient Israel during the Second Temple period, starting from the 2nd century BC through the destruction of the Temple in 70 AD. The sect was identified by Josephus with the upper social and economic echelon of Judean society, and may have been comprised originally of members of the priestly clan. As a whole, the sect fulfilled various political, social and religious roles, including maintaining the Temple. Their sect is believed to have become extinct sometime after the destruction of Herod's Temple in Jerusalem in 70 AD.

The religious responsibilities of the Sadducees included the maintenance of the Temple in Jerusalem. Their high social status was reinforced by their priestly responsibilities, as mandated in the Torah. The Priests were responsible for performing sacrifices at the Temple, the primary method of worship in Ancient Israel. This also included presiding over sacrifices on the three festivals of pilgrimage to Jerusalem. Their religious beliefs and social status were mutually reinforcing, as the Priesthood often represented the highest class in Judean society. It is important to note that the Sadducees and the priests were not completely synonymous. Cohen points out that 'not all priests, high priests, and aristocrats were Sadducees; many were Pharisees, and many were not members of any group at all.' As mentioned above, it is widely believed that the Sadducees were descended from the House of Zadok and sought to preserve this priestly line and the authority of the Temple.

The Sadducees oversaw many formal affairs of the state. Members of the Sadducees:
- Administered the state domestically
- Represented the state internationally
- Participated in the Sanhedrin, and often encountered the Pharisees there.
- Collected taxes. These also came in the form of international tribute from Jews in the Diaspora.
- Equipped and led the army
- Regulated relations with the Romans
- Mediated domestic grievances.

According to Josephus, the Sadducees believed that:
- there is no fate
- God does not commit evil
- man has free will; 'man has the free choice of good or evil'
- the soul is not immortal; there is no afterlife, and
- there are no rewards or penalties after death

The Sadducees rejected the belief in resurrection, which was a central tenet of the teaching of Jesus. This often provoked hostility between the two groups. Furthermore, the Sadducees rejected the oral law as proposed by the Pharisees. Rather, they saw the written law as the sole source of divine authority. The written law, in its depiction of the priesthood, corroborated the power and enforced the hegemony of the Sadducees in Judean society.

A SUMMARY OF DIFFERENCES BETWEEN THESE JEWISH GROUPS

Differences between Saducees and the Essenes:

The Dead Sea Scrolls, which are often attributed to the Essenes, suggest clashing ideologies and social positions between the Essenes and the Sadducees. In fact, some scholars suggest that the Essenes began as a group of renegade Zadokites, which would suggest that the group itself had priestly, and thus Sadduccean origins. Within the Dead Sea Scrolls, the Sadducees are often referred to as Manasseh. The Scrolls suggest that the Sadducees (Manasseh) and the Pharisees (Ephraim) became religious communities that were distinct from the Essenes, the true Judah. Clashes between the Essenes and the Sadducees are depicted in the Pesher on Nahum, which states 'They [Manasseh] are the wicked ones... whose reign over Israel will be brought down... his wives, his children, and his infant will go into captivity. His warriors and his honored ones [will perish] by the sword.' The reference to the Sadducees as those who reign over Israel corroborates their aristocratic status as opposed to the more fringe group of Essenes. Furthermore, it suggests that the Essenes challenged the authenticity of the rule of the Sadducees, blaming the downfall of ancient Israel and the siege of Jerusalem on their impiety. The Dead Sea Scrolls brand the Sadduceean elite as those who broke the covenant with God in their rule of the Judean state, and thus became targets of divine revenge.

Differences between the Saducees and the approach of Jesus

The New Testament, specifically the books of Mark and Matthew, describe anecdotes that hint at hostility between Jesus and the Sadduceean establishment. These disputes manifest themselves on both theological and social levels. Primarily, Mark describes how the Sadducees challenged the Jesus' groups belief in divine resurrection. Jesus subsequently, defends his belief in repentance against Sadduceean resistance, stating 'and as for the dead being raised, have you not read in the book of Moses, in the story about the bush, how God said to him 'I am the God of Abraham, the God of Isaac, and the God of Jacob?' He is God not of the dead, but of the living; you are quite wrong.' The tone and content of the passage are indicative of theological and sociopolitical dispute. Jesus challenges the reliability of the Sadducees' interpretation of

Biblical doctrine, the authority of which enforces the power of the Sadduceean priesthood. In addition, the Sadducees address the issue of resurrection through the lens of marriage, which hinted at their real agenda: the protection of property rights through patriarchal marriage that perpetuated the male lineage. Furthermore, Matthew depicts the Sadducees as 'brood of Vipers,' and a perversion of the true Israel. The New Testament thus constructs Jesus as being in opposition to the Sadducees.

Differences between the Saducees and the Pharisees

The Pharisees and the Sadducees are historically seen as antitheses of one another. Josephus, the author of the most extensive historical account of the Second Temple Period, gives an extensive account of Jewish sectarianism in both Jewish War and Antiquities. In Antiquities, he describes 'the Pharisees have delivered to the people a great many observances by succession from their father which are not written in the law of Moses, and for that reason the Sadducees reject them and say that we are to esteem those observance to be obligatory which are in the written word, but are not to observe what are derived from the tradition of our forefathers.' The Sadducees rejected the Pharisaic use of the Written law to enforce their claims to power, citing the Written Torah as the sole manifestation of divinity. Furthermore, the Rabbis, who are traditionally seen as the descendants of the Pharisees, describe the similarities and differences between the two sects in Mishnah Yadaim. The Mishnah explains that the Sadducees state, 'So too, regarding the Holy Scriptures, their impurity is according to (our) love for them. But the books of Homer, which are not beloved, do not defile the hands.' The Sadducees thus accuse the Pharisees as the opponents of traditional Judaism because of their susceptibility and assimilation into the Hellenistic world. When synthesized, one can discern that the Pharisees represented mainstream Judaism in the Hellenistic world, while the Sadducees represented a more aristocratic elite. Despite this, a passage from the book of Acts suggests that both Pharisees and Sadducees collaborated in the Sanhedrin, the high Jewish court.

ROMAN OCCUPATION

The other thing that we should note of course is that all of this is in the context of Roman occupation. The whole country is being governed by Romans, something that is resented by many and actively resisted by some groups of zealots.

THE LIFE, MINISTRY AND TEACHING OF JESUS

So to return to our narrative of the Gospel attributed to Mark, the story begins with the baptism of Jesus by John the Baptist. This is an unusual experience for Jesus, somewhat akin to Paul's Damascus Road experience. Immediately on coming out of the water, Jesus sees heaven opened and hears a voice saying 'You are my beloved son in whom I am well pleased' and immediately he feels compelled to go to the wilderness where he stays for forty days living among the wild animals. Here he has more unusual experiences considering himself tempted by the devil and ministered to by angels.

John the Baptist is arrested on Herod's orders for his own protection and it is at this time that Jesus comes to Galilee and begins to preach and teach. His message:
- the time is fulfilled
- the kingdom of God is at hand
- repent – turn away from your present ways and turn to God
- believe this good news

He begins to gather followers and his teaching in the synagogue astonishes people in terms of both the new doctrines he presents and the authority with which he presents them. A synagogue is a Jewish house of assembly or house of prayer. When broken down, the word could also mean 'learning together'. Synagogues are consecrated spaces that can be used only for the purpose of prayer, however a synagogue is not necessary for worship. Jesus being permitted to speak in a synagogue would indicate that he was a respected figure and also that he could speak Hebrew in addition to the Aramaic that was the common language of the area. There is further amazement as he begins casting out unclean spirits and healing people. The crowds quickly grow as they bring those who are sick and possessed for healing. Jesus links this healing to forgiveness of sins.

272

From the crowds of followers, he ordains twelve of them as his disciples and with the charge that they:
- should be with him
- would be sent out to preach
- would have power to cast out spirits
- would have power to heal sicknesses

But Jesus very quickly finds himself at odds with those in authority in the synagogues such as the priests and scribes, who begin to challenge his teaching and authority and the sort of company he keeps. Jesus says that he has not come to call the righteous but sinners to repentance: to turn from their present ways and thoughts to God. Other Jewish religious groups like the Pharisees also begin to challenge his teaching and behaviour by using doctrinal technicalities and Hebrew tradition against him, or by accusing him of performing his healing by the power of the devil.

When his family arrive amongst the crowds pressing to see Jesus, he declares that the spiritual-minded people around him are his family. The crowds become so great that he is forced to preach and teach outside the synagogue but he does so only in parables: illustrative stories of every day life that are used to declare a few spiritual ideas. This is a deliberate use of spiritual discrimination to obscure spiritual matters from those outside who are not really spiritually inclined and likely to ridicule the message and the messenger. He explains the meanings of parables only to his disciples. When the twelve asked him about parables he says to them, 'To you it is given to know the mystery of the kingdom of God: but to those outside, all these things are done in parables: so that in seeing they may see, and yet not perceive; and in hearing they may hear, and yet not understand; in case at any time they should be converted, and their sins should be forgiven them'. He continues his preaching and healing as he moves about the area from town to town. He talks about:
- a coming judgment when all secrets will be revealed.
- the growth of the word of God from something very small to very large.
- The impossibility of putting new doctrines into old frameworks and traditions.

He appears to have power of the wind and storm and performs more healings and more casting out of spirits and in many cases, the spirits,

through those they have possessed, call Jesus 'Son of the most high God'. The crowds are astonished at his teaching, wisdom and abilities. The crowds think that Jesus is:
- Isaiah risen from the dead or
- A new prophet or
- Someone come as one of the old prophets

Meanwhile, King Herod had respected and feared John the Baptist as a holy and righteous man and had watched him and heard him gladly. But Herod had married his brother's wife and John the Baptist had condemned him for this. Herod's new wife wanted John killed so in order to protect John the Baptist, Herod had him imprisoned. However, Herod was later cornered into making an oath that turned into an obligation to have John the Baptist beheaded. News of Jesus reached Herod who was convinced that Jesus was John the Baptist risen from the dead.

The fame and popularity of Jesus increases even more, with people laying out their ill and sick relatives and friends in the streets that they might be touched by him. There is an incident of Jesus walking on the water. The Pharisees return to criticize him but Jesus condemns them as hypocrites or play actors speaking good words but their hearts being far away. They are accused of putting forward the ideas of men as the commandments and word of God as rejecting the word of God or making it of no effect in favour of human tradition. Jesus indicates that he has come primarily to the Jews, not to the Gentiles or non-Jews.

He continues his travels and preaching and healing and there are a couple of instances where he feeds the crowds with what appears to be little food.

Jesus asks his disciples who they think he is and they repeat what the crowds are saying, that he is Isaiah risen from the dead or a new prophet or someone come as one of the old prophets, but Peter says that Jesus is: the Messiah.

The word 'messiah', means 'anointed' and is a term used in Judaism, Christianity and Islam for a redeemer figure expected in one form or another by each of these religions. More loosely, the term 'messiah' denotes *any* redeemer figure and the adjective 'messianic' is used in a broad sense to refer to beliefs or theories about an improvement of the state of humanity or the world at the end of the age, that is a figure concerned with what are believed to be the final events in history, or the ultimate destiny of humanity. The word 'messiah' is used in the Old Testament to describe priests and kings, who were traditionally anointed with holy anointing oil as described in Exodus 30 v 22-25. For example, Cyrus the Great, the king of Persia, though not a Hebrew, is referred to as 'God's anointed' (messiah). People and things are anointed to symbolize the introduction of a sacramental or divine influence, a holy emanation, spirit, power or god. In later Jewish messianic tradition and eschatology, 'messiah' refers to a leader 'anointed by God', and in some cases, a future King of Israel, physically descended from the Davidic line, who will rule the people of the united tribes of Israel and herald the Messianic Age of global peace. In Judaism, the messiah *is not* considered to be God or a Son of God. The translation of the Hebrew word *Mašíaḥ* as Χριστός (*Khristós*) in the Greek Septuagint, the oldest of several ancient translations of the Hebrew Bible into Greek, became the accepted Christian designation and title of Jesus of Nazareth, indicative of the principal character and function of his ministry, thus Jesus 'Christ', or Jesus 'Messiah'.

This statement by Peter that Jesus is the Messiah introduces a series of statements about the suffering, death and rising of Jesus and about his coming in glory and power at the end of the age.

Then we have the *vision* of the transfiguration of Jesus who appears in garments of the brightest and purest white, with Moses and Isaiah. The disciples hear a voice out of the clouds saying 'This is my beloved Son: hear him'. Then suddenly Moses and Isaiah vanish leaving only Jesus who instructs them to say nothing till the Son of man is risen from the dead.

The ministry of Jesus continues, with talk about the *meaning* of rising from the dead, the return of Isaiah, faith and the rigours of discipleship, divorce, riches and the kingdom of God and servant-hood.

Jesus then enters Jerusalem on a donkey with the crowds laying down palms and saying 'Blessed is he who comes in the name of the Lord! Blessed is the Kingdom of David that comes in the name of the Lord! Praise in the highest!' Then Jesus enters the Temple at Jerusalem and angrily overturns the tables and chairs of those changing money in order for people to buy sacrifices and of those selling doves and so on for sacrifice, condemning them all as a den of thieves.

The religious leaders want to be rid of him now because they are afraid of him and because he is gaining popular support with the people who are astonished at his teaching. Jesus has further theological confrontations with the Jewish religious leaders, but they are afraid to arrest him because of his popularity amongst so many people. When asked what is the greatest commandment, Jesus is portrayed as stating that the first two commandments and the greatest, are:

a)   One should *love* God with one's entire heart, soul, mind, and strength

b)   One should *love* one's neighbour as one would *love* oneself

Once again religious leaders seek to trick him with theological questions but in the temple, when Jesus preaches, he condemns the scribes as lovers of status who are full of pretence. Jesus seems to advocate material poverty in the spiritual life. Though quite radical to the Pharisees and Sadduccees, non-ownership was the normal way of life for Essenes, who lived at varying levels of asceticism and this is one of the reasons that many scholars suspect that Jesus was originally part of an Essene group. More teaching about the end of the age follows. By now the chief priests and scribes are deeply envious of him and want him secretly abducted and killed, but the Passover feast is near and they fear the reaction of the people. Secretly, Judas Iscariot goes to the priests and offers to betray Jesus.

Following the Passover supper and a night of intense outdoor prayer by Jesus, Judas arrives with a crowd of religious authorities who are armed with swords and sticks, and Judas betrays Jesus with a kiss. The disciples flee and Jesus is taken in custody to the high priest who has with him the assembly of chief priests, scribes and elders. But they cannot find a witness against Jesus in order to legally have him convicted. There are many false witnesses but their testimonies do not agree. Finally, after remaining silent during these proceedings, Jesus is asked by the High Priest: 'Are you the Messiah, the Son of the Blessed?' Jesus replies 'I am, and you will see the Son of man sitting on the right hand of power and coming in the clouds of heaven'. At which point the High priest tears his clothes in anger and says 'Why do we need any further witnesses? You have heard the blasphemy. What do you think?'. They all condemn Jesus as guilty and pronounce the death sentence and they begin to spit on him, slap him, push him about and mock him. The chief priests consult with the elders and scribes and they tie Jesus up and take him to Pilate, the Roman Governor. Jesus hardly speaks. Pilate knows that the religious officials are envious of Jesus so he offers the people the chance to release one person – a common thief named Barabbas or Jesus, but the chief priests then stir up the crowd who shout for the crucifixion of Jesus. So, wishing to keep the people content, Pilate releases Barabbas, whips Jesus and delivers him for crucifixion. The chief priests and scribes are smugly content – 'He saved others; himself he cannot save. Let messiah the King of Israel descend from the cross so that we can see and believe.'. Jesus dies on the cross.

The day before the Sabbath, Joseph of Arimathea goes to Pilate and begs for the body of Jesus. Pilate is amazed that Jesus is already dead and after checking this fact with his soldiers, Pilate gives the body to him. Joseph wraps Jesus in fine linen and lays Jesus' body in a stone sepulcher and rolls a large stone across the entrance. After the Sabbath, Mary the mother of Jesus and Mary Magdalene and Salome bring spices to anoint the body at sunrise. When they get there, the large stone has been rolled away and inside they see a man clothed in white who says: 'He is not here – go to Galilee and you will see him there as he said'. They are amazed, trembling and afraid and dare not speak to anyone.

Jesus preached the resurrection of the dead reflecting the common Jewish belief of the time that the righteous and unrighteous await Judgment Day in peace (in the bosom of Abraham) or in torment, respectively. The belief in the resurrection of the dead was largely a late innovation in ancient Jewish thought and the Sadducees, who considered only the Pentateuch to be divinely inspired, considered it to be a false teaching. Since Deuteronomy decrees the obligation of Levirate marriage, (Deuteronomy 25 v 5), i.e., the brother of a dead man must marry the dead man's wife if the wife is childless, the logical conclusion is that if there are seven brothers, each dying for some reason, the wife could potentially have been married seven times, and hence if the dead were resurrected she would find herself in a highly polygamous situation. According to Mark 12 v 18 – 27, the Sadducees used this logical conundrum to challenge the idea of the resurrection of the dead, but Jesus argues that the resolution is simple—there will be no marriage after the resurrection and the people will be like the angels in heaven. Jesus is described by Mark as going on to justify the doctrine of resurrection, by referring to the story of the burning bush, in which God is described as stating, at one moment in time, that he is the God of each of the three Patriarchs—Abraham, Isaac, and Jacob, using the present tense—*I am* ... not *I was*. Mark portrays Jesus as stating that, since God is God of the Living and not of the dead, Abraham, Isaac and Jacob are still living, i.e., resurrection.

In Mark, with the discovery of the empty tomb we have no definite statement regarding the presence of an angel, but just of a man in a white robe; but by Matthew and Luke we have references to angels and by the time of Luke's writing, this seems to become two angels.

'When the Sabbath was over, Mary Magdalene, Mary the mother of James, and Salome bought spices so that they might go to anoint Jesus' body. Very early on the first day of the week, just after sunrise, they were on their way to the tomb and they asked each other, "Who will roll the stone away from the entrance of the tomb?" But when they looked up, they saw that the stone, which was very large, had been rolled away. As they entered the tomb, they saw a young man dressed in a white robe sitting on the right side, and they were alarmed.
"Don't be alarmed," he said. "You are looking for Jesus the Nazarene, who was crucified. He has risen! He is not here. See the place where they laid him. But go, tell his disciples and Peter, 'He is going ahead of you into Galilee. There you will see him, just as he told you.'"
Trembling and bewildered, the women went out and fled from the tomb. They said nothing to anyone, because they were afraid.' (Mark 16 v 1 7)

Mark, says nothing more concerning the resurrection of Jesus. There are some extra verses in some later manuscripts but it seems that this is where the original gospel attributed to Mark ends.

A SUMMARY OVERVIEW

In an overview summary of the gospel attributed to Mark we find:

Jesus – His person and identity –

Jesus' identity:

demons to keep secret: Mark 1:25, Mark 1:34, Mark 3:12
people to keep secret until resurrection: Mark 9:9, Mark 1:44, Mark 5:43, Mark 7:36, Mark 8:30

Jesus – His work and mission –

Jesus has come to give life as a ransom for many: Mark 10:45
Jesus has come to serve: Mark 10:45
Jesus has come to teach: Mark 1:38

Jesus – His message/Gospel –

Parables given to those outside synagogue: Mark 10:1, Mark 4:11-13, Mark 4:34, Mark 6:34, Mark 4:2
Jesus taught in synagogues: Mark 1:21
Jesus taught on Sabbath: Mark 6:2
Jesus is light not to be hidden: Mark 4:21-25
Jesus preached outside: Mark 2:2, Mark 2:13, Mark 4:1
Repent: Mark 1:15, Mark 6:12

Jesus – His Names

Bread is Christ's body: Mark 14:22
Servant: Mark 10:45
Bridegroom: Mark 2:19,20
Christ or messiah (by Jesus/high priest): Mark 14:61,62
Christ or messiah (by Peter): Mark 8:29
Holy One of God: Mark 1:24
King of the Jews: Mark 15:2
My Son (by God the Father): Mark 9:7
Rabbi (by teacher): Mark 11:21
Ransom: Mark 10:45
Shepherd: Mark 14:27
Son of God (by centurion): Mark 15:39
Son of God (by unclean spirits): Mark 3:11, Mark 5:7
Son of Man: Mark 10:53, Mark 2:10, Mark 2:28, Mark 8:31, Mark 9:30
Teacher (by crowds): Mark 10:35
Teacher (by disciples): Mark 10:17

279

Jesus – His Miracles –

Miracles could not be done in home town because of lack of faith: Mark 6:5

Jesus – His Excorcisms –

Casts out evil spirits: Mark 1:26, Mark 1:39, Mark 9:25-28

Jesus – His Healing –

Healed diseases: Mark 1:34, Mark 1:40-42, Mark 2:10,11, Mark 3:5, Mark 6:56, Mark 7:35
Healed fever: Mark 1:31

JESUS – THEMES AND THREADS IN HIS TEACHING –

Approaching God –

Believe the good news about God: Mark 1:15
Repentance: Mark 1:15, Mark 6:12

Prayer and Worship –

Jesus Prays: Mark 1:35, Mark 14:32, Mark 6:46

New Covenant –

Blood of New Covenant poured out for many: Mark 14:23,24

Law and commandments -

Law and commandments supported by Jesus: Mark 1:44
Eternal life obtained by following law and sacrifice: not possible with man, but possible with God: Mark 10:8-25

Tradition, Rituals and ceremonies –

Love to God and man more important than ceremony: Mark 12:33

Critical of Tradition: Mark 7:6-8

Standing/relationship with God –

Elect: Mark 13:20,22
Predestination, preparation: Mark 10:40

Heaven/spiritual realm and earthly/material realm and authorities –

Moneychangers expelled for trading in the temple: Mark 11:15
Spiritual and material contrasted: Mark 12:17, Mark 8:33

Kingdom of God/ Kingdom of heaven – (The spiritual realm within) -

Kingdom of God is near: Mark 1:15
Kingdom of heaven is like a seed growing into large tree: Mark 4:30-32
Kingdom of heaven is like sown seed - it grows, ripens, then harvest it: Mark 4:26-29

Eschatology (Last things) -

Jesus returns in clouds at the end of the world: Mark 13:26
Punishments after death: Mark 12:40
Rewards after death: Mark 9:41

Eternal life -

Eternal life obtained by following law and sacrifice: not possible with man, but possible with God: Mark 10:8-25

Faith –

Faith heals the person: Mark 10:52, Mark 5:34
Faith: When God sees faith He forgives sins: Mark 2:5

Jews -

Jews are like tenants: Mark 12:1-11

Prophecy –

Jesus Prophesies his own death and resurrection: Mark 10:33,34
Jesus Prophesies Peter's denial: Mark 14:30

CONCLUSIONS

So what do we make of these summaries and overviews of the Gospel attributed to Mark? Certainly what we have here is a Gospel that is more down to earth than that say of the later gospel attributed to John. There is no mention of the virgin birth, no mention of the Divine nature of Jesus, a focus on faith healing rather than on miracles, no mention of visions of the risen or resurrected Jesus or of his ascension to the clouds. There are various debates about aspects of Jewish religion – what it is lawful to do on the Sabbath, what is the primary commandment, how tradition relates to the Law of God, how effective ceremonies and rituals are, condemnation of the hypocrisy of some Jewish leaders in imposing heavy burdens on followers of God, ethical teaching about marriage and teaching about humility and faith. There are debates with Jewish leaders about the authority of Jesus, especially in terms of his proclaiming forgiveness of sins, coupled with debates as to the source of his power to heal. Yes, there is mention of the forgiveness of sins, especially in relation to healing and mention of his death as a means of forgiveness, there is also support for the idea of a resurrection of humanity after death and the idea that Jesus will return at the end of the age. There are prophesies concerning his betrayal, death and resurrection and the circumstances of the end of the age. But taken as a whole, this is certainly less miraculous and transcendent than the other, later gospels and the writings of Paul.

Prior to visions of Jesus risen from the dead, we find his disciples in a state of fear and dejection. At this point they considered that:

Jesus was a prophet
Jesus was powerful in what he said and did before God and all the people.
The chief priests and our rulers handed him over to be sentenced to death
They crucified him
We hoped that he was the one who was going to redeem Israel.

282

There is also a record of the reaction of the religious leaders to the empty tomb and missing body of Jesus: the elders and priests bribe the soldiers who were supposed to be guarding the tomb….'When the chief priests had met with the elders and devised a plan, they gave the soldiers a large sum of money, telling them, "You are to say, 'His disciples came during the night and stole him away while we were asleep.' If this report gets to the governor, we will satisfy him and keep you out of trouble." So the soldiers took the money and did as they were instructed.'.

However, as we know, quite a number of the followers of Jesus had *visions* that Jesus had risen from the dead and that he eventually ascended to the clouds and out of their sight. These visions gave the Disciple/Apostles hope, strength and courage given their understanding that what they had seen was the literally existing objectively real resurrected Jesus. Thus the movement that Jesus had started survived his death and was carried on by his brother James the Just and also by the other Disciples/Apostles of Jesus who also proclaimed Jesus' resurrection. The movement became a Jewish sect – one of many – and became based in Jerusalem where these Jewish Christians regularly attended the Temple.

Post visionary experience their message seemed to be:

Jesus is God's servant
Jesus is holy and righteous, the Righteous One—the Messiah
Jesus is the author of life
You Jews betrayed and murdered Jesus
But God raised him from the dead, and we are witnesses of this (by reason of the visions that we have had of an objectively real resurrected Jesus)
What you Jews and your leaders did to Jesus was done in ignorance
God was fulfilling what all the Jewish prophets had foretold about the Messiah
Therefore repent of your sins, have a new mind and turn to God
He will *again* send you Jesus, your appointed Messiah.
Because Jesus must remain in heaven until the time for the final restoration of all things
Jesus the Son of Man is standing in the place of honour at God's right hand.

Already we see the beginnings of the deification of Jesus and with that will come the need for the Virgin Birth, the Word made flesh and so on, all arising from this reification of the contents of their visions.

AN OUTLINE OF THE TEACHING OF JESUS

What do we seem able to say about Jesus? What did he teach? The original perception of him seems a little more down to earth:

He was possibly an Essene.
He submitted to the baptism of John the Baptist which inaugurated personal spiritual visions and experiences.
At John the Baptist's arrest, he commenced his ministry, travelling the countryside, preaching in synagogues.
He was a prophet, foretelling his own death, suffering and resurrection
Jesus was powerful in what he said and did.
The crowds considered that he healed and cast out evil spirits and thus he gathered a large following.
Faith heals the person and when God sees faith, he forgives sins.
He came to give life as a ransom for many, to serve and to teach.
He preached that the time is fulfilled: the kingdom of God is at hand, therefore repent – turn away from your present ways and turn to God and believe this good news
He was variously referred to as Servant, Bridegroom, Holy One of God, King of the Jews, My Son (by God the Father in a vision), Rabbi (by a teacher), Teacher, (by crowds and disciples), Ransom, Shepherd, Son of God (by centurion and unclean spirits), Son of Man.
He believed in and practiced prayer, particularly solitary prayer
He supported the Law and Commandments with a view that what was impossible for human beings was possible with God. But he was critical of tradition and ceremony, especially when burdensome or placed on a par with God's Word.
The Jews are like tenants - they are custodians of divine things
The Kingdom of God seems to be the spiritual realm within and it is near, and like a small seed growing into a large tree.
He believed in election, predestination and preparation of people by God

He believed eternal life was obtained by keeping the Law and maintaining sacrifice

He advocated material poverty and despised materialism in the temple

He antagonised religious leaders of the day

He was eventually condemned to death by religious leaders on charges of blasphemy out of envy

His followers hoped that he was the one who was going to redeem Israel – the anointed one or messiah.

He believed in the resurrection of the dead and in the Judgment and punishments and rewards

He believed he would return in clouds in power and glory

A BASIC SET OF CHRISTIAN VALUES AND BELIEFS

Thus a follower of Jesus would accept:

The need for repentance - turning around from our present ways and turning to God.

The ceremony of Baptism for repentance.

The need to follow Mosaic Law – moral and ceremonial, with faith in God to cover personal failings and shortcomings.

Prayer – especially solitary prayer.

The spiritual kingdom within and the importance of its cultivation.

Election and predestination by God.

Asceticism – material poverty and a selling of possessions to give to the poor.

Faith healing

Believe in eternal life gained through obedience to the Law and personal poverty.

Believe in the resurrection of the dead.

Believe in a future Judgment by God with rewards and punishments following.

Believe in a period of false prophets and messiahs and a period of suffering before the culmination of all things.

Believe that Jesus was anointed by God.

Seek to follow the teaching of Jesus.

Believe that Jesus will return in the clouds in power and glory.

Celebrate the ceremony of the bread and wine until Jesus returns.

Tend to have non-conformist attitudes to and be critical of hypocritical, presumptuous, man-made religious traditions, leaders, practices and institutions.

It is these kinds of ideas that would have to form the basis of any revised neo-orthodox Christianity. Even though I have questioned the nature of the experiences whereby the Disciples and Apostles 'saw' the resurrected Jesus, we still end up with a commitment to a post-death resurrection, because this is something that Jesus plainly believed in and taught. How far we agree with the ideas of the theology listed above is of course up to us but I would suggest that anyone calling themselves a 'Christian' would have to subscribe to most if not all this outline theology since at the bare minimum, this is what Jesus appeared to preach, teach and practice. To move away from these ideas is to move away to a different spiritual path – which according to what we have seen is perfectly acceptable – since we all worship our personal Lord – but in making such a move, we do move away not only from the sort of Christian orthodoxy that the Apostle Paul developed, but also we move away from the teaching of the founder, leader or teacher whose name we claim to take and whose teaching we therefore claim to follow.

A PERSONAL CONCLUSION

For myself, much as I would at times like to join a community or fellowship with shared symbols and meanings in spirituality; and much as Christianity has been the heritage and tradition of my country for hundreds of years, I find that I cannot subscribe to many of the precepts above. My own experiences, like those of the Christian Gnostics and the broader Gnostic movement and world-wide mystical spirituality in general has taken me out of Christian Fundamentalism and on a different path which I have elaborated in some of my other studies. I do not throw the baby out with the bathwater – there is much that is insightful and profitable in Christianity – I still delight in reading and studying Christian mystics such as Meister Eckhart; and I still gain profit from reading Christian theologians – but I also profit from reading Sufi Islamic thinkers such as Ibn al-Arabi, and Rumi, and from reading Hindu Advaita sages such as Shankara and others.

THE SPIRITUAL LIFE OF A MANIC DEPRESSIVE

P_____ S_____ was a graphics computer operator for 33 years. In his late thirties he studied with the Open University and obtained a Bachelor of Science honours degree. He subsequently gained a Certificate and Diploma in Counselling. Since his early fifties he has worked in a retail store. He enjoys photography, jazz, crime novels, tracing his family tree and Badminton.

I was born in 1951, in the north Midlands of England the only child of working class parents living in an industrial town. I remember my childhood as happy and secure. I went through the then-usual gamut of childhood illnesses – measles, mumps, chicken pox and so on. There was also a period when I had scarlet fever and was placed in an isolation hospital for three weeks at the age of three and a half. This was quite a traumatic experience for an only child of this age and did leave a few problems in later life, such as overwhelming feelings of isolation even on a crowded room. It was an experience that proved to be interesting to explore as part of my self-development in my counselling studies years later. I went to the local school with my friends and played in the local park. There were day trips to the coast and holidays in Wales. Neither of my parents were churchgoers, though they considered themselves to be Christians and encouraged me to go to Sunday School like many parents did with their children in the mid fifties. I had attended the local Church of England Sunday school (St. J____) as an infant, and during a period of unhappiness there when I was about six or seven years old, I was encouraged by my piano teacher to go to a local Congregational church which I attended until I was about twelve years old. I remember having a respect for church and I refused to fool around or misbehave in church like some of my friends but nevertheless, by the age of twelve I found the whole thing very boring and drifted away. That was in 1963. I was not a 'sporty' child – I hated football and cricket – and was a thin boy, slightly underweight and slightly shy and introverted.

My first experience of what we might call mental disturbance was at the age of ten or eleven. In those days, in England, a school exam called the 11-Plus was a very important milestone in a child's education. It consisted of a day of exams – in maths, English and so on – that determined what level of education the child was to progress to for their secondary education in their teen years. Failure to pass the exam meant that one was sent to 'senior' school – grouped together with low achievers who would eventually go into some sort of lower paid manual work. Success in the exam meant entrance to a grammar school or high school – with more opportunities, higher standards, and therefore an opportunity to obtain a higher quality job or profession – even a chance at University. The pressure to pass this exam was quite intense in those days, and all school work was geared to rehearsing the kind of questions and answers needed to pass this exam. Parents put pressure on their children to succeed and to gain opportunities for a better job in the future. My parents were by no means excessive in this, but encouraged me to do my best. Due to the date of my birthday within the year, I was one of the youngest in the class and at this age, that year makes quite a difference in one's maturity, skills and abilities. In this, I was at a disadvantage. Neither am I quick learner – it takes time sometimes for ideas and concepts to sink in, thus, I was at another disadvantage. Nevertheless, I got a reasonable result and went on to a Technical High School. But the pressure was undoubtedly there and I certainly felt it. For a few days during this period, I went to bed and my parent's activity around me seemed to 'speed up'. I guess I was suffering from some sort of feverish activity in my mind – feeling overwhelmed, mithered and distracted by this general pressure. It felt very disturbing and I would not go to sleep on my own for about a week. The experience only lasted for a few seconds or a minute, but was a little frighteneing for a 10/11 year old. It was bad enough for me to be taken to the doctors by my parents, but it was dismissed as a reaction to the pressure of this 11-Plus exam and after a few days, this mithered distraction passed. I believe now that this was my first encounter with a borderline manic episode.

My first encounter with Christian fundamentalism was at the age of 16. Fundamentalism is term that covers both religious and secular areas, but I use the term here with reference to Christian protestant churches which insist on the inerrancy of the Bible. They contest that the Bible is the inspired word of God, and that therefore it is without any mistakes or errors, Thus they use the Bible as their authority in matters of faith and conduct, with frequent appeals to it's texts and verses. Despite their shared this view of Biblical inerrancy, different fundamentalist churches hold to different and even opposing views. This is because these churches emphasise different verses of the Bible and draw out different interpretations of Biblical passages. Thus, though sharing a common belief in Biblical inerrancy, these groups have different systems of government and practice, and draw out different systems of belief. Some are Arminian, some Calvinist; some believe that extraordinary gifts like tongues prophecy and healing continue today, whilst others do not; some are democratic, some are not. These groups include Christadelphians, Pentecostal churches, both Elim and Assemblies of God, Brethren churches and Evangelical Reformed churches, which may be Baptist churches or local independent churches.

By 1967, a new minister, B_____ T_____, had arrived at the local Congregational church following the merging of the Congregational church with the local Railway Mission, whose building had been burnt down. Many of my friends were impressed with this new Pastor, a young man in his early twenties who came from a working class background in Manchester and was fresh from Bible College. He developed an instant rapport with the young people and the church youth club had grown in popularity as a result. It was about six months after his arrival that I started to attend the youth club with my friends. Being a church youth club for the youth of the church, it was expected that those who attended the youth club should also attend church services or Sunday school on Sunday mornings. No one ever challenged me on this, but I felt obliged to attend church and began to do so, a little begrudgingly since the youth club seemed worth it. I attended with an open mind, considering myself a Christian, with the same sort of respect that I used to have before. Over a period of six months it became clear to me that the message being preached by this new minister was different from what I had heard before. These sermons were preached from the Bible passages and texts and it appeared that they were faithful to these verses and passages. The messages declared that I appeared to be in danger of a 'lost' eternity, because a Just and Pure God demanded that failures and disobedience against God be punished. I saw that my failures and disobedience against God demanded such punishment and weighed against me when put in the balance. I saw the sword of God's justice hanging over me, rightly and fairly because I had offended a Just and Pure God. But I also saw the Love and Mercy of God in the offering of His Son Jesus Christ to take my deserved punishment on my behalf, and therefore an opportunity for deliverance by trusting in Jesus Christ to that effect.

Through August and September of 1968 these things occupied my mind and I sincerely wanted to believe and trust in Jesus and 'asked Jesus into my heart' many times. But I was not sure that I had obtained deliverance or forgiveness. I began to change my behaviour; to shun things that I felt were displeasing to God and to seek to do those things which it appeared that God approved of. At that time I bought a gospel record by Little Richard, the Rock and Roll singer of the 50's. It still remains an excellent Gospel album of spirituals by the likes of Thomas Dorsey. Whilst listening to that album and particularly the track 'Peace in the valley', I had, for the first time, the *experience* of assurance of salvation. All of a sudden, I knew that I was going to have 'peace in the valley some day' and that my sins were forgiven and that I was welcome by Jesus. These ideas were no longer theories or doctrines out there, but I felt that they became personal: they applied to me: I had a personal interest in them. I wept with joy as my salvation anxiety fell away and I felt assured of a place in paradise for all eternity. Eternal, Invisible, Spiritual things seemed Real and True to me. This was my 'conversion' experience – I was 'born again'.

I continued to attend church and became enrolled as a member. Some of the young people, myself included, asked for a young people's Bible study. We spent three years going through Paul's Epistle to the Romans once a week. During this period I also to attended evening services and mid week Bible studies. By 1971, I was asked if I would serve as a deacon, a sort of church administrator in more secular matters, which was considered at that time to be a role that lasted one year and which was then open for election again by the membership. Deacons deal with various odd jobs around the church, organised the bread and wine for communion and dealt with things like decorating, heating, maintenance and so on. With some reservations, I agreed. Looking back, this was a big mistake: I was not mature enough or educated enough in spiritual matters, but this was in many ways still a young church and not very large in membership, and the minister had introduced a tremendous sense of community and fellowship. These were happy days for me: full of humour, exploring together, playing together and working together. The structure and organisation of the church was moderately loose and informal and there was room for spontaneity and flexibility.

During this time I developed a growing respect for Scripture, but it was not until two or three years after my 'conversion' that I considered the Bible to be the inerrant word of God. I remember sitting through a sermon on Paul's letter to the Romans, chapter 5, where Paul talks about the first and second Adam. The Adam of Genesis is referred to as a real person, not a parable or symbol and it was pointed out that Jesus himself regarded Adam as a real human being. If the Apostles and Jesus the Son of God taught this, then it must be so I thought. This literalism, this dismissing of analogy or metaphor except where plainly intended, such as in parables, is a typical feature of Christian fundamentalism. The creation story in Genesis for example, is often taken quite literally by fundamentalists, who often believe in a literal, seven 24hr day creation of the universe and a young earth only tens of thousands of years old rather than millions or billions of years old. I was no exception and it was arguments like this coupled with an increasing faith and commitment that moved me to an acceptance of Scripture as God's inerrant Word and eventually to a position of being a young earth creationist, that is one who believes that God literally created the world in seven days about 6,000 to 10,000 years ago. I was encouraged to lead the occasional Bible study and to preach and these meetings obviously met with some approval since I was asked to preach and lead again at various occasions.

291

By now I was also beginning to seriously read Christian books. I had read introductory booklets to the Christian faith, but over a few years I had begun to read more deeply. Christianity really began my love of books and my love of philosophy. Over about five or six years I progressed from booklets, to modern book length studies, to Victorian works and eventually to the writings of the puritans. I sometimes had to have a dictionary on hand as I became aware of deeper, more thoughtful and more 'technical' works of theology and philosophy. I developed an increased love of the English language, grammar and the preciseness of the use of words in philosophy. Trips to second-hand bookshops became a joy.

I continued in this direction for about two years, but by late 1970 or early 1971 I began to suffer from tension and anxiety. The anxiety was what psychologists and psychiatrists call 'free floating anxiety': in other words, there wasn't a particular issue or event that was causing my anxiety, but rather, I suffered from waves of anxiety in which my mind would latch on to some small or irrational concern and blow it out of all proportion. My stomach would tighten and I would get 'butterflies' in my stomach. Waves on unsettlement and worry would sweep over me and I would feel distracted, 'mithered' and cluttered in my head. It is not clear to me even now what triggered this condition, though it may just have been pressures of work, course exams and so on.

At lunch times I took to going to a local open space and sitting in the long grass for half an hour, to escape the hustle and bustle of the working day. One particular day during the summer, I became deeply aware of the beauty of my surroundings. The sunshine, the tall grass blowing gently in the breeze, the sound of the grass as it moved, the patterns of the wind on the grass and the peaceful solitude all conspired together to produce in me a sense of natural harmony and simple beauty that seemed richer and fuller than I had ever experienced before. This open space seemed like a little paradise on earth, pure and unspoilt, and I felt deeply calm and peaceful and sensed the power and beauty of the God who must have made such harmonious nature.

However, my anxieties continued and I visited my doctor who prescribed the then wonder drug of Vallium. I was to learn ten years later that this drug causes me to become depressed about twenty-four hours after taking it. At this time though, I thought my depressions were a reaction to my anxieties. This condition was bad enough for me to be absent for a few days from work occasionally and generally disrupted my life making me introspective, lacking in confidence and morose.

The world sometimes appeared to me to be a scary, unpredictable place and there was a feeling of things being slightly out of control. It is not surprising then that the issue of whether God was sovereign or not was exercising my mind: Was God in control? Was God effectively ruling the world or had God wound the world up like a clockwork toy such that it was now winding down in it's own way? If God was in control, why was there so much evil and suffering? It was in this frame of mind that I read a book called 'The sovereignty of God' (A. W. Pink. 1968). Using Biblical texts, this book proposed that God was indeed a sovereign God, in full control, ruling believers and unbelievers, events and circumstances to accomplish His purposes. As I read this I remember suddenly seeing this sovereignty of God very clearly as True and Real. In what was to be a common factor in many of my experiences, it was as if a door in my mind opened and I saw things clearly. My heightened spiritual experiences often arose from an apprehension of some doctrine in a deeper and fuller way than before. In this case I saw clearly that God was a King of kings, ruling in power: He appeared as truly God to me. I was so empowered by this apprehension of God and the perception that He was MY God and that I was watched over by Him, that I threw away my Vallium tablets, knowing that I had nothing to be anxious about with such a God organising the circumstances of my life. My irrational anxieties were overcome and I recovered from my anxious state.

About a year later I remember coming home from a church service with an increased sense of the love of God towards me. This had probably arisen from something in the sermon, though I cannot remember exactly what now. I walked home in a state of energised praise and contemplation on God and decided, when I got home, to spend some time in prayer. I went to my bedroom to pray alone and was increasingly filled with a sense of God's love for me such that I could no longer put my words together, because the sense of God's love was so great. I lay on the bed enraptured by the immediate sense of God's presence and His loving condescension to me and all I could do was bathe in God's love as I continued in a state of bliss, taken up as it were, to a spiritual realm in close communion with God for about half an hour.

It was at this time that I met my first wife, W___, who was also 'converted' under the church ministry. Though about twenty years old, I was still quite naïve and inexperienced with members of the opposite sex. During my mid teens, many of my friends had started to go to local nightclubs and discotheques, but these never appealed to me. My mother and father had been keen dancers and won competitions. Mt father was a qualified dance teacher. But they liked the Old Tyme and Modern sequence dancing which by the late 1960's was seen as old fashioned. My parents used to host dancing at a couple of local workingmen's clubs every week, and as a child I had been taken to these events. By my early teens I grew to dislike the cigarette smoke-and-beer laden atmosphere. I just grew to dislike such clubs and public houses...I never was and never have been a big drinker or a smoker. Neither have I been a fan of contemporary popular music. My tastes turned to mellow Jazz, Blues and Latin music from Brazil, Cuba and Puerto Rico. So nightclubs and discos never held any fascination for me. As a result, the 'swinging sixties' partly passed me by and always seemed to be happening 'somewhere else'. In any case, I always think that I must have seemed a bit of an oddball – wrapped up in Christianity, studious and introverted, not liking modern popular music and still remaining physically thin and slightly underweight. Nevertheless, I was and still remain a bit of a 'hippy' at heart – at this time my hair was shoulder length like many other males of my age, I had a 'goatee' beard and liked the sanitised version of flower-power and psychedelia. I had met and dated a couple of girls but to my frustration at times, nothing came of these brief relationships. It was therefore natural that I would gravitate to someone within the church circle who shared to a great degree my spiritual views.

At the end of 1971, the Minister of the church received an invitation to pastor a church at Bridgnorth in Shropshire and after prayer and consideration, he accepted. He helped us in our search for a new Pastor and following a few months where the Deaconate looked after the church, our new minister, H_____ M_____ arrived in January 1973. Thus it was that I had found myself leading and preaching in church services along with other deacons during the period between our minister leaving and a new minister arriving.

The new minister, was a different man altogether from our previous pastor. A schoolteacher in his mid twenties, he had come up through the

294

ranks of an independent reformed church at Brighton, where served as an assistant Pastor. Very quickly, the cold wind of a more austere Calvinism swept into the fellowship. Our previous pastor had taken a Calvinist stance, but H____M____ introduced a more intellectual and emotionally cold approach and by now, I was already locked into a worldview that had Scripture as God's inerrant Word: an authority that shaped my view of everything. It was no longer an easy thing for me to dismiss apparently Biblically based ideas. The young people's flamboyant humour and the church's free and open structure was interpreted by this new minister as he later admitted, as a form of Antinomianism: too free and liberal in it's approach to morals and having to much licence. Thus a stricter, more disciplined approach began to take shape.

The new pastor had also seen problems in the then-emerging Charismatic movement. This was a movement that laid stress on spontaneity and inspiration in worship and on spiritual gifts, such as speaking in tongues and prophecy. It emphasised the personal experience of Baptism in the Spirit and centred on experience and joyous emotional displays in worship. This movement was critical of what it saw as the cold, dead formality of traditional English church services in the late 1960's and early 1970's. Our new pastor had seen at least one church divided and broken up by this clash between Charismatics and traditionalists and this had produced in him an acute wariness of 'experiences' or emotional displays; of hand clapping; chorus singing; tongue speaking or other such practices.

He also a more reasoning, intellectual approach to Scripture, though like all fundamentalists, this intellectual approach was strictly within the bounds of fundamentalist ideology and the Bible as the inerrant Word of God. For example, everyone was encouraged to have their Bible open during sermons so that they could check that what the preacher was saying really was Scriptural. The bookstall was checked to ensure that only 'sound' literature was available, that is, material which conformed to the fundamentalist Calvinist ideology. This was not seen as censorship, but as a preservation of the 'Truth'. It would soon extend to comments made about the sort of books that appeared on church member's bookshelves, or the sorts of films they went to see or television that they watched. I remember a considerable uproar for example when some of us decided to go and see 'The Exorcist'. The new pastor made it his aim to work through the whole Bible within ten years via the two Sunday services and midweek Bible study, which he succeeded in doing. His aim was to give a balanced Biblical view, not over-emphasising his favourite verses and not avoiding difficult or controversial passages. He soon began to wear a minister's black gown in the pulpit to help assert his authority and he insisted that he be addressed as 'Pastor' rather than by the more familiar and informal use of his Christian name.

A new church manse was built via member's contributions, the men of the fellowship built a Baptistry and the church was redecorated. A church constitution was worked through and adopted, with the authority of the minister or 'Elders' being more firmly established together with the importance of respect for and submission to Elders in so far as they follow Scripture. An integrated doctrinal system took shape, based very much on protestant reformers like John Calvin and the high Calvinists like B. B. Warfield and A. A. Hodge. The church became fully independent, not relying on any grants, or on any special meetings which relied on public donations. In this way, it supported it's own full time minister with provision for pension in retirement. 'Unseemly' humour was clamped down on and standards of behaviour began to be imposed which were seen as consistent with Scripture. This imposition was effected in various ways. Members who acted or spoke in an inappropriate way were likely to be taken into the church vestry for rebuke by the Pastor, or later into the Pastor's study, which became affectionately known by us as the 'Sin bin', much to the minister's annoyance. If a member desired to achieve a particular role within the church, they might not get approval from the minister. The shift was made from a spontaneous, natural fellowship to one where the Law of God and the Commandments were paramount. But it was as if the Holy Spirit of God was being denied and stifled.

Matters had to be seen to be done 'decently and in order' - and that is an accurate portrayal: they were only 'seen' to be done decently and in order - under the surface and away from formal services, there persisted a quite surreal and zany humour, inspired by such programmes as 'I'm sorry I'll read that again', 'Monty Python', and Spike Milligan's television programmes. There was often an irreverent and bawdy humour, serving I think as a compensation for imposed decency and order of formal services and as an outlet of our real personalities.

For me, these first few years under the new minister made Christianity become a burdensome affair. The joy and spontaneity that we previously enjoyed was repressed and suppressed and a soberness and seriousness descended on us all. The sense of community continued, as did a sense of achievement and growth. But it seemed to me that if things were bad, or we weren't seen to be enjoying this repressed, formal, legalised version of religion, then it was portrayed by the minister as basically our fault, our sin, our transgressions, our fallen human nature, because, after all, this version of religion was 'True', God's Law was perfect and delighted in by a righteous man. The implication was that doubt was being expressed concerning whether we had righteousness imputed by Christ, whether we had integrity, whether we had salvation. We had descended into a legalistic form of Calvinism, one of its heights being the placing in the church hall of a poster of the Ten Commandments. Someone wrote at the bottom of it, 'the letter kills, but the Spirit gives life' (II Corinthians 3 v 6) and other similar verses.

This tension between freedom in the Spirit and the continual application of Law which made me feel guilty and weak as a Christian continued to grow. As an antidote I began to read yet more fundamentalist Christian literature and I was particularly shaped at this time by Dr. Martyn Lloyd-Jones's writings, especially his Romans 5 volume. I had a number of meetings with the minister, both by myself and with one or two other like minded individuals to try and address our concerns, but the outcome was always the same: no real movement. There was an inability on my part to get him to see the problem, and he had an inability to see the difficulty. Tensions came to a head when a group of us went to an evangelical meeting called 'Come Together' in 1974, they year I got married. This was an American originated evangelism type of event. For the first time in a few years I saw people actually enjoying themselves in worship. Those of us who went to this meeting decided to meet together for prayer, both to get ourselves 'right with God' and to pray for the church.

Fairly quickly, house meetings began to be held each Friday evening, though it took some persuading to get the Pastor to agree to these meetings. Though we were not conscious of it at the time, we were setting up a situation where the minister did not have quite the same authority, since the meetings were taking place in someone's house and not the church. But this was not our intention: we were seeking unity and

297

blessing for the whole group and were constantly seeking to avoid division and schism from the rest of the church membership. These meetings ran for about two years, after which many of the young people who attended got married and moved a bit further away or went to university. These meetings were the source of almost a mini revival for some. There appeared to be at least one 'conversion', a sense of liberty and spontaneity and a deepening of spiritual fellowship and communion with each other and with God.

The weight of concern over the formal, legalistic and dead state of the church was for me overwhelming. I spent much time in prayer, anguish, discussion, frustration, depression, concern and study and for me 1972-75 was a very frustrating and difficult time. I was also struggling with my personal walk with God: various habitual behaviours, which I felt to be displeasing to God and against the code of Scripture, were present in my life and I could not shake them off. I felt a poor and unworthy Christian and sometimes I wondered if I was a Christian at all. The 'Come together' meetings led me to read about the Welsh revivals of 1859/60 and 1904. I wept. Here seemed to be truly joyful and awesome Christian spirituality in practice: here were people moved greatly by an understanding of the Bible and a movement of the Spirit; here was the opposite of our dry state... lively and vital encounters with God. About half a dozen of us set out to pray for revival in our church.

The first Sunday of September 1975, (about six months after the Come Together meetings) was unlike any other. I give two accounts of it below, written at different times and from slightly different perspectives and emphasis, to try and give a flavour of this event:-

Here is the first account:-

This state of affairs changed on the first Sunday morning in September 1975. It is interesting to note that I had been struggling all that summer with a book by Dr. Martyn Lloyd-Jones, an exposition of the Apostle Paul's Epistle to the Romans. (Lloyd-Jones 1974). I had read about a third of the book and somehow could not get past one particular chapter. This was unusual for me: I tried many times to read it, it was not hard, but somehow, my concentration was not there. It was our habit to have a prayer meeting before each Sunday service, to seek God's blessing on the service. I arrived this particular Sunday morning with all these issues still on my mind, and still with a heavy heart for the church. During the course of the prayer meeting, the pastor prayed as usual, but I noticed a change in his words and attitude. Suddenly this man had shaken off some of his legalistic tone and seemed to embracing the Holy Spirit. It was as if I was being transported upwards out of the room. My heart and mind lifted as I was filled with the perception that God had changed this man. I was filled with a perception of the power of God over men's hearts and minds. It was like the floodgates of heaven were opened and a torrent of blessing was poured into my soul. I walked out of the prayer meeting as if my feet were six inches off the floor... I was filled with optimism, expectancy, energy and joy. The service that morning was as many had been before it in form: the pastor briefly opened in prayer and we then sang a hymn. Alas I cannot remember what the hymn was, but it was a typical school anthem type hymn of praise. All I can remember now is that I sang the words of that hymn as I had done many times before, but now, again, it was as if a door in my mind had opened and I perceived clearly and plainly the depth and reality of the words of praise and descriptions of the character of God. These qualities of God, His Power, His Omnipotence, His Love, His Eternity, were so immediately Real, Deep and Powerful, so Clear to my mind that I groaned under the weight of the perception of them and could barely physically stand under the glory of what they described. I could barely sing because of my strong emotions and tears filled my eyes. It was as if God was pouring out not just a shower of blessing but also a flood of power into my soul. At the end of the hymn I all but collapsed into my chair and the minister then lead us in prayer. He was a university-educated man, a qualified teacher, and by no means lacking in eloquence. Even so, the prayer was like many that had been uttered before it, yet this time, my perception of the meaning of the words was so great that I was groaning under the weight of them. Words like Immortal, Sovereign, Merciful, Eternal, Lord, Love, Pardon, Ransomed, Healed, Forgiven, were so Rich and Deep, and I felt their meaning keenly in my heart and mind. I was hardly conscious of anything else. I felt their application to the Church and to me. I KNEW I was saved from the just deserts of hell, and that my heavenly Father who seemed very near and loving to me loved me without question. After the prayer, the experience subsided, the immediate experience lasting about fifteen minutes. I don't think I have ever felt so clear headed and balanced as I did then. The immediate perception was of God's Almighty Power: that at any time, as it pleased Him, He could pour out such a torrent of blessing and turn people's hearts no matter how indifferent or rebellious they were to Him. A revival and awakening could occur in the time it takes to snap one's fingers and the Holy Spirit could pour out his blessing on one or a thousand with irresistible power, and this no matter how dark or oppressive the circumstances seemed. Though powerful, this experience was in no way frightening. It was coupled with such a sublime sense of God's supportive and protective Love that my heart opened and rejoiced in this experience. At no time was I afraid. I should point out also that there was no self-exaltation or pride in this experience. Rather there was an experience of lowliness, of humbleness and unworthiness. This was a gift of God to me, an unworthy and undeserving servant.

Some secondary effects have lasted to this day, others diminished over about six months. Immediate secondary effects included a falling away of the habits that I felt were so displeasing to God. They literally just fell away and had no power or attraction for me for some time. I was given to much time in prayer and conversation with God in much earnestness of concern for others and the church. I devoured as much as I could read on spiritual matters, particularly a number of works by the New England Calvinist Jonathan Edwards. The Lloyd-Jones book that I was struggling with was read within a week, and most interestingly dealt with the very experience I had just received. It gave a doctrinal explanation, and a number of testimonies by other Christians to this experience throughout church history. It gave tests to sift out false experiences, and mine passed every one, so this was a great reassurance to me even though the experience was so direct as to appear to be self-evidently from God. I felt very much the unity of mankind and Christians in particular, for they were bound together by Christ. When I heard fellow Christians in dispute or being sarcastic with each other, my heart was in great pain. I wondered how people could be so cruel to each other, especially Christians and at how lightly they treated God and spiritual things and I wished for Unity and Concord and for my fellow believers to share in the weight of glory that I had seen. I was aware of the Unity of the whole of creation, how everything, and every living creature were important.

Other people saw these changes in me too and commented on my increased seriousness, intensity and involvement. My experience of God during the months that followed rose and fell and then rose again. These were not serious roller coaster out-of-control situations, but a gentle, undulating petering out of the intensity of these experiences. There was one occasion when I set out for work and there was a glorious rainbow in the sky. Again, I was lifted up to God as I considered not only the beauty of the rainbow per se, with it's proportion and symmetry, but also its spiritual significance as a sign by God that He would not destroy the earth by flood. Thus again, qualities of God's Mercy, and Love and the quality of His sign filled my mind and heart and lead me to heavenly contemplations.

Here is the second account:-

I entered the morning prayer meeting of our church anniversary service very much with these concerns on my mind. I had given our Pastor a book to read which seemed to express my feelings, in the hope that in some way, he might perceive the problem. As he prayed, I sensed immediately a difference in his approach. For the first time it seemed, he talked about the presence of the Holy Spirit and the need for his blessing. My heart and mind soared. We entered the service and sang the opening hymn, one of the traditional ones and I had such a perception of the Power and Awesomeness of God, together with His mercy and Gentleness that I could scarcely stand under the weight of such a view. The Pastor then led in prayer and this perception continued with such a weight that I felt completely melted, humbled and in awe. I KNEW the power of God to bring an Instant revival. This experience led to increased study, prayer and diligence. Old habits that I felt God disapproved of fell away for months, yet before, I could not shake them with all my efforts. Bitterness and animosity that had grown towards the pastor fell away and the sense of a need for Christians to unite in love filled my mind and heart. Studies by Dr. Martyn Lloyd-Jones in Romans 8 seemed to confirm this as a genuine Godly experience and I moved on to study the works of Jonathan Edwards, which had a great influence on my thinking, particularly his works on revival and on the religious affections.

It still remains the most potent spiritual experience of my life.

One of the questions that emerge from this is whether these are genuine spiritual experiences or whether they can be explained purely as products of bi-polar disorder. I was not to be diagnosed as borderline manic-depressive until 2009, and one of the symptoms of mania is a lack of insight into the condition. The person in a manic or hypo manic phase feels great, euphoric, but this appears quite normal and a reasonable response to what is going on to the person themselves, even though others may not be so sure. Are the sort of experiences that I have been describing merely a form of religious or spiritual mania? It certainly never entered my mind that this could be so. But of couse it may well be that I am deluded by these mystical experiences and that I am rationalising them after the fact into an unfalsifiable hypothesis and world-view. It appears that neither side can prove this one way or the other. What I do know is that these experiences have given me depth, meaning and orientation: they have made me feel eleveated and euphoric and I have never felt so clear headed and perceptive as when I have them. Sometimes they have been unsettling and caused a sense of flatness and emptiness at the loss of the experience. They have altered my priorities and made me less materialistic generally and during and near to the experiences, I have become much more altruistic and selfless for example. I believe that though having some similarities to psychosis and some symptoms of bipolar disorder, they are nevertheless distinct from them and for me, as a bipolar sufferer, thay have had a rich, stabilising effect. Whether it is true or not, I believe in the Divine as diffuse literal Spirit/Energy as Essence of all that is and expressed in all that is. It makes me feel orientated, healthy and gives me a sense of purpose.

I have found the following to be true of myself as a bipolar sufferer who has had mystical experiences:

Only small evidence of thought disorder or disorganised thinking. Though entering a receptive or passive mode of consciousness, I am able to return to the active, rational mode of being. There is as a result an integration or synthesis of these two modes of being.
I enter the passive, receptive, mystical mode as a mature adult and return to the rational mode. The experience is trans-rational and paradoxical.
I am able to continue functioning in daily life, despite bipolar mood fluctuations.
I do not suffer from visual or auditory hallucinations.
Mystical episodes are generally brief, maximum about fifteen to twenty minutes.

Mood swings last for about two to three weeks, sometimes, a few months.

I have no impairment to my social relationships beyond my natural introspective nature. I respond empathically to the needs and concerns of others.

I have a history of mental health problems with bipolar disorder.

The mystical event often has a positive outcome, resulting in improvement in my functioning, social relationships and growth. It has a healthy effect.

I am probably one of 0.1% of people who experience mysticism.

I have a supportive social network

The mystical experience is no longer unsettling or disorientating

I have a sense that the material world is 'real/not real' whereas Spirit is Real

I have the following indications as common both mysticism and psychosis:

I can enter the receptive mode

The experience appears unmediated or Immediate and Real

There are biological effects in my brain

The content is non-rational and cannot be construed or remains unconstrued

My experience involves a unified perception and loss of boundaries

The boundary between inner and outer can be lost

My experience involves a deeper quest for meaning and stable foundation.

The experience may give rise to a loss or orientation of the self momentarily

I feel marginalized by modern western secular society and fear being marginalized by health professionals

The experience leads to a heightened sense of perception and insight

In terms of mysticism and bipolar disorder:

Both may lead to euphoria, ecstasy, elation and joy, but mystical content is always spiritual, whereas bipolar content is not.

Both may lead to preoccupation and withdrawal, even depression.

The following list gives indications of schizophrenia as opposed to mysticism:

The person's thoughts are not easily understandable i.e. what they say doesn't make sense. They are irrational.
The person has difficulty functioning, or is unable to function, in everyday life: they are stuck in a passive mode of functioning that does not deal with practical issues. They lose touch with material reality and are stuck in a world of fantasy or delusion.
Auditory hallucinations are more common than visual hallucinations.
Episodes are generally prolonged.
Social relationships are impaired due to the person withdrawing socially. They may respond inappropriately to the needs and concerns of others.
There may be a history of mental health problems in the individual or the family.
The person has usually exhibited mental health problems previously.
The event often has a negative outcome: hallucinations and delusions are considered a disruption to the normal functioning of the person's consciousness.
The tendency is one of regression and pathology
1% of people suffer this disorder
They may feel alone and isolated
The 'ego' or 'self-system' may break down or become fragmented

I think that in these sorts of ways we can begin at least to differentiate a little between 'madness', 'mental illness', 'mania' and 'manic depression' or 'bipolar disorder' on the one hand, and 'mystical', 'gnostic', 'transcendent', 'immediate spiritual' experience on the other. Though there are differences there are also similarities. Some of these issues will be dealt with as we move through this account.

Back in 1975, for me, these were genuine spiritual experiences and were exactly what they appeared to be. They confirmed the theology that I was embracing, reinforced it, established it and made it more deeply Real. In this atmosphere of heightened spiritual awareness, of expectation of revival/awakening, of change at church, and house groups and so on, an interest in spiritual gifts arose. Some experimentation had gone on in the house groups concerning prophecy and a word of knowledge and dreams and revivals seemed to have some of these elements, even with notable puritans, the fathers of present day fundamentalism. Our austere Calvinism considered such influences to have ceased, yet here were some of the people that we looked to such as John Flavel, C.H. Spurgeon, John Knox and Howell Harris encountering or experiencing these phenomena. We attended a few healing rallies, though I came to the conclusion that there was too much show and not enough substance and that these were in some cases positively harmful. I agreed with our Pastor that these 'healers' were like spiritual cowboys, riding into town, kicking up a storm and riding out again, leaving damage and lack of spiritual aftercare in their wake. Thus began, in 1976, a study on spiritual gifts that was to continuing into the new millennium. I worked excessively on this study in 1976, to the point of mental exhaustion by early 1977.Too much study had made me mentally exhausted and vulnerable.

Again there are two accounts of this period written at different times. Here is the first:-

Back came the free floating anxiety with a vengeance and following a visit to the doctor, I was on Vallium again. 1977 became and remains the worst year of my life. Vallium-induced depression led me to a foretaste of hell. Many have said to me that they consider this depression to have been a reaction to my ecstatic experiences but I do not accept this. I was simply so involved in intense study that it exhausted me mentally and physically. I overworked, studied too hard, did not give myself proper sleep and found I could not stop, and suffered a return of anxiety states, palpitations and so on. Vallium, prescribed to alleviate this anxiety, plunged me into depression, particularly in the summer of that year. If the ecstatic experiences were a foretaste of glory, this was a foretaste of hell. I was regularly, for hours each day, in a state of anguish, fear, blackness and inner torment. My thoughts, especially during the summer, were often of suicide, but the potential upset of my parents and wife was a restraining influence. An even greater restraining influence at times was the fact that I might fail in my suicide bid – that really would have depressed me. On one occasion I actually seriously gave in to the desire to kill myself. I thought that it was far better to be with Christ, in glory and that all my suffering could be ended quickly. I accordingly decided to kill myself and as I submitted to this desire, the words: 'You are not your own, you are bought with a price' (I Corinthians 6 v10) were forcefully impressed upon my mind. I immediately and strongly perceived the meaning of these words and used them as a weapon to fight off my suicidal desires. This seemed most unusual at the time. I did not realise that the words were Scriptural and could not recall hearing or reading them before. They felt like the words of God to ME. I later realised their Scriptural origin and also realised that I must have read these words before as we had worked through I Corinthians in a series of studies about five years earlier. At times I thought I was going mad, something which I had a real fear about. I suffered from illusions, (a bundle of waste paper in the street looked like a dead sheep) The world seemed mad... with lots of violence, conflict and a breakneck pace. At one point, having barely got through the day, the sheer noise of the dishes being washed by my wife caused me to collapse on all fours deeply sobbing with despair. I could hear this noise and wondered what it was and then realised it was myself sobbing uncontrollably. I stood outsider of myself as it were and could see myself defeated then suddenly being overwhelmed with terror because I thought that men in white coats would soon be arriving to drag me away to a mental hospital. For six weeks I experienced no sense of God's presence whatsoever. No one knew how to help me. This was the withdrawal of the sense of God's presence as described for example in Lamentations in the Old Testament. I felt completely and absolutely alone and frightened. It seemed to me (and still does) that sometimes when a schizophrenic commits suicide it is a last act of complete sanity.

This period ended with another spiritual experience arising from a sermon delivered one Sunday morning by our minister on the text 'My God, my God, why hast Thou forsaken me?' I knew that the experience of separation from God was like hell, but then I saw that Christ, who had been in the bosom of the Father from all eternity and who then became the God-Man and suffered this separation at Calvary too, I felt His cry as my own, but new it was infinitely more terrible than my own experience, because I had not dwelt with the Father in heaven. Then I saw that this separation was endured for the elect, that Christ had endured it for me out of His great Love for me, that Christ willingly came as a sacrifice, and I was melted to tears by His love, condescension and mercy to me, who was unworthy dust. My sense of separation ended at that moment.

Here is the second account:-

1977 was a disaster. I suffered severe anxiety, was given Valium by my Doctor, which I was later to discover, caused me to suffer severe depression. During 1977 I became suicidal, my thinking hopelessly distorted by the effects of Valium and exhaustion. I tried to continue my church duties, but it was very hard. Irrational fears would overwhelm me, such as a dread of being called up to National Service in the army, even though there was no conscription at that time. I found it difficult to eat. It was a major event to get through a single day. In the summer, for six weeks, I encountered what the puritans call spiritual desertion: all sense of the presence and comfort of God disappeared and I despaired. I felt cast off and cut off from God, and had no evidence or assurance of my salvation. I clung desperately to the Scriptures, still believing them to be the inspired Word of God which promised grace, though all my experiences testified that I was lost and without God. I also clung to my experience of 1975, when I had full assurance and felt that I saw things very clearly. This desertion experience came to an end one Sunday morning when our minister preached on Christ's saying 'My God, my God, why hast Thou forsaken me?' I saw how much more agony Christ had suffered in his separation from the Father on the cross and coincidentally, my condition began to be relieved.

During this time, my wife, the pastor and the members of the church struggled to cope with me. They did not know how to help; they had never experienced anything like it before. This was very much a cognitive battle against powerful emotions. It was a matter of continued obedience. Christian theology, especially of this Calvinist kind, subtly devalues feelings and sensations in favour of obedience to authority. Though fundamentalism helped in some ways, it caused further problems at other levels. It insists that man is a sinner who can do nothing to save himself. Indeed, ALL ATTEMPTS AT SELF HELP ARE VIEWED AS INDICATIONS OF PRIDE, which only deepen sin. I was never the same again.

As I emerged from my depression at the end of 1977, all the bitterness, frustration, anger exhaustion and hurt boiled over. Just as I thought I had overcome, I was overwhelmed by these negative feelings. The church and the Pastor in particular became the focus of my venom, (rightly so I felt at the time). I resigned from the Deaconate and left the church in early 1978, with my longsuffering wife as well as a close friend and his wife, who interestingly enough had gone through very similar problems at the same time. We left very much under a cloud: it was not possible to leave with dignity – the Pastor was too worried about us causing division in the church and branded us as backsliders and perhaps not even saved by Christ. For six months we attended a local Pentecostal church where initially, I found it's more spontaneous meetings fresh, positive and enjoyable. Eventually though, my friend and his wife drifted back to our original Church; I ceased going anywhere and my wife then returned to our original Church too. My returning friend, desperate to be accepted again and to be involved in preaching and leading never seemed to be himself again, but to always be putting on a mask in order to gain the approval he needed from the minister, and which was so begrudgingly given or more usually withheld. Just occasionally, when the minister was absent, his real nature and character surfaced again, but ultimately, after about ten to fifteen years, he moved to another church again, never to return, and never to gain the appreciation that he so desperately needed from the minister, not even at his funeral.

My involvement in Christianity after this became erratic. By 1978 I was not thinking too clearly and in any case, with regard to the church, the whole place seemed very oppressive because despite all, it still had an emphasis on duty, law, doing things properly and in order and such like. For two years, on and off, I attended the Pentecostal church. Pentecostalists are like the New Agers of Christianity: the experience is the thing but there is little in the way of a critical approach or in the way of testing the genuineness of various phenomena. I loved the emphasis on praise, openness and spontaneity. It was such a great release from the legalistic restraints of my previous church. I mention this as a side note, because of course, spiritual gifts were also present and I had a considerable interest in them. Every week without fail, one or two would speak in tongues and there would be an interpretation of each of these. The tongue speaking was, I think, a form of automatic speech, which was claimed to be a heavenly tongue. But there was ALWAYS an interpretation. Interpretations were always vague, in the sense that newspaper horoscopes are vague… they were either general praises, general injunctions to holiness, or vague promises of blessing… no one said anything like 'Next Tuesday morning Fred Jones will have an unexpected visitor.', or anything specific like that. One Sunday morning a man prayed in a tongue that appeared quite superior in quality to the usual stuff: it had a greater variety of phrases and syllables and I then realised that this was an Italian man speaking in his native tongue. Significantly, this was the only occasion that no one interpreted and the only time that such an event could have been tested easily.

I finally rebelled in 1979 after all my depression and exhaustion. I was spiritually exhausted: I could not stand to see theological books on my bookshelves, God appeared monstrous and sadistic to me after all my suffering in depression. I became bitter, especially concerning the pastor of my first church, yet at no time did I consider that God did not exist. Despite resting, I entered a cycle of rebellion then return, further rebellion and return again. The conservative nature of reformed evangelicalism sat increasingly uneasily with me. I asked too many questions, became too individual, but it was to take fifteen years to leave Calvinism. My spiritual experiences still seemed very Real and they were difficult for me to explain outside Calvinism and I could not be deny them, but my heart left Calvinism in the early eighties. My mind would not shake it off until the 1990's, so this time was a period of inner conflict and a searching for truth and growing interest in psychology. 1979 was also the year that my father died.

Christian Fundamentalism proved inadequate at dealing with my depression: I was told I did not have the right faith, or enough faith or something similar; so I turned to self-help psychology literature. To Fundamentalists, these books had far too much emphasis on the self or had an atheistic philosophy or both. I was continually being told to deny myself and this seemed increasingly absurd. During my depression and subsequent conflicts I became more introverted and withdrawn and felt like a square peg in a round hole when it came to fitting in to the fellowship on my periods of return. Nevertheless, if it had not been for my heightened experiences prior to my depression, I think I would have gone under: I would have gone mad or committed suicide. I just would not have had the inner resource to cope.

During this time my two daughters were born.

The five years immediately following my depression WAS a roller coaster ride. I fluctuated on a monthly cycle from a mentally taut, near manic state to days of depression. Normal life was difficult. During all this time I never sought medical help or counselling... I was far too scared during my intense depression period in 1977 when I thought I was going mad and would be locked away. The one apparently sane anchor was the Bible, which I felt to be absolutely, unquestionably true in the light of my previous ecstatic experiences. Even if I did not now feel it to be true, in my mind I knew it was true, and clung to its word and testimony. I did not seek counselling in case anyone sought to undermine this one anchor of steadfastness and hope. Even in my greatest rebellions I could not shake off the idea that the Bible was God's word and that God really existed.

It was only as time distanced me from the immediate effects of these experiences that I eventually sought medical help and by 1982, I ended up on a years course of antidepressants, to help stabilise my condition. The antidepressant was Triptizol and worked wonders, but also caused new problems. The day before I started the tablets, I found myself most irritated by the Tannoy announcement system at work. I took the tablets and the first effect was pins and needles in the brain. Then, I became very relaxed and the Tannoy system was just not important anymore. I developed a ready sense of humour, became quite giggly and I remember thinking that this new mood was how I used to feel as a child. The problem was a philosophical one: Within a week, things 'out there' ceased to irritate and annoy me and I developed a ready sense of humour. My moods began to stabilise and I became relaxed and easy going. But what had changed? Nothing 'out there' had changed. Only my perception of reality had changed and the problem was which perception was correct? How did I know what reality was? We all think that what we perceive is correct, but now I became aware of just how much we interpret reality

During this time I perused a number of self-help psychology books and my slight interest in psychology deepened as some of these books provided positive help in remedying my low self esteem, guilt and lack of confidence. There is increasing evidence that reliance upon church or state or astrologer or some other external authority fosters a passive-dependent lifestyle in which responsibility for personal growth is evaded. I decided that I had to take some of that responsibility on board and I felt that no one had a right to deny me or anyone else access to views and arguments that in promising to help also promised to challenge me.

I went through periods of spiritual and religious rebellion and then through attempts to re commit myself to the Christian life. In the early

80's, I began to try and sort out my difficulties by study of Scripture. I wrote a church constitution clarifying my role with Elders and the extent of their authority, together with the scope of my own duties and responsibilities. I wrote a study of evangelism that differed from the accepted orthodox view. In my spiritual gifts study I had adopted a position that gifts still continued at certain times and seasons as special providences of God and that they had in themselves their own evidence as to their Authorship: an argument drawn from John Owen and John Calvin and for quite some time, this was enough. This argument is closely related to arguments and evidences for the Authorship of Scripture, which is the highest spiritual gift in many ways, being supposedly inerrant inspired revelation.

However, despite the antidepressants, I still remained somewhat unstable in mood and opinion. I went back to the church for a while, but I was like a square peg in a round hole. Even though I still accepted the Bible as the Word of God, I placed a different interpretation on much of the practical outworking of it. I became aware of what I thought of as too much superficial thinking and hypocrisy in these fundamentalist circles. I also knew that I would only be accepted if I conformed to the orthodox fundamentalist view. I recognised that my interpretation was my opinion: just one view of reality and that I could not be dogmatic about it, but neither could I accept the dogmatism of others. I was beginning to become dissatisfied with the 'established church dogma' in other words. When I presented cogent Biblical arguments for my views, these were rejected with statements like 'You cannot prove everything from the Bible!' This from fundamentalist leaders! I resented anyone telling me what books I should or should not read and it was becoming clear that for a fundamentalist, a lack of firm dogma meant a lack of commitment. All the various Christian views were just competing shades of grey to me: nothing was black or white. If things were not so certain, then I felt that I could not give a great commitment to them. There was an increasing dissatisfaction and a growing feeling in me that I had been wrong in my life choices and that I had missed out on various worldly pleasures. Events would happen like some church members being involved in a car accident but escaping severe injury. They came back praising God for His mercy, but I thought, if God is God, why did he let it happen in the first place? All the strain of these changes and uncertainties finally took their toll. I entered another period of rebellion against God and everything.

My marriage broke up in 1984 under the strain of all these events and I had a wild and passionate affair. I visited the Pastor with the woman I was going out with just to upset him and many of my Christian friends supported me during this confused emotional time by refusing to talk to me, or walking across to the other side of the street to avoid me. Needless to say, that hurt me, though I know I hurt others as well. Within three years my new relationship broke up and following the death of my mother I lived alone. In sincere repentance I began to return to God and Christian interests, not to my old church, but to another fundamentalist church, under the gentle and friendly persuasion of my second wife to be, B_____.

I also began studies with the Open University in social science. Because of my experiences, psychology had interested me for some time and I decided to seek a degree in psychology. I was introduced to thinkers like Karl Marx as well as a wide variety of psychologists. I then regularly attended B_____'s church at Astley, near Leigh. This church was in some ways very much like my original church in its early days with B____ T____. At this time, rather academic matters like the nature of the soul occupied my mind. After our marriage, we attended W____ H____ B____ Church, another fundamentalist church. Open University trained me a little in critical thinking and introduced me to a wide variety of theories and I eventually came away with a B.Sc. (Hons.) degree. Open University also sharpened, (though some may say dulled) my political awareness. I emerged as a working class Marxist/Pluralist. I was no longer sympathetic to right wing, middle class traditional values. Of course, right wing middle class traditional values are the very values that infuse most fundamentalist churches. So, even more, I was now a square peg in a round hole, unsympathetic to much of the social agenda in fundamentalist churches.

I'm sure that many of my fundamentalist friends would like to blame Open University and psychology for my eventual withdrawal from fundamentalism, since this would provide a ready target of some alternative philosophy to Calvinism. But this is not so. My withdrawal actually came as a result of my continued studies on the theme of spiritual gifts and from fundamentalism's own inadequacies and contradictions. In terms of psychological theories, the nearest I came to accept was George Kelly's Repertory Grid theory. This is not a philosophy but a way of measuring people's beliefs and examining them. Open University

312

encouraged an eclectic approach, where appropriate theories with regard to the problem were used. I did not come away with a global psychological worldview.

The crunch issue was this: if spiritual gifts such as tongues and healing, like Scripture, were self evidencing; if they contained within themselves their own irrefutable evidence as to their Godly authorship, it seemed reasonable to ask: exactly what is this evidence in particular? I began to study widely. My first shock came on reading 'The mind of the Bible believer' by Edmund Cohen. Here was a critical essay on fundamentalism by an ex fundamentalist. I had never read anything by an ex fundamentalist before. All the people I knew who had 'left the faith' had either faded away or left in rebellion. Either way, it was considered that either they were 'backsliders' and would return eventually, or if not, they were never 'true' Christians in the first place and had never really understood the doctrines of grace. Here, in Cohen's book, for the first time for me, was an ex fundamentalist actively criticising fundamentalism. It was clear that he understood fully the doctrines of grace and had once embraced them. He was now clearly and eloquently rejecting them. Quite why it surprised me I do not know, because Jonathan Edwards had given clear indication that such a thing was possible in his work on the religious affections. Alongside this, the inadequacies of fundamentalist arguments for inspiration, inerrancy and the authority of Scripture were becoming clear. I began to take the view that if Scripture really were the Word of God and that the doctrines I had drawn from it were correct, then they would stand up to human argument. It would not be possible for humans to effectively criticise God. What good would a faith be that cannot stand up to these simple questions and criticisms?

However, Calvin, Owen, Luther, Packer, Young, Strong, Warfield, the Westminster Confession, Sword and Trowel and the rest were all failing to supply adequate arguments for Scripture inspiration and inerrancy. It occurred to me that rarely was this subject dealt with in fundamentalist circles. If it was, specious arguments were often given, which when combined with existing beliefs and commitments, seemed to be sufficient. Other books such as Lane Fox's 'The unauthorized version' compounded the problems where inconsistencies in Scripture were outlined. The final nail in the coffin was James Barr's book, 'Fundamentalism'. Further inconsistencies of Scripture and other problems in fundamentalism were outlined, many of which I readily identified with. The arguments against fundamentalism seemed unanswerable. Furthermore, fundamentalism seemed now to be a stagnant, dogmatic, right wing conservative authoritarian structure. It was censorious and closed to open debate.

The axe had been laid to the root of the tree of Christian fundamentalism. Without the authority of inspired revelation in the form of Scripture, the entire edifice began to collapse. It was not a pleasant experience and by 1994, I was in the middle of it. My whole orientation and identity appeared to collapse. I was not sure who I was, where I was going or why. I alternated between bitter resentment of fundamentalism and a longing to return to its cosy security. But every time I returned to it, the doubts and evidence against it soon caused me to reject it. Yet it was also a liberating experience, a freedom from constraints and standards which I no longer agreed with or which no longer reflected my views, or which no longer seemed to work. At times I was afraid of eternal damnation. At times I returned to prayer and found comfort. It was still by no means clear to me that God did not exist, but the evidence, as with gifts, was hard to find. I remembered my experience of 1975. It was the highest of at least three similar experiences and it's impressions were difficult to deny.

The end result was that my interpretation of the experience was questioned. This was because other believers in different, contradictory religions had received similar experiences couched in their own religious framework. Even non-religious people had received similar experiences. The experience is beyond doubt: a transforming, elatory, humbling and transcendent experience, which language is insufficient to capture: and it just happened to be framed by my world view at that time, as on the other occasions.

I left W_____ H_____ B_____ Church, since I found myself increasingly unhappy there and attended Christ Church, a Church of England fellowship near to home. This was a very relaxed fellowship and gave me time and opportunity to think a little more. I studied outlines of Biblical criticism and then did a personal study on authority in the church and the place and nature of Scripture. I looked at other early Christian writings such as the book of Enoch and I Clement. Whilst happy with such ideas as two authors for Isaiah, and Paul not being the author of the Pastoral Epistles and so on, the authority of Scripture as a cohesive document was undermined. To move to a context where I understood the

314

writers to be writing in their own historical perspectives meant a depreciation of the authority of Scripture as God's truth. To begin regarding Genesis as figurative and the so called words of Jesus being rather what early Christians thought or wished or summarised what they thought he had a said all seemed to me to be a greater difficulty of harmonisation than the more literal approach. The main thing was that the coherent authority had gone and though the Scriptures may be remarkable documents, with many wise sayings and insights, they were no longer authoritative in a way that I could understand or build on. I had been trained in the view of plenary inspiration as promoted by B. B. Warfield and this had been for me internally coherent and logical. But now, the evidence for such a view was lacking and even more, was positively against such a view, but the alternative view of the Scriptures for me was that they were simply men's opinions, and though the ideas and literature were in many ways superior for me to books like the Koran, they nevertheless were exactly of the same nature. I began to see the Bible as a collection of contradictory, discrepant books that had been written by superstitious ethnocentrics who thought that the hand of God was directing the destiny of the Hebrew people.

I explored other philosophies such as existentialism with which I identified to a moderate degree. For about twelve to eighteen months I sought to adopt a liberal Christian position, but found this impossible: I was just selecting bits of Scripture that I liked and none of it had any real authority for me. I explored the history of the reformation by writers other than fundamentalists and found much that I did not like: its cruelty, narrowness and censoriousness, but I still enjoyed that sense of revolution and overthrow of corruption. I spent some time looking at diverse religions like Judaism, Hinduism and Islam, but found these to be inferior to Christianity in my opinion. By late 1995, attendance at Christ Church had wavered. Other, more modernistic approaches to Christianity seemed to distort the meaning of Scripture into something else and I could not accept these either.

My continued studies of spiritual gifts and psychological explanations of false gifts had led me to the U.K. Sceptics. From them I discovered C.S.I.C.O.P., the Committee for Scientific Investigation of Claims Of the Paranormal. Their articles proved interesting and I subscribed to the 'Sceptical Inquirer', a monthly publication where scientists of various specialisations investigate U.F.O.'s, new age thinking, astrology, spiritual gifts, healing meetings and so on, encouraging scientific thinking and exposing superstition and fraud. For a while I began to adopt their worldview. The fundamentalism that I experienced had a cohesive, integrated worldview. Once one accepted certain assumptions it was quite logical. It was not like some fundamentalist groups where mere affirmation of certain 'truths' was enough without a sense of integration. If one part of my fundamentalist worldview was altered, it often affected other areas. Leaving fundamentalism left an empty void in the sense that for a while there was no integrated, cohesive worldview. I did not know how to orientate myself on various issues or on what basis. I had to start from scratch. Liberal Christianity did not fit the bill. Secular humanism involving a reasoned, logical scientific approach seemed for while to fill the gap.

Following this brief period of secular humanism, which in the end just felt inadequate, I was discovering people like Roberto Assagioli. I really like his writings, for their depth, balance, definition of self and embracing, in a psychological way, of spirituality. Then I discovered Ken Wilber and transpersonal psychology whose model seemed to cover all my experiences and also to present spirituality within a stage model of development that was broadly accepted by a number of modern psychologists and thinkers. I did not have to deny my experiences and I did not have to distort them. Neither were they were dealt with as though they were the products of poor mental health. I was able to embrace these experiences in a positive way.

Despite leaving Christian Fundamentalism, spirituality, in it's broadest sense, remained an important dimension in my life and one that had to be acknowledged, though it could no longer be done so at a Christian fundamentalist level. Following obtaining my degree with the Open University, I went on to study for my Certificate and Diploma of counselling at Keele University and it was here, that I explored more fully the area of Transpersonal Psychology, of which Assagioli and Wilber were a part. For a while, I found myself quite absorbed about New Age thinking. Tucked in amongst the dross of uncritical New Age material were some interesting books. I toyed with the Qabbalah, the Tarot, Feng Shui, T'ai Chi and other similar areas. Much of it was either unsatisfying because it was immature, or elusive: leaving a vague feeling of truth but difficult to pin down. But this period of gaining a degree and studying a new subject also introduced a hypo-manic phase. This meant that my second marriage to B_____ collapsed. Despite this upheaval, spirituality still dominated my thoughts.

For a few years, Ken Wilber became the theorist who provided me with orientation, including spiritual orientation. His model, or map embraced ALL my experiences, in a positive way, without recourse to fundamentalist type religion. He provided a scheme that positioned fundamentalism and the New Age in relation to logic, existentialism and mysticism, and differentiated genuine Transpersonal experiences from false, regressive ones. He produced a scheme that had a differentiated view of levels of spirituality.

A further period of mystical exploration began however at the turn of the millennium when I also got married for a third time. After leaving Christian fundamentalism, I entered upon a period of spiritual near-hermitage. I did not become involved in any fellowships or religious groups apart from one weekend Buddhist retreat in the Lake District and peripheral work in the spiritual area during my studies for a Certificate and Diploma in Counselling. I trod an individual path, carrying out personal studies on different religions and in Transpersonal psychology. I developed my relaxation and guided imagery practice and found new thinkers such as Ken Wilber, Roberto Assagioli, Arthur Deikman, Julian Jaynes and Ibn al-Arabi. This involved the use of Free Imagery: an extension of Guided Imagery, but without the pre-planned script or template. An opening situation was planned, (the desire to see God) and then the Imagery was allowed to take its own course. I kept a journal recording the mystical experiences that occurred during this period, and a personal spiritual philosophy has been elicited from this journal that feels right for me.

Intense spiritual experiences occurred again, but this time, they were not framed in Christian terms such as this example:

I tried my key, which fitted the lock, and before I knew it, I was in a vast, cathedral-like room. 47. Pews were laid out on a black and white tile floor. The vaulted roof was resplendent in gold and blue. There were ornate gold carvings everywhere, and at the front of the room, covering the ceiling and made of black stone, there was a huge eagle with wings outstretched. Etheria flew around the room. In the place where one would expect the altar to be, there was a stone table. From each corner of the table there rose a column and these supported a polished stone slab and dome. 48. Between the four pillars was a glass globe, blue in colour, in which specks of light were swirling around. I became aware of a pulsating humming sound, like the sound of an electrical generator or vast electrical power. 49. I asked Etheria what this was and she told me that it was the Hub of the Universe. I felt impelled to touch the globe, and this overcame my apprehension about getting an electrical shock or being hurt in some way. To my surprise, my hand went through the globe into the blue energy, and in a moment, I had entered it completely. 50. I became the energy, and expanded out being the specks of light that infused the whole Cosmos. I began to lose my centre of being and feel that I was in all places at once. 51. I heard Etheria say 'As God fills the Universe, so God's energy fills the Universe as the source of all life.'. 52. Then, the light seemed to dissipate and I found myself standing by the globe again. Etheria began flying in front of me and said 'Come!'. 53. I grabbed her ankles and together we flew out of the Treasure Room, high into the sky, until the Golden City appeared as a small dot below us. Up we went, beyond the Earth, the Solar System, the galaxy, to the outer reaches of the Universe. 'All this is God's Treasure' said Etheria.

Or this:

I decided, with their approval, to open the chest. 29. As I lifted the lid I saw that the chest was filled with an incredibly bright white Light that seemed to fill the whole room. Despite my apprehension, I wanted to enter this Light, to step into the chest, to get behind the light. I put one foot in the chest and seemed at times to become part of the Light itself. 30. This perception happened only momentarily, for fractions of a second. 31. When it did, I lost for a moment my sense of being in a particular place, the sense of being an object in a particular location. I seemed to fill the space in the room, indeed, to fill the space beyond it, and instead of being a central entity, I seemed to be distributed across all dimensions, to be in all places, both there and here. 32. I felt momentarily expansive. Then the whiteness of the light faded and I was back

Processing the information that occurred during these Free Imagery sessions has now taken over nine years and the most recent writers that I have come across that most closely reflect these ideas are the Sufi mystics Ibn al-Arabi, and Rumi; the Hindu commentator Shankara; to a lesser extent the Christian Mystic Meister Eckhart and some modern writers adopting the non-dualist Advaita Vedanta philosophy. I got a couple of articles published, one in 'Transpersonal Psychology Review' at the British

Psychological Society, and a couple in 'De Numine', the magazine of the Alister Hardy society.

After ten years, this left a feeling of not being involved with any spiritual group or people. Friends would say that I should be teaching, or counselling, or involved in some religious organisation and indeed, career guidance had suggested lecturing or teaching and I was in many ways a trained and qualified counsellor, though counselling had left me a little disillusioned regarding a certain overall lack of coherence.

It was in this frame of mind that I decided to carry out a Repertory Grid Analysis in order to see the way in which I perceived these different options and why I seemed to be a little stuck with regard to moving into any of them. Initially, fourteen options were compared.

1) No fellowship: I learn from books, websites, lectures, television.
2) Attend a Calvinist Christian fundamentalist church
3) Attend a Pentecostal Christian fundamentalist church
4) Attend an Anglican/Methodist Christian church
5) Attend an informal house fellowship/experience meetings.
6) Go to a Buddhist retreat. E.g. Lake District.
7) Attend a Multi faith or Inter faith centre.
8) Go to a spiritual retreat, e.g. Findhorn, Counselling workshop.
9) Attend a Liberal Christian fellowship
10) Try something new and exotic. E.g. Islam, Hinduism.
11) Start my own meetings/lead own group.
12) Attend a spiritualist fellowship
13) Practice Transpersonal counselling/lecturing/teaching.
14) Go to a Yoga course/or meet a guru/leader.

By comparing these options, bi-polar constructs were elicited, with further, deeper, core constructs being elicited from them. In all, thirty two constructs were elicited:

Preferred pole   Contrast pole

1) Intuitive, spontaneous, informal warm.   Cold formality
2) Receptive to mystical experience.   Closed, restrictive.
3) Reward, satisfaction, achievement   Frustration dissatisfaction
4) Fulfilment of my potential.   Poor performance

319

5) A sense of social purpose — Aimless, meaningless.
6) Uplifting, energising. — Numbness, depression
7) Accepted, belonging. — Disapproved of, outcast.
8) Truthfulness, integrity — Charlatanism, deceit, lies
9) Orientation, I know where I am. — Constantly wrong-footed.
10) Confidence — Bewilderment
11) At ease, relaxed, peaceful — Guarded, uneasy, tense
12) Long lasting commitment — Drifting, temporary
13) Involved in meaning behind religion — Indifference
14) Reach depths of my being, real me. — Empty, superficial
15) Affirming of life and self — Nothing, death.
16) Clear perception of God and Reality — Things stay as they are.
17) Sense of self-control, Independence — Manipulated, dependent
18) A position of power and strength — Weakness, draining.
19) Mature, Adult — Put into child, patronising
20) Stable, level, good foundation — Unstable, unsettled.
21) Able to stand in storm and tempest — Collapse in difficulty.
22) Structure, discipline and boundaries — Undisciplined, chaos.
23) Being happy and comfortable — Restless, uncomfortable,
24) Not accountable to others — Accountable disapproval
25) Able to build (on good foundation) — Not able to build
26) Participation. Originality — Following by rote
27) Part of my context, culture. Fits — Unfamiliar, foreign, alien,
28) Able to function well — Distracted, restricted.
29) Originality, Freshness — Restricted to system.
30) Diversity, multiplicity, plurality — Restricted to ideology.
31) Involvement in spiritual teaching. — Hiding ones light
32) Tendency to altruism — Self interest

Each of these was rated in importance, and then evaluated for each option in terms of how likely one or the other side of the construct would be fulfilled. This produced a network of figures, totals for each option and each construct and so on. But at the end of this exercise, I still felt that I had not quite grasped the essence of the problem, so a further set of options were drawn up for comparison:

1) Attend a Pentecostal House fellowship
2) Practice Transpersonal counselling in hospice or Mind.
3) Transpersonal counselling: own practice
4) Be a lecturer in a college following their syllabus

5) Set up my own lectures in a college or library
6) Be a spiritual mentor or guide
7) Teach or lecture in a Pentecostal/Quaker fellowship
8) Do occasional teaching or lecturing
9) Writing for spiritual magazines.

The bi polar constructs elicited were:

Preferred pole	Contrast pole
MEANINGFUL, DEEP	EPHEMERAL, LIGHT
SAFE, WITHIN MY LIMITS	OUT OF MY DEPTH
HEALTHY SELF-PROTECTION	RISK OF EMOTIONAL HURT
HAPPY, SETTLED	UNHAPPY, ANXIOUS
ORIENTATED	BEWILDERED
IN CONTROL EMOTIONALLY	OVERWHELMED
CAN FUNCTION	CANNOT FUNCTION
RELAXED, SPACE	CLUTTERED, TENSE
EVEN TEMPERED	MOODY IRRITABLE
GOOD RELATIONSHIPS	STRAINED RELATIONSHIPS
WITHIN MY FINANCES	BEYOND MY FINANCES
NO GUILT	FEEL GUILTY
LITTLE WEIGHT TO CARRY	HEAVY BURDEN
IN TOUCH WITH OTHERS	DISTANCE, BARRIER
GOOD FOUNDATION	BASELESS
ORDERED, STEADY	TOSSED ABOUT
FOCUSSED	DISTRACTED
AT EASE WITH MY SELF	PERSECUTE MYSELF
ENERGISING	DEPRESSING
EMOTIONALLY SAFE	EMOTIONALLY CRIPPLING
MY AGENDA	SOMEONE ELSES AGENDA
SENSE OF LIBERTY	BOUNDED, CLOSED IN
AWAY FROM HOUSE	AT MY HOUSE
GIVING INFO	PROBLEM SOLVING

NO QUALIFICATIONS	NEED QUALIFICATIONS
NOT OPEN TO BLAME	OPEN TO BLAME
TOUCH LIVES	DO NOT TOUCH LIVES
STUDY AT OWN PACE	PACE SET BY OTHERS
COMPANIONSHIP	LONELY
HELP AND SUPPORT	UNSUPPORTED
UNMONITORED	MONITORED
THEORETICAL	PRACTICAL

All of these two groups of constructs were rated highly: they were seen as important.

It was during the elicitation of the second group of constructs that a fundamental and deep-rooted conflict within myself emerged. My counselling training had revealed a problem left over from a stay in an isolation hospital when I was just over three years old. I sometimes get in touch with a deep seated and uncomfortable sense of isolation and loneliness. The way to remove this deeply uncomfortable feeling is by contact, often, just a handshake, a hand on a shoulder or hug. Thus I sometimes feel quite keenly my need for spiritual fellowship with like-minded people. However, this conflicts with another deep-seated emotional issue: I find being with people can be quite overwhelming emotionally; I feel out of my depth, distracted and unsure quite how to behave. Thus I can feel quite uncomfortable at social gatherings, parties e.t.c., and especially when I am first meeting people or in a new situation with people, such as working in a new place. Also, tied up with these emotional issues is a need for approval. When these sometimes quite powerful emotions arise within me, I am taken back to being three years old again: I either feel isolated and distant, or I am overwhelmed with churning emotions of uncertainty and anxiety, or I become very sensitive to a need of approval by others, and am deeply hurt and isolated when not approved of or criticised. It is this trio of emotional states, deeply imprinted by my hospital stay at the age of three that form a core problem. Knowing the issues, and working through them in my counselling self-development has not made them go away. Neither has staying with the feelings and trying to ride them out. This is a major reason why I could never be a professional counsellor: the emotions are too much like a roller coaster, and too exhausting. Similarly, if I were to stand in front of a fellowship or group of students as a leader or teacher, the strong need for approval would kick in. And that is what it is like: being kicked in the stomach. Not to be approved is to be isolated, and once again, the roller coaster emotions begin.

This second set of constructs got in touch with some of these issues.

In the end, the results of the analysis were:

1) The best option was the one that I was in: the semi-hermit; the individual walk. (42%)
2) The next best options were:
a) Writing (37%)
b) Pentecostal House fellowship/experience meeting. (36%)
c) Going to yoga class. (31%)
d) Starting my own meetings. (16%)

3) The constructs that scored negatively, in other words, areas of dissatisfaction, in the main option of keeping an individual walk and not attending any fellowship were:

-40 No participation
-40 No involvement
-40 Lonely
-40 Isolated
-36 Unsupported
-28 Socially aimless
-19 Do not touch other people's lives
-16 Sense of distance from people, barrier
-16 Depressing
-14 Unhappy
-14 Moody
-14 Burdensome
-12 Self-interested
-12 Poor performance
-12 Drifting socially

4) The second option, Writing, does not satisfy or overcome these areas. Though not significantly related to the first option of the individual walk, it nevertheless scores negatively on most of the same constructs, so taking up writing, though an interesting area to begin, would not solve the feelings of dissatisfaction that I have listed above. These

323

disadvantages are most countered by going to some sort of house fellowship or meeting. However, if I attend say a Pentecostal fellowship, I would have to attend Sunday worship and tolerate the narrow or restricted view of spirituality that they have, and I would find this difficult and if I lead a meeting myself, than I have all the disadvantages of the burden of the need for approval and the resulting emotional roller-coaster ride. Attending a weekly meditation/prayer group with the Pentecostal/Quaker context is quite appealing, but attending weekly church services is less so.

5) The fourth option, attending a Yoga class, I found to be surprisingly high up on the list of favourable options. The Yoga that I have in mind is not the keep fit stretch-and-bend variety, but the meditative variety. This does begin to give a sense of involvement with like-minded people if it is in the form of a class as opposed to a one-to-one session.

6) Finally needless to say, all counselling options scored negatively because of the emotional involvement, and they should be avoided. They scored highly in the areas of contact and purpose, and that is why they sometimes seem attractive to me when I feel isolated and purposeless. Teaching and lecturing offers orientation, purpose, meaning and some involvement, but being more distant, these options are more emotionally safe. They scored in the mid range, some slightly negative, some more positive. This trend encapsulates the main problem: I want to be involved and in contact with people, but the result is an emotional rollercoaster that is draining and produces tension and anxiety, together with a need for approval. Counselling provides most contact and most unsettlement. Teaching gives a certain distance but begins to create with that a certain sense of isolation, but it is emotionally safer. However, I only feel really safe more or less on my own, but then I am more isolated still. This reflects upon my whole social life: I much prefer having a few close friends to being plunged into a pool of being surrounded by many people and being out of my depth.

7) The Calvinist option was put in as a test. Bitter experiences of leaving a Calvinist church mean that I feel quite negative to this option, and indeed, it came out quite negatively as it should have done.

I felt that this exercise really did get into some of the nitty-gritty of the issues involved in my spiritual walk and I have come away understanding my dissatisfactions more clearly together with an understanding of options realistically available to me.

Then, in 2009, I was diagnosed as being hypo manic-depressive following a period of exuberant but not spiritual activity throughout 2008. This was as a result of finally arriving at what I felt to be a stable, coherent, integrated spiritual philosophy. I felt released from a long quest and the resulting euphoria led to a manic phase. I love these phases, but I do not always have proper insight into what they are and everyone around me seems dull and staid while I want to have fun. My third marriage collapsed.

Being diagnosed as a Bi-polar sufferer led me to an extensive personal study on the differences between mysticism madness and mania which can also be found on the web at:

http://www.scribd.com/doc/14800812/MYSTICISM-MADNESS-AND-MANIA-AN-EXPLORATION-OF-EXPERIENCES-OF-GOD-AND-MENTAL-DISORDER

The instability that arises from manic depression, with the accompanying shifting sands of changes of perspective have led me on a spiritual quest to find a spiritual philosophy and orientation that is deep enough, strong enough and stable enough to endure such changes and the trials that the world brings. It has lead to a position that embraces the expressions of all religions, Christian Fundamentalism included but which recognises that the Divine cannot be contained by any of them. It recognises that the Divine meets us where we are, and uses our imagination to create metaphors and analogies to explain and comprehend the Formless Incomprehensible Absolute.

REFERENCES AND FURTHER READING.

Assagioli, R. (1975) ' Psychosynthesis' Turnstone. London.

McKinsey, C.D. (1994) 'The encyclopedia of Biblical errancy' Prometheus Books.

Porterfield, K.M. (1993) 'Blind faith. Recognizing and recovering from dysfunctional religious groups'. CompCare publishers.

Psychological approaches to Fundamentalism:

Sargant, W. (1957) 'Battle for the mind' Pan London

Porterfield, M. (1993) 'Blind faith – Recognising and recovering from dysfunctional religious groups' CompCare U.S.A.

Hassan, S. (1990) 'Combatting cult mind control' Park Street Press Vermont U.S.A.

Cohen, E.D. (1986) 'The mind of the Bible believer' Prometheus Books New York U.S.A. (Neo-Freudian)

Thouless, Robert H. (1983) 'Straight and crooked thinking' Pan London.

Christian critique of psychology:

Vitz, Paul C. (1977) 'Psychology as religion: the cult of self worship' Lion. U.K.

Cosgrove, Mark P. (1979) 'Psychology gone awry – Four psychological worldviews' IVP U.S.A.

Liberal Christian critiques of Fundamentalism and leaving Fundamentalism:

Barr, J. (1984) 'Escaping from Fundamentalism' SCM Press London

Barr, J. (1977) 'Fundamentalism' SCM Press London

Humanist approach to Fundamentalism:

Kurtz, P. (1994) 'Living without religion' Prometheus Books New York U.S.A.

Historical context of Fundamentalism:

McManners, J. (Ed) (1993) 'The Oxford history of Christianity' Oxford University Press, Oxford.

Testimonies of former Fundamentalists:

Babinski, Edward T. (1995) Leaving the fold – testimonies of former fundamentalists' Prometheus Books New York U.S.A.

Critique of Bible:

Lane-Fox, R. (1992) 'The unauthorised version: truth and fiction in the Bible' Penguin London.

From the same author on Feedbooks

THE RESURRECTION - A BIBLICAL PERSPECTIVE *(2011)*
The resurrection, the idea that sometime after death we are physically restored and made alive in order to stand before God and the Final Judgment is a central idea in Christian theology and particularly the teaching of the Apostle Paul. Over the centuries, many different interpretations have been placed on this event and so this study seeks to return to what the Bible actually says about the resurrection: what it is, what events lead up to it and what follows afterwards.

Basic Christian teaching for beginners *(2011)*
This book covers the elementary or basic teachings of Christianity - the foundation of repentance from acts that lead to death, faith in God, instruction about baptisms, the laying on of hands, the resurrection of the dead, and eternal judgment. Hebrews 6 v 1 - 3.
It is intended for those people who are beginning to make a commitment to the Christian faith and describes an orthodox Biblical perspective on the themes listed above. Following these articles, there is an outline of the gospel itself, and this is covered at a slightly more advanced level.

NON DUALISM KARMA, REINCARNATION AND PAST LIVES *(2011)*
Some religions hold to the idea of Karma: the idea that a person almost endlessly recycles through death and reincarnation until at last they achieve release. But I consider that at death the Essence and Ground of our being, our True Self, returns to God as Expansive Pure Spirit.
This short study explores this non-dualist position.

MODERN SPIRITUALITY *(2011)*
Pilgrim Simon considers over fifty questions related to the theme of spirituality drawing from a number of respected spiritual writers and mystics, different religious traditions and modern Transpersonal Psychology as well as his own experiences in order to create an introductory but comprehensive spiritual world-view for the 21st century. Issues such as spiritual authority, the existence of God, the relationship of morality to spirituality, the nature

of the spiritual path and the problems of evil and suffering are all considered in this wide-ranging study.

THE SPIRITUAL LIFE OF A MANIC DEPRESSIVE *(2011)*
This is the spiritual biography of Pilgrim Simon with special consideration and relation to his mystical experiences and bipolar (manic-depressive)disorder. Pilgrim Simon presents his spiritual life story as a sufferer from manic depression and as a person who has had a number of mystical encounters with the Divine. This story charts his entrance into and eventual leaving of Christian Fundamentalism and his quest to find a deep-rooted, stable and relevant spiritual orientation in the light of his mood changes. This document covers a forty year period of Pilgrim Simon's spiritual quest for the Divine.

CHRISTIAN MARRIAGE AND THE PRINCIPLE OF HEADSHIP AND SUBMISSION *(2011)*
An overview of the theology of Christian marriage, the biblical principle of headship and submission and the roles of husbands and wives.
In this study the author draws out Biblical principles surrounding the relationships and roles of husbands and wives in Christian marriage. The spiritual significance of marriage in its reflection of the relationship of Jesus Christ to the body of believers that make up the Church is explored, with attention given to the sometimes thorny issue of the husband's headship and the submission of the his wife.

GROUPS, CULTS, SECTS AND MIND CONTROL *(2011)*
A set of outline notes highlighting the techniques and processes used in dysfunctional groups in order to dishonestly persuade their members to adopt the group philosophy and remain as members. Though the main references here are to religious groups, these methods are also used by any dysfunctional group - be it religious, political or whatever.
Using these notes, readers should be able to quickly detect the degree of dysfunctionality in any group to which they belong.

The local church: Administration, government and practice *(2011)*

How is a local church governed? Who makes the decisions - is it a democratic organisation or is it directed by Elders? What is the role of women in the church? How are Elders appointed and what are their qualifications? How should the church deal with disputes? What does church membership entail? What does a deacon do? Should a local church have a constitution?
These and other important questions are addressed by drawing out the examples, commands and principles contained in Scripture, and as such those forming a new local church should find this study of practical help.

SPIRITUAL QUESTIONS *(2011)*
The author asks a series of a questions related to spirituality and philosophy: Who am I?, How does morality relate to spirituality?, If God exists then why is there suffering?, How do I equate my desires and passions to the spiritual life?, What is Detachment?, What role does surrender have in spirituality?, If God is in control, do I determine my own actions?, What is the point of doing anything? Why bother?
This study takes a non-dualist position in addressing these issues. Answers are also drawn from the personal spiritual journal of the author, 'The Song of Simon', which is a record of his own mystical encounters.

CHRISTIANS SEEKING GUIDANCE FROM GOD *(2011)*
Even for Bible-believing Christians, seeking God's guidance in every day circumstances can sometimes seem to be a difficult task. On some issues, the Bible is plain but in other areas, Christians seem to be on less certain ground and may resort to methods and approaches that lead them into error and difficulty, or they may sub-consciously interpret their own desires and preferences as God's will for them with equally disastrous results. Sometimes, these mistakes can cost the believer emotionally, financially and in terms of personal relationships and faith cause many difficulties. This study seeks to cut through some of the potential pitfalls to offer a more considered Biblical view of seeking God's guidance and will for the Christian.

MYSTICISM, MADNESS AND MANIA *(2011)*

Drawing from his own personal experience as a sufferer from bipolar mood disorder and as a person who has had a number of mystical, spiritual experiences, Pilgrim Simon explores the themes of religious mania, so-called 'mental illness' amd immediate or mystical experiences of the Divine. In so doing he seeks to draw out distinguishing features that differentiate mystical experience from manic mood phases and from schizophrenic displays of religious delusion. He draws from the Transpersonal model of Ken Wilber and also from the approach of Personal Constuct theory and the research of Julian Jaynes on the Bicameral mind. This study leads to questions about the very foundations of psychology and psychiatry and the forms of analysis and diagnosis that they may make concerning mystical or transcendent spiritual experience.

Pilgrim Simon has studied spirituality and religion for over forty years. He has an Honours degree majoring in Psychology and Post graduate qualifications in counselling.

CHRISTIAN REVELATION *(2011)*
This study is concerned with that area of Christianity known as 'spiritual gifts', or 'charismata' and particularly the gifts of revelation and inspiration - and God's guidance.
Initially, these gifts are explored and defined in Biblical terms with a Calvinist interpretation, but as the study progresses it becomes more and more evident that tests are needed to be applied witrh regard to claims of experiences of spiritual gifts in order to prevent the Christian believer from being decieved, mistaken or deluded by false gifts and influences.
Where better to look then than to THE outstanding example of Christian God-inspired revelation - the Bible itself. In taking this course we are led to a critical exploration of the very foundations not only of Christian Fundamentalism and the Bible, but to the foundations of Christianity itself.

SPIRIT, SELF AND EGO *(2011)*
Who are we? What is our 'self'? What do we mean when we talk about 'ego'? Are 'ego' and 'self' the same thing? Exactly what is human nature? Do we have a spiritual dimension to our nature? Do we have a soul? Or are we just material, physical bodies? The answers that we give to these questions affect our assumptions

331

and understanding in practical disciplines of social science such as psychology and psychiatry as well as affecting our approach to spirituality.

In this study, Pilgrim Simon seeks to answer these questions and provide a foundation for theories of understanding ourselves.

EVANGELISM: AN ALTERNATIVE BIBLICAL PERSPECTIVE *(2011)*
Evangelism - spreading the gospel of Jesus Christ - can be big business, with large crusades and campaigns - or it may be a local church initiative to attract new vistors. But what does the Bible say about evangelism and outreach? Is it every believer's duty to evan gelise? Should the church be seeking to spread the gospel to everyone in their neighbourhood? Should a believer feel guilty if they do not get involved? What methods of approach should be used? What is the message that should be conveyed?

Pilgrim Simon explores the approach of the Apostles and compares them to modern approaches and attitudes and finds some interesting lessons to learn.

THE CHARACTER AND NAMES OF GOD *(2011)*
What is God like? What sort of characteristics, qualities or attributes does the Divine have? Many spiritually-minded people picture God using the Names ascribed to the Divine: God is Love, Mercy, Father, Judge and so on. Some tend to think of God as 'Big-Person-in-the-sky' looking down on us, ordering events around us and keeping a record of all that we do and say ready for us to give an account of our lives.

In this study, Pilgrim Simon gets beneath these ideas to find something far more transcendent and intimate, resulting in a view of God that challenges many religious and orthodox ideas about what God is like, and suggests a way through religious division, conflict and dogma.

THE SONG OF SIMON - A SPIRITUAL JOURNAL *(2011)*
The 'Song of Simon' is a spiritual journal that faithfully records the content of a series of mystical encounters experienced by Pilgrim Simon over the course of a few months at the turn of the millennium. Though allegorical and mythical in its symbolism, the philosophical and theological content is at times quite profound. In

332

general, it resonates with the approach of non-dualists and core views of spiritual thinkers such as Ibn al-Arabi, Shankara and Meister Eckhart - though at the time of writing this journal, these authors were unknown to Pilgrim Simon.
The text provides a rich reservoir of spiritual philosophy and provides the springboard for the spiritual studies written by Pilgrim Simon over the last decade.

FOUNDATION FOR CONTEMPORARY SPIRITUALITY *(2011)*
Older, traditional religious ideas are being questioned and challenged, but this does not mean that we have to reject the very notion of God or the Divine, or throw out all religion as useless. But it does mean hard and searching questions into the foundation of spirituality and religion, and particularly orthodox religion and spirituality which declare themselves as the one true path to the Divine. A contemporary approach is needed which can accommodate our modern world and its discoveries. Paradoxically, such an approach reaches back to some very old ideas indeed.
What is set out in this study is a set of articles dealing with the foundations, the ground, the base, of spirituality, stripping away inadequate ideas and theologies that are no longer tenable in an attempt to get to a more sure foundation for contemporary spirituality.

LEAVING CHRISTIAN FUNDAMENTALISM - THE BIBLE AND AUTHORITY *(2011)*
The rallying call of the Protestant Reformers was 'sola sciptura' - Scripture alone. For modern Christian Fundamentalists, The Bible forms THE tangible spiritual authority as God's inerrant Word and therefore it forms the ONLY rule of faith and conduct. All beliefs and conduct are brought under its searching light.
But is Christian Fundamentalism correct in taking this position? In this study, ex Christian Fundamentalist and Calvinist Pilgrim Simon considers over sixty questions concerning the foundation and ground of authority for the Christian's faith and conduct and in doing so lays the axe to the root of Fundamentalism and begins to question the very basis of orthodox Christianity itself.

THE END OF THE WORLD - A BIBLICAL PERSPECTIVE *(2011)*

What does the Bible have to say about the last days before the return of Jesus Christ? There have always been some rather wild, alarmist and fanciful interpretations of what these last days are supposed to be like and when this period begins. At the same time, the events of Biblical prophecy are often notoriously difficult to anticipate and interpret before the events themselves occur. Even so, Pilgrim Simon seeks to cut through these extremes and problems in order to give a balanced overview of just what the Scriptures say about these last days, the man of sin, the period of persecution of Christians and the return of Jesus Christ.

THE WORLD: AN ILLUSION OR REALITY? *(2011)*
Some spiritual traditions argue that the world, indeed, the entire universe is just an illusion. Is this correct or does the world and the universe have real substance? What do we mean by the term 'real'? Taking a non-dualist position, Pilgrim Simon explores the concept of the universe as a manifestation of the Divine. In so doing, the nature of illusions and reality, substance and reality, free will and predestination and the nature of the self are all explored in the light of a panentheistic perspective where the Divine is simultaneously Transcendent of and Immanent in all that exists.

LIVING THE CHRISTIAN LIFE *(2011)*
What does it mean to live the Christian life? A lot of emphasis today is put on what Christians believe and on defending those beliefs against opposing views. There is also a great deal of emphasis of worship - on music, gospel groups and choirs, singing praises and enjoying a sense of fellowship and community with like-minded believers every Sunday at church. There may also be an emphasis on reaching out to unbelievers - on evangelism and spreading the gospel. There may be an emphasis on healing campaigns and rallies. Sometimes there is an emphasis on teaching - on theological debate in Bible study groups. Or there may be an emphasis on young people and on youth groups within the church. Is this what the Christian life is all about? Or does the Bible give us another emphasis? In this study, Pilgrim Simon explores Biblical aspects of Christian living.

THE FOUNDATION OF CHRISTIANITY *(2011)*

We often turn to the Bible as our authority and foundation for the Christian faith. Christian Fundamentalists go as far as to say that the Bible is God's Word and therefore without substantial error of any kind.
But are we correct in this reliance upon Scripture? What did the believers in the early Christian church rely on before the writings of the Bible were collected and agreed on as being suitable for a rule of faith? In any case, what qualifications did a piece of writing have to exhibit before it was included in the Bible?
In this study, Pilgrim Simon gets back to the basics of Christianity to try and establish a broad outline of the foundation of Christian faith and practice.

Essays on spirituality - Volume 1 *(2011)*
'Essays on spirituality' consists of over a dozen short and medium length articles on spiritual themes. They were written as the author was coming to an understanding of his own mystical experiences and the theological and philosophical content that they displayed. References are made to the Journal of these experiences - 'The Song of Simon' - also available on Feedbooks.
The themes covered in this volume include:
ABANDONING MATERIALISM
CHARACTERISTICS OF MYSTICAL EXPERIENCE
CHRISTIANITY AND MODERN SPIRITUALITY
DEATH AND THE AFTERLIFE
DEGREES OF IGNORANCE
EVIL – ITS ORIGIN AND PERSISTENCE
THE EXPERIENCE MEETING
THE SPIRITUAL WISDOM OF THE CHILD?
GOD, TRUTH AND PERPETUAL TRANSFORMATION
GOD'S WILL AND PLEASURE...IN THE BEGINNING
HARMONISING RELIGIONS
THE HEART
THE INTRINSIC PATH
KNOWING ME, KNOWING GOD – AHA!

THE SOUL - A BIBLICAL PERSPECTIVE *(2011)*
The orthodox Christian view of the soul and spirit is to regard them as very similar if not the same. They are words used to describe what is seen as an eternal spiritual entity that together with

the body makes up the nature of a human being. After death, it is largely considered that the soul/spirit continues to exist as a rational, thinking, desiring, purposeful entity - the essential personality, brought to stand before God.
In this study, Pilgrim Simon examines how well this view stands up in the light of Biblical texts, and argues that the grounds of this view are weak, if not unsupportable.

SPIRITUAL FELLOWSHIP *(2011)*
Should spiritually minded people gather together for devotion, worship and praise of God? Should they gather together for teaching? Who is it exactly who teaches? What do they teach? What is it exactly that they worship? What happens when individual understandings of what God is like different from or even contradict the views of other spiritual travellers? How should any such meeting be structured and organised? Given that there are different levels of transcendence in spirituality, which is the most appropriate spiritual path to follow?
In this study, Pilgrim Simon addresses these issues of practical spirituality.

THE MEANING OF PERSONAL REVELATION *(2011)*
In the course of engaging in spiritual exercises such as contemplation, prayer, mindfulness and meditation some people may experience an immediate encounter with the Divine - a mystical experience in which they may receive teaching and guidance in spiritual matters.For some in Christianity, the whole Bible is declared to be inspired revelation.
What principles shouls we use in seeking to understand the meaning of such literature and experiences? What is the meaning of a spiritual dream? If the Absolute makes a representation to us in metaphor, allegory or symbol, how then do we understand this content? What is the sense or significance of mystical literature? What is the purpose underlying or intended by such accounts? What is the true interpretation, value, or message that such and experience and literature seeks to convey?
In this study, Pilgrim Simon seeks to address such questions.

SPIRITUAL QUESTIONS VOLUME 2 *(2011)*

In this second volume of spiritual questions, Pilgrim Simon asks: What is the nature of the universe? What do we mean by manifestation, illusion and ignorance? Is reality Ultimately Two or One - duality or non-duality? What happens after death? What is the mind? What role, if any, does sex and sexuality have in spirituality? What do we mean when we talk about material and spirit?

Spiritual Questions Vol. 3 *(2011)*
In this third volume of 'Spiritual Questions', Pilgrim Simon continues to seek answers to various common questions on the theme of spirituality. The questions covered in this volume include:
What are Angels or Spiritual guides?
How important is it to belong to a Community or Fellowship?
Is Worship, Praise and adoration of God necessary?
Where do Rules, Laws, Commandments and Moral Codes fit in to spirituality?
What about Personal Revelations of God?
How important is Ritual and Ceremony in spirituality?
What is Scripture and sacred writing?
How important are Teachers, Leaders, Founders of movements, Gurus e.t.c.?
What role does Tradition play in spirituality?
How important is Ideology, Theology, Philosophy and Rationality in the spiritual life?
Why does God allow suffering, pain and evil?
If there is One God, why are there so many different and contradictory religions?

THE STING OF DEATH *(2011)*
What happens with regard to the lack of moral balance when we die? Does guilt just evaporate and perish with the death of the person? Does death mean that we escape the penalty that our moral transgressions should incur? Some religions promote reincarnation - a near endless cylcle of birth and rebirth until such guilt is purified and purged away. But what of the Christian position? The sting of death is sin - but what does this mean? How is the guilt and debt of moral transgression worked out in Christianity? Pilgrim Simon looks at these issues from a Christian and Covenant perspective.

COVENANT HISTORY AND THE HOLY SPIRIT *(2011)*
This study began with the question: 'Did the Holy Spirit indwell believers in Old Testament times?' Many modern Christians place an emphasis on the regeneration and indwelling of the Holy Spirit as an essential part of salvation. If this is the case, in what sense was the Holy Spirit given at Pentecost? In seeking to answer these kinds of questions, the author, Pilgrim Simon, found himself exploring the history of just how God dealt with his people via a series of 'covenants' or relationships leading up to the New Covenant in Christ. The progression through these covenants reveals changes in relationships with and discoveries about the Divine as the plan of redemption is unfolded. It also questions some of the assumptions made by some Christians today.

WHO DO MEN SAY THAT I AM? *(2011)*
Who is Jesus? The answer may seem obvious to those in the west brought up in Sunday Schools and thus reasonably familiar with the Bible tales of Jesus. But in fact, things are more complex than that because the Bible documents are not quite what they appear to be at first sight or face value. Yet we have little knowledge of Jesus outside of these Biblical texts. To make things worse, we have centuries of church tradition which in some cases masks and hides a more accurate picture of what Jesus was like.
In this study, Pilgrim Simon, an ex Christian Fundamentalist, explores the very foundation of Christianity itself in seeking to get to the roots of just who Jesus was.

WHERE IS JESUS NOW? *(2011)*
Many of us are familiar with the story of Jesus, his crucifixion, resurrection and ascension. Ask many Christians today where Jesus is and they will reply that he is seated at the right hand of God the Father. But where is that exactly? If the resurrection of Jesus was a physical one - or at least had physical characteristics - then where exactly is Jesus now, following his ascension up to the clouds?
In this short study, Pilgrim Simon ponders this theme within an orthodox Christian viewpoint together with some of the practical implications involved.

THEY NEVER HEARD THE GOSPEL *(2011)*

The Bible and many modern Christians place a great emphasis on the gospel - the good news of Jesus Christ and the grace procured by his life, death and resurrection for those who believe. The importance of this message motivated many attempts at missionary and evangelistic work, in order that hearers may have the opportunity to believe and be saved.
But what of those people who have never had the opportunity to hear the gospel? Are they doomed to a lost eternity? Are they condemned because of their situation to eternal condemnation?
In this short study, Pilgrim Simon explores this subject and its implications from a Biblical point of view.

A CRITIQUE OF CHRISTIAN FUNDAMENTALISM *(2011)*
Many of us are familiar with the term 'Christian fundamentalism'. It is a term that that through constant use in the media often creates in our minds a stereotypical image of a naive literalistic faith coupled with a somewhat dogmatic and intolerant attitude - especially with regard to modern science.
In this short study, ex Christian fundamentalist Pilgrim Simon gives an outline critique of the Christian fundamentalist system and believer.

Detachment and the spiritual life *(2011)*
The idea of detachment, of withdrawing from the world and society, of abstaining from worldly interests and pleasures, even denying the self, has a long tradition in spirituality and is expressed in many religious systems. From simply abstaining from certain behaviours to living the life of an Ascetic - detachment is present in spirituality in a wide degree of intensity and scope.
In this study, Pilgrim Simon takes a look at detachment and the ideas that underpin it from a non-dualist stance. He asks if detachment is necessary to walking the spiritual path. If it is, what are to detach from? And to what degree? He draws on the thoughts of Shankara and Meister Eckhart and outlines the theology of the spiritual path.

LAYNTON LAINTON FAMILY HISTORY *(2011)*
An outline one-name study and history of the Laynton/Lainton family originally from the Staffordshire/Shropshire borders in England.

The history of the family is traced back to the 1500's and reveals a typical working class story from the beginning of the reign of Elizabeth the first, through the English Civil Wars, the industrial revolution and two world wars, with family members spreading all over the world. This study would be of interest to anyone with the Laynton/Lainton name as their own name or in their familiy history and also to students of social history, since a great percentage of the Laynton/Lainton's in the world are included in this one name study.

The appendix contains wills and census records, apprenticeship records and a full chronological index of births, marriages and deaths from the 1500's up to 1995.

You should note that some parts of he appendix are intended for computer display and may not be spaced correctly on mobile devices.

MORALITY, NON-DUALISM AND THE SPIRITUAL ASCENT *(2011)*
Non dualism, typified by Advaita, is often criticised for failing to address morality and failing to direct spiritual pilgrims in terms of how to act in the world. It is even accused of detaching spirituality from morality altogether. This study looks at the whole issue of morality with regard to non-dualistic spirituality and argues, as do the non-dualist traditions themselves, that morality is an essential foundation for the spiritual life. This study traces seven broad stages of spiritual development – the spiritual ascent – and shows how morality is integral to each stage. In so doing, the study also suggests an outline spiritual path for the spiritual traveller – regardless of the particular religious system that may be embraced.

TOWARDS A 21ST CENTURY CHRISTIANITY *(2011)*
In the light of textual, historical and scientific criticism and resulting re-evaluation of the Bible, can we actually begin to form any sort of view about what Christianity is and who Jesus was? Is there anything left after these radical deconstructions?
Ex Christian fundamentalist Pilgrim Simon makes a personal evaluation of Christianity today, cutting through fundamentalist thought and years of orthodox theology and practice to try and arrive at what the essence of Christianity really was and is and what theology it would embrace in the light of these modern criticisms.

The Visions of St. Paul and the Judeo/Christian orthodox tradition *(2011)*
The visions of the resurrected Jesus experienced by the Apostles and the Apostle Paul in particular form the basis of new Testament and earcly Christian orthodoxy. On the basis of his Damascus Road experience and other, similar spiritual experiences that followed it, Paul received a theology that formed the basis of his message to the non-Jewish community or Gentiles. Paul's writngs and the writings of his associates or followers make up most of the New Testament. This essay explores the context and content of these visions and draws out implications for any contemporary Christian faith.

Do mystics become God? *(2011)*
Some mystics, following their transcendent spiritual experiences, claim unity or oneness with God - to the point of declaring that they themselves are Divine or an Incarnation of God. This short essay explores this theme of Deification and asks if such mystics and gurus are correvt in their assertions.

The Spiritual Matrix - Questionnaire and results analysis *(2012)*
How spiritual and transcendent is your thinking and behaviour? Where would you place yourself on the spiritual landscape? This questionnaire lists 72 statements about spirituality and asks you to rate them in terms of how much you agree or disagree with them. It then gives you guidance on how to analyse your ratings and gives you a personal spiritual profile and indicates your degree of transendence. It also places your position on a spiritual map. The questionnaire takes about 20 - 30 minutes to complete and ful details of how to understand your ratings are given.

The Spiritual Matrix - Mapping spiritual transcendence - Full study *(2012)*
The spiritual landscape can sometimes be daunting and confusing such that approaches to spirituality that seem on the surface to promote personal growth and insight may in the end turn out to be regressive and a hindrance. It can be useful to have some sort of 'map' to help us to orientate ourselves in this sometimes bewildering scene.

341

In exploring commonly accepted categories of spiritual ideas and spiritual pathways, the author builds up a spiritual matrix in which various points of view and practices with regard to spirituality can be rated to provide us with our own personal spiritual code. This matrix reveals the depth and scope of our reactions to spiritual ideas and practices, whether we support or oppose them as well as indicating the degree of transcendence of our spiritual philosophy and practice.

This study is divided into three parts – Part one: A questionnaire to rate your own spiritual views and practices, Part two: A discussion of the theoretical approach, Part three: An analysis of your questionnaire results.

Along the way, the author discusses proto-science, pseudo-science, souls, ancestor veneration, spirits, fairy folk, deities, magic, alchemy, materialism, mysticism, Astrology, Mediums, religion and non-dualism.